GUNPOWDER TREASON AND PLOT

PUBLISHING HOUSE

GABRIOLA, BC CANADA V0R 1X4

Copyright © 2023, H.B. Dumont
All rights reserved.

WITHOUT LIMITING THE RIGHTS UNDER copyright reserved above, no part of this publication may be reproduced, stored in or introduced into a retrieval system, or transmitted, in any form or by any means (electronic, mechanical, photocopying, recording or otherwise), without the prior written permission of both the copyright owner and the publisher of this book.

GUNPOWDER TREASON AND PLOT
ISBN 978-1-990335-19-8 (PAPERBACK)
ISBN 978-1-990335-21-1 (CASEBOUND)
ISBN 978-1-990335-20-4 (EBOOK)

Printed on acid-free paper. Agio Publishing House is a socially and environmentally responsible company, measuring success on a triple-bottom-line basis.

10 9 8 7 6 5 4 3 2 1

DEDICATED TO JUDY

Books by H.B. Dumont

THE NOIR INTELLIGENCE SERIES

The Black Hat

Spine of the Antiquarian

Kiss of the Death Adder

Assassin in My Bed

Gunpowder Treason and Plot

GUNPOWDER TREASON AND PLOT

A Novel

H.B. DUMONT

PROLOGUE

5 NOVEMBER 1978

He gasped as he grabbed Constable Olivia Daniels' arm with a gorilla-like grip, pulling the constable's face to his own. Blood was pulsating through the field dressings that Daniels had applied over the .303 calibre rifle wound to his abdomen. He cringed in excruciating pain as his gut convulsed.

"She did it," he gasped, his eyes revealing alarming panic.

"Who is *she*?" Daniels asked.

"*They* shot me!" His voice was raspy but piercing.

"Who are *they*?"

He hesitated as he laboured to take a shallow breath. "She wanted it!" His resolve was terrifying.

"Wanted what?"

He gasped again from the agonizing pain. His breathing was fast and shallow. "Inside metal box."

Daniels sensed that she didn't have much time to gather specifics. "What box? Where?"

"Corner barn... 321 degrees... fencepost."

"Who shot you?" Daniels pressed for crucial details.

Then a brief, slurred utterance in a barely distinguishable Slavic-Germanic inflection, beyond a faint lilt, projected his fear, panic: "Nein, nein, nyet, nyet," he whispered, scarcely audible through the gurgles in his throat of bright red blood bubbling into his mouth. He knew his death was imminent. His expression was vacant. His eyes were unreadable. His face was gaunt.

"No, what? Nein, was? Nyet, chto?" Daniels repeated.

He gaped in a contorted grimace, seemingly surprised that the constable had acknowledged the languages of his repeated pleas. His grip gradually loosened. His arm slowly dropped. He paused as if hesitant before expelling a broken breath, slurring his words, "Sheenataish ... Mig ... Tavish." Then his voice vanished.

Daniels made a mental note of the phonetics of what she thought his last utterance had been. She then checked for a pulse. There was none, just the hauntingly empty stare of his blank dark eyes riveted on her like the crowning signature of a Shakespearian sonnet. She took a moment to write in her new notebook in phonetics all she thought he had breathed in his final slurred words.

"Paramedics are en route," announced Daniels' partner, Constable Stan Polanski, from outside.

She called back from the barn door. "No pulse, no breath, no need to rush on the ambulance. Suggest we call to confirm Ident and GIS are coming."

She retraced her steps into the barn, bent down and searched the deceased for identification. His driver's licence read John Robert Hackett, date of birth 7 April 1931. His chronological age seemed inconsistent with his current appearance, accentuated by wary eyes masking what they wished to hide, she thought. Perhaps the violent circumstances of his death could explain the apparent discrepancy, but the photo on the driver's licence seemed oddly mismatched also.

Constable Mike Davidson arrived into the farmyard, and rolled down a window. "Just passing by," he called out. "Need any help?"

Polanski gazed at Davidson and his shiny new cruiser. "Slow day at the office for highway patrol?"

"You might say," Davidson grinned.

"Best we protect the scene. Can you block traffic entering the farmyard except for authorized vehicles? Even then, direct them away from the entrance to the barn where there appear to be fresh footprints," Polanski requested. He then joined Constable Daniels in the barn.

"A suicide?" Polanski speculated.

"Could be but perhaps not," Daniels replied. "A female and someone else may have shot him. He whispered a name to me as he was gasping for a final breath. But I couldn't make out the name clearly. It sounded something like Sheena Tavish or McTavish but I could be mistaken. Not exactly admissible evidence."

Daniels sat down on a feed box, the only place in the cow barn that wasn't covered in manure. She recorded the time and date of death: *11:57 a.m. 5 November 1978. Location: Hammonds Plains, Halifax County, Nova Scotia.* With an apprehensive expression, she mumbled to herself the words that her father had recited annually on this day:

Remember, remember!
The fifth of November,
The Gunpowder treason and plot;
I know of no reason
Why the Gunpowder treason
Should ever be forgot!

Guido Fawkes, also known as – a.k.a. – Guy Fawkes had conspired to blow up the British House of Parliament on 5 November 1605. His chosen means was gunpowder, his motivation was treason, to kill King James I. His plot had been contrived with fellow Catholic conspirators. Today, the means was a rifle, the motivation was unknown, as were the details of the plot including the identity of the conspirators. Daniels shrugged her shoulders as a shiver of ill omen ran the length of her spine. But a menacing sensation lingered in its wake like a stain of red wine spilt on a new white linen tablecloth. Even if it washed out, its presence would be eternal.

"Cancel Ident and GIS," a voice crackled over the radio.

Polanski squinted as his brow tightened. He ground his teeth and took a guarded breath. "Damn. I know that venomous voice all too well," he muttered. The hair on the back of his neck lifted up as Scrooge's would have done when Charles Dickens' ghost from Christmas Past came to visit.

"Who was that?" Daniels asked.

"Inspector J.P.R.C. Leblanc from Security Service. He took over the Security Service – the secret squirrels – this past summer. Came in from 'C' Division, Montréal. You want to keep your distance," Polanski cautioned as he nodded at the deceased. "You could end up like him if you got on Leblanc's bad side. In fact, everyone starts out on his bad side. He has been instrumental in prematurely ending a few promising careers."

"Why would he cancel Ident and GIS when he isn't even here?"

"With Leblanc calling the shots, I can say with a high degree of certainty that there is something *untoward underfoot*. He promotes his own brand of arrogance and disdain unlike any you may ever encounter. We need to tread very carefully."

Daniels' forehead furrowed as she walked hurriedly over to their patrol car where she retrieved a Pentax 35mm camera from her private briefcase. Scurrying back to the barn, she took a series of sequential photos for a 360-degree panoramic perspective. She then took several close-ups of the body and the .303 Lee Enfield rifle lying beside the deceased. The camera flash drew Polanski's attention. He sprinted back into the barn and looked directly at her with an inquisitive yet wary expression.

"Something untoward underfoot," Daniels mumbled, shaking her head as she looked up. "I've got a funny feeling on this one." She sensed her intuition and initiative would be rewarded.

Polanski looked at his partner, his eyes guarded, his lips set tight. "Be careful," he repeated. "Be very careful."

Wheels skidded to a hurried halt, causing a cloud of farmyard dust to swirl, some seeping into the barn between cracks in the weathered wall boards. The vehicle drove over and stopped on the footprints he had asked Davidson to warn drivers entering the farmyard to stay away from. Polanski peered at the lone occupant through the eddy of farmyard dust rising from the wheel wells. His name wafted on the periphery of Polanski's memory. He quickly whispered over his shoulder to Daniels, "Hide your camera under your coat, *fast*. Secret squirrels are here. Remember what I said. Play dumb. I'll explain later."

Polanski had recently been transferred to Bedford Detachment after a discreet plain-clothes assignment with what he had described as working with interesting people, doing interesting things in interesting places. While on that clandestine assignment, he had learned well how those operating on the fringe conducted the business of espionage and intelligence gathering, and how they looked down with utter contempt at uniformed officers. It became readily apparent that intelligence, unlike defence, was not entirely peacetime work. Instead, it was a constant war, the parameters of which were continually morphing as was the battlespace. Yet espionage was played out in mostly humdrum scenarios. Low-level contacts were the currency of virtually all intelligence work. The nimble and perilous world of James Bond and Goldfinger were limited to Ian Fleming novels and the Hollywood silver screen. Often, agents did not know if they were chasing actual spies or shadows of ideological polarization within the prism of disinformation and utter lies.

"I'm Corporal Werner Hartmann from Security Service. I'm taking over." His tone fell with a disparaging snarl behind an acrid sneer. "Report to your Detachment Commander immediately," he abruptly directed in no uncertain terms. There was something sinister in his demeanour that was all the more menacing. His voice was exacting with a discernible trace of the cruelty inherent in his accompanying malevolent personality. The weight of his stare was like a medieval curse that would need a priest to perform an exorcism to expel.

Polanski recognized the plainclothes officer from his venomous reputation, which would have fitted in well within the ranks of the Gestapo or Stasi. He was one of Inspector Leblanc's rising stars who, like himself, had earned his rusting spurs in 'C' Division, Montréal. There was neither room for debate in his blunt dictate nor space for a summary synopsis of what Polanski and his partner had noted when they first arrived at the farm, including the fresh footprint now obliterated under his car.

Hartmann's menacing presence engulfed Daniels with his own brand of arrogance like no ill-omened aura or wraithlike apparition had done before. She felt momentarily violated, exposed. Her heart pounded in reaction to the ghoulish threat she perceived. She would not fight. She would not run. She would, instead, stand her ground in silence with an expressionless bearing. She had never acted as a victim of abusive behaviour by school-yard bullies and wasn't prepared to start now.

"Mount up, Daniels," Polanski directed in a forceful tone, not quite an order but not a simple request either. "We need to report to Sergeant McNeill."

Daniels understood the implications of the furtive communications and severity of unknown potential consequences should she so much as hesitate in contemplation.

She slowly backed away from Hartmann all the while holding his harrying stare with her own mounting confidence. He wasn't aware that her camera was concealed from his view under her winter coat, yet within his grasp. Her inner voice told her that she needed to protect that photographic record of what she had witnessed, at all cost.

Once in their patrol car, Polanski said to his partner, "I commend you for taking your stance, but this is neither the time nor the place to engage with Corporal Hartmann." He nodded his head slowly. His communication was clear. "There are times when discretion is the better part of valour, Constable Daniels. This is one of those occasions."

"Lesson learned," she replied. She sighed deeply as she nodded her head in acknowledgement of her partner's words of wisdom. This was one of those times when she needed to close her eyes for a brief moment in order to see.

"Rest assured, the day of reckoning will come, Olivia, it just won't be today, nor will it be tomorrow." His voice brought with it a sense of tentative comfort and confidence.

※ ※

AT THE DETACHMENT, DANIELS TOOK the film out of her camera and stealthily slid it into her pocket. She then replaced it with a new roll of black and white Tri-X film. In her customary jovial voice, she announced to all in the office, "Smile, you're on *Candid Camera*," as she took a few shots. "For posterity," she kidded in the event someone had seen her remove the one roll of film and replace it with another.

"Polanski, Daniels, in my office," Sergeant McNeill directed in a stern yet guarded voice. "Security Service from Halifax want to interview everyone remotely involved with the case. They will be here shortly. Make yourselves available."

Polanski whispered to his partner while maintaining his focused stare. "Strongly suggest that you only report what you observed at the scene when we arrived and nothing of what the deceased may have said to you. Understand? I'm deadly serious, Olivia." *A Freudian slip with that expression*, he reflected, *but most appropriate under the circumstances.* "Don't say anything more. Play dumb. Say that you are only a probationary constable under training. Minimize your involvement. I'll back up your story."

Daniels drew her eyebrows together, subtly tilted her head, and shot back a confirming yet questioning expression. She was good at covering up, of saying nothing, of washing unblemished linen stained with red wine. She had done it so many times, keeping secrets about secrets.

"You thought you might have heard something but you have no proof," Polanski continued. "You admitted to me that you weren't certain. Better yet, say that the person was dying when you entered the barn. As you were placing the field dressing on his wound, he took his last breath. If they ask how you knew he had taken his final breath, say that you checked for a pulse on both carotid arteries. There was none."

"I'm just a dumb junior constable," she mumbled with a resigned tone, "but a wiser one now, and time will tell." She reflected on her partner's sage words of advice: *"The day of reckoning will come, Olivia, it just won't be today or tomorrow."*

Inspector J.P.R.C. Leblanc called Constable Polanski into the interrogation room first. Daniels could hear the one-sided conversation from outside the door where she stood reflecting on her partner's advice while making mental note of the few single syllable words Polanski had been allowed to utter to the inspector – "Yes, sir. No, sir." She knew what awaited her, even as the junior probationary constable. She would quote Sergeant Schultz, Stalag 13's memorable rotund comedic character from the TV series, *Hogan's Heroes*, "I see nutingk. I hear nutingk. I know nutingk."

Although just a junior constable, her inquisition alone with Inspector J.P.R.P Leblanc seemed longer than Polanski's. He demanded to see her notebook which she obediently handed over. He admonished her for poorly maintaining her notes as there was no record of the incident or anything else, not even today's date. He hadn't realized that she had inserted a new notepad into the holder when she removed the original and changed the Tri-X film in her camera. He was correct in commenting that she had not made any link to the final time and date of a previous notebook, which there wasn't. She hadn't had time before being called into the interrogation room. After another flurry of one-sided forceful remarks by Inspector Leblanc, some under his breath, but all implacable, she left the interrogation room clearly flustered.

"Everything OK?" Polanski asked. A cloak of compassion overshadowed his concern.

She nodded as a terse acknowledgement but without eye contact.

Polanski watched her hurry out of the detachment. Although they had been working together for only a few weeks, he had become aware of many of her mannerisms. What he noted today was out of character, worrying. He wouldn't press the issue at this time. He was confident she would confide in him in the fullness of time, in the privacy of their patrol car.

Polanski reflected on the first time he had been called into his supervisor's office to account for decisions he had made that the corporal believed were inconsistent with operating procedures. As a junior constable still on probation, he had never had to stand at attention in front of an officer. While in training, corporals were demi-gods. Inspectors and superintendents were gods with whom you dared not make eye contact let alone say anything more than yes sir, no sir, with a vacant façade. The Commissioner was a fabled character from a storied existence like gargoyles adorning steepled spires and gothic abutments on medieval cathedrals. On the one hand, Polanski wanted to protect her. On the other, he knew that she would gain wisdom from this experience. The ancient Athenians referred to two distinct types of wisdom: *phronesis*, the more practical, and *sophia*, the more general. He could teach her about one but she would have to learn the other on her own.

Both Daniels and Polanski knew she would have to endure Inspector Leblanc's torment: officers in the Force were all cut from the same hubris dinosaurian cloth.

CHAPTER 1

SEPTEMBER 2005

"Olivia Daniels! Stanislaw Polanski. Haven't seen you since Bedford. That must be almost 30 years ago."

Olivia looked up from her seat in the Air Canada Maple Leaf Lounge at the Toronto Pearson International Airport. Recognizing the face behind the voice, she immediately stood, smiled and extended her hand. "Stan, you are a pleasant sight for a traveller's weary eyes. Where are you coming from, flying to? Do you have time for a java?" She found herself holding his hand for a little longer than normal. "God, it's good to see you."

The tone of her voice emphasized her sincerity. How many times had she reflected on the shifts they had worked together, sharing aspirations, exchanging tales of childhood adventures, engaging in the conversations that a young girl might have had with an older big brother. Banter began to flow as if no time had passed since their last shift together as a team at the Bedford Detachment.

"I have a few hours. Heading back home to Victoria via Vancouver. What about you?"

"Same. My flight to Calgary doesn't board for two hours."

He was taken aback by her natural yet still youthful appearance. She was not one of those narcissistic women who spent hours preening themselves in front of a mirror attempting, often in vain, to recapture their fleeting youth. When they worked together in Bedford, he had found her presence to be compelling, their times together on and off the job so unassuming. He conceded that there was discrepancy in perception and his perception had been influenced by his own rose-coloured lenses. Much water had passed under the bridge since then.

"You haven't changed a bit," he complimented her.

"Only my hairdresser knows," she jested. Hair colour was a socially acceptable means of masking, of covering up both good and hard times.

He rubbed the palm of his hand over his balding head. "I'm follicly challenged. Otherwise, none the worse for wear."

She chuckled at his amusing self-assessment. There was something about the way he held himself, an ease, a confidence, a neatness, a semblance of presence. She recalled being drawn to these attributes when they first met. But the years had fogged her memory leaving only a remnant of a *je ne sais quoi*.

Aware of the silence between them resulting from her reflection, she re-engaged. "I've often thought about you and wanted to express my gratitude so many times for teaching me a few tricks of the trade, especially the artful connotation of *something untoward underfoot*. I've muttered your sage words many times."

He stood in silence, smiling, captivated once again by her company.

She gazed around looking for eavesdroppers. Despite the fact that this section of the first-class lounge was all but vacant, she beckoned him to occupy the padded leather chair beside her where his voice would project against a wall, not the open lounge.

She lowered her voice. "After the shooting in the barn, life went sideways for me. I mean the mysterious murder case at the farm. But in retrospect, I had a relatively successful career although on the periphery of the orbit and gravitational influence of the Great White Buffalo in Ottawa."

"That case impacted both our careers," he admitted. "I did well in my first few years before I was transferred to Bedford. There, I was able to shake free of Inspector Leblanc's intrusion."

Olivia huffed. "You may recall that within a few days of Hackett's death, I was swiftly transferred to Ottawa to guard tulips with the cardboard Mounties on Parliament Hill. It wasn't so bad. I managed to wrangle my way into Carleton University and ultimately completed a PhD in Slavic Studies that the Force paid for. My great grandparents were Russian immigrants. My grandparents and parents spoke Russian so I had a rudimentary understanding of the language. I applied for Security Service after graduating, but was turned down. I concluded that I was still *persona non grata* so I left the Force within a couple of years and ended my working career as faculty at the University of Calgary. I'm now on an open-ended sabbatical."

Stan smiled, acknowledging with a slight nod her brief yet optimistic autobiography. "I can see you leading the brightest of bright minds in a classroom. You entered this galaxy a star destined to become the nucleus of a constellation."

"Thanks for that artful compliment." A faint blush accompanied her smile. "But hardly so." She savoured the gracious accolade as she had done many times as his trainee in Bedford. Those assessments had meant a great deal to her. Other men in her life had acknowledged her effort with what she interpreted as a hollow expression based on ulterior motives.

"Both our transfers had J.P.R.C. Leblanc stamped all over them," Stan followed up. "About the same time as you departed Bedford for Ottawa, I was transferred to Assumption Detachment in Northern Alberta. It was said that if the country needed an enema, the insertion point would be Assumption. I received a reprieve for my sins, whatever they might have been, ending up in Identification Services and ultimately as a Crime Scene Analyst where I spent the next ten years or so of my less-than-illustrious career. After that, I accepted an offer to work with some old friends who were providing consulting services to private sector national and multi-national clients. I retired from that lucrative gig a couple of years ago."

Olivia added to her abridged summary. "I can't remember if I mentioned before I left Bedford that someone had snooped through my briefcase about the same time that Inspector Leblanc was reading the riot act to us. I know that because whoever it was opened my camera and the light spoiled the few pictures I had taken in the detachment. Unbeknown to the intruder, I had replaced the roll of film with the pictures of the deceased in the barn. On a subsequent trip to visit my family in Calgary, a friend developed them. I kept the prints and the negatives in my father's bank safe deposit box."

"I'm not surprised to hear that. You were known for going nowhere without your camera. They probably thought you had taken photos in the barn."

Again, with a lowered voice and glancing around warily, Olivia admitted, "Your warning that there was something untoward underfoot certainly rang true."

"Do you remember Mike Davidson?" Stan asked.

"Highway patrol, arrived at the barn just before Corporal Hartmann, the secret squirrel."

"Yes. Inspector Leblanc interviewed him after us. Apparently, Davidson had stopped Hackett on the road close to the farm a few hours before the elderly man was shot. For whatever reason, Davidson was suspicious that something just wasn't right."

"That might have been why he just happened to be in the area and asked if he could help," Olivia speculated, intrigued, curious.

After a solemn moment of reflection, Stan added with lament, "Shortly after I left Bedford, Davidson drowned while fishing in Pockwock Lake just north of Hammonds Plains."

Olivia's mouth dropped in utter disbelief and abruptly exclaimed, "No way, no damn way."

"Why?" Stan asked, instinctively drawing back in response to her brusque rebuff to his account.

"Davidson hated fish and despised fishing with a passion. He got seasick just thinking about water. Do you remember the time when he was supposed to supervise the recovery of a stolen truck that went off the road and into Stillwater Lake? That day, the wind was blowing hard and the waves were whitecapped. He started to vomit. We had to supervise the recovery for him while he rested in the back seat of his patrol car."

"I forgot about that. You're right," Stan acknowledged.

"Davidson had previously banged his head in a car accident. Thereafter, he suffered from sporadic episodes of vertigo, spiking headaches, nausea and occasional blurred vision."

"Right again. The Force eventually took him off highway patrol and stuck him in headquarters driving a desk."

They sat in brief meditation staring at each other.

Stan was the first to break the silence. "Are you thinking what I'm thinking?"

"Is your retirement seemingly as boring and uneventful as mine, particularly with the prospects of having to acknowledge the approach of the body's autumn season?" Olivia countered. "Looking for a part-time post-retirement career where we call the shots? Sorry about the pun."

"Two Old Farts Investigative Services, TOFIS, only limited by our arthritis," Stan responded with a contemplative chuckle and a mischievous grin to her tantalizing invitation. They were both silent in the fleeting moment that followed.

"Louis, I think this is the beginning of a beautiful friendship," Olivia uttered in hopeful jest.

"Bogie. Casablanca. 1942! One of my favourite classic Hollywood heroes," Stan crowed with adoration for Humphrey Bogart and for Olivia's proposal to become partners once again.

She could see the enthusiasm in his reaction to her invitation. Seeing Stan again after all these years, if only by happenstance, brought back a flood of regretful emotional memories. She had contacted a friend who was in RCMP headquarters staffing to expedite her application to attend Carleton University. From her, Olivia had learned that Stan had been transferred to Assumption Detachment in Alberta. She had thought about writing him or at least making note of his address so she could send him a belated Christmas card. She had second thoughts. He had not contacted her so she concluded he wasn't interested in becoming pen pals.

Life got complicated thereafter. She had looked at his address each year as Christmas rolled around but failed to do more until she received her acceptance letter as faculty at the University of Calgary. By then, he had left the Force and Alberta. Her contact in staffing at RCMP Headquarters had moved on also. The last known address was somewhere in Montréal. They had passed each other like ships in the night. Life seemed to remain complicated. On the fifth of November each year, she looked at his outdated address with increasing regret. There were other occasions when she kicked herself for not reaching out. No doubt he would have been married. Would she have been able to hide her true emotions? Wives were good at picking up on such sentiments. It would have been awkward, she surmised.

CHAPTER 2

"Thanks for agreeing to meet in Calgary. Coffee? Tea?" Olivia asked.

"Coffee would be great, double double."

While Olivia went to the kitchen to summon the coffee pot into action, Stan surveyed her living room with curiosity for the eclectic decor and admiration for the excellence of her furnishings.

"You have more bookshelves than most people have books." He continued to scan the paperbacks and hardcovers that were organized from classics to contemporary, from Virgil to Shakespeare, Austin to Whitman and Hemingway to Le Carré, all in chronological order for select series. Other books were lying on their side in various piles, perhaps by dates acquired but not yet read or filed. "If I remember correctly, you were a prolific reader back in the day. You had several novels on the go at any one time," he commented when she returned from the kitchen with the coffee.

"It's a hazard of the academic profession and affiliation with the ancient guild of the avid *antiquarian*. It's a fancy word for those addicted to the collectable classics which I started as a child. You'll find a complete first edition set of Charles Dickens, in addition to Alexandre Dumas in French, and Leo Tolstoy and Fyodor Dostoyevsky in Russian."

"I'm impressed." He was also drawn to a fencing foil and mask, and other accoutrements of the fine art of the Sabreuse, amid numerous trophies that attested to her considerable talents. "Do you fence?"

"I do, have for several years. I find it better for mental and physical exercise than yoga which seems to be more popular among most of my domesticated female friends in their well-intentioned

but misguided endeavour to shed the pregnancy pounds after years gone astray."
"Remind me to keep on your good side," he jested.
"What about you? What occupies your spare time?"
"Since moving to Victoria, I've become a devoted gardener in pursuit of the Great Victoria Night-hopping Marrow Looper that consumes my tomatoes among other prized veggies between dusk and dawn. Like the Loch Ness monster and Ogopogo in Lake Okanagan, no one has ever seen one, but they leave their calling cards in their wake. I spend the rainy days solving crossword and Sudoku puzzles."
"Once an analyst, always an analyst," Olivia chuckled. It had been a while since she had laughed and teased with someone so relaxed.
"I also volunteer with the local American Sign Language Society."
Olivia gave him an inquisitive gaze.
"My mother was born deaf so sign language was how we communicated as a family."
"Any problems getting away?" Olivia asked as she poured the coffee.
"Widowed two years ago. Brain cancer. One daughter and one son, both married with budding careers of their own. No grandchildren. No problems getting away."
Olivia acknowledged his loss. "Thanks for sharing." She sensed he was still dealing with his wife's death and rattling around the empty nest.
Stan simply smiled. "And you?"
"Divorced. No kids." Her matter-of-fact terse accounting indicated there were no outstanding emotional strings.
"So where do you suggest we start?" Stan asked.

"Let's go back to square one. Do you know who called it in, the shooting at the farm?"

"I never did find out," Stan replied, noticeably frustrated. "I enquired in order to annotate my notes. First, I was told by the shift supervisor that I didn't have to complete a report because Security Service had taken over the case. Second, and more puzzling, there was no record of who reported it, no C238 Daily Occurrence Report, not even a reference to the Security Service handover. It was as if the shooting had never occurred."

"Can you recall who was on the desk?"

Stan paused, searching through his mental Rolodex file. "Brian Hamilton. Off the record, he told me that he had been ordered to say nothing, ordered as in threatened with a fate worse than a permanent transfer to Hades, or worse – Assumption Detachment. He substituted our C238 occurrence number with a supposed anonymous call that was registered as unfounded for uniform crime-reporting purposes. That way it was immediately cleared off the books by the shift NCO. The Detachment Commander liked those calls – reported one, unfounded one."

"What about Davidson's drowning?"

"By then, I was at Assumption Detachment counting mallard ducks under the *Migratory Bird Convention Act*. I only heard about his death through the grapevine. I do recall he was buried in the RCMP Cemetery in Regina."

"OK, first stop Regina," Olivia responded in an authoritative tone. "There will be a verification of the interment with date of death. I'll get a copy of the *RCMP Quarterly* which should have a record in the obituary section. If we're lucky, there will be a reference to the circumstances surrounding his death. I'll also research obituary records for Halifax County because it will list where John Robert Hackett, the deceased, was buried. The coroner's office should be able to provide a cause of death."

"I'll contact one of the crime analysts I trained. He will be able to dig up contact information for Hamilton which we cannot easily access. Hamilton should also be less close-lipped now and not so easily intimidated."

"Not easily accessed or not accessed at all," Olivia added with a tinge of sarcasm in her voice. "I recall one of my Depot training instructors in Regina insinuating that discipline meant not telling anyone outside the Force about what went on inside. To do otherwise would be tantamount to heresy. Corporals were demi-gods so I never thought of challenging their authority or the veracity of their reasoning. I grew out of that false belief when I was researching for my PhD dissertation at Carleton, and challenged every denial under Access to Information while faculty at the University of Calgary. I even challenged redacted information and was occasionally successful in squeezing out additional details. I just surmised that I didn't trust anyone within the RCMP. I didn't know anyone else and concluded that I probably didn't want to know them. I needed to be cautious about anyone who claimed to be a part of the fraternity or anyone who seemed like a favourite uncle not showing any of the expected norms yet showing up for a family dinner unbeknown to other family members."

CHAPTER 3

The drive from Calgary to Regina allowed them to get caught up on forty-five years of collective career highlights embellished with tall tales. At Depot Division in Regina, the record of Davidson's interment was limited to his service number, date of birth, date of death, and burial plot number. Notation in the obituary section of the *RCMP Quarterly* was equally sparse.

Olivia scanned incoming messages on her cell phone. She pursed her lips and grunted in dissatisfaction. With a passion, she disliked bureaucracy. She had learned the fine art of circumventing university hurdles with the aid of a few select administrative colleagues with senior service. Government was another unwieldy beast that often left her reaching for antacid medication. Drinking glasses of warm water with baking soda was her next best option when she had exhausted her supply of over-the-counter medication. She unwrapped her last few pills.

"What's up?" Stan enquired. Trepidation accented his tone. He had learned when you were confronted early in an investigation with road blocks, it tended not to get easier. It wasn't Murphy's Law but instead Stanislaw's Law.

"My request for records from Halifax County regarding Hackett's death has come back negative. There is no record, not even a reference to a coroner's report. Nor is there an obituary in any Halifax newspaper of his death or funeral. No record. No photos. No references. No details. No correspondence. *Persona non grata* as in disappeared without a trace."

"How can that be?"

"Not sure," Olivia muttered. She had conducted countless online searches for academic papers and research projects. Occasionally, she would have to modify the words or the search sequence but she invariably came up with some responses. From these initial findings, the snowball effect produced exponentially more leads. She could not ever remember coming up with a blank slate especially when the search string focused on individual names or aliases. The challenge was typically quite the opposite, having to vet too many extraneous hits.

"Perhaps he had a different name," Stan suggested.

"But his driver's licence is an official government document. The name I wrote down in my notebook clearly stated John Robert Hackett."

"You have a point there. I'm not aware that names of deceased can be lawfully altered *post mortem*. There might be an addendum for also-known-as – a.k.a." He paused in reflection. "The operative phrase being *lawfully altered.* If you simply disappear and no one reports you absent, who is to know otherwise?"

"His wife would know." Olivia furrowed her eyebrows as she searched her mind for possible explanations. "Unless his wife didn't want him found," she added. "Hackett had first gasped, '*She did it.*' Then he said, '*They* shot me.' I distinctly remember writing down in my notebook what he slurred."

"One person, his wife, suggests premeditated murder. Two people, his wife and this other person, equates to conspiracy to commit murder," Stan suggested. "Now we add in secret squirrels, one being Cpl. Werner Hartmann, and another being Inspector J.P.R.C. Leblanc." He inhaled a slow deep worrisome breath. "I don't like where this is leading in the slightest. We aren't just looking into suspicious circumstances surrounding Davidson's death."

Her father's lyrics resonated in her mind. *Remember, remember, / The fifth of November, / The Gunpowder treason and plot; / I know of no reason / Why the Gunpowder treason / Should ever be forgot!*

Stan was amused by her odd expression. "And?"

"And the circumstances surrounding this case." Her voice trailed off. "Too many inconsistencies, perhaps cover-ups." An ill-omened shiver ran the length of her spine. She recalled Stan telling her to say nothing when asked about what she had seen and heard in the barn where Hackett had been murdered. She was good at covering up, keeping secrets about secrets. She hesitated and then reiterated Stan's observation. "Lawfully altered. If a student came to me with a research paper that had inconsistencies or unconnected threads, I'd tell them to explore with broader depth and breadth."

"So, we dig further for the facts."

"I had one student who responded to my comment to research further by asking how to investigate intuition, the gut feeling."

"And what did you say?"

"If you can't find an explicit, the fact, seek the implicit, the intuitive. Explain objectively why you have subjective reservations."

"So, why do you have reservations about this case beyond the apparent disappearance of Hackett and the questionable circumstances surrounding Davidson's reported drowning?" Stan probed.

Olivia dwelt on his question. "I can't put my finger on it… might have been something that Hackett whispered to me just before he died. Or maybe it was something I saw in the barn. It's been too long." She raised her head scanning for a single image projected on the monitor of her mind or a series of connected clues which alone might mean nothing but in sequence could lead to a potential solution or another viable clue or lead to follow, something, anything.

Her cell phone buzzed with an incoming message, interrupting her train of thought. She studied the screen with a puzzled expression. Her smile morphed into a frown. Once more, she slowly shook her head from side to side.

Stan watched her reactions. A double road block he surmised. Murphy's law and Stanislaw's law.

"My request under Access to Information has been denied under the *Official Secrets Act*. We would need written authority from the Director of Canadian Security Intelligence Service or the Minister of Public Safety to access any details, even a mere verification of the incident, let alone specific details pertaining to Hackett's death and apparent disappearance."

"I don't like the sound of that," Stan replied, sharing his partner's growing frustration. "I'm sensing that Inspector J.P.R.C. Leblanc is still pulling some strings in order to maintain a cover-up. We need to tread ever so carefully as we proceed."

"In the words of a wise colleague, there appears to be something untoward underfoot," Olivia muttered. "Have you received anything back from your friend regarding the whereabouts of Brian Hamilton?"

"Nothing yet. I'll call my contact again. At this juncture, I think it would be wise to minimize any electronic email record that can be tracked by any associates of Leblanc or someone else. Not paranoid. Just careful."

Olivia grumbled under her breath as she conducted a first-level online search. "There are over ten thousand references for the name Brian Hamilton on the internet. No help there. Hopefully, your friend can assist us, as Hamilton is now our last known tangible link."

It was Stan's turn to grimace as his colleague replied to his call regarding Brian Hamilton. His face changed from hopeful anticipation to wary speculation. His guarded expression was contagious.

Olivia took a slow deep breath. "Don't keep me in suspense."

She smiled inwardly at the thought of this renewed relationship with her former trainer and mentor, now partner.

"Strike three." Stan paused. "My friend apologized for taking so long. When he initially enquired about Hamilton, he was grilled by his superior officer as to why he wanted to know. His initial enquiry was denied. Through a friend of a friend, he was advised that Hamilton supposedly committed suicide with a bullet to his head from his own service revolver. I say 'supposedly' because circumstances were suspicious. My friend advised me to be very careful."

"We are being confounded at every turn. If I didn't know any better, I'd suggest some black-hatted bad guys are masquerading as white-hatted good guys," Olivia concluded, mirroring Stan's recommendation for vigilance. "Perhaps we need to find some good-bad guys and exploit their talents."

"Leblanc is really irritating me. Let's re-evaluate our strategy. I'm not suggesting we dissolve TOFIS. Quite the opposite. Two of our friends associated with this case have died under suspicious circumstances. If for no other reason, we owe it to them to find out what really happened and who is responsible. I'm more than ever committed. We just need to come up with a different, better game plan."

"*De l'audace, encore de l'audace, et toujours d l'audace,*" Olivia declared. "Audacity, more audacity, and always audacity. In the *lingua franca*, Leblanc is also pissing me off. As a strategy, I'm inclined to confront the devil on his own turf, but on our schedule, not his. We stay one step ahead of Leblanc and his legacy until such time as we have something irrefutable to hold over their heads."

"We have exhausted all our standing, breathing potential contacts. What do you suggest?" Stan asked.

"I have one bit of information that they don't know about and don't know that I have. Next stop, Hammonds Plains, Halifax County, Nova Scotia. Can you get hold of a surveyor's map of the farm, a compass, or better still a surveyor's transit?"

"Probably could. Why do you ask?"

She smiled. "First a bit more research that cannot be thwarted."

Stan stood erect staring at his new business partner, appreciating her tenacity once again. "If nothing else, my time in Ident and crime analysis taught me to observe. In perceived chaos, randomness and confusion, search for patterns and anomalies, and patterns of anomalies. Even in the apparent absence of anything, there is something: what is not said, not seen, not heard, not done. Anything sensed always leaves a pattern that will get us closer, wherever closer is."

"Closer to what? Further from where?" Olivia queried, appreciating the craving for candour and need for vigilance.

"We'll find out. I'll follow your lead," Stan replied as he bobbed his head. As Olivia's trainer, she had obediently followed his lead. The tables were turning and he liked the thought of being a partner in an equal relationship. It was refreshing.

"I very much appreciate your confidence. But please don't follow without asking why or offering alternative options even if it is just your hunch. I am a firm believer that our intuition is never wrong. It's just our misinterpretation of our intuition that gets us into trouble, or outright dismissal of the implicit that sends us on the wrong path. A mistake on an academic paper could easily be remedied through debate or corrected in a subsequent draft if needs be. An error in this malicious game of cat and mouse has a higher probability of being disastrous."

"Deal," he replied with a warm smile. As an identification technician and later as a crime analyst, he had mostly worked alone. There was a certain level of satisfaction when he was able to link all the dots together, but it was a distanced objective feeling of gratification. Rarely did he ever meet the victim or families of the victim if a death was involved. This case was different. He was emotionally invested. He knew Davidson and Hamilton. He had seen Hackett, his lifeless body wedged against a structural beam in the barn. And then there was Olivia. He had thought about her just about every day since they were separated. Now they were partners, together.

CHAPTER 4

"What research?" Stan asked.

"Land Titles," Olivia replied. "The land where the farm was situated all those years ago has been sold twice since then. That's good news because the probability the current owner is aware of this case is infinitely small, let alone that a murder took place on their property. The current owner is listed as living in Toronto and has been there for over fifteen years. That means there is a good chance that the farm may be vacant or at minimum just rented."

"So, what are we surveying?"

"Hackett, or whatever his name was, whispered something to me just as he was taking his last breath. He gasped, *'321 degrees from the corner of the barn, a fencepost.'* That is where your surveyor transit and compass skills will come into play. You need to point us to a fencepost under which a metal box is supposedly buried. That was something else Hackett said just before he took his last breath."

As they approached the farm, Olivia muttered with hesitation in her voice, "Finally, luck may be on our side. The farm appears to be vacant."

"Never underestimate luck," Stan replied. "I am humble enough to admit that luck, more so than skill, helped me find evidence that contributed to convictions in a few cases."

Like a seasoned land surveyor, Stan directed Olivia along the compass bearing of 321 degrees from a corner of the barn.

"Spoke too soon," she said with rising frustration and a hint of irritation in her voice. "No fencepost, not even a damn fence."

Stan joined her and focused along the reverse bearing from where she stood, her shoulders heavy with disappointment. "Either corner of the cattle barn, over this distance would lead us to this approximate point, at least to a fence." He lingered with a contemplative expression, searching left and right. He then gave her an oblique look. "Correct me if I am wrong but wasn't there another smaller barn back then? It probably held foxes – fox and mink farming were all the rage back then until the furry four-legged inhabitants contracted ringworm which destroyed their pelts. The animals then had to be exterminated and the barn burned down to contain the fungal infection outbreak. Give me a moment to scan my map."

Olivia's hopes were marginally renewed but still reserved. The lyrics of the Righteous Brothers' melody, *Ebb Tide*, reminded her that change of luck was a cyclical process and overdue:

First the tide rushes in,
Plants a kiss on the shore,
Then rolls out to sea,
And the sea is still once more.

Stan exclaimed with a re-energized voice. "Not all lost. An experienced modern-day surveyor goes nowhere without a remote GPS."

She watched as her partner traced a compass line along an old map of the region.

"Eureka!" he uttered. The ebb tide had turned. "Back to the fox barn, not the cattle barn. We run a new bearing."

Low shrubs of Nova Scotia blueberries filled the interior of what remained of the foundation of the fox barn and adjacent outdoor pen. The round juicy fruit had been prolific in the decade following the extermination and fire, from the natural fertilizer left behind. But even Mother Nature needs a helping hand after a few years, certainly decades. In every adversity there are the seeds of its opposite.

Olivia braced herself for further frustrations and disappointment after a first false lead. Again, she followed the surveying signals this time to a fence and fencepost. She jubilantly signalled Stan to join her. With an audible clunk, the spade struck a metal object buried under a rotting fencepost held partially erect only by the strands of rusting barbed wire extending to adjacent posts still standing.

Olivia's eyes lit up. "That could be it," she exclaimed as she scratched the soil with her fingers exposing a rusted metal box. She wrenched it from its secluded grave. Something tugged at her instinct as she held onto it momentarily.

With the edge of the spade, Stan forced the corroded lid free. "What the hell!" he exclaimed as he unravelled what appeared to be an oilskin burlap fabric, exposing its contents.

"Back to the car, *NOW!* Let's get away from here before anyone sees us," Olivia directed with an urgency in her voice that Stan could not recall having experienced before. It suited her well. He liked it. He obeyed her directive.

At their hotel and in the privacy of his room, Stan opened the lid a second time. Again, he carefully unfolded the oilskin material and removed the contents.

Olivia briefly examined the cache. "I need to make a quick phone call," she announced, "to my ex. I think I know what it is and what the Cyrillic script on the document says. The severity of the consequences dictates that we err on the side of caution and get an expert opinion from someone we can trust. If I am correct in my assessment, we now hold the high ground over Inspector J.P.R.C. Leblanc and his cronies."

"You said you can speak Russian? What about reading it? Your ex?" Stan prompted with a combination of curiosity and concern. Proficiency in a second language, even Russian, would be feasible, even commendable given her doctoral credentials in Slavic Studies and family background. Contacting her ex could also be reasonable, even pragmatic.

He felt uncomfortable, uneasy. What had Olivia experienced when he mentioned that his wife, Betty, had died from brain cancer not so long ago? There had been an awkward moment in their conversation regarding previous spouses. But his wife was absent, deceased. Her ex was present, apparently very much alive. A third cog? He took a slow silent breath of resignation.

"To your first question, I studied Russian while at Carleton University. To your second, his name is Uri. He is Ukrainian. He had served with, been conscripted into the Russian army and later the Spetsnaz, their special forces. We met at Carleton, and married when I was starting my PhD in Slavic Studies. I learned more Russian from him than I was ever taught in class. We divorced the year I graduated. He moved as far east as he could while I went west. By chance, he is teaching at Dalhousie University here in Halifax. That's the *Coles Notes* version of my bizarre university and brief married life."

Becoming proficient in Russian was commendable. Being married to a Ukrainian, a former Cold War foe with whom he had engaged in electronic intelligence combat, left a sour taste in his mouth. He continued to feel uncomfortable, uneasy. "Do you want me here when he arrives?"

"Absolutely. I want you here." She reached over and touched his arm. "You and I are partners, always have been, always will be." Her thought of an embrace to confirm her need for him and commitment to their fledging yet growing relationship felt awkward under the circumstances. It had been too long since Bedford and too short since their meeting in the Air Canada Maple Leaf Lounge at the Toronto Pearson International Airport to show such closeness, despite her longing. Instead, she held his gaze hoping he would recognize her feelings and reciprocate her sincerity.

Within an hour of the phone call, Olivia, Stan and Uri were huddled around the table in Stan's room.

"It's a Russian Makarov PB pistol with silencer, the weapon of choice of the former KGB and now FSB, and Russian special forces, the Spetsnaz," Uri stated emphatically with a faint but still noticeable Russian lilt as he glared at Olivia.

"Don't ask," she abruptly cut him off. The acrimony of their marriage remained as strong as it had been on the day of their divorce decree. Olivia said sternly, "I must warn you that if you speak to anyone about what we are showing you, the consequences could be fatal. Two of our former colleagues are already dead, we suspect murdered. One other person is also deceased and missing in action." She then showed him the four pages of Cyrillic script.

Uri scanned the pages. "St. Cyril's Byzantine alphabet," he mumbled. His expression changed from annoyance to vulnerability. "There is no love lost between us," he flicked a glance over at Stan, "but there is even less affection between me and my former Russian employer because of what Moscow did to my fellow Ukrainian citizens in the years leading up to the Second World War and following the defeat of the Nazis. The genocide of the Jews and others perceived as less than human in the concentration camps is equivalent to the unspeakable atrocities committed by Russia against the Ukrainian people. The only difference is the Ukrainian mass murders were never widely publicized. So, you can rest assured that I will speak to no one."

"I need you to verify what I believe the four pages state," Olivia uttered. There was an absence of compassion in her voice also.

Uri frowned with anxiety as he once again read each line. "What were you involved in back in your RCMP days? You told me that you were just a junior constable assigned to general detachment duties."

"That's the truth, Uri. That's all I was doing before I was transferred to Ottawa." She gazed over at Stan. "Stan was my trainer and can verify that. By happenstance, we became involved in a murder case, connected to this metal box and its contents."

Stan nodded, acknowledging her claim. "Can someone tell me what the script says?"

"The first page is a Russian cypher code used to translate highly sensitive communiqués from Moscow to Soviet agents," Uri explained. "I would say the recipients were part of a network of Russian spies here in Canada. Her Russian name was Lada and his was Nikolai. More than likely a sleeper cell. There is reference to another senior agent name of Ruslan. He appears to be the controller of this sleeper cell in addition to several other Russian agents. Lada and Nikolai were involved in negotiating the transfer of the FLQ separatists to Cuba after the Québec Deputy Premier, Pierre Laporte, and British Diplomat, James Cross, were kidnapped in October 1970. These two Soviet agents, Lada and Nikolai, were ordered by Moscow to murder Laporte. This Russian Makarov PB pistol you found in the metal box was more than likely the weapon used."

Olivia and Stan stood in stunned silence. They looked at each other with wide eyes before focusing back on Uri, then back to the pistol and documents, and finally back to each other. Their heartbeats increased tempo in unison.

With a dour frown of black humour, Stan summed up Uri's precise geopolitical analysis, "In the immortal words of U.S. Marshall Matt Dillon from the black and white cowboy TV series, *Gunsmoke*, 'It only takes one bullet to kill a man and one gun to fire it.'"

"And you cautioned me not to say anything about this to anyone!" Uri barked at his ex. "I'll see your cautionary bid for silence in this lethal game of poker you are playing and raise your bet with an equally scary warning. You will be highest priority targets of Russian FSB, Canadian CSIS, and American CIA snipers and a host of other nefarious non-state players if this gets out. I'm torn between thanking you and cursing you for asking me to verify what you have found. I'm leaning toward cursing. I will just be anonymous collateral damage without any footnote in the resurrection of the Cold War. Now I leave you to figure out what you are going to do. I need a stiff drink of Vodka and a few more as chasers. Remember not to call me next time you're in town, Olivia," he snarled.

After Uri left the hotel room, Olivia transferred her attention exclusively on Stan. "I need a stiff drink too. Care to join me?"

"So, what's our strategy now?" Stan asked as he poured two drinks from the mini bar in the room.

"It's an understatement to suggest that we hold the high ground over Inspector J.P.R.C. Leblanc and his co-conspirators," Olivia replied with a serious yet sarcastic tone. A Sunday school silence filled the space between them as they attempted to make sense of what lay on the table.

"Better yet, partner, we hold the high ground over those who yearn for the good old days of the Cold War," Stan countered with a grim tone. "Now Version 2.0 would have exponentially more ramifications on international relations and be much more lethal. We are back in the fray, deeper than we ever could have imagined, whether we like it or not. We have unknowingly crossed the Rubicon, the point of no return."

"Can you lift any fingerprints from the pistol and silencer, in addition to the paper? I am thinking about further potential evidence we might need to incriminate god knows who or use as surety to negotiate if we find ourselves having to fortify our ramparts and bastions."

Stan thought for a moment, still trying to make sense of the circumstances churning in their midst like erratic eddies of flotsam and jetsam at ebb tide.

"*Si vis pacem, para bellum* – If you want peace, prepare for war," Olivia translated. "I can only imagine what the battle space may encompass and the myriad of armaments available in the armouries of the combatants, some – more than likely *many* – aimed directly at us."

His stare morphed into a faint yet buoyant smile. "Theoretically, I should be able to lift a print. The environmental conditions are a factor, though. A major consideration is the porousness of the surfaces. The gun barrel, the silencer and the magazine should be ideal surfaces. The paper, possibly, depending on its composition. Because the metal box was sealed tight and the contents wrapped in oilskin, we may be in luck."

"I was exhilarated that the ebb tide of our luck had reversed when we pulled the metal box out of the ground. There is the old adage – be careful what you ask for because you just might get it. Well, we got it in spades. How can you do this, lift the prints given the fact you have been out of Ident for such a long time? Don't you need your special bushes, powder and tape for lifting the prints?"

"Let me ask one of my former associates who has a summer home up the coast from Antigonish toward the provincial border. It will be a long shot. If I can, and the operative word is *if,* I will be able to take a photo of any latent prints on the pistol and the paper with the camera on my cell phone. It actually has better resolution than the cameras we used twenty years ago. I'm reluctant to store any e-pics in the cloud because nothing is completely secure from someone who really wants to access digital data. So, I may just copy the file to a thumb drive for you and another for me. Even that has an elevated risk factor."

Olivia nodded. "I wouldn't be surprised if red flags have already been raised with the Canadian Security Intelligence Service and a few other agencies in Ottawa based solely on our preliminary enquiries to date, like my Access for Information request."

"And in Moscow," Stan added. "Ottawa is awash with spies, including some who have infiltrated our CSIS Watcher Service, their sole purpose being to monitor any variation in routine activities including e-traffic."

"I suggest we find an obscure place locally where we can hideout," Olivia proposed. "I say locally because we want to avoid public locations where facial recognition surveillance cameras have been installed clandestinely to monitor persons of interest. I suspect that the CSIS already has our respective homes under surveillance. Any suggestions as to where we can lie low until we can come up with a revised strategy? If at all possible, I'd prefer to have someone else return our rental car to the airport before we rise to the exalted status of number one on the ten most-wanted lists of who knows how many nefarious players."

"Now that you ask, I do," Stan offered.

As a child, Olivia would ask her grandmother to tell her stories of the old country. She would always start off, 'Now that you ask,' in an almost dutiful manner. Her grandmother would talk about the sparse letters regarding Communist oppression that her relatives wrote to her about. They were always intriguing. And then the letters stopped coming altogether. As Olivia grew older, she saw similarities to what she read in Tolstoy's *War and Peace* and fables of other Russian authors like Dostoyevsky and Turgenev. All were similar to those that Uri had recited to her when they were first married, on those rare occasions when he would reveal rarely disclosed details from his past, specifically from surreptitious Spetsnaz missions. They too were ominous although sparse in specifics and few in number. They stopped when his nightmares became overwhelming.

Accounts by her grandmother and Uri, and now the Russian Makarov PB pistol and the Cyrillic script wove a pattern of premonition. Together, they triggered recollections of the annual recital of her father: *Remember, remember, / The fifth of November, / The Gunpowder treason and plot; / I know of no reason / Why the Gunpowder treason / Should ever be forgot!* She shrugged her shoulders as the familiar ill-omened shiver ran the length of her spine.

Time to listen to her own advice. *Your intuition is never wrong. It's only your misinterpretation of your intuition that gets you into trouble.* There was more at stake now that she had a partner to consider. Leblanc had been responsible for separating them before. Until they met at the Toronto Pearson International Airport, she hadn't realized how much she resented Leblanc's intervention, how much she missed Stan being by her side. When they met at the airport, she had meant to tell him, emphasize her feelings, not just her gratitude for the lessons he had taught her. But she never got around to it, now regretted it. That time didn't seem to be right. Now, it didn't seem to be the right time either. They were together again. That is all that mattered. She would find a time. She would not regret her inaction again.

From a time-management perspective, she would make note in her university calendar of appointments made and time needed to complete tasks. She would remind people, especially students, the day before their scheduled appointment. Time was of the essence. Her colleagues both envied and admired her for her discipline. Non-scheduled time allowed her flexibility to do as she wanted, to bring balance to her life. She would chuckle at the reality of scheduling in unscheduled time for relaxation. It seemed like an oxymoron. She reflected on an old Yiddish proverb: *man plans and God laughs.* With maximum flexibility, they would need to plan their next steps with contingencies and mitigation strategies in the event the gods started to laugh.

CHAPTER 5

Traffic was sparse as they drove north with Bedford in the rear-view mirror in their nondescript retro SUV. The registered owner was following behind in their rented vehicle which he would park in the vacant rental car space at the Halifax Stanfield International Airport. There he would leave the keys in the overnight drop-off box. He would then take the airport shuttle bus back to Halifax. Stan would see the rental charges on his credit card invoice next month. He wondered which intelligence agency or other alerted non-state players might monitor his mail delivered to his home as a means of establishing an audit trail or a trail of Hansel and Gretel bread crumbs to follow. He could contact his credit card company and just ask for an e-invoice, but that might leave yet one more trail of bread crumbs, more evidence regarding their profiles leading to their whereabouts. A paperless invoice was still a better option.

"You never cease to amaze me, Stanislaw Polanski. When you were my trainer, you seemed to know someone who knew someone," Olivia grinned. For whatever reason, she seemed more relaxed with Stan as a partner than she had ever experienced with other colleagues or even closer associates, including Uri. She again wondered how their relationship might have advanced had they remained together in Bedford. Some other members of the RCMP married and seemed to stay together despite the Force that demonstrated tacit intolerance for such relationships. Indeed for much of the Force's existence, a member was strictly forbidden to marry at all, without obtaining prior approval from his superior officers.

Stan glanced over with an equally affable smile. "We will pick up some groceries in Truro and be in Oxford within the hour.

Then on to Port Howe via Kolbec with the River Phillip on the right. Then left onto the Amherst Shore Road. We will be putting on the teapot within forty minutes. On a clear day from Amherst Shore you can see across Baie Verte to the peninsula with Cape Tormentine at its tip. Ferries from the mainland once crossed the Northumberland Straits to Bordon, Prince Edward Island until it was replaced by the Confederation Bridge. Today, there is a quaint ferry that runs from Caribou, Nova Scotia to Wood Islands, Prince Edward Island. Once this case is solved, we can drive over the bridge and return via the ferry. Nothing else happens along this stretch of the coast. The perfect place to get away. No security surveillance cameras to worry about via the roads we will be taking. There is a security CCTV network around the farmhouse which the owner refers to as 'the ranch', in addition to outer buildings. Yes, it even has facial recognition software that is state of the art. It comes in handy for identifying intruders or online photos. I'll show you."

The road to Amherst Shore had once been the only coastal artery but today was devoid of any traffic except the odd farm vehicle lumbering along at speeds that would allow the tortoise to squander the race. This prompted Olivia to ask with a tinge of glibness but also with cautious curiosity, "What's there at Amherst Shore that requires this advanced level of CCTV security surveillance?"

"My friend is a retired lobster fisherman according to Canada Revenue Agency, but a computer techie by hobby. He inherited a century-old ranch house with a clutch of outer buildings on a sizeable plot of farm land, today mostly forested. He has fixed up the house on the inside with the most up-to-date satellite surveillance technology in the secure garret. He drives his cherished grey antique F-100 tractor around the few fields as a means of stress reduction and for show. If not being driven, it is stored with loving care in the secure garage. From all outward appearances, you wouldn't suspect anything. However, there is no point in tempting providence so we will park our retro SUV out of sight in the garage beside the tractor."

Olivia felt more relaxed. "Stan, what do you do to pass the time?" she asked.

"We will be able to conduct internet searches without being traced. The log-in sequence can be found in the barn, to the right as you enter the main door. I'll show you. The property also has some other features that enhance security including two clandestine tunnels, one to the garage and the other to the barn. I will show you them also."

Her stress level rose slightly at the explanation that there were additional advanced security features including tunnels but not to the point that she needed to drive the F-100 tractor around the property. *Why would that be necessary,* she mused. On second thought, perhaps having enhanced security wasn't such a bad idea given the fact that they were in possession of the metal box, containing the Russian Makarov PB pistol, silencer and the Cyrillic script which now connected them to Nikolai, Lada, his wife, and Ruslan, their KGB handler and God only knows who in the Canadian Security Intelligence Service hierarchy in addition to untold senior mandarins in the government bureaucracy. Although Uri, her ex, was relatively nearby in the event he might be needed again, he did not know where they were, nor would he. She had no intention of telling him, given his employment history and other associates from the Cold War.

After they placed the groceries on the kitchen counter and put on the teapot, Olivia surveyed the interior of the ranch with its circa turn-of-the-last-century rural decor and refurbished retro kitchen wood stove, in addition to modern fixtures and furnishings and other artifacts of an earlier simpler era. She anticipated being greeted with dingy windows and a dreary dismal structure engulfed in a dank smell of mold that had infiltrated every porous surface.

Instead she was pleasantly surprised at the somewhat opulent surroundings attended to on a scheduled maintenance basis by professional cleaners. A scent of fresh-baked bread and cinnamon buns seemed to linger. Her initial thought suggested that it would be an ideal location for someone seeking isolation from the distractions of a hectic life style such as a contemplative philosopher, fiction writer or a serious antisocial introvert. *Or a retired spy seeking solitude from other spies*, she pondered. The sophistication of technology housed in the secure office left her almost speechless.

"Lobster fishing must be lucrative," she commented in jest. She couldn't recall anyone in the agrarian or fisheries industries she had ever known having the means or wherewithal to invest in such high-level technology. They just drew unemployment insurance during the off-seasons when snow covered the corn fields or the fishery had been closed down by the government due to decreasing stocks resulting from over-fishing. She supposed being a techie was as good a pastime as repairing lobster traps and fishing nets, or getting caught up on the most recent publications regarding the best practices in the art and science of Atlantic Canada husbandry.

"He has private sector clients who supplement his income with compensation for services rendered," Stan added. "He goes fishing for them but not for marine crustaceans. Instead, he hauls in big data, and from it he extracts information, intelligence. For some, secret sins of their pasts can become a harsh mistress. If exposed, it can demand a handsome recompense, like fine Côtes du Rhône AOC wine or exquisite VSOP cognac. And the more illicit the information, the higher the remuneration. That is where the sophistication of his technological system allows for unfettered access to an abundance of such knowledge. That's what pays the bills. The lobster boat is just a convenient cover. Such is the lifestyle of someone who resides in the growing community of Cyberville and works in the online spyosphere metropolis."

"Interesting. No lobster traps to maintain. I recall you saying that prior to being transferred to the Bedford Detachment, you had worked with interesting people doing interesting things in interesting places. I'm sensing a little déjà vu?"

Stan maintained his subtle smile that hadn't migrated from his lips. "He is indebted to me for favours – like a few other acquaintances you and I may have to tap on the shoulder after we map out version two of our strategic plan."

"You mentioned the RCMP Watcher Service. It's not common knowledge so how do you know about it?"

Stan was short on detail in his response to this question. She recalled him being a master of preferential disclosure when they first worked together. It initially annoyed her. She later found it intriguing and now alluring.

"I played in that sandbox while at university before I joined the Force," he elaborated. "That is where Bernie and I first crossed paths. I never formally met Inspector J.C.R.C. Leblanc, but I learned about his exploits, both above and below board. It was like eavesdropping without wiretap warrants, and sometimes skating on the periphery of legal authority." He lowered his voice and dipped his forehead as if paying homage to the technology gods. E-eavesdropping added the necessary leverage, tended to bring balance to the playing field which otherwise leaned in favour of the bad guys. A reed-slim smile expressed his true sentiments.

OLIVIA HUMMED AS SHE SIPPED her cup of steaming hot green tea. "There seems to be a common, perhaps coincidental theme emerging in this case."

Without commenting, Stan cast a curious gaze and subtly nodded his head in acknowledgement.

"Barns," she proposed. "Hackett was murdered in a barn. The

FLQ cell planned to kidnap Laporte and Cross in a barn that the RCMP subsequently burned down. We located the metal box and the contents by following a compass bearing of 321 degrees from the corner of a barn that no longer exists. Now, we are hiding out from the CSIS and possibly the FSB, the CIA and God knows who else in a ranch house adjacent to a barn like the one in which Hackett was killed, as we create our own stratagem to thwart them all. And this barn hides the log-in sequence to what I can only speculate. What else might have Hackett's barn hidden that we did not find in the brief time we were there on 5 November 1978? I wouldn't be surprised if, today, it is also monitored with CCTV cameras. And in 1978 also but not nearly as sophisticated as today's technology."

Stan raised his bushy salt-and-pepper eyebrows and crooked his head ever so slightly. "I like your line of thinking, particularly your differentiation between our strategy as opposed to their conspiracy, whoever *they* are."

"The distinction is delicate but essential," she reinforced. The tone of her voice identified unambiguously the gravity of her intent.

"We need to find out all we can about John Robert Hackett. Part of a partnered Russian sleeper cell with his wife, Lada, and their supposed Russian handler, Ruslan? OK. Maybe? But there has to be more to Hackett, much more," Stan speculated.

"I'm looking forward to exploring your friend's secure internet and its research potential. I sense that I would have been able to write some brilliant research papers in my university days had I had access to this sophisticated level of technology and multi-layered covert databases."

"And you would have been even more frustrated because you would not have been authorized to publish anything due to the high security level of the sources and means of access."

"Ahhhh, the double edge of the intelligence sword," Olivia

uttered with an impatient sigh. She was gaining a better appreciation of Stan's expression to level the playing field. *What the codebreakers at Bletchley Park could have done with Bernie's computer housed in the garret of this rural Nova Scotia ranch house*, she mused.

The first casualty of war is the truth, Winston Churchill had stated. But the truth by whose standards? From her all too brief conversations with Uri when he infrequently spoke about his experience with the Spetsnaz, there were truths, partial truths and make-believe truths. From which of these three playing fields was Inspector Leblanc, the covert croupier, dealing cards – the fixed deck that he could draw three aces off the bottom of the pack? Or was there a fourth field, outright lies being divulged in order to gain and maintain power, in addition to wealth wagered to manipulate that power at a macro geopolitical level. Was that the fifth column veiled in the Trojan Horse, part of their fifth of November treasonous plot?

CHAPTER 6

Stan navigated the labyrinth of carpeted hallways that led to an office in the ranch house illuminated only by the moon shining through the reinforced skylight. He squinted through blurry eyes at Olivia as she sat erect with an elegance he had often dreamed about. "It's the middle of the night. What are you doing up so late?" He squinted at his watch. "Or so early?"

When confronted with cognitive challenges, she often awoke in the early morning hours with abrupt revelations. Trying to figure out who murdered constables Davidson and Hamilton, and whether Leblanc was a good cop or a corrupt cop were no exceptions. Without breaking her concentration from the blue glow that emitted from the triad of over-sized monitors that surrounded her like a horseshoe, Olivia replied, "I researched John Robert Hackett a.k.a. Nikolai associated with his wife Sylvia Hackett a.k.a. Lada and their comrade controller, Ruslan."

"And?" Stan prompted.

"And Hackett has a German connection in addition to Russian. He had been a senior Nazi SS officer, Oberstleutnant, who went by the name of Brandt Felix Schmidt. He was taken prisoner by the Allies, more than likely allowing himself to be captured, whereupon he was transported to the POW camp in Lethbridge, Alberta. Life as a POW would have been harsh but significantly more pleasant with higher probability of survival than in the rear echelon let alone the forward edge of any battlefield. He remained in Canada after the war and changed his name to John Robert Hackett. I'm sensing that the maneuvering was purposeful and strategic, and aided by Russian spies already embedded as senior bureaucrats, the start of a well-established communist network."

"Nazi SS lieutenant colonel. You don't rise to that rank overnight," Stan commented, his eyes now wide open and his attention fully focused on the data on the multiple monitors. "Every Nazi was someone else before the March 1933 election when Adolf Hitler became the Chancellor of Germany. Heinrich Himmler, having been previously appointed by the Führer in 1929 as *Reichsführer*, the leader of the Nazi SS, was confirmed in that position in 1933 which morphed into the dreaded Nazi Security Service, the SD – *Sicherheitsdienst*. We must assume that Hackett a.k.a Nikolai, a.k.a. Oberstleutnant Brandt Felix Schmidt had already been endorsed by *Reichsführer* Heinrich Himmler or some other highly influential Nazi party official for him to rise in rank so quickly. Lenin's Cheka, his own secret police, must have been strategic in their vision for communism shortly after the Bolshevik revolution as they focused on the fall of Germany after WWI and its mercurial rise in the late 1920s and early 1930s. It would not be unrealistic for the Cheka to embed a mole within the Nazi SS during this bewildering tenuous period, in order to forge Hackett's credentials."

"*Eto pravil'no, tovarishch* – That is correct, comrade." Olivia read the screen of a subsequent search sequence. "The plot thickens. More germane to our case, his father had been a Russian Cheka spy, sent by Lenin to Berlin and later Munich. There Hackett learned to speak German fluently with a flawless Bavarian lilt. Around this time, he joined the Nazi Party, but as a Russian agent. Hackett had allegedly murdered another German prisoner of war who had become suspicious of his forged double identity and questionable rank. Hackett was never charged with this murder because there was insufficient conclusive evidence to substantiate the charge let alone convict."

"You *have* been busy," Stan commended. "That raises the stakes exponentially. I have a better appreciation why your ex, Uri, was so worried about what we had unearthed literally, and had surreptitiously drawn him into. But why did Hackett's wife, Lada, and comrade controller, Ruslan, kill him as we suspect?"

"Why does anyone kill? For fear of loss or opportunity for gain, primarily in the arena of love, lust and power, money being intrinsically linked to power."

"OK. But what about Mike Davidson? Why was he murdered, as we also suspect?" Stan probed.

"He pulled Hackett over supposedly as a routine traffic stop on the road close to the farm on Hammonds Plains Road just hours before Hackett was murdered. Was it just routine or had Davidson and Hackett engaged in previous conversations under the guise of routine motor vehicle enforcement? Great cover scenario but careless on Davidson's part to do so that close to the farm. Why was Davidson suspicious? Of what? Had Hackett alluded to something? Is that what motivated Lada and Ruslan to murder him? Were they, whoever *they* are, fearful that Hackett was about to defect and turn them in? That brings us back to our initial question: Who killed Davidson? The same person who killed Hamilton?"

Stan drew his hand over his five-a.m. shadow as he considered possible answers. He focused on another question, the answer to which might connect some of the dots. "Do we have any evidence that links Lada and Ruslan to Hackett's death, murder, beyond just speculation at this juncture?"

"Hackett had blood gurgling in his throat as he uttered his final words to me. I wrote them down phonetically, at least what I thought he said, 'Sheenataish Mig ... Tavish' or 'Sheena Tavish or McTavish.' What if he really said Zhena Tovarishch and I transcribed it incorrectly? That would be the definitive evidence, the link."

"I'm not following you." Stan seemed puzzled.

"Zhena is Russian for wife and Tovarishch is Russian for

comrade, a term used within the context of the Cold War. There can only be one explanation. Hackett was telling me that his wife, Lada, and comrade controller, Ruslan, shot him."

"Ten out of ten on intelligence. You are brilliant, Olivia Daniels," Stan replied. His enthusiasm piqued. The ebb tide had definitely turned. "Less so on irrefutable evidence admissible in a court of law. But we aren't gathering evidence. Instead, we are trying to find out what happened to Davidson and Hamilton. We are getting closer to the truth with each revelation. Question: was Inspector Leblanc aware of this? If he was, I understand why he had Corporal Hartmann take over the crime scene at the barn on Hammonds Plains Road while Leblanc cancelled our request for Identification Services and GIS to attend the scene. The political implications would have rumbled on for a long time with far-reaching Cold War international implications, especially south of the border. The CIA would have gone into spin dry as would many of our NATO allies and several foes."

Stan squinted as an isolated yet speculative grin crept from his lips to define his eye brows and ultimately his forehead.

CHAPTER 7

Stan brought Olivia a cup of green tea and placed it quietly on a side table so as not to disturb her train of thought. She was in her element, fully immersed in offensive cyber research operations with the aid of his friend's electronic intelligence architecture. She was searching for clues on anything that might shed additional light on the deaths of their colleagues, Davidson and Hamilton.

She smiled her thanks, only resting to formulate another empirical search sequence. Stan's admiration for her grew. He considered how they might have lived their lives together rather than separately. He lamented the fact he had not kept in contact with her. It would have been easy enough. Did she have similar regrets? He never felt depressed, just remorseful for not having been completely truthful with his wife, Betty, about his innermost feelings. Pragmatically, he was now simply aware that Betty was dead, no longer here. He searched for reasons why his and Olivia's lives had taken different trajectories and were now travelling on separate albeit closer orbits. Like Olivia, he now dwelt on search patterns for evidence to help make sense of the deaths of Davidson and Hamilton and find answers to a myriad of other related questions.

"Anything new?" he asked when she paused in contemplation.

Olivia huffed in frustration. "Nothing of consequence. Not yet at any rate. I just need to hit on the best search sequence. The chilling fog currently wafting off the Northumberland Straits has shrouded my Pooh Bear mind like an impenetrable veil. It happens on occasion." She stared up beyond the ceiling, marshalling her thoughts.

The sound of her voice accompanied with her jesting humour projected a reassuring warmth that he savoured. "Let's explore another angle," Stan suggested. "Anything related to J.P.R.C. Leblanc? There was one facet of his career that amazed and annoyed everyone who knew him, including me."

Olivia withdrew her fingers from the keyboard, reached for the side table, wrapped them around the mug of steeping hot green tea and raised it to her lips. "Hmmmmm, good, thank you. What are you thinking?" she queried, anticipating that his suggestion might lead to a productive gold seam in her mining for clues and, better still, answers.

"Leblanc was promoted faster than anyone in the Force," Stan remarked. "To corporal at five years, sergeant at seven and commissioned as inspector at just over nine."

"Never knew that," Olivia acknowledged. "I can see why that would piss off a few people. If I remember correctly, the average promotion service from constable to corporal was about nine years at minimum and eleven on average. He must have dug up some dirt on someone senior in the Force whom he could blackmail."

Her response triggered a thought in Stan's mind that initiated an intriguing thread. But he lost it as he gazed upward. He returned his attention to her and, as he did, the truant thought manifested itself.

It was Olivia's turn not to disturb him, but to offer a supportive expression. She sat erect and elegant, gazing at him. Unfortunately, her precise pose again became a distraction to him.

He shook his head, eyes averted. He grunted, mimicking her in a futile effort to rid himself of his exasperation. The silence surged around him bringing with it an opaque mist akin to the Northumberland fog that surrounded the farmhouse, in place of the clarity he sought. But silence wasn't always synonymous with peacefulness and certainly could not guarantee it. By the time it cleared, the thread was gone like a caboose that had become uncoupled, drifting away onto a siding. There was an elephant in the room and he knew they should talk about it sooner rather than later, if they were going to work effectively together as TOFIS sleuths.

He picked up on another tangential thought. "Rumour had it that someone senior in the Québec government had links to the Montréal crime mob. The octopus had a ninth tentacle that reached deep into the not-so-hallowed halls and backrooms of Parliament in Ottawa."

"Was there a connection to Security Service? The October 1970 FLQ Crisis? Nikolai?" she thought aloud.

"Hopefully you can find something. I do know that whatever it was eventually caught up with him." Stan hovered over her shoulder, anticipating that Olivia's initial search queue would fill the screen with a treasure trove of answers. Instead, she reached up to him with her empty mug and a don't-crowd-me expression. "Another cup, please."

By the time Stan returned, Olivia had some preliminary results. "There had been a number of investigations into corruption in the Montréal region, some more enlightening than others. One scandal was associated with Leblanc but only on the periphery. It suggested Leblanc had used effective investigative techniques as a member of an anti-crime taskforce. If you dress up intelligence with bullet-proof provenance, you can appear like a saint."

Stan's tone was irritable. "He was never formally linked to any corruption, although his mercurial rise in rank fizzled out shortly afterwards. For unknown reasons, he remained an inspector for the remainder of his career. Unusual to say the least. But a plausible conclusion. Even today, if you get promoted to inspector, the next step to superintendent is almost assured." Stan dwelt on that revelation. "Unless you get tarred and feathered with the same brush that got you mysteriously promoted with contrived merit in the first place."

Olivia locked eyes on Stan, while analyzing the mounting

information. As she was thinking, he turned on his heel and blurted out, "The elusive thread!"

"Excuse me?"

Stan elaborated. "Perhaps it wasn't blackmailing as such. Perhaps something else, not really sinister but not completely Sunday school innocent either. We have assumed thus far that Leblanc was a corrupt cop who took his brass knuckles to confession. What if he wasn't corrupt but found himself navigating the perimeter of a criminal cesspool that others in the Force and/or government were frequenting?"

Olivia returned his stare with wide eyes. Their fuzzy theory started to take on the trappings of the vagueness of discernable details.

"Another unknown," Stan muttered with a sarcastic sort of a smirk. "But then again, he could have been part of a Security Service cover-up. Or an ongoing investigation into infiltration by Moscow-motivated crime involving sleeper cells like Nikolai and Lada, all coordinated by their comrade – tovarishch Ruslan." He blinked. "I just don't know. We need more hard facts."

Olivia joined him in reflection before speculating, "I haven't found any concrete links, yet. Maybe he was a good cop, just abusive, arrogant and obnoxious. But perhaps that was part of his evolving cover one way or another, lacking in benevolence in social interactions."

"I think we need to have a tête-a-tête with Inspector J.P.R.C. Leblanc and on our chosen turf and timetable. His invitation to meet needs to link him conclusively to something that demonstrates we hold the high ground but doesn't reveal that we have just a smattering of not necessarily related facts. Thus, he would have no choice but to meet with us so we could either smoke him out if he was a dirty cop or bolster his work if he was a good cop."

"Nikolai, Lada and Ruslan," Olivia proposed. "If he takes the bait, that will be more telling evidence and the missing link – certainly to Nikolai and Lada, and hopefully to the deaths of Davidson and Hamilton. But if he is clean, who is dirty? There had to have been someone, at least one. Corporal Werner Hartmann? But he was subordinate in rank to Leblanc, had no influence over him. Who was above Leblanc in his secret squirrel organization within the Force or government within the political bureaucracy? And who might have been pulling Hartmann's strings if not Leblanc?"

"OK, but we need to consider the consequences of all scenarios. It could go sideways pretty quickly," Stan cautioned.

"At this juncture, we are not advancing on the Rubicon merely to test the temperature by dipping our toes in the rushing water. You know Leblanc better than I do." Olivia passed the baton to Stan. "What do you suggest?"

"If I was Leblanc, the clean cop, the probability of me responding to an invitation to have coffee with two retired junior constables who I once treated like crap, would be infinitely small. If I was Leblanc, the corrupt cop, I would be arriving with backup. More so if I was the RCMP Security Service now CSIS-KGB double agent about to be exposed because of my association with John Robert Hackett a.k.a. Nikolai, the Moscow sleeper cell agent a.k.a. Nazi SS Lieutenant Colonel Brandt Felix Schmidt who killed a fellow POW to keep his true identity a secret. I think we need to call in our landlord to help with the planning."

"Agreed. Three heads facing off against Cerberus, the multi-headed hound of Hades, are better odds." Olivia's cell phone vibrated. She eyed the time, then focused on the sender ID, finally at the text: *"I feel obliged to caution you to be very careful. Don't reply. S U."* She showed Stan. "Better the devil you know than the devil you don't know," she mused.

"What does it mean – S U?"

"S U, Spetsnaz Uri. Someone has poked the Russian Ukrainian

City Centre
URGENT PRIMARY CARE CENTRE

~~tbd-journal~~ Euro 1.49
Scotia 1.4712
NBC 1.4712
BOC 1.44

tbd-journal.com

"To Be Decided" Journal

Volume 8 –
Alternatives & Potentialities

"Reverence and Revolution"

qu3uv2u3w7

1290 Hornby Street ✚ Vancouver, British Columbia ✚ V6Z 0A3

FLT 221   5.05 arrival

778 882-1614

email the Path

MEDIPAC travel insurance
1(877) 633 4722

1) List of traffic types
2) Questions for the Port
   — restrictions
   — nighttime? etc.
3) Other users
   1) Log booms.
   2) Chip barges.
   3) Work barges.
   4) Gravel "
   5) Recreational users.
   6) Fishing (commercial/_____)

Walnut House

bear to test its reaction. He is letting me know that Moscow is calling. Knowing Uri, he would not have responded in any way that would suggest we had recently crossed paths."

Stan was bothered by the text and unsure of its consequences. "You said and he agreed that there is no love lost between the two of you. I need to ask if push came to shove, would he be there for you, for us?"

"Not out of obligation to an ex but out of a sense of duty and loyalty to a former professional academic colleague. That is one of the traits that attracted me to him. Loyalty. If he believed that someone had demonstrated integrity or courage, he would fight alongside them. He would respond if you sounded the bugle because I sense that he respects you as a fellow warrior. Grudgingly, he would be there for me if I sent up a flare. One last point to remember, he subscribes to no religious faith. Instead, just faith in himself."

"Thanks, good to know," Stan acknowledged. "I like people who stand by their word and are who they appear to be."

"That's it!" Olivia exclaimed.

"That's what?"

"One unknown has been bugging me. In the barn, I checked Hackett's pockets for identification. His driver's licence read John Robert Hackett, date of birth 7 April 1931. Initially, I concluded the violent circumstances of his death could explain the incompatibility I perceived in his age, but the photo on his driver's licence also seemed oddly mismatched. He appeared older. His date of birth must have been changed when he became John Robert Hackett after being released from the POW camp as Nazi SS officer Oberstleutnant Brandt Felix Schmidt."

Stan half-smiled. "Constants aren't constant and variables don't vary. That's just a given. There are contradictions and falsehoods in intelligence, in evidence and simple fact."

"Constants aren't and variables don't! Haven't heard that before," Olivia exclaimed.

"It was one of my wife's expressions," he replied.

Olivia smiled, at a loss for an appropriate emotional response in an awkward moment.

"Betty was a micro-biologist," Stan explained.

Olivia sensed that he wanted to talk about his wife so she took what she thought was an open invitation. "Tell me about Betty. What attracted you to her?"

"We met while working on a murder case, a partially decomposed body of a man and his dog had been unearthed in the same shallow grave. Betty had been called in to collect biological samples. Did you know that no two decomposing corpses are exactly alike?"

"Never knew that," Olivia replied.

"Our first dinner date was not a romantic candle-lit Parisienne meal of Boeuf Bourguignon with a 1967 Côte du Rhône followed by crème brûlée and Cognac. Quite the contrary, it was at a truck stop. We dined at a table covered with a sticky clear plastic sheet and paper napkins, not a white linen tablecloth. The only quasi-edible choice on the menu was a deluxe cheese burger with equally greasy fries washed down with coffee made with the beans that Juan Valdez had swept off the table onto the floor."

Olivia appreciated his humour but responded to the mention of a white linen tablecloth by pulling back, increasing slightly the distance between them. She was good at keeping secrets.

Stan noted her reaction. Perhaps his description was inappropriate, too intimate. He quickly summarized in a more rational manner. "Apart from being a talented crime scene analyst, Betty was a crossword puzzle aficionado like me. I was fascinated by the macro linguistics of the puzzles, the words. She analyzed the micro pattern of the overlapping letters. She had considered writing a book someday on the letter patterns but cancer intervened too rapidly. She was dead within five months of the diagnosis."

Olivia felt even more awkward for asking and reacting the way she did. On occasion, students would blurt out candid facts about their personal lives and relationships. She replied to Stan in the same neutral yet supportive manner. "Thank you for sharing."

"Sorry for being a bit too personal. Believe it or not, you are the only person to have asked me that since her death. Thanks for enquiring."

Olivia did not reply but instead continued to hold his gaze with a supportive smile. She needed to get back on track. Hackett's identity was evolving first as a Russian spy, then a Nazi SS officer, and finally a sleeper cell partner in a quiet Maritime community where everybody knew about their neighbours or thought they knew. More importantly, what was Leblanc's involvement, then and now?

Stan re-engaged on the trail for facts. "Let's map out what we know with a link analysis. Hammonds Plains, Montréal and Ottawa are locations in common. Hackett a.k.a. Russian sleeper cell agent Nikolai a.k.a. Nazi SS officer Brandt Schmidt, his Russian sleeper cell wife Sylvia a.k.a. Lada and their Moscow handler, Ruslan, in addition to Inspector J.P.R.C. Leblanc and Corporal Werner Hartmann are common players that we have thus far been able to identify. On the periphery are Davidson, Hamilton and you and I. We can safely surmise there are others directly or tangentially involved perhaps not in Hammonds Plains, but more than likely in Montréal and Ottawa, perhaps elsewhere, including south of the border."

CHAPTER 8

"Olivia, meet Bernie Allen. Bernie, my new partner, Olivia Daniels. You may recall me mentioning her."

"Yes, a few times. In fact, several times if I recall correctly," Bernie replied as he bowed his head and smiled graciously as if greeting an old friend whom he hadn't seen for far too long.

Olivia's customary reply was interrupted. She gazed down in response to wet licks from an oversized tongue.

"This mutt with questionable social etiquette is Digger," Bernie explained. "Appropriately named because he presents visitors with a sundry of gifts that he digs up. Although his heritage is of dubious ancestral lineage, he appears to have a streak of bloodhound and retriever."

Olivia patted her newest friend on the head. "Very much enjoy the internet potential of your service provider," she conceded as she extended her now-moist hand to Digger's master.

Bernie not only didn't mind Olivia using his system sporadically, but encouraged it, as he did Stan. Different keyboard signatures tended to distract electronic eavesdroppers, especially when intermittent and with search subjects and strings running from Walt Disney to George Gershwin. It was all about confusing the e-fingerprint of the sender of the codes.

"The WiFi comes complimentary with the accommodations. Apologize for the lack of housekeeping services, though," Bernie added with a jovial manner.

A warm smile lit up Olivia's face. The cozy rustic farmhouse in rural Nova Scotia had a charm that surpassed any urban expectations. It reminded her of her own upbringing on the prairies where her great grandparents had been among the first settlers in the Cyprus Hills in southeastern Alberta at a time when the North West Mounted Police were establishing a foothold. How life had changed for citizens of the fledging Dominion and its burgeoning federal police presence whose purpose it had been to maintain law and order while detering foreign aspirations for territorial acquisitions. Today, it was less about defending physical borders, and increasingly more about alien ambitions for geopolitical gain brought about through ideological disruption and distraction – law and order in another context.

"Brought some extra groceries in the event you wish to extend your vacation at Amherst Shore. How else can I help? A day out lobster fishing, perhaps?" Bernie offered in jest.

"Fishing for two-legged creatures as opposed to ten-legged crustaceans," Stan replied guardedly. "We need your assistance to provide security for a tea party we are planning with an ex-colleague who has a rather unsavoury reputation with international implications."

"We have met a few of those in our day," Bernie acknowledged in a tone that signalled previous involvement with dubious characters of questionable conviction who they had stealthily outmaneuvered with practiced craft and cunning.

Stan unspooled a comprehensive analysis with emphasis on the chronology of events concerning the unsolved murder of John Robert Hackett, and the mysterious intervention by RCMP Security Service, specifically Inspector J.P.R.C. Leblanc and Corporal Werner Hartmann.

Olivia briefed him on the equally mystifying deaths of their two colleagues, constables Davidson and Hamilton, and finally on the enhanced research results delivered by his search engine. Some delivered more results but not necessarily better, like big data including National Security Agency foreign signals intelligence SIGNET.

What she was seeking but what seemed to elude her was accuracy verification for all search sequences.

A faint frown creased Bernie's forehead. "I agree with your assessment that there appears to be much more to this case than what you have discovered thus far," he commented. "I suggest we step back and consider the geopolitical factors, starting with the early days of the Cold War. Some of the cases we worked on, Stan, may be tangentially relevant."

Olivia watched the two friends who had what she imagined was a close collegial relationship. She correctly surmised some of those escapades would remain between them. It was nothing against her, but just the way it would remain. She too had secrets not to be revealed.

Bernie glanced at Stan. "I sense you haven't filled Olivia in on what we were working on back in the day?"

"Not all, not yet," Stan conceded.

"Perhaps you can do that while I put on a fresh pot of java and stow away the groceries."

Stan regarded Olivia with an apologetic grin. He was still a bit reticent about divulging all aspects of his life. Each time he mentioned anything related to his late wife, Betty, Olivia seemed to became uncomfortable. He wasn't sure how to approach the subject. His feelings. Her response. Their emerging relationship. This ranch house at Amherst Shore had become a sanctuary for him, a place to run away to, away from Betty, their strained marriage. He needed to face those and other ghosts from the many Christmases Past of Charles Dickens.

"The interesting people doing interesting things, in interesting places?" Olivia commented, aware of his hesitancy.

"I've mentioned the RCMP Watcher Service and how I scrutinized Leblanc's antics from the electronic sidelines. Bernie and I met at McGill University. He was also working with the Watcher

Service but as a computer geek before the term 'geek' was a common noun. Like Bill Gates, he had a vision of the potential of computer technology. But unlike Gates, he saw the probable consequences, good and bad, that cyber security would bring to spy architecture. In the wrong hands, the threat of offensive cyber operations was clear. The Cold War was a nuanced force that was about nuclear parity made all the more threatening by the vast advancements in technology. Winning the Cold War would be based on your ability to exploit tactical opportunities undetected, like those Nazi wolfpacks accomplished during the early years of the Second World War. Technical advances in sonar and communication codes ultimately changed what some perceived to be the inevitable outcome."

"And you?" Olivia gently pressed, with a warm inviting smile.

"Bernie took the technical route while I joined the Force to gain a better understanding of policing and investigative techniques. We kept in contact and, after my brief stint with Ident and crime analysis, I left the Force to work with him full-time. By then, he was an expert in all things cyber, specifically counter-espionage electronic surveillance such as cyber-hacking and code-breaking. That is the Coles Notes quick study version."

Olivia was consumed by questions but did not interrupt. She knew Stan had more background details to explain and would do so in the fullness of time. She was getting used to the tentative steps that bolstered his confidence in their emerging professional and personal relationship. She had lived alone too long. Now she needed to make a concerted effort not to take him for granted.

Bernie returned with the coffee. "Let's focus on the background and how that will help us to prepare for your tea party reunion with your enigmatic Inspector Leblanc. After the liberation of Paris in 1944, the Kremlin's initial raison d'être was to form political parties throughout Europe under a common communist doctrine, in the wake of successive Allied victories. They soon realized that forming governments wasn't in the cards. So, in response to the U.S. Marshall Plan, Moscow decided to modify the tactics of their political doctrine. Their new philosophy would be to create disruption in order to derail democracies by strategically inserting active agents and passive sleeper cells among other clandestine initiatives."

"That was a long time ago," Olivia suggested.

"Not that long for political manifestos. The roots of the Cold War reach even further back. In this century, the seeds were sown in the Bolshevik revolution two and a half decades earlier. Now fast-forward fifty years. In July 1967, French President Charles de Gaulle took the initiative to take France out of NATO. The KGB – reporting to their Politburo masters – alluded to their involvement in this political divorce. The same month, President de Gaulle gave his now infamous speech in Montréal: Vive Le Québec Libre. Coincidently, Moscow took advantage of the emerging Québec separatist movement by increasing the number of French- and English-speaking Soviet agents and the apparent awakening of Soviet sleeper cells such as Nikolai a.k.a. John Robert Hackett and his wife Lada a.k.a. Sylvia. These cells had been implanted to undermine and destabilize the Québec government, among others, which was consistent with the revised communist disruptive ideology."

"That was never discussed in my political science classes," Olivia muttered with an agitated tone. "The more you think you know, the more you realize you don't know, and the more you learn, the more you realize that you need to learn more."

"Let's muddy the waters and consider the CIA wild card," Bernie continued. "The FLQ Crisis caused a big security reaction south of the border. Three American mechanized military brigades were deployed, one to New Brunswick at Canadian Forces

Base Gagetown under the guise they were participating in joint American/Canadian military exercises. A second mechanized brigade was deployed to northern New York state within a stone's throw of the Québec border, and a third moved into northern Vermont. Two up one back – typical U.S. military ORBAT – order of battle."

"I questioned back then and still wonder today," Stan interjected. "If the FLQ Crisis was just a few disgruntled Québecois raising stink, it would have been assessed by the Americans as local low-level political rumbling. So, why deploy a modified military task force composed of three mechanized brigade groups in addition to placing other air and land rapid response resources on standby?"

"The U.S. must have had reliable information suggesting Russia was involved," Bernie replied. "More importantly, Moscow's perceived incursion in Québec posed an immediate and present threat to American national security. So, what caused the U.S. to perceive it as a Soviet military foray, a vanguard, at the height of the Cold War? Would the reason have been because the Cuban Missile Crisis a decade earlier was still fresh in the U.S. psyche? The potential strategic deployment of a few clandestine medium-range missiles in la belle province de Québec, as occurred in Cuba, would do more than raise their hackles."

Olivia interjected. "The documents in the metal box referred to Nikolai and Lada being directed by Moscow to engage in political disruption. Kidnapping and murdering Pierre Laporte, a political hostage, by members of the FLQ would certainly get the attention of a few folks, particularly those south of the border. But why and why then? There has to have been more."

"What's the common denominator?" Bernie asked. "What would have occurred in Montréal and Ottawa that was connected to the quiet rural community of Hammonds Plains, Halifax County, Nova Scotia?"

Bernie was the first to break the pensive silence that had filled the room. "Let's look at it from a slightly different perspective. If you have something that others don't have but desperately desire, they may want to keep you alive, at least until they get it. Then again, they may be prepared to kill to ensure that their competitors don't get to it first. A tangential question. What do the two of you have that others want because it links Montréal, Ottawa and Hammonds Plains to Washington and Moscow and possibly elsewhere in the international arena?"

"The documents that were in the metal box," Olivia suggested. "And why? Because they identify Montréal, Ottawa and Hammonds Plains as strategic locations where Moscow had inserted Soviet sleeper cells, amongst other locations."

"The Americans weren't too far off the mark when they feared the FLQ Crisis was a new front for Russian offensive action after the aborted Cuban Missile Crisis in 1962," Stan concluded. "That had been the Soviets' modus operandi in Southeast Asia, specifically Vietnam and Korea, and on the African continent, including the Democratic Republic of the Congo. There were others."

"Sleeper cells were the Soviet Fifth Column. Lada and Nikolai would not have been their only Trojan Horses," Olivia speculated. "Do you remember that three days after World War II ended, Igor Gourzenko, a cypher clerk in the Russian embassy in Ottawa, defected? That woke up both Canadian and American intelligence agencies, more so the latter, to the significant expanse of Russian intelligence networks. Let's not overlook the vocal campaign initiated by Senator Joseph McCarthy in the early 1950s against alleged communists in America, earning the label: A Red under every bed. Defections are invariably tinted with tragedy and some defectors are gnawed with guilt. Igor Gourzenko was no different."

Bernie continued his threat assessment. "In response to Stan's assertion, the Russians were prepared to kill Nikolai to ensure their competitors – the Americans and Canadians – wouldn't get to him first. That would strongly suggest Nikolai had been murdered because Lada and their controller comrade, Ruslan, truly believed the traffic checks by your highway patrol colleague, Mike Davidson, were not just routine community-based policing initiatives. They were, instead, convenient opportunities to exchange information."

"Let's assume for a moment that we have established a motive – it doesn't answer the question who killed Davidson," Olivia pondered out loud. "And Hamilton?" That was her and Stan's primary motivation for forming a light-hearted two old farts investigative services – TOFIS – partnership. Buoyancy morphed into deadly consequences when they pried open Pandora's metal box under the fence post.

"I recall Davidson and Hamilton hanging out together. If Davidson had told him about his conversations with John Robert Hackett, Davidson may have unknowingly signed Hamilton's death warrant," Stan suggested.

"Was Leblanc involved, directly or indirectly?" Olivia queried.

Bernie qualified, "Tangentially, if for no other reason than he took over the supposed investigation and assumed responsibility in so doing. Motivated more than likely by Moscow's manoeuvrings as a marauding player in the Cold War." Bernie lifted his shoulders, raised his hands and cocked an eyebrow. "Was he a good cop or a turncoat? I'm not sure at this time. He could conceivably be either but not both. And his emissary, Corporal Werner Hartmann, where does he fit in, if at all?"

Stan conjectured, "Hackett's hidden documents strongly suggested the possibility that the Russian Makarov PB pistol and silencer we found in the metal box had been used to assassinate Pierre Laporte, the Deputy Premier of Québec. We can correctly conclude it would have been used before Hackett was murdered because he would have to have buried it before he was fatally shot. We do know the documents are the key. Is the pistol also linked to the Montréal, Ottawa, Hammonds Plains triad? It has to be significant somehow. Why else would he have gone to such lengths to hide it with the documents? For someone to find? Hackett whispered to Olivia with his final desperate breath the coordinates: 321 degrees from the corner of the barn to a fence post."

Their train of thought was interrupted by persistent barking at the back door.

"Oh, you have been blessed, Olivia," Bernie grinned.

She bent down to Digger who had something in his mouth that looked like an earth-covered root.

"You are Digger's newest best friend," Bernie commented. "This is his favourite prize. He doesn't present this special gift to just anyone. If you throw it, he will retrieve it and then bury it for another day, another newest best friend."

Olivia followed the instructions, and immediately washed her hands in the kitchen sink, twice. In the distance, she watched Digger traipsing off to find another secreted place to hide his favourite treasure. She gazed after him. Bury it for another day, she mused. Is that what John Robert Hackett did with the metal box? Is that why he whispered in his dying breath the coordinates for me to follow?

"I know that contemplative look," Stan said as he stared at her. "What's the trigger? Talk to me, partner."

"Hackett had buried the metal box containing the Makarov PB pistol and the Cyrillic documents for another day, the day we dug it up. Did he bury something else under the same or another fence post?"

"Do you recall him saying something else? Did he point at anything in the barn?"

Olivia reflected back on her foggy recollection. "I wish I had made better notes," she muttered, slowly shaking her head from side to side as she stared forward with squinting eyes hoping to bring clarity to a shrouded memory. "He had his left hand on his gut over the shell dressing I had applied. He had grabbed my coat with his right hand and pulled me down toward his face with every bit of strength he could muster. I distinctly remember his vice-like grip. It was so tight it left bruises around my neck. He could not have physically pointed at anything." Olivia hesitated before continuing as if possessed by a spirit from another time and place. "His stare," she uttered as if a revelation had unexpectedly emerged for the first time from a fogbank. "He stared into my eyes with a desperate riveting intensity that I remember as clearly today as if it was the 5th of November 1978." She lingered again. "He knew the Grim Reaper was dragging him from this earthly world. "His gasp, his frantic final words hold the key somehow."

Olivia dwelt on an apparition. "Someone had buried Hackett. By now, his body would have decomposed with only his bones remaining, unlike Digger's favourite prize. The scent would be too old, too cold for even Digger or another equally gifted tracking dog to trail. The intuitive sensing scent would still be fresh, though, still out there for us to find and follow."

CHAPTER 9

"When you are up to your ass in alligators, it is difficult to remember that your initial objective was to drain the swamp," Bernie quipped.

"And that initial objective is to solve the mysterious deaths, perceived murders, of Davidson and Hamilton," Olivia reconfirmed, nodding as if as much for her own ratification in their mission as for Stan and Bernie. "It is safe to say that Leblanc is involved somehow. I am confident he is the nexus. If not at the nucleus, he knows who is. His connection presents two critical challenges. First, how do we contact him after all these years? Once we determine that, we need to confirm he received our invitation to meet. Second, where do we meet? We need to be sure that the locale will provide maximum surveillance and security for us, with a strategy for an easy exit if we need one."

"How we contact him is relatively easy," Bernie replied. "I have created an e-persona, an avatar who does not exist in reality, instead lives in a world of duplicitous motivations, a prism of misinformation as needed to counter double entendre.

This person already has a social media profile on Facebook, Twitter, and LinkedIn, in addition to an email and a physical snail mail address. Today, the e-world allows anyone to create an online identity in minutes unlike the old world of Cold War spies and sleeper cells that often took months, even years to establish."

Such anonymity raises the specter of the mission, Olivia considered. She caught her image in the partial reflection of the darkened ranch house window. Intelligence gathering had advanced exponentially since she first met Stan at Bedford Detachment. The

Canadian Police Information Center was in its relative infancy back then.

Bernie continued. "I suggest we use the physical post box because electronic means leave audit trails that will flag alerts for anyone covertly monitoring networks. Stan, you will recall one of our previous associates who worked in the Truro Post Office. He will intercept incoming mail and forward it to me in a nondescript envelope care of a second PO box at the Amherst Canada Post Office. In response to your second concern, we can be confident that the invitation has been received via a registered mail receipt."

"We can be more confident that someone at that address has received it, perhaps someone signing for Leblanc," Olivia qualified.

"We can be less confident about how it will be interpreted," Stan speculated with reservation, "given the fact that so much water has flowed under the bridge since we last crossed paths with him."

"For location to meet, I recommend we use a two-step process," Bernie suggested. "We direct Leblanc to go to Mount Pleasant Cemetery and to the headstone of Matthew Edward Brownell. There, we affix a note to a small bouquet of flowers that will instruct him to proceed to Riverview to the intersection of Kolbec and Dickson Roads. If he is being followed by agents of different political persuasions, or by his own backup, we will be alerted by our associates who will be watching the cemetery. The Riverview rendezvous site will provide 360-degree cover from the adjacent woods. That is not to say this strategy is foolproof. Leblanc could be wearing a wire and be in communication with his own confederates. In either case, he could also have a GPS tracker. Our contingency plan for that scenario is simple. We abort the mission at the first sign of a compromise."

Olivia nodded warily, reflecting on the scheme. "From a risk management perspective, there are two unknowns – Leblanc and possible third parties. Given the history of this case thus far, there is a higher degree of probability that agents of different political persuasions, as you say, will be present."

How Leblanc might react was a lesser concern. He would pose no threat if he failed to attend. They would consider an alternate plan to lure him into their snare. He would pose a minimal threat if he did show up. There would be enough of Bernie's associates to negate any immediate potential menace. Olivia started to focus on mitigation strategies to deal with agents of different political persuasion.

"To what lengths would Leblanc or foreign proxies go to ensure that the meeting either takes place or does not take place?" Bernie asked. His rhetorical posture prompted a guarded response from both Stan and Olivia.

"I am considering viable options as we speak," Olivia replied. "The probability is lowest that he will shoot first and ask questions later if he arrives alone and our letter to him suggests that we have evidence involving him in the shooting of Hackett. He won't know exactly what we know or if we have irrefutable incriminating physical evidence. He will still be inquisitive if he arrives with his own people. That is the best-case scenario. If he is being followed knowingly or otherwise by those of other political persuasions like the subtle shadows of night, including some of Uri's expatriates, there is an exponentially greater risk that they will shoot first. In either case, we need to be prepared."

"Just asking," Bernie speculated. "I'm sensing there is an off chance that Leblanc could be the sacrificial lamb. He's been out of the game for a while. If I were his former boss, I'd be asking if he could still keep a secret about secrets." He allowed the thought to percolate. "Alternately, the two of you could be the intended targets. It is apparent that you were rapidly transferred away from Bedford after Hackett had been shot in order to ensure you had no further involvement and ideally would forget about this case altogether in the fullness of time."

Stan monitored Olivia's reaction. "You seem unsure, hesitant. What are you thinking?"

"In the words of a wise man, there seems to be something untoward underfoot. The facts as we know them just don't add up."

"If you are worried, I am worried and I don't like being worried. What's sticking in your craw?" he pressed.

Olivia mulled over Bernie's proposition in the context of other unknowns. "I'm bothered because I still don't know if Leblanc is a good cop or a corrupt cop." She shook her head warily in frustration. "Is he a double agent, a Soviet spy who subverted the RCMP Security Service? That is close to a worst-case scenario. Or is he one of our agents who infiltrated the KGB when Soviet intelligence was distracted during its transition to the FSB? The latter seems less likely because Canada did not have legislation that allowed Canadian agents to spy within foreign jurisdictions. Any offensive or defensive action taken by the RCMP Security Service would have to have been within our borders..." She allowed the thought to hang for a moment before clarifying "... supposedly. Just because there was no formal legislation doesn't mean it did not occur, perhaps under another guise. Stuff happens. People don't always comply with the law."

"In either case, we agree that Leblanc is an obnoxious jerk or he was – back when we were confronted by him alone in the Bedford Detachment interview room."

Stan agreed. "That meeting in Bedford has influenced my perception of him and the circumstances overshadowing this case. I'm sensing it has influenced you similarly."

Olivia reflected on ghosts from Christmases Past. "After we returned to the detachment following the shooting, Leblanc grilled us both. I could hear him reading the riot act to you. Then he did the same to me. But he lowered his voice at one point and asked if I would like to join him on the case. I was frightened because I thought that he was putting the make on me. I took it as an unsolicited sexual invitation."

It was Stan's turn to reflect with regret. "I recall you coming out of the interrogation room looking quite flustered. I didn't press the matter, thinking that you would eventually tell me when the time was right. That time never came because we were speedily transferred and separated so quickly. It crossed my mind over the years but then just faded away like other distant memories I have been reluctant to resurrect. I deeply apologize for not immediately following up with you."

Bernie was all too aware of the sentiment that had taken over the moment, based on underlying emotional threads in the fabric of their early relationship which seemed to be simmering at an increased temperature. He refilled the coffee mugs before getting back to the trail. "We keep returning to the unknown haze in the room. If Inspector Leblanc wasn't a corrupt cop, was he playing the role of Robin Hood seeking to recruit Olivia into his band of Merry Men? I don't recall there being any females in RCMP Security Service back then. Or was he Al Capone trying to conscript her into his gang, or worse as Olivia had expressed?"

An ill-omened shiver ran the length of Olivia's spine as she remembered her father's words. *Remember, remember, / The fifth of November, / The Gunpowder treason and plot; / I know of no reason / Why the Gunpowder treason / Should ever be forgot!* She found herself focusing on three words – gunpowder, treason and plot.

She mused momentarily. *What would constitute the gunpowder, the means used by the traitors to achieve the end state? The treason would be the duplicitous deeds of the players, the nefarious traitor – Leblanc and possibly Hartmann. The plot would be the plan, the sequence of events, covertly contrived by the treasonous traitor. The king pin, the link for all three is the traitor,* she surmised. *In this case, traitors in the plural, others associated with Leblanc and his comptroller yet to be identified.*

Both Stan and Bernie waited silently, neither wanting to disturb her train of thought. In the short time they had worked together in Bedford, Stan recalled the occasions when Olivia had retreated into herself as she reflected on potential scenarios for cases. Bernie followed Stan's lead. On numerous occasions, he too had experienced the fruits of uninterrupted silent contemplative deliberations, in addition to frustrations when others interrupted at the exact moment he was on the cusp of envisioning solutions.

"You are deep in thought," Stan suggested in a low voice as she refocused.

With a terse nod, Olivia replied. "Our discussion thus far has centered on Leblanc as the one good guy or singular corrupt cop. I doubt he could have been acting alone. If he was a good cop, he could have been working with others like Corporal Werner Hartmann, reporting to a lone supervisor. If he was a corrupt cop, likewise more than likely he must have been working with others. At minimum, he would have been reporting to a supervisor. If a spy, he would want to keep his contacts to a minimum, ideally one person. A third scenario, if he was a double agent, he would have had two supervisors, one in each camp." She gazed at both Bernie and Stan seeking feedback.

"You're correct," Stan acknowledged.

Bernie hesitated, then nodded in agreement.

CHAPTER 10

"You have mail," Bernie announced, "but it's not from Leblanc or at least I don't think it is. The sender mentions Canadian Security Intelligence Service as the source, curiously close-lipped. From my past dealings with the CSIS, initial contact has traditionally been subtle with a tinge of the inquisitive, yet shrewdly reassuring." He paused rationalizing his thoughts. "Marshall McLuhan coined the expression that the medium is the message. The medium of this message is in itself a caveat that dictates prudence. I strongly recommend we err on the side of caution."

"Specifics?" Olivia probed.

"There is reference to Hammonds Plains, a sudden death on a farm, an unforeseen intervention by a non-uniformed investigator, and a curious reference to the letters K and A. I'm not sure what the latter references mean."

Stan replied thoughtfully, "K could signify 'K' Division which is the RCMP designation for Alberta where I was banished. Likewise, the letter A could signify 'A' Division, Ottawa, where Olivia was exiled. Whoever sent this note is acutely aware of some of the circumstances surrounding this case and our involvement and the inner workings of the Force. This suggests that the author could be Leblanc or the CSIS testing the veracity of our previous probes. Or it could be another party, an agent of a different political persuasion, as you so aptly put it, who knows some of the background details. Regardless, the expressions and level of detail might indicate potential coercion."

Bernie looked at Olivia. "Thoughts?"

Olivia hesitated. "I agree with Stan's analysis, especially the choice of words and reference to these specifics. It begs the question: why were other details not mentioned? I'm leaning toward it being Moscow-related. Could be the FSB directly or indirectly."

"I'm curious. Why do you think so?" Bernie asked.

"A bit of background. I was briefly married to a Ukrainian who had served with the Russian Military Special Forces, the Spetsnaz. He told me that an interrogation technique taught to the Spetsnaz was to give out excessive detail, truthful or otherwise, in a frontal encounter. The sole purpose was to intimidate. The author of this note is purporting to be a CSIS agent yet is providing us with too much information, more than the CSIS might know and would divulge. Perhaps this supposed CSIS agent isn't CSIS. Instead, he or she is a Moscow-trained agent or perhaps a sleeper cell awakened by the sound of the Russian bugle." She reflected for another moment. "Or another nation's trumpet."

"Interesting, especially your reference to the Spetsnaz," Bernie commented. "Whoever wrote this note is aware that we have been digging for something. Or they have figured out we know something they don't know but desperately want. My experience with the CSIS, although slightly dated, suggests the security and intelligence folks would just hide under the cloak of the *Official Secrets Act* and not come out because they don't have to. They can stay silent forever. The author of this communiqué is anxious for a reason, and your continued good health may not be one of those considerations. I suggest we just sit tight and wait for whoever sent this letter to make their next move. With each response from them we gather more intelligence, more about their strategies and tactics, and potential identity. Likewise, each time we withhold our response, they have less to analyze, less to learn about us."

Stan nodded slowly but with cautious assurance. "It's all about the end state, gathering evidence as opposed to intelligence. Police are constantly concerned with the admissibility of indisputable evidence throughout an investigation with the end state being a trial, and ideally a conviction. The politics of uniform crime reporting of statistics drives police procedures because statistics equate to budgets. In contrast, intelligence rarely if ever ends up in the public domain. Intelligence agents do not read suspects their rights before they question them. Their end state isn't always driven by the truth, the whole truth and nothing but the truth. The gathering of intelligence is also politically driven but its motivation is national security. Therein one finds the difference. For that reason, I agree with Bernie's assessment. The CSIS is not the author of this correspondence. We are looking at the opening bid in the game of cat and mouse."

"So, let the games begin," Olivia proclaimed.

"I'm thinking we need to open up a new front with a feign, a false intention, a distraction," Bernie proposed. "We can safely surmise they know something. So, let's send them on a wild goose chase to waste their time and consume their resources. I have a long-in-the-tooth associate in Montréal who has perfected the art and science of being a court jester, which happens to be his *nom de guerre*. He doubles as a private sector researcher and consultant for small to medium sized organizations. Occasionally, he is awarded shorter provincial and federal government contracts where the unwritten terms and conditions stipulate compensation that will be forthcoming from a third party and, most importantly, without financial audit trails to the primary contractor."

Olivia's inquisitive stare suggested she was not completely aware of such arrangements. "Compensation without compensation. Ultimately, everyone needs to bring home the bacon and pay the butcher."

"The employer, *per se*, refers them to other respectable organizations who can compensate handsomely with cash. Importantly, they do not mind having audit trails. These businesses receive preferred moderately priced government contracts so as not to attract the undo attention of auditors. It's the name of the game."

"Money laundering? The mob? Biker gangs?" Olivia muttered.

"Just taking care of business," Bernie replied. "Money laundering is illegal. It attracts the police and nefarious characters who complicate the marketplace. Under such transactions, information is the product and the safe transmission of the information, the service. No one likes trade wars, worst of all the warriors and the collateral damage they cause. Certainly no one wants a body count. Having said that, virtually all politicians need to get things done. It's how some private and public sector business is transacted."

"A thought," Stan interjected. "Can you ask the court jester to fish around his Montréal contacts for anything related to Inspector Leblanc, and a Hammonds Plains connection with a link to Ottawa, perhaps elsewhere? We know Moscow is still very active. It is highly likely John Robert Hackett and his supposedly devoted wife had been replaced by another sleeper cell. If we are lucky, we may be able to find out where Hackett was buried. If not in an actual marked grave, how and where his remains were disposed of."

CHAPTER 11

"We have mail again, and I'm more confident that it's from Leblanc this time. That strongly suggests the previous contact is confederate," Bernie announced. "I have called on the services of a select few of our former associates, Stan."

Stan nodded. "Rural communities are both the best and the worst places to track and be tracked. They tend not to be overwhelmed by hordes of anonymous people who neither know their neighbours nor care about their communities. In contrast, locals know if someone new has arrived and is loitering too long or enquiring too much. Recommend we proceed with Plan A."

They rehearsed the strategy for the meeting with Leblanc and the signal to abort at the slightest indication of an ambush. The first check point would be the Mount Pleasant cemetery. Assuming Leblanc finds their note among the flowers left at the gravesite of Matthew Edward Brownell, they would ready the rendezvous site at the intersection of Dickson Road and Kolbec Road.

Both Bernie and Stan had been trained as Watcher Service agents to observe and be aware of others watching them, but in sprawling urban centers. In the country, Olivia had more experience in rural communities having grown up on a farm, albeit in High River south of Calgary famous for former Prime Minister Joe Clark and not much more. Casual urban attire, including designer jeans, stood out like neon lights on steroids in a retro Tijuana bar. They changed into weathered coveralls and sweat-stained baseball caps advertising local garages or popular farm equipment retailers.

The owners of the coffee shops in Amherst and Oxford reported new customers the evening before D-Day. It was not totally uncommon but a matter of curiosity for the residents, nonetheless.

One licence plate was framed in a rental car holder, the second issued in the Halifax region. They spent the night in local hotels, rising early but spending more time than other travellers at breakfast in the same coffee shops they had visited the evening before. They said little not wanting to be identified by their accents as not being from the Cumberland County region. Not entirely uncommon but curious for the proprietors, nonetheless.

One individual meeting Leblanc's description was observed by Bernie's associate retrieving the note from a bouquet leaning against the headstone of Bernie's avatar relative, at the Mount Pleasant Cemetery. Leblanc left a small wreath. No one else was seen in the vicinity either before Leblanc arrived or after he departed. Phase one of the strategy appeared to pass without incident.

At the Riverview rendezvous, the second phase of the plan started without incident. Stan, Olivia and Bernie waited in the woods. One other local associate was dredging a ditch with a backhoe. They watched as Leblanc parked his car on Dickson Road meters from the Kolbec Road intersection, consistent with the instructions in the note. He sat in his car chain smoking, constantly checking the rear-view mirror.

The backhoe operator sauntered up to the driver's window. "In the immortal words of Smokey-The-Bear, only you can prevent forest fires." He reprimanded Leblanc for throwing the cigarette butts out the window. The operator removed his cap and wiped his brow with a red checkered handkerchief as he returned to his backhoe. This was the signal that all appeared safe although he could not see into the back seat through the heavily tinted windows.

Olivia left her hiding spot and walked toward the rear of his vehicle. Leblanc followed her approach from the rear-view mirror. Stan walked out of the woods in front of Leblanc's vehicle. Leblanc could be seen transferring his gaze between the two.

Bernie remained hidden providing surveillance and commentary to Olivia and Stan who also wore two-way communication devices.

Earphones crackled and Bernie's cautious voice said: "Heads up. We have company, a black SUV approaching from the north on Kolbec Road. It is turning onto Dickson Road. I only see a driver, appears to be male."

The backhoe operator reported the same single occupant driver noting that the licence plate was local but the driver was not. Potentially more worrisome, he could not recall the plate being consistent with the shiny black SUV. "Best be cautious," he announced.

Stan and Olivia acknowledged the communiqués with a brief nod and a verbal confirmation. Stan kept the SUV in view as it approached slowly.

The backhoe operator yelled, "the tinted rear window on the driver side has just been lowered. There is someone in the rear seat with what looks like a handgun."

Bernie confirmed. "Take cover! Take cover!"

Semi-automatic gunfire rang out from the back window as the alien SUV pulled alongside Leblanc's vehicle. Both Olivia and Stan were grazed by bullets, forcing them to sprint for cover into the ditch and back into the woods. The passenger jumped out and motioned with the barrel of the Beretta for Leblanc to exit his vehicle and get in the back seat of the SUV. Leblanc hesitated, looking confused, then followed the direction of the waving weapon. Within seconds, the SUV raced off in a cloud of dust, and smoke from a canister that had been ignited and dropped on the gravel road. Both blocked a clear line of sight of those who had organized the intercept rendezvous.

Olivia drove Stan back to the farmhouse in their vehicle which they had parked in an adjacent driveway. There, she bandaged his wound and her own which was less severe. Bernie followed in a second vehicle. The backhoe operator reversed into the intersection providing cover for their retreat from any other foreign intruder.

Olivia prepared a pot of tea while monitoring the patient who was lying on a day cot in the kitchen a few feet from the kitchen stove with its crackling fire. Digger lay on the floor monitoring the movements and anxiously awaiting the arrival of his master. He raised his head when Bernie drove into the yard and parked between the barn and the farmhouse adjacent to the woodshed, out of sight from anyone approaching from the highway.

Digger rose to his feet and whimpered. He licked Bernie's hand as his master admired Olivia's First Aid skills.

"How's the patient?" he enquired.

Olivia nodded as she walked around to the right side of the cot where she placed a cup of green tea on the only side table.

Bernie stretched out his hand to Digger who gave him a second confirming lick. Again, he whimpered his concern for the patient laying on the day cot and the cautious ambience. For now, he would stand sentinel at the foot of the cot with ears alert for any unusual sounds that stirred his distress.

Stan awkwardly reached over for the steaming mug. "Bit challenging for a south paw in a right-handed world, otherwise relatively good!"

"And you?" Bernie transferred his gaze to Olivia.

"OK. It's just a minor flesh wound. More importantly, what happened to Leblanc?"

"He disappeared in a cloud of dust and smoke. Or worse, has been captured, kidnapped, or shot and dumped along the road somewhere. My associate operating the backhoe followed but saw nothing that suggested Leblanc had been ejected forcefully from the SUV. Given the rate of speed the SUV departed the scene, he concluded that Leblanc was being transported to another location relatively close by, probably a barn or a garage."

"Damn," she muttered.

"Was it Leblanc who shot you? My line of sight was blocked," Bernie questioned. "Or someone else who didn't want you talking to him? Perhaps whoever it was that sped off."

"I couldn't see clearly either but I believe the shot that hit me came from the backseat of the SUV," Stan replied.

"Did Leblanc jump into the SUV voluntarily or was he following the shooter's non-negotiable directions at the point of the barrel?" Bernie pressed. "I couldn't see for the dust and smoke from the camouflage smoke cannister which the passenger jettisoned. I think that Leblanc was the actual target, now a reluctant hostage. Shooting the two of you merely made his abduction and their subsequent escape easier."

"I hadn't seriously considered that scenario, although we had talked about it," Stan confessed.

"We know that two shots were fired," Bernie confirmed. "Leblanc was there in addition to the two in the black SUV, a man driving and a woman with a handgun in the back seat."

"Is there an off chance that we were being set up?" Olivia asked after a moment of worried reflection.

Bernie shrugged. "If the two of you were the intended targets, I think whoever it was just wanted to wound you. They wanted to keep you alive so they could interrogate you later because they suspect you know something and/or possess something they don't have but want."

"The contents of the metal box?" Olivia reconfirmed. She could think of nothing else to append to her response at this juncture.

"A distinct possibility," Stan responded. "We can safely conclude that they don't know where we are though. If they did, they would be beating down the door as we speak."

"That reminds me, Stan. Do you remember where the entrances are to the escape tunnel?" Bernie asked.

"Yes, and I've already shown Olivia both doors from the in-law suite in the back and the woodshed off the kitchen."

Bernie frowned as he monitored an incoming text message. "Got a reply from the Mount Pleasant Cemetery surveillance team. It suggests that Leblanc has been kidnapped, not just gone AWOL. By whom, my source isn't sure. Those involved have vanished off the radar as quickly as they appeared. The black SUV could be hidden in a barn locally where the occupants picked up another getaway vehicle. This whole takedown was professional, that's for certain."

"Was Leblanc a bigger prize for what he knows and might divulge?" Olivia asked as she transferred her gaze to Bernie.

"Like Hackett?"

"Or bigger bait to identify and subsequently entrap us," Stan speculated, less a question to ponder and more a fact to consider seriously.

Bernie contacted his local associates asking them to beat the bushes in order to identify potential hiding places for the black SUV. He concluded that whoever was behind the abduction of Leblanc would not have had time to familiarize themselves with the region given the relatively brief period between us contacting Leblanc and the interrupted rendezvous on Dickson Road. Their only option would have been to bribe a naïve local who saw an opportunity to make an easy dollar by renting out a secure location to hideout. For his sake, I sincerely hope he received his short-term property rental fee in cash and in advance.

Remember, remember, / The fifth of November, / The Gunpowder treason and plot; / I know of no reason / Why the Gunpowder treason / Should ever be forgot! Olivia mused. "We have forgotten or are overlooking something," she muttered, frustrated because she couldn't explain why she had misgivings. The fog of war beyond the dust raised on Dickson Road by the spinning tires and smoke from the ejected canister was impairing her thought process as she threaded her way through the events as she recalled them from the moment she stepped out of the woods that had provided her with camouflage and into the line of fire. It was less than a minute before she leaped back into the foliage, yet it seemed much longer. Her rapid reaction was synonymous with survival, competencies she had finely tuned in preparation for fencing competitions, practiced by others in the courts of Kings and Queens in bygone eras that belonged to history and wisdom. She lamented her inability to recall. She sighed, *what the eye doesn't see the mind doesn't recall.*

If she was back in Calgary, she would pick up her foil and practice her basic fencing techniques – lunge, parry and riposte. She would attack imaginary opponents with thrusts – high outside, low outside, high inside, low inside, while replaying perplexing scenarios in her mind. It was her singular skill, her proven method of relaxation to improve her concentration. Perhaps she could teach Stan. For now, she would keep that thought within her own reflective monologue.

CHAPTER 12

Leblanc awoke face up on a cold cement slab, his arms outstretched and his wrists tied to bench posts, the arthritis in his hip and shoulder ached. The unmistakable fumes of oil and gas filled his nostrils. The air felt fetid as if the room he was in had been abandoned for a very long time. He listened for sounds of anyone inside or outside. There was none. He could not even detect the singing of song birds like those he had heard while at the Mount Pleasant cemetery, or the screeching seagulls in competition with shrieking ravens that noisily announced his arrival at the intersection of the Kolbec and Dickson Roads, the intended rendezvous. He perceived a single window partially boarded up against any direct sun light. He did not know how long he had been unconscious but estimated it was early afternoon so it must have been two to three hours. *How had I ended up here, what careless mistake had I made?* He pondered. His up-scale condo in Montréal in the shadow of Mount Royal Cross was a lifetime away. Immediate assistance seemed implausible at this moment. There was just his exchange note and follow-up letter sent via alternate means. Redundancy was a necessary contingency for such communications. But they would take time to reach their intended recipients.

The hood that covered his head had been replaced with a burlap blindfold tainted with battery acid. He yelled his objection to the burning sensation that made his eyes pour tears. They failed to flush the irritant but instead mixed with it, helping to further distribute the acid. His shouts were incoherent through the gag in his mouth soaked in rancid oil. "Where am I? Who are you?" he demanded once the gag had been removed.

"Inspector Leblanc," a man said in a deep baritone voice. It was vaguely familiar somehow.

"Why are you treating me like this?" Leblanc blurted out between gasps of increasing pain. He heard the man ask with what resembled an East European or Germanic inflection to his voice, "Would you like to do the honours?" The question did not appear to be directed toward him but to another person in the room.

A woman's soft voice replied, "*Da.*"

"My eyes are burning," Leblanc objected again.

"Not as bad as they may," the female replied, her tone callous and devoid of compassion. He recognized her distinct Slavic accent.

"Whoever you are, I have very influential friends who can compensate you exceptionally well."

"Not quite," the man interrupted. "You have become a liability to your colleagues or should I say former best friends in Ottawa. You left too many loose ends that are now being dredged up. They sent me here to let you know they are displeased with you. As a result, they no longer require the pleasure of your services or association."

"I was just following their orders," Leblanc screamed.

"The judges at the Nuremburg tribunals ruled that just following orders isn't a lawful defence. It didn't save the Nazis in the makeshift courtroom prisoner dock in Nuremberg and it won't save you here."

"He's all yours," the male voice said. His enunciation emphasized the coldness of the consonants. Leblanc heard his shuffling footsteps fade away.

Leblanc jerked his head from left to right and back again in a futile attempt to find his bearings. "Why are you doing this?" he demanded.

The soft female voice became crisp. She replied, "your superiors need to make an example of you to ensure that other associates know not to act indiscriminately, especially not to leave politicians and other bodies behind in their wake."

"No, no, please no more," he pleaded as acid was poured on his hands and his blindfold. He fell unconscious as the acrid fumes seared his lungs and the resulting pain overwhelmed him.

Images of pagan gargoyles and medieval high church rituals of inquisition and torture consumed his semi-unconscious mind. This was not Cold War battles of the titans but sociopathic martyrdom.

※ ※

THE ROLLING OF THE BOAT jolted Leblanc into a quasi-lucid state of mind.

"You are awake, just in time. Do you like lobster?" The same slightly accented male voice from the garage enquired as the boat headed out into the Northumberland Straits bouncing off the waves that splashed over the bow. The chilly night air crawled along his naked body.

"No, I hate lobster," Leblanc cried, confused by the question and the context, and the pain that continued to remind him of his mortality. *I know that voice with its hint of cruelty*, he concluded. "We met somewhere. Montréal? Ottawa? Untie me."

"Perhaps the lobster will like you better," the vaguely familiar voice replied. "Recent live bait is their preferred hors d'oeuvre." Leblanc felt the cold jagged steel cable that confined his movement suddenly tighten around his neck as a dead heavy weight splashed into the water, abruptly jerking him off the gunwale and into the desolate black depths. The claws of the giant crustaceans awaited him. His stubborn thrashing was futile. His final desperate pleas were muted barring a last guttural scream which would have been recorded as a sonar pulse had anyone been monitoring the final underwater sounds of protest.

Faint recollections swirled gently in his mind like serene eddies at ebb tide. Who were you going to meet? Why did they want to meet with you? What would you have told them? A final thought brought into focus his own search for clarity as his mind foresaw the ultimate outcome. *I know who that voice belongs to, Herr ... Gospodin.* His final conscious thought faded away. The perfidy of memory and all consciousness once intuited ceased as did all the pain that accompanied him into anonymity. He was then vaguely observing motionlessness, just floating.

His father had served in the Canadian navy during the war. The first frigate he had served on had been torpedoed by a Nazi submarine manoeuvring among others in a wolfpack, all spurred on by the adrenalin of the hunt. On a very few occasions his father spoke of comrades taken to their watery graves. Leblanc had asked him what it was like to flounder in the cold grey sea while fellow seamen disappeared under the surface one by one, their voices forever muted yet their spirits never forgotten. His father became solemn. His reply known only to those who had made the ultimate sacrifice. Leblanc stopped asking. He now heard his father's long-awaited yet muffled response.

CHAPTER 13

"You asked me why people kill. For fear of loss or opportunity for gain," Olivia stated in a matter-of-fact expression.

"Or both loss and gain, motivated perhaps by greed, a mixed message?" Stan speculated. He guessed as much from his own proficiency as an experienced Identification Technician, but wanted to bolster his own assumptions.

"So, who is trying to find us, FSB? CIA? CSIS? Someone else? I think in that order but not to the exclusion of others. Who wants what we have or does not want others to get from us first?" Olivia muttered as much as a mental prompt for herself as a tactical prod for the others.

"I agree with Bernie," Stan conjectured. "We were wounded because we have something they want. If that were not the case, there is no doubt in my mind that we would be among the deceased. We were only feet away from the shooter. Leblanc was the primary target, this time because he needed to be kept from talking to us. His capture begs the question: Why did they not kill him on the spot? Is there something he knows that they don't? Perhaps. Or was he bait? Perhaps not. I'm thinking that if we were the primary target, they had us at gunpoint. They could have quite easily captured us. Perhaps they want both of us for what we know and/or have, but Leblanc first."

Olivia delayed her response as she considered a potential scenario. "Now that they have him, we move up from second on their most-wanted list to top priority, a position I am not particularly enamoured with. Like Hackett, Davidson and Hamilton, we need to conclude that we will also be disposable once they get the Russian

Makarov PB pistol and the Cyrillic documents, or our first-hand knowledge."

Stan added. "Unfortunately, that now involves you, Bernie."

Olivia followed up, "there is strength in numbers. The more who know what we know, the greater the probability that we will live longer and more prosperous lives." She lingered on that assumption, sharing a thoughtful look. "Let me qualify that statement. The more good guys who know, the greater security we will have. Alternately, the more bad guys who suspect us, the more people will be on our tail."

Stan filled the gap. "Finding the truth about what happened to Davidson and Hamilton is still our priority. As gracious a host as you have been, Bernie, we can't remain here at the ranch forever. We have only one alternative and that is to seize and hold the high ground. Solving the mysterious deaths of Davidson and Hamilton has moved beyond the local arena and local resources."

Stan glanced over at Bernie who responded with a faint smile and a subtle nod.

Neither escaped Olivia's observation. "Care to share?" she said less of an inquisitive question and more of an emphatic statement.

"Someone, perhaps a CSIS agent, has requested a meeting with you, with us," Bernie said. "Apparently, there is an increase in e-traffic into and out of the Russian Embassy in Ottawa and also in Washington. There is a suggestion the FSB is seeking the whereabouts of some misplaced property. The associate said Leblanc had been kidnapped by the Russians who may be interested in a trade. For what, the source didn't know. To validate the contact, the agent confirmed that the two of you were investigating the mysterious deaths of two former colleagues. They strongly suggested you both need to come in from the cold, so to speak, and work with the CSIS."

"Have you heard from our other associate?" Stan asked.

"Not yet. I suggest we hold off replying to this supposed CSIS enquiry until we have confirmed a detailed Plan B with a validated risk-mitigation strategy. The recent flesh wounds which the two of you have incurred warrants some down time to recuperate. Saint Michael may be the patron saint of the police but I won't call on him in my prayers this evening," Bernie concluded in jest but with a solemn tone."

Olivia paused in silence which carried with it a fleeting clue. As a child without siblings, she had spent summers on the family farm in the Cypress Hills of southern Alberta making her own entertainment. She often wandered to a special place on a bluff overlooking a grove of prairie diamond willow trees. The place was imbued with a mystical gift like the power known to the youthful King Arthur who could draw Excalibur from the stone. She slept under the willow trees shading her from the stifling heat of the summer sun and the parching impact of the prairie winds that her grandfather and other farmers had cursed. Solutions to perceived problems appeared as imprecise aberrations, some as mystical images – clues that required interpretation. Nowhere else had she experienced such sensations of the mind. It had been years since she had wandered the fields of the farm, but now she felt an urge to return. Alas, it was nine provinces and nearly 4,000 kilometers distant from the ranch house on Amherst Shore.

"I need to do some research," she murmured as she retired to Bernie's office. There had been more than one person involved with Guy Fawkes, a.k.a. Guido Fawkes, a.k.a. John Johnson when he devised the treasonous Gunpowder Plot to blow up the English parliament and King James I. Did Leblanc also have a *nom de guerre*? She pondered. Guy Fawkes was known for unwavering loyalty to his close friends, members of a group of English Catholics. Leblanc was a devoted Catholic Québecois. Who would he have held unwavering loyalty for, besides the Pope? Would he have befriended someone to the level he might have confided in, as Guy Fawkes and his co-conspirators had done?

"While you are immersed in your research, I'll go into Amherst to pick up a few groceries and meet a man about a horse," Bernie announced.

※ ※

"HAVE YOU HEARD THE NEWS?" a friendly voice whispered to Bernie as he entered the Amherst post office. "Not good. Folks are on edge."

Bernie dwelled on the question as he thumbed through advertisement flyers, not making direct eye contact but paying close attention.

"Billy Allen's body was found in his old abandoned garage. He had been shot in the head, twice. I guess that the shooter wanted to make sure he was dead. Police also found a black SUV in the garage, apparently stolen. The original licence plates had been removed and a different set attached. They had been reported missing, not necessarily stolen."

As previous case files evolved, similar unfortunate events also occurred. But they were in other communities, in other countries on other continents. Bernie felt the closeness and associated stress as never before. His farmhouse, the ranch, was an inconspicuous oasis as safe as any safehouse could be. He had developed strategic and operational plans with contingencies like the escape tunnels from the in-law suite and woodshed in the ranch house to the barn which held the machinery. He had reinforced and extended the berm that connected the back entrance of the machinery barn to the forest with its labyrinth of secreted trails. Unless you were on top of the berm, you would not have been able to observe anyone scurrying along its veiled paths. He had often thought that such mitigation strategies were too extreme. Today, he felt that these measures were minimally adequate. He would walk each of the routes to confirm their readiness. He would also ensure his full system remote shut down was operational. He sent the standard code to Stan to raise his radar.

CHAPTER 14

Bernie checked his mailbox. A lonely letter contained in a larger non-descript envelope elevated his curiosity and caution. He was wary because of the surreptitious identity of the sender and the fact it had been written in some kind of code. It was addressed to Olivia, care of the avatar, and supposedly signed by Leblanc. He promptly returned to the ranch, stopping only briefly for a few essential provisions.

"I don't like the tacit implication of the message," Stan commented as he stared at Bernie with a worrying concern.

Bernie related the news regarding the discovery of the body, missing licence plates and the black SUV. He then handed Olivia the letter. All three stood in silence exchanging blank stares while thinking about their initial reactions and forming their own responses and that of their colleagues. The content of the invitation had left them cautiously hopeful, yet curiously skeptical about the prospects of receiving a reply. Now, they were wary about reading the response and even more guarded about misinterpreting Leblanc's potentially malevolent intent. Deciding not to react to the first letter allegedly from the CSIS was simple because of its perceived fraudulent nature. In retrospect, none truly believed they would receive a reply to their RSVP.

Digger interrupted Olivia's initial assessment of the cryptic script with frantic barking and whining, and scratching at the back door. He dropped a gift at Bernie's feet, his paws soaked and smelling of seaweed. Bits of ebb tide debris clung to his fur.

"Good boy. What have you got there?" Bernie patted him on the head.

Digger sat wagging his tail and nudging Bernie's pocket with his nose. He knew his master kept treats there for just such an auspicious occasion. As he crunched the dog biscuit, Stan, Olivia and Bernie stood in horror, looking obliquely at a reminder of the presence of death cutting like the scythe of the grim reaper. There was no mistaking the identity of Digger's prized gift, a mangled hand scarred with deep burns that had corroded the skin, in places exposing bone. The remaining fingers were tightly clinched into the palm, fused together in the grip of a tightened fist.

"Can you retrieve a print, Stan?" Bernie asked with muffled trepidation. "Your gear is still in the attic where you left it."

On preliminary examination, he muttered with a tinge of skepticism, "Should be able to get something. The quality will be another matter though. While I'm at it, I'll try to lift any prints from the Makarov PB pistol and the Cyrillic scripted letter contained in the metal box." He surmised it was highly doubtful the latter would surrender any prints from the external surface. He delicately separated the middle and ring fingers from the palm, careful not to disturb what remained of the impression of the friction ridges and the pores.

"We will pay homage to the fingerprint gods," Olivia uttered in jest. She was trying to make light of an abysmal situation. "Can I observe your Merlin magic? I promise not to interfere with my pestering presence or peppering questions of a novice."

"I would welcome your company. Questions would not be interpreted as pestering. There's no Merlin magic of an alchemist transforming metals into gold or sleight of hand to create a universal elixir. Instead, just tried and true forensic science lifting prints from cadaveric fingers and alien surfaces."

She recalled the pristine conditions from her Identification lecture while in training at Depot Division decades before. They had washed their soiled hands and all the equipment to meticulous standards of the instructor. This was completely different. While Stan delved into the task at hand with the enthusiasm and finesse of a master craftsman, she observed from a distance hoping the circulating air would lessen the repugnance of the odor emanating from the rotting flesh of what remained of the mutilated hand.

Within the hour, Stan looked up with satisfaction from his detailed examination. "The gods are with us. We have confirmed prints from two fingers of the mangled hand which I surmise was only recently severed from the owner's wrist. I also lifted a partial print from the barrel and a couple of full prints from the magazine of the Russian Makarov PB pistol and silencer which seem to match some on the document. There is no match between the mutilated fingers and the latent prints on the pistol, magazine or silencer."

Stan passed the fingerprint algorithms to Bernie.

After a series of keystrokes, Bernie relaxed with a smug smile. "Don't you just love technology when it works to your advantage?" he chuckled. "Commit to memory not to a memory chip if you want a secret to remain secret. The folks in charge of fingerprint records in Ottawa either don't know or are too arrogant to care." He returned to the keypad and with each search sequence, he grew more alarmed.

"What have you got?" Olivia asked, not sure she really wanted to know the results but supposed she should prepare herself for the revelation. Responses to some of her questions to date had been double-edged swords with one blade being sharper than the other. Nonetheless, the results could be evidence or intelligence, both useful in separate contexts.

Bernie rubbed his index finger against his temple. The results of his digital search appeared on the monitor. "If there was any doubt, I can verify that we are not dealing with nice people."

Olivia and Stan looked at him. Other results had borne both good and bad news. They had no reason to believe that this would be different. How much more horrific or alarming could this information be in comparison? Neither would be surprised given the trajectory this case had taken since they had formed their fledging partnership under the Two Old Farts Investigative Services, TOFIS banner.

"I can validate with a high degree of probability that we are Number One on someone's most-wanted list. The prints from the hand belong to Jean Paul Richard Claude Leblanc or should I use the past tense – belonged to the infamous enigmatic Inspector J.P.R.C. Leblanc."

"The meek may inherit the earth, but Leblanc will not be a benefactor." Olivia struggled to make sense of Digger's discovery within the context of the cryptic writing in the letter addressed to her care of the avatar from the late Inspector Leblanc. It had been mailed without a return address or post box number. The date of the mailing was equally cryptic.

"Prints from the pistol and documents are unavailable. Words blocked in bolded script and large font appeared on the monitor with the designation: ACCESS DENIED."

"You are the Ident expert. What does that mean?" Olivia queried as she looked at Stan with exasperated astonishment. The news regarding the late Inspector Leblanc was still reverberating in her flustered mind.

"*Access Denied* as a designation is only used for top-secret files. I've only seen it a few times and they were associated with national security. Only a few cabinet ministers and senior mandarins of the select few in the prime minister's closest circle could gain access, and then only on a need-to-know basis. It just doesn't get any more secret than this, sometimes colloquially referred to as *Cryptic Secret*."

Bernie sat back, his eyes flickering like an early rendition of a silent Hollywood black and white movie. He purposely slowed his breathing to calm his heartbeat. "Not all is lost. It's just a detour on the e-highway. Can you two work on decoding Leblanc's letter while I pursue some electronic backroads along the less-travelled but occasionally telling hacker highway?" He tenderly rubbed the tips of his fingers together like a safe breaker about to make ever-so-delicate love to the dial that would align the internal tumblers of a combination lock safe.

"It will take a while to decipher. Your guess is as good as mine at this juncture," Olivia replied with a trace of irritation in her voice. "The process is similar but different from translating language. Do you have another associate who can help?"

"Yes and no. Yes, but it will take a while. One is out of the country. The other will take a few days to get here. I am reluctant to send a code by encrypted message. The meaning can get lost in the interpretation," Bernie explained. "More importantly, I want to keep our e-traffic to a minimum regarding this file so we don't attract undue attention. In the early days of Special Operations Executive during the Second World War, SOE agents in occupied Europe disabled phone wires, forcing the Nazis to use wireless radio communications which could be more easily accessed by the code breakers at Bletchley Park and elsewhere by embedded Allied agents. This ultimately led to breaking into the German Enigma Code which the Nazi tech experts of the day arrogantly assured their Teutonic superiors could not be done, certainly not easily. I do not want my system to become the focus of hackers as a result of overuse. That is the primary reason I revert to other means. At times like this, I am reluctant even to use snail mail."

"Crime analysis is all about solving riddles, clues left behind to be found and mapped out in a logical sequence. As such, Ident folks are cryptologists," Stan explained. He glanced at Olivia. "Time to amass the multitude of our collective talents, partner."

"Once again, I bow to the senior senator," Olivia said as she slid Leblanc's encrypted letter over to Stan. She relished the opportunity to put their heads together from both a professional and personal perspective. On the horizon, like the rising sun they needed to deal with the emerging personal issues before the professional. But personal would take much longer, a life time of regrets of lost opportunities of dreams to personally resolve or at least acknowledge. There were elephants in the room which she had no experience herding. But that was more time than the current circumstances would allow. She did not have her personal calendar to schedule in those impromptu intimate moments, the eternal embraces which could only occur without a confining scripted calendar. She had held love at bay so long she had forgotten how to deal with such intimate emotions. For now, she would put all her effort into solving what appeared to be a pragmatic derivative of the Pope's Code.

Stan followed her distant focus. She was in her space which he suspected was occupied with other thoughts intrinsically linked to related tangential factors. He wanted to ask where she was, how he could help. Yet he needed to organize the stuff he too was feeling, what was occupying his own mind. But that would have to wait. Interpersonal codes were more difficult to decipher because they did not have flawless legends that changed at set times like scheduled enigma machines or other military code books. People were just fickle and their emotions subject to intervening variables operating in the environment either intuitive or counter intuitive to circumstances known only to the gods and not necessarily the mortal souls. Such were the ambiguous characteristics of human nature.

Most cryptologists, intelligence analysts like those who worked at Bletchley Park, had strong backgrounds in mathematics. Olivia was proficient in the maths but superior in languages. Fencing had honed her skills at analysis of pattern recognition for individual behaviours. Know the coder and you know the code. She was gaining an understanding of Leblanc.

CHAPTER 15

"Virtually all codes are based on some kind of numeric sequencing. Get on the keyboard, Bernie," Stan requested. "We need brain power and artificial intelligence to help solve this one. There are two factors in our favour. First, I'm thinking Leblanc's arrogance would not allow him to bow to anyone who might know more about any subject, let alone code breaking. He is supposed to have said on several occasions that he knew everything there was to know about policing. Second, Leblanc was French Canadian and, more importantly, a devout Roman Catholic who would have studied Latin in school and perfected it at mass."

"But Latin is not the only language of the Catholic Liturgy and it is not confined to Rome," Olivia added. "Russian Orthodox scriptures are steeped in Latin. Based on our preliminary characterization of Leblanc, can we safely assume that he would move as close to Russian agents as he could for no reason other than *chutzpah* – audacity. Keep your friends close and your enemies closer is the old adage. In the game of backgammon, if you have to expose your player, the safest position is next to your opponent because it exponentially reduces the probability of being hit, temporarily bumped to the bar and, as such, suspended from the game."

Olivia paused with an abrupt wince as if responding to an ominous omen as she rubbed her chin with her steepled index fingers. She slumped into her chair, searching for clues masked in the meditative mist, only to find more seemingly isolated traces.

"You're troubled," Stan prompted. "What's wrong?"

After a moment of hesitation, she responded, "It's something Leblanc said when he was interrogating me in the interview room at the Bedford Detachment after the shooting. He was overbearing and aggressive at first, then became marginally more approachable. He asked me if I wanted to join him, work with him. I mentioned before that I thought he was putting the make on me so I recoiled rapidly, declining his offer. But what if he really wanted me to work with him because he figured I could keep a secret about a secret? What if he was accepting me – his invitation a benediction, a blessing for me to join him?"

Stan maintained his gaze, not wanting to interrupt her train of thought, mesmerized by her deductive contemplative process.

"Just an idea," she eventually added. "There is something missing, nagging at me." *Remember, remember, the fifth of November* drifted through her fogged recollection like a semi-opaque mist at times allowing an imprecise outline to be teased into focus while at other times only suggesting an implicit presence.

Bernie joined Stan in supporting her exploration down Lewis Carroll's white rabbit tunnel. He stepped back not wanting to crowd her nor abandon her with the impression he wasn't interested. Like Stan, he was still learning where on the periphery the optimum fulcrum could be found.

"It will come," Olivia responded. Within seconds, she emerged from her contemplative trance, her intuitive consciousness. She found herself imagining the family farm in the Cypress Hills of southeastern Alberta and the bluff overlooking the shading grove of prairie diamond willow trees.

"One confounding White Rabbit hole leading to a labyrinth of secondary tunnels may shed light on a maze of cognitive passages, each potentially providing implicit clues. Let's go for a walk through the tunnel from the woodshed to the garage." *What did the decrypting ladies of Bletchley Park do for cognitive stimulation?* she pondered. *Seek out a silent supportive ambience – a space to engage in conversations that mattered with like-minded colleagues?*

Once in the garage, she meandered through the machines of husbandry, some of which had come off the assembly line during the Great Depression over a half century earlier. Others had bid farewell to the nineteenth century. They reminded her of the family farm where she had spent many summers watching the horse-drawn combines, visionary technology in its time. She listened to stories her grandmother had told her of the old country. Her mother had related other tales. Many of the sagas were awash with allegory that Olivia had learned to decipher. She knew there was more truth in story than detail in fact. Perhaps the years of loving care bestowed on the machinery by previous owners of this farmstead in Nova Scotia would reciprocate with fabled clues of their own.

She found herself standing perfectly still, her eyes staring at everything yet focusing on nothing, her mind wandering yet analyzing data and sequences. She had come to the realization that there were different forms of consciousness, plant, animal, and spiritual intuitive awareness. We are the mindfulness of the Earth, she surmised. Our consciousness exists influenced by intuitiveness which molds our characters. How different her life, her character, might have been with the man now standing sentinel beside her. In her thought, she leaned over and kissed him tenderly, relishing the mythical image of a reciprocated gesture and a warm supportive embrace of eternity. Reality of passion replaced fanciful imagination. Inspiration flowed.

They rejoined Bernie in the kitchen around the coffee pot. Stan was standing close beside her, his presence reassuring and encouraging, his vitality welcoming.

"So, what can we conclude?" Stan prompted.

Bernie was the first to reply. "Everything about everything smells of a spy architecture about trusted friends, unproven associates to be cautious of, and known foes to be neither, yet more – *doveryay i proveryay* – trust and verify."

Olivia joined in. "Leblanc was known for both lying and telling the truth at the same time. He appears to have left some genuine facts out, while putting other false details in. I think he purposely did that as a clue for us to warily find, figure out and follow. In the context of a previous global conflict, he seems to have been an operator like Mata Hari, a master of deception, ultimately executed. And as you suggest, Stan, for spurious reasons, yet unknown, he has kept secrets about a secret with dire consequences."

Bernie remained thoughtful. "Having played on the edge of this sandbox myself, I think he was very much aware that he might be killed before he could communicate vital information to both of you. That would have been his motivation for sending us this cryptic letter by snail mail which he no doubt suspected would raise the ire of his current and duplicitous former foes. Perhaps it was necessary, essential redundancy."

Olivia again withdrew, this time massaging her forehead with her fingertips. *Remember, remember the fifth of November*, she reflected. Digger approached and rested his chin on her lap, staring up at her with his deep brown eyes. She patted his head as she gazed down. "Oh, you are a clever dog," she whispered.

"And?" Stan quizzed, noticing the change in her complexion and composure, and the tone in her voice.

"Let me explain. *Beneficium* is the Latin term for conferring of a blessing, *per se*. In a figure of speech, the laying on of the hands. During the Renaissance, the Vatican employed cryptologists, *cifristi*, under a cypher secretariat to code and decode the Pope's secret dictates to the papal nuncio. They used what became known as the Code Book of the Pope, a celebration of papal power. It was simple but not simplistic because you still needed to remember the keywords. Leblanc would keep it as simple as possible, not using pre-coded numeric sequencing because we would not have a parallel decoding key. In its absence, we should be able to figure them out. *In alia forma* – in another format, his invitation to join him was a Beneficium, a blessing in disguise."

"Paper, please, Bernie," Stan asked. "No artificial intelligence of algorithm sequencing needed at this preliminary stage, just basic brain-cell sequencing."

"A strength taken to an extreme has an elevated potential of becoming a weakness," Bernie acknowledged. "It's a rudimentary skill lost to an increasing number of aspiring graduates from academic and technical institutions these days. Their weakness is their unquestioning devotion to technology which itself can be fraught with errors. The programmers are their disciples. The hardware is their religion. The software their bible. The apps their scriptures. The algorithms their gospels. Common sense acquired by brain-cell sequencing is quickly going the way of the flightless dodo bird – like an extinct species lost to those who cannot think independently." He handed Stan a pile of blank paper, unlined, to avoid placing limitations on any potential solutions. "OK, put your heads together and make it happen."

Stan felt a smile emerge on his face like a flower opening its petals in response to the sun's first warmth of a spring day. A season of fertile nourishment was on the cusp. All they had to do was to tweak the clues to ensure a match. Easier said than done like scanning a crime scene for microscopic physical evidence, present yet not present. What was the intent of the perpetrator? Once tentatively identified, the trail would reveal its hidden treasures like the Easter egg hunt.

The Pope's Code was the trail. Leblanc was the Pope. Olivia and Stan the cifristi, the Papal cryptologists. The encrypted message the treasure. But what was the damn key to open the code? Stan was the best forensic criminologist there was. He had studied the behavioural patterns of countless interlopers. Then, under Bernie's tutelage, had mastered the art and science of mapping behaviours of the e-intruders.

The criminal mind was the same. The interpretation of the treasure was a different skill altogether. It helped if there was a personal relationship, an intuitive bonding of the psyche. Leblanc's tentative invitation for Olivia to join him might be that connection. They just needed to tap into it however minuscule the sense might have been.

Stan detected that Olivia had implicitly connected with Hackett's spirit in the barn whether she knew it or not. The essence was older than time itself premised on the truism of mythology, known to Celtic and Druid allegory amongst other traditional cultures mostly ancient not mired in only the pragmatic. The Celtic word for oak is *duir* from which the word Druid is derived. The Druids firmly believed that the Oak Tree was the source of all wisdom and strength. This was the infancy of future forensic identification services, Stan surmised, identifying the olden essence of the spiritual finger-print.

CHAPTER 16

"God love the Pope and his covert cell of cyber clergy," Olivia exclaimed with a rich chuckle. Most of Leblanc's decoded message lay on the table for all three to contemplate. Several numeric sequences each with six digits remained unidentified. Under the text was a sketch of a flower and a short sentence following. It seemed out of place as content within the context of the pragmatic yet cryptic numeric categorizations unless it symbolized another algorithm. It seemed like a kaleidoscope of ever-changing intelligence some meant to inform, others meant to mislead. She placed the envelope beside the raw enigmatic and decoded documents.

"The text is grammatically correct and revealing. Whoever is chasing us for the metal box containing the Russian Makarov PB pistol and the Cyrillic text documents would also want this letter even without a complete translation. I expect these numeric sequences refer to either places, people or events," Stan speculated.

Bernie's fingers flashed over the keyboard. "If we look for associations among all the players and places in this case, the event locations, and the repeated frequency of use, we end up with these possible scripts!" He printed them out. "Which makes the most sense, in order of priority?"

Olivia and Stan shuffled the pages initially settling on five before whittling the possibilities down to three. They were unable to agree on any priority, not knowing what criteria to use.

"We might not have a complete list of all the people, places and events," Bernie noted. "If we agree on John Robert Hackett a.k.a. Nikolai a.k.a. Nazi SS Oberstleutnant, Brandt Felix Schmidt, his wife Sylvia a.k.a. Lada, and their Russian tovarishch – comrade controller Ruslan, Leblanc's message becomes clearer. We cannot confirm for certain that we have identified all the locations and people and events involved."

Stan separated two of the three possible options. Olivia shifted her attention in a series of infinite loops while considering his choices. She nodded tentatively regarding his final selection.

"Let's consider two known places – the farm at Hammonds Plains and Montréal. A third possibility could be Ottawa. Subsequent unknown locations we identify as X," Bernie recommended.

Olivia and Stan reshuffled the options. They adjusted the possibilities from two back to three piles. Bernie selected two unidentified numeric sequences and labelled them 'shooting at the barn' and 'FLQ Crisis'. Subsequent unknowns were identified as Y. Olivia and Stan immediately separated a third option, leaving the initial short list of the two previously chosen.

"Not knowing all potential players, places or events, can we live with this tentative translation for now?" Bernie asked. He did not want to become stymied in the quagmire of overthinking or missing a key element by being too superficial at this preliminary stage. The death knell in any analysis was the false positive and its opposite, the false negative.

"We strongly suspect that there is an Ottawa connection, more than likely senior mandarins and politicians. Other known knowns are the CSIS and the CIA, and a generic reference to Washington. Leblanc refers to two victims. We know of Laporte in Montréal, and Nikolai in Hammonds Plains." Bernie selected two more numeric sequences and aligned them with reference to Montréal and Hammonds Plains. That left three unidentified and apparently unrelated numeric sequences. He figured there was a high probability that two would be people, possibly Davidson and Hamilton, and the final one, a yet to be identified location.

"If it was Leblanc wanting to communicate with Olivia, why would he make this difficult?" Stan asked.

"Perhaps Leblanc suspected other players but didn't know their names. He only knew that Olivia needed to be cautious."

"I'm more apprehensive and guarded, now," Olivia admitted quietly. She sensed that she was close to the southeastern Alberta shading diamond willow tree solution. Possibly the depiction of the flower at the bottom of the note with a brief sentence following was a clue drawing everything in accord or it could be completely separate.

"We must err on the side of caution, then," Bernie suggested, "if that is Leblanc's intent. We need to view this analysis from his perspective. He would have been reluctant to come right out and say so in the event that this letter fell into the wrong hands."

Olivia paced the floor of the kitchen under the watchful gaze of Stan and Bernie, and Digger who whined faintly. She stopped in guarded silence as she looked upward, scanning her memory and listening to her intuition in hopes of seeking inspiration.

Stan followed her eyes searching. He remembered her doing the same when they worked together in Bedford. He knew that patience was a virtue and he needed to await her enlightened re-engagement. In Bedford as now, he admired her uncanny ability to conduct mental gymnastics in the analysis of ostensibly unrelated facts.

"I'm more convinced now than ever before that Leblanc holds the key," she muttered for her own benefit as much her two colleagues.

"Was it something he said? Did? Insinuated?" Stan pressed. "What is your intuition saying?"

"Et je restai là, morne, avec les yeux pensifs, et j'entendais en moi des marteaux convulsifs, renfoncer les clous noirs des intimes Calvaires."

"I get the gist but a full translation and interpretation within your cultural context would help," Bernie remarked.

"*And I stood there, dreary, with pensive eyes; and I heard in me convulsive hammers, reinforcing the black nails of intimate Calvaries,*" she replied "It is the last stanza of a poem entitled *Christ en Croix* or Christ on the Cross, written by a French-Canadian poet, Émile Nelligan. Leblanc muttered it just before I escaped his interrogation in Bedford. I don't know if he recited it for my benefit or as a reflection for himself. Given what has transpired in the past few days, I think he may have recited it for strategic reasons. I had a feeling he had read my personnel file before interrogating me."

Stan looked at her inquisitively. "Why do you think that?"

"He mentioned that he was impressed with my undergraduate degree in linguistics and courses in French literature, particularly the Culture of French-Canadian poetry. After he muttered this last stanza of Nelligan's poem, he must have seen me smile because he shrewdly nodded, acknowledging I had recognized the lyrics and their potential context. It's not the poem as much as the culture of the poetry. The medium is the message, Marshall McLuhan."

"Do you sense it contains an encrypted code or is it a link, a key to the code?"

"It could be either or both. Let's look at the unsolved numeric sequences in his encrypted letter in the context of this stanza and the entire poem if need be."

"To know Leblanc is to know of him. Is your perception of Leblanc blinding you? Just asking," Bernie speculated.

"He may not have been a bad cop, just an arrogant jerk with an obnoxious attitude. But maybe that is what was needed to survive," Olivia proposed. "But why would he not follow up his furtive offer to me to join him? I had applied for the Canadian Security Intelligence Service after I completed my PhD in Slavic Studies, but I wasn't accepted."

"I don't know the answer," Stan admitted. "Perhaps because

of your marriage to an ex-Russian special forces guy. Or maybe because Leblanc had lost favour with his superiors in Ottawa or Montréal by then. We may never know. Then again, he might have realized that you were too nice, didn't possess the cold killer aptitude and the requisite thick rhinoceros hide. The potential wasn't there for you to be a hubris jerk, like him. Without it, you would have been devoured by those wolverines in the Canadian Security Intelligence Service and by the KGB later FSB with the same personalities, the CIA, or other players."

Olivia raised her eyebrows. "An arrogant jerk but a wise arrogant jerk," she mumbled.

"With our two, possibly three unsolved sequenced options, what can we conclude with any degree of certainty?" Bernie asked.

Olivia pondered before responding. "There is a cryptic clue that Hackett is buried somewhere but not in a lawfully registered cemetery, perhaps back at the barn in Hammonds Plains. There was someone else directing Leblanc, possibly his superior or another up the chain of either Canadian or Russian command. Within the former, perhaps it was a politician, or someone masquerading as a mandarin who pulled the puppet strings." She sought their agreement before continuing.

They delayed their responses before slowly nodding, encouraging her train of thought as she eyed a distant horizon of her memory.

"We are dealing with different thought processes. We have Leblanc and his encrypting mind, Hackett a.k.a. Nikolai and his Russian sleeper cell mentality, Lada and Ruslan who we are confident conspired to kill Nikolai. We also have the Cold War players from their respective paranoid environments, all employing their own brands of deceit and covert skulduggery."

Again, the others considered this angle of analysis before briefly nodding in continued support.

"Washington and the CIA had similar and conflicting interests in the 1970 FLQ Crisis. Common to both was a perceived threat to U.S. national security. But that begs a question: why after all these years? There were Russian sleeper cells in Canada and in the U.S. but what was the common denominator or connection? Whatever happened on the farm in Hammonds Plains was both the nexus and the nucleus of something else occurring at a higher geopolitical level. Davidson and Hamilton were merely unfortunate casualties in the Cold War, in the wrong place at the wrong time."

As much as she discounted the obvious, Olivia realized that she needed to have a second discussion with her ex about the content of the Cyrillic pages from the metal box and possibly the Russian Makarov PB pistol. She was missing something that had a cultural context. The unknown carried in it the unstated furtive answer. After their first meeting in the hotel room in Halifax, Uri had warned her the Russian bear had poked the retired Ukrainian Spetsnaz. It was readily apparent she could not contact him directly. That would have to be left to one of Bernie's friends who had no association with Olivia, yet could communicate as her. She looked at Bernie as she pursed her lips.

"I'm sensing a tentative question," Bernie responded.

"You mentioned that you could draw on the services of two possible associates to help with the decoding. One was out of the country. The other was available at this time but a farther distance away. Would the latter be female and open to convincing my ex, Uri, to meet with us?"

"Yes, to both questions. I've already asked her to join us. She should be here by tomorrow or the next day at the latest."

"Yvonne?" Stan asked.

Bernie nodded.

"Uri doesn't have a chance," Stan whispered to Olivia who concluded that Yvonne must be not only physically attractive but decidedly intellectual and remarkably charming, the triad of Uri's vulnerability. When Olivia would catch Uri gazing at other females, he would say that it didn't matter where you worked up an appetite as long as you came home for dinner. She held a differing perspective of devotion to their marriage vows. That wasn't cultural. Instead, it was respect and loyalty, plain and simple. In retrospect, she knew that his behaviour was a fatal flaw and she should have acted. But she was too focused on completing her PhD which consumed every ounce of her energy and every breathing moment of her life. She didn't need the added stress. Focusing on her graduation while waiting for a divorce decree was the lesser of the evils.

CHAPTER 17

"I would like to introduce you to Yvonne Simpson," Bernie said to Olivia. "We all worked together at the Watcher Service in Montréal."

"Nice to meet you, Olivia. Very much looking forward to working with you on this case," Yvonne replied with a charisma that permeated the room like an affable apparition. Digger greeted her as an old friend with a wet kiss from his loving tongue even before she patted his head and scratched behind his ears.

Olivia calculated that if Yvonne was a colleague from the 1970 FLQ Crisis era, she would be approximately the same age as Bernie and Stan, yet she seemed years younger. Either Yvonne was one of those women who was the envy of all her female friends because she never aged, or her hairdresser, dermatologist, physiotherapist, and fitness coach were professionals who Olivia would like to add to her own list of preferred VIP contacts. Her first impression based of Stan's whispered comment was absolutely correct. Yvonne would be the perfect agent provocateur. Uri would be immediately smitten by her stunning beauty, disarming yet piercing azure eyes, and mesmeric elegant charm.

"Back in the day?" Olivia mirrored Bernie's brief introduction as she continued to gaze at Yvonne.

"I worked with the Watcher Service while at Laval University from 1968 to 1972. Immediately afterwards, I joined the Canadian Forces as an Intelligence officer and spent the majority of my 20-plus-year career in Europe, mostly Germany. That was my old stomping ground because my father had been stationed in Baden-Soellingen with the Royal Canadian Air Force's Air Defence Command in the early 1960s. Benefits of the Cold War. Bernie,

Stan and I, plus a few other close colleagues, have kept in contact since our Watcher Service days. We all knew that we would work together again, and here we are."

Over green tea, the details of the case became more harrowing as Olivia briefed the newest member of the group. She only omitted precise details of the communiqué that had been secreted away in the metal box for the better part of three decades. Yvonne's mission would be to lure a reluctant Uri away from the tranquillity of the halls of academia at Dalhousie University in Halifax and the suspected surveillance of Slavic agents, to a neutral locale where he and Olivia could translate the cultural connotations of the Cyrillic script.

※ ※

YVONNE KNEW FROM HER TRAINING and practiced precision how to seduce a target like a Red Sparrow, without such a formal designation, in order to get what she wanted – mission success. People are puzzles. You first have to identify the missing piece in the puzzle, then become that piece and make it believable. That meant being able to read people quickly and accurately employing intelligence, sophistication, cunning, discipline, at times to be cold, violent, scheming, and then be seductively sincere and passionately desirable, yet unreachable. To lie until it becomes the truth. To push yourself beyond all limitations including the dilemma of morality – the perceived duality of the soul. Such was the religion, the creed and the gospel of the Russian Red Sparrow.

"Uri," Yvonne said in a satiny voice as she extended her hand in a way so alluring that her intended target could not resist.

He stood captivated by the audacious behaviour of this petite woman who had effortlessly wended her way through the scrum of students by conveying a command presence. He first looked her in the eye and then at the rest of her. The inferior apprenticing students seemed to step aside like the biblical story of Moses parting the waters of the Red Sea.

Before Uri could respond, Yvonne continued, "You may not remember me as a PhD student at Carleton. I was in the Slavic Studies program. I had asked to read your copies of Leo Tolstoy's *War and Peace* and Fyodor Dostoevsky's *Crime and Punishment*. In no uncertain terms, you said no one could touch these almost mint first edition first print copies let alone thumb through them. But if I read other copies from the library, you would be pleased to debate the contents with me, especially the cultural connotations. I did that, and as a result of your invaluable tutoring, I received an A+ grade on my paper, the highest grade ever awarded to any student in any previous class for that assignment. I just wanted to thank you again."

Uri continued to stare, enthralled by her presence. But he now had to recollect details of a meeting that he could not remember ever having taken place with her, but with someone else once very close to him.

Yvonne continued, "I heard that you are very partial to lobster. As a gesture of gratitude, can I entice you to join me in Antigonish this weekend? I have a friend who has a lobster boat and he will be heading out into the Northumberland Straits to catch a few of the crustaceans and boil them up in his marine cuisine." She leaned forward and slowly whispered into his ear while allowing Uri to breathe in her natural scents, and feel her moist lips and subtle curves that up to this moment he had only imagined. "Yes, lobster fishing season is over," she added, "but that simply means any catch will be garnished with mystery and tenderness of the succulent flesh." As she was describing the details of the chef's culinary talents, she pulled out her cell phone and showed him a picture. "This is the lobster boat."

Uri felt himself being drawn into the gravitational allure of this woman. For the first time since Yvonne had commandeered his attention, he broke eye contact to look down at the e-pic. His mind stopped spinning the Rolodex of his memory files as he read the last wary text message he had sent to Olivia.

Yvonne again closed the intimate distance between them and smiled seductively. "*Poka my ne vstretimyasnova* – until we meet again," she whispered a second time into his ear, but purposely with a harsh American-Russian accent, as she slowly blinked her azure blue eyes. *Hooked*, she concluded with confidence.

"I'll be there." Uri spoke for the first time. *I need to get to know this mirage,* he reflected. Greek mythology suggested that Helen of Troy's beauty could launch a fleet of a thousand ships. The tantalizing mystery and sheer beauty of this goddess in my classroom could launch a thousand fleets each with a thousand ships. He dwelt on the context of this first encounter. *Have we met before? Why do I not remember*? He asked himself. There was something about her that told another story, a slight softening of an armour he had once known, perhaps. As Yvonne departed his company with the same finesse and genteel eloquence as she had approached, the ambient noise of clucking students like farmyard hens rose to its previous irritating level. He stared after her. He blinked once then repeatedly as he became aware of the imposing distraction of the unruly pupils in his classroom once again. He feverishly focused on committing to his long-term memory the circumstances of this spontaneous encounter and the mosaic of her image.

The balance of his class was a blur. The singular anticipation of lobster, Chardonnay, and an opportunity to engage in an uninterrupted conversation with Yvonne occupied his consciousness. More puzzling and potentially more worrisome was the message she had conveyed replete with the e-pic of the email and his text. If it was Olivia summoning him, given his previous warning, it would have to be very serious and associated with the contents of the unearthed metal box.

Uri had briefly dated, Sofia, a fellow student while at the University of Rostov in southern Russia, which was an academic finishing school for Moscow's Red Sparrows whose mission it was to identify strengths, and most importantly, weaknesses of their targets. In retrospect, he wasn't certain if Sofia had initiated their relationship or he had, with her encouragement. At a subliminal yet instinctual level, he knew she was a force of nature. Regardless, he was confident Sofia hadn't really ended the relationship. She simply disappeared one day. He was left wondering if he had been an intended target of this seductive Red Sparrow, as it preened its soft feathers and imperceptibly transformed into a lethal black hawk, a final test of her advanced espionage training before being sent on her first operational mission.

Likewise, Olivia had initiated their divorce, another sad day in his life of seemingly endless failed relationships. If Yvonne was also a coquettish Red Sparrow of the tradecraft, always the predator, constantly vigilant, he would need to rehearse his responses to the anticipated FSB questions. For now, he would be cautious before entertaining thoughts of pursuing a potential relationship with Yvonne. Faith reshapes the way the faithful perceive the world. He had been self-ordained into the faith of Uri and singularly focused on his own Zen-styled raison d'être.

He chuckled to himself. *All three – Sofia, Olivia, now Yvonne are compellingly charming, exceptionally intelligent and stunningly beautiful blondes – the triad of my weakness, my nemesis.* Today, Olivia had become the primary contributing source of his extant attack of painful acid indigestion. She owed him.

CHAPTER 18

Yvonne met Uri on the wharf and guided the way to the lobster boat where she introduced him to Captain Bernie. They then maneuvered through the maze of secured lobster traps and a sundry of fishing gear lashed to the deck, before descending into the galley where Olivia and Stan were sitting around the table.

"Not your average lobster boat," Uri commented as he scanned the luxurious décor of the cabin, noting the tinted windows that obscured any scrutiny from outside. At the bow was a flat sealed waterproof compartment that protected a satellite dish from the corroding elements of the brackish environment. On the roof of the cabin, an extended antenna lay flat in its protective sheath. The RPMs increased as the boat headed north into the Northumberland Straits.

Uri glanced at Stan and abruptly glared at Olivia, before resting his gaze on Yvonne. "I'm a bit perplexed," he admitted. "I never planned on meeting you again," he bluntly admitted to Olivia. "But I couldn't find any rational reason to turn down an invitation to dine on succulent fresh lobster in a private maritime bistro. Your messenger was convincing. You know me well," he concluded as he transferred his gaze from Yvonne and back to Olivia, acknowledging Stan with a brief cordial glance. "Am I correct in concluding that we are meeting once again because of your involvement in this case, which has prompted the Russian bear to pay more attention to my professorial academic credentials and competencies?"

Olivia acknowledged his accurate assessment with a terse nod. *"Da"* – Yes.

He transferred his stare back to Yvonne and raised his eyebrows. "Best stay away from my classroom as one of the students is an FSB agent supposedly auditing the course. But unknowingly she is being observed by another interesting student whose tuition is being paid, I suspect, by either the CSIS or CIA. Once in a while, I team the two of them up on an in-class assignment. The machinations are entertaining if nothing else." He smiled warmly at Yvonne once again. "If I didn't know anything different, I would surmise that you were trained by the best in the art and science of clandestine communication techniques. I'm confident that my auditing students are none the wiser. Nonetheless, best we keep it that way."

"Noted. Thanks for the tip," Yvonne acknowledged with a nod. "Perhaps I left the impression that I was a coquette in pursuit, competition beyond their experience and naïve adolescent aspirations. The blind wisdom of youth is no match for the practiced acumen of maturity and proficiency."

Stan concluded that he and Olivia had secured the tentative loyalty of a Slavic partner albeit initially reluctant and reserved. Better that than a coiled foe.

Stan and Olivia grabbed hold of a handrail to steady themselves as the boat bounced off the first few waves once they had passed the protection of the fortified breakwater at the entrance to the harbour. They immediately winced and took a short breath. Bullets might bounce off a select few who have a gifted ability to leap over tall buildings but they were left with a reminder of their mortality.

"Am I also correct in concluding that your plans for a long and healthy retirement together have been challenged? I've had to nurse a few dents myself while serving with the Spetsnaz." His tone became more conciliatory. "How can I help, Oli?"

Sympathy had been a rare commodity in their turbulent marriage, Olivia reflected. He had only used her nickname, Oli, when he was sincerely concerned for her safety and wellbeing. She picked up on his intimation that the relationship between her and

Stan was evolving beyond old cold case partners. It was this *je ne sais quoi* that had been absent in their brief marital rapport.

Olivia replied, "I'm missing something in the text of the documents we found. Not so much the actual pragmatic translation but the cultural connotations only you can help me with. It is for that reason I have asked you to join us."

"You remembered my tutoring from our Carleton University days. I'm honoured, I guess," he said. "It was the clincher for me to accept Yvonne's invitation for a lobster feast! It was also the reference to Tolstoy and Dostoevsky and the A+ grade you got on the final paper for the Interpretation of Russian Literature course, after our many discussions on cultural innuendoes."

Olivia reciprocated the further warming of East/West relations with a humble bow and appreciative smile to her former mentor in Russian culture, the Ukrainian Yoda.

"Let's work together, again, Oli. We'll need to clear the table for lobster à la Capitaine Bernie. Both are imperatives but the cuisine will take precedent at some point."

Olivia briefed him on the details and cover-up of the shooting in the barn, the subsequent suspicious deaths of their colleagues, and the aborted meeting with Leblanc, his abduction and the suspected murder.

After considerable reflection, Uri broke the silence. "You fell into this Cold War initiative in Sleepy Hollow Hammonds Plains and now you are being hunted down like rabid animals. I am not surprised given the circumstances. It goes without saying that my previous employer knows no limitations when it comes to getting what they want."

This reality struck home. It felt like the final cubic millimetres of air had been sucked out of them by a high-powered commercial vacuum. Unfortunately, the removal of the deadly threat to their lives could not be diminished by similar modern-day technology.

"You already have a comprehensive appreciation of nineteenth and early twentieth century Russian culture, Oli. There are two aspects of contemporary culture you should consider, both impacted by Cold War scripting of political thèâtre. Today, they are often interpreted within the context of Cold War versus Cold Peace. First, Cold War political events of the 1960s leading up to FLQ Crisis in 1970 prompted this Hackett sleeper cell to awaken. Second, macro global events contributed to the transition that the Cold War underwent pre- and post-collapse of the USSR. In a nutshell, it's all about power and control. Who has it, who doesn't and who wants it? Who are winners and who are losers? What price are people ultimately prepared to pay? Some have already paid the ultimate price. I refer to your deceased colleagues. I am confident others will follow suit as your investigation progresses."

Olivia listed off the following: "In addition to constables Mike Davidson, Brian Hamilton, the dead include John Robert Hackett a.k.a. Nicolai a.k.a. Oberstleutnant Brandt Felix Schmid, Pierre Laporte, and, most recently, J.P.R.C. Leblanc. Missing in action are Comrade Ruslan and his co-conspirator Sylvia Hackett a.k.a. Lada." She then raised her hand. "Hold on. I need to write something down before I forget." She scribbled a quick note to herself, then nodded to Uri to continue.

"I can understand the fate of these players in the broader context of the Cold War," Uri acknowledged. "Given the international implications, you could have been killed as easily as Davidson and Hamilton. That begs the question: why were you not?"

"Because the Cold War is not over. Instead, it has merely mutated like viral superbugs for which there are no known antibiotics," Yvonne speculated. "Moscow, specifically Nikita Khrushchev, used the supposed era of devious détente of the 1960s as a cover for massive Russian military expansion. This cover-up was achieved through the deception of trust as the strategic initiative. The West either could not or had great difficulty quantifying and verifying the final figures of inter-continental ballistic missiles, ICBMs with nuclear warheads, amongst other offensive armaments."

Uri added, "I agree, but there is more. Put it into context. Delve into the genesis of Communist culture. This was the manifestation of the Lenin adage: the West are wishful thinkers so we will give them what they want to think. Boris Pasternak was a Russian poet and author best known in the West for his novel, *Doctor Zhivago*. He summed up communism the best. *'The communist regime wants you to hate things you love and love things you despise. Winners and losers.'*"

Olivia interjected slowly yet deliberately. "Winners and losers, assets and liabilities. With the exception of Laporte, the others like Davidson and Hamilton had nothing more to add. They were no longer potential assets but threats by happenstance. In contrast, Laporte was separate, an intervening variable, a tool that was conveniently available to press the communist agenda. His assassination accomplished just that by creating a disruption."

Uri pointed at Olivia. "Yes, absolutely. But why?" He continued without hesitation. "Because, at a global level, it is an extension of the communist culture to disrupt and thereby distract. If the Cold War was discovered to be a hoax, it would call into question current Russian and American political processes, the myriad of lies to the proletariat, the masses, let alone the justification for billions of dollars spent. Best to keep it all a secret and protect the secret at all costs. That means this document that you and Stan dug up. The Russian Makarov pistol is the smoking gun, literally. It shows depth and breadth of Russian interference, influence in foreign domestic politics, likewise American politics. Then mix in American intrusion in Canadian politics including the Avro Aircraft debacle, among other nefarious and criminal activities."

"Neither side can tolerate these secrets being divulged," Yvonne speculated. "So, both sides are hunting you because you are exhuming the Hackett file and all its dirty deceitful details. That could be an advantage because neither may want you dead without first interrogating you and ideally securing the evidence. It is actually to your advantage to spread the news amongst more players without surrendering to anyone."

Uri nodded again. "It's too late to put the geopolitical genie back in the bottle because the genie is the game changer. You are being chased by the CIA, FSB and CSIS concurrently, in addition to other emerging nation-state powers, the most prominent being the Chinese. One cannot allow the other to win. That is the tentative advantage to a Cold War stalemate as long as equal stress and pressure on all sides is maintained. Adjust the balance one way or another and someone will have to be eliminated in order to re-establish stasis, balance. That someone is the two of you because finding the Makarov PB pistol and documents has altered the fulcrum."

Olivia and Stan exchanged both pensive and worrisome glances. Individually, they had considered such strategic consequences. Together, they had toyed with the reality but never seriously debated its impact, perhaps because they had suddenly stumbled onto it in the context of an idyllic pastoral setting. Perhaps John Robert Hackett had that in mind when he whispered Zhena and Tovarishch and the compass bearing into Olivia's ear.

Uri added, "At the opposite end of spectrum, are other unknown parties with political agendas who want Hackett's secrets exposed for their own advantages. Ask yourself, who would be the winners if the U.S. and Russia suffered, fell from grace on the world stage? China for certain. Other non-Nation-State actors who see their stars ascending on the world stage?"

Yvonne nodded. "I second Uri's analysis. The two of you were not killed or haven't yet been silenced because they, whoever they are, are convinced that you have something more dangerous than any megaton atomic bomb. If it is the Makarov PB pistol and the documents, it cannot be left unaccounted for. We also need to consider CIA interests circa the 1970 FLQ Crisis."

"But why now after all these years?" Olivia pressed.

"My turn to support Yvonne's points," Uri said. "There have been Russian spies in Canada and U.S. since the 1920s. Examine the murder, assassination of Peter 'Lordly' Verigin in the interior of British Columbia. Ask why his file is still under lock and key in Ottawa?"

"Let's go back to Leblanc," Stan suggested. "We still don't know if he was a good cop or a corrupt cop. Two possible scenarios. Good cop: Thinking strategically, Leblanc went out of his way to protect us because he suspected we knew or would be able to identify the whereabouts of the missing pieces of the puzzle, literally the smoking gun and the document which would implicate others. We can safely conclude that only Hackett and Olivia knew where it had been hidden. I say this because if Leblanc had known, he would have secured it himself. Corrupt cop: Thinking strategically, same reasoning, same conclusion. Together, the contents of the metal box are the common denominator. But the key to what lock? Pandora's box, as Uri and Yvonne propose?"

"Or peace?" Olivia suggested. "Follow the money trail. Weapons manufacturing is a trillion-dollar industry. Add in other interrelated industries that support war, be it hot war or cold war, and you have a motivation. Peace doesn't pay. Disruption and war do pay and they pay well. Add in these industrialists to the list of those who want us out of the picture and our odds of surviving are becoming less attractive."

"The next logical step in the sequence of events is the repercussions of the FLQ Crisis," Yvonne proposed. "There were virtually no consequences for the ringleaders, Paul Rose, Jacques

Rose and Francis Simard. They were never charged but instead were banished to Cuba, a nation state designated as *persona non grata* by the United States. For these FLQ conspirators, Cuba was Club Med in comparison to a federal penitentiary. No one crossed into or out of the U.S.-imposed Cuban blockade without permission of the U.S. State Department and with the President's knowledge and consent. So, who was in bed with whom? It must have been someone at the highest level in Ottawa – the PMO, and Washington – The Whitehouse."

"Time for a lobster feast?" Uri enquired with anticipation as he glanced over at Yvonne.

Bernie reached into the fridge and pulled out a container brimming with the flesh from claws, tails and succulent legs. "Already cracked and dressed. All you can eat. Wine, beer or a sample of local shine to pair with your seafood entrée?"

Uri found himself drawn to both Olivia and Yvonne, like two prevailing planets passing within the periphery of his own constellation and shadowing his orbit. Each was exerting differing gravitational forces from their respective trajectories, one seemingly influencing while the other toying with influence. He sensed the latter was trailing a black hole which, by definition, could not have been seen, instead only detected by the presence of their absence.

Future affiliations were fraught with as many unknowns as the circumstance which had drawn them together on this voyage in uncharted waters. If torpedoed, he was unsure if it would be better to be in one lifeboat charting a collective course to the safety of a singular port or in separate dinghies adrift at the mercy of the winds and currents. He and Olivia had been separated too long for him to decipher her encoded intent with any reasonable degree of accuracy. Reading her mannerisms had never been his strong suit when they were together. It was less so now. He would have to rely on indications of others in her company and his own intuition.

He knew virtually nothing about Yvonne so attempting to draw any reliable conclusion was fraught with suspicions. At this juncture, she could potentially still be a Russian agent, a Red Sparrow. Based on the working relationship with Bernie, Stan and Olivia, he concluded that the likelihood of that scenario was infinitely small. He refrained from using superlatives like never. Instead, he suspected that something else was at play. Thus, he would not pursue the possibility of a more formal relationship at this juncture. He would merely observe from his quiet perch on the sideline even if that meant having to maintain closer ties with Olivia who potentially posed less of a threat. But that would be a double-edged sword.

CHAPTER 19

"We have at least one more player who appears to be AWOL," Olivia suggested as she examined the brief notes she had made while reflecting on the mental minutes of their maritime meeting with Uri aboard Bernie's lobster boat.

Stan inclined his head toward her and squinted with curiosity.

"The secret squirrel who arrived at the barn and told us to report to the Detachment Commander. Corporal Hartmann if I recall correctly. But, where is he?"

"One of the unidentified sequences in Leblanc's coded letter," Bernie proposed. "If Hartmann is one, then we are just left with a final unsolved numeric sequence. Good and bad news. Good, we may have reduced the unknowns by one. Bad news, who or what is the remaining unknown sequence? Possibly Leblanc's superior in the RCMP Security Service or within the government?" He lingered momentarily. "Or someone else?"

"Could be if we have concluded correctly that Leblanc has been murdered for what or who he knew. What about other secret squirrels? They could have been as close to him as anyone especially if he had personally selected his closest colleagues like Robin Hood and his merry band of men, plus one woman, Maid Marion." Olivia looked at Stan. "Did you ever find out the names of others who were working out of the Halifax office?"

"Never did, never asked," he replied. "An oversight on Leblanc's part, and mine? I should be able to find out relatively easily. There would have been an 'H' Division nominal roll of all those serving in Halifax in 1978."

Olivia's attention focused on the sketch of the flowers that Leblanc had drawn at the bottom of the letter. "Art is a form of communication. *Les Fleurs du mal,"* she muttered. Then the first lines of her father's words again came to mind: *Remember, remember, /The fifth of November, / The Gunpowder treason and plot...* "We have the smoking gun. We are confident there is treason at the highest levels. We just have to figure out who all the players were and perhaps still are, so we can better identify all those collaborating in the plot and those on the periphery. Their unsavory motivation drives the plot. We need to identify the conspirators." She smiled inwardly. Yet, something continued to gnaw at her – an inconsistency, a cover-up that was impairing her ability to clearly identify the truth, the whole truth and nothing but the truth.

Stan couldn't help noticing the change in her mood. At another time, another place, they would talk. He had to admit that Leblanc might have been a good guy with laudable although questionable intentions. Yet he would never forgive him for separating them. He threw Olivia an inquisitive glance. *"Les Fleurs du mal?"*

"A poem by Charles Baudelaire, a French poet," she clarified. *"Les Fleurs du mal,* evil flowers in the garden?" Leblanc has already alluded to the fact there is corruption, evilness in government among common senior bureaucrats, provincially and federally.

"Bernie, what did your contact at the Mount Pleasant Cemetery say about Leblanc? He obviously retrieved our note directing him to go to Kolbec Road," Stan prompted.

"Leblanc just bent down and left a second bouquet of flowers. He then paused in what appeared to be a respectful moment of reverence while furtively reading our note. He then departed without fanfare."

Olivia raised her eyebrows and grinned. "Are you thinking what I'm thinking? He picked up our note and he left his note." She looked at Stan. "I recall from my Identification course the instructor stating at every crime scene some evidence is left by the perpetrator while other evidence is taken away. Correct?"

"Correct," Stan replied.

Bernie responded. "Individual grave sites in the Mount Pleasant Cemetery are maintained by relatives of the deceased. Matthew Edward Brownell is a fictitious avatar. I am his sole grieving relative and, as such, I am responsible for grooming the grave site."

"Leblanc would have left another communiqué somehow concealed in the flowers he laid at the grave? If anyone had had him under surveillance, they would not have necessarily second-guessed his behaviour."

"I'll have my contact collect the flowers he left and bring them to the farmhouse. He's a computer geek. He makes a living by providing drone surveillance for a select clientele. On these types of assignments, he sets up his video surveillance system as a backup in the event that the world goes sideways. He reported that he had reviewed the footage but there didn't appear to be anything unusual before, during or after Leblanc's visit. I'll ask him to send a copy to me."

"A tool to augment I-spy-with-my-little-eye is always useful, a visionary," Olivia commented. "We are gaining a better understanding of how Leblanc thinks. I wouldn't be surprised if he purposely left us more bread crumbs for Hansel and Gretel to follow in the event we missed other clues. At this juncture, I'm not thinking that Leblanc is paranoid. To the contrary, he is telling us we need to be meticulous yet very careful. The opposition is ruthless. So, redundancy is necessary."

"Another friend," Stan nodded at Olivia with a sly smile.

"When we were with the Watcher Service at McGill, I envisioned changes to every aspect of our lives as a result of technology," Bernie added. "I recall presenting a paper in one of my classes arguing that the impact of technology would be greater than the industrial and agrarian revolutions combined. I received a very low grade because my professor, who I felt was a Luddite cut from a dinosaurian cloth, said that my thesis wasn't based on fact but instead on emotion."

Olivia replied with a smile that rose from her lips to her eyes, "Fact that incorporates intuition analyzed with logarithms and good old fashion brain power reigns supreme."

"It would be a great deal easier if we knew Leblanc was a good guy or a corrupt cop," Stan reflected. "Would he have swept the immoral dirt under the carpet or merely swept it aside with the intension of recovering it at a later, safer time? Each of us must confront morality from our own perspective. You dress it up with a believable provenance that will make you look moral. I am thinking that Leblanc had a penchant for a selective truth regardless of whether he was a good cop or a corrupt cop. Perhaps, that is what it takes to survive in a swamp inhabited by agents of villainy of the spyosphere and criminality."

"Yes and no," Bernie suggested. "If we supposed one way or the other, that could bias our thinking. If we don't know, we need to consider all options with equal weight. That provides a more comprehensive analysis. We need to be continually asking what the good Leblanc would be thinking and the same for the bad Leblanc. Of equal importance, we need to ask why he was thinking that way. The answer to the why question, will provide us with a clearer psychological profile of those who wanted him dead, who are now after the two of you, want both of you disposed of after they have interrogated you. From that, we will be able to glimpse into their culture, their psyche. We might never know their names but we will know who they are by the nature of their bread crumbs – their political rhetoric."

"By the way, the collective you, includes all of us," Yvonne added with a realistic somber tone which all warily conceded. "On a positive note, the more good guys who know, the more security and protection we have from our collective and separate voices."

"Voices from the grave where no grave exists except those of the choir whose voices have been muted," Bernie muttered. In response to their inquisitive stares, he added, "The avatar. Leblanc left flowers and bowed his head in reverence to the avatar, representing the choir which Leblanc leads, their voices growing in unison yet unheard, and whose members are not fully accounted for, hitherto missing in action."

CHAPTER 20

The bouquet of slightly wilted flowers was on the back porch to greet them. There was no card providing written condolences or a signature. Olivia carefully untied the bow that bound the paper wrapper around the stems. On the inside of the paper, several dual groups of sequenced numbers were listed in two columns.

"It appears to be a Pope's Code but with a different code book key than the letter Bernie had retrieved from the Amherst Post Office," she suggested after comparing the two documents.

"Would he use the same key for both?" Yvonne enquired.

"There is one way to find out. We apply our best result through a process of elimination," Olivia replied.

"Coffee pot is on," Bernie announced. "It could be a long night."

"I agree with your logic for a simplistic but not a simple code based on Leblanc's Catholic affiliation and his reciting of Émile Nelligan's poem," Yvonne offered. "It's Occam's Razor – the simplest solution is probably the correct one. Another Catholic connotation. It's a good starting point, in the absence of an actual code book. Just because it didn't work with the letter doesn't mean it won't work with the bouquet message. Leblanc, from how you have described him, could have used two keys from the same poem, Christ on the Cross. That could be the common code book."

Olivia and Yvonne juxtaposed permutations and combinations of Catholic-referenced words in the final stanza and eventually the entire poem, all with negative and frustrating results. Olivia responded with a puzzling sort of stare. As a last-ditch effort, she used the poet's first name and last name spaced, first and last names together without a space. No combination worked. Finally, she keyed in last and first names without a space.

"Eureka," She exclaimed.

"The elegance of simplicity in some codes," Bernie yelped gleefully.

Digger raised his head and wagged his tail. He liked it when his master was happy. It usually meant treats from his pocket would be forthcoming if he rubbed against the pocket with the strongest scent. He was not disappointed. His master then reached down and gently tickled his stomach. Life was good in this dog house.

A series of first and last names rolled down the monitor, many of which he recognized and all of which they collectively identified. A back-translation confirmed the entire encryption. It wasn't simplistic but simple once the combination to the lock was applied. Finally, she interpreted the short sentence under the drawing of the flowers at the bottom of the page. A shiver ran the length of Olivia's spine reminding her of the first time she experienced such a tactile sensation. She was standing next to the barn where Hackett lay dead. The voice resounded ordering both her and Stan to report to their Detachment Commander. The translation they starred at: a dire warning by Leblanc to be very cautious of Corporal Werner Hartmann. An elusive scent of treachery lingered.

"Hartmann must be still alive and a clear and present threat," Olivia uttered in a convincing yet worrisome declaration. She gazed up, capturing the moment with her deep breath. "What if." She hesitated. "What if we have been influenced by our self-imposed paradigm of analysis within our mind sets of rank and structure within the organization? What if the corporal is the leader of the Moscow ring, not the inspector? The perfect cover for Hartmann. That could mean that Leblanc is a good cop after all, not a corrupt cop. Just a thought, a different perspective," she speculated.

Stan slowly nodded his head in affirmation of a thought that had been nagging him since that morning all those years ago. "When Davidson asked if he could help, I requested he limit access to vehicles entering the barnyard close to the barn where Hackett had been shot. Yet Hartmann drove speedily into the yard and came to a skidding halt over the prints beside the barn. I thought he was just being arrogant. I spoke to Davidson about it just before we departed for the detachment. He stated emphatically that he had specifically mentioned it to Hartmann. Hartmann wasn't being arrogant. He drove over the prints purposefully to destroy any trace of evidence."

Reality set in. An ominous hush hung over the room like the premonition of a pandemic about to descend upon the world. Finding the Russian Makarov PB pistol and the Cyrillic script with their implications buried under the fence post paled in comparison. We feel guilty about our small indiscretions because we find it exponentially too difficult to acknowledge exceptionally large errors in judgement. Breaking the Pope's Code was small in comparison to the potential implications now facing them. No one wanted to be the first to fill the enormity of the vacuum.

Stan ultimately led with a broad conceptual assessment. "If you ask the question, you had better be prepared to handle the answer. The genie is now completely out of the proverbial bottle. Each breakthrough brings with it an exponential consequence, not just one more individual Russian doll revealed but an entire set of dolls. I suspect each successive set will contain additional sets."

"We have identified the conspirators. We have the gunpowder, the treason and the plot," Olivia whispered as if they were being covertly monitored by cameras and microphones planted by the CSIS, CIA, and MI6, past and current agents of the KGB and FSB, Mossad, and God only knows who else.

"As Uri said, we fell into this Cold War collusion in Sleepy Hollow Hammonds Plains. So, where are Ichabod Crane and the headless horseman?" Stan jested. "I now have a crystal-clear understanding of why we are being hunted down like rabid animals."

"We're on a roll," Yvonne announced as she glanced over at Olivia. "You are good. No, you are damn good at judging people and their characters. It is the Pope's Code together with Émile Nelligan's poem that is the key. Let's use the same process to identify the key for the unsolved mysterious numeric sequences. It has to be a derivative. What do you suggest?"

"I'm not certain. It was a lucky guess."

"Luck is an extension of intuition," Stan followed up. "You mentioned that if a student came to you with an incomplete researched paper, you would ask them to seek the implicit, the intuitive and then objectively explain why."

Olivia pondered like Pooh Bear over a pot of honey. "You usually have the code book first and then apply it to the encrypted sequence. Our code book is the poem. We apply the encrypted sequence to the first and last names in a single column and then back-translate."

All eyes were on the monitor once again.

"You are hot, lady," Stan exclaimed. He hugged her with all the empty years of emotion. The others seemed not to notice. Olivia reciprocated Stan's coded embrace.

"Hot is an understatement," Bernie repeated. "How would you like to work with us full time?"

All the locations, events and players flowed like a stream temporarily blocked by a beaver dam but now allowed to find its natural course once again. No sequence was incomplete. Known events with known dates were verified. The cyber interpretation of the Pope's Code was itself a *nom de guerre*.

"Leblanc is a good cop, perhaps Ichabod Crane, not corrupt but still obnoxious," Olivia whispered to Stan before openly admitting it to the others. "Or is Leblanc the handless horseman, at least one-handed for certain, not the headless, metaphorically speaking?"

The video surveillance of Leblanc leaving the flowers at the grave site that Stan's colleague had sent him, in addition to leaving the flowers, showed no one else at the grave site after Leblanc departed. As Bernie's contact reported, Leblanc stood by the tombstone in a respectful pose.

"Go back," Olivia said sharply. "Watch his right hand."

Bernie replayed it.

"He's pointing, tapping his finger on a lapel pin on his jacket. Is that a RCMP crest? What is he trying to communicate? To us? Someone else?" Olivia asked inquisitively.

"An unknown remains an unknown," Stan said with a tinge of uncertainty in his voice that dropped off, "good cop or corrupt cop." He stood shaking his head. "I still don't know which."

"How about we celebrate the solving of the code at least with still-fresh lobster and Chardonnay?" Bernie suggested. "There will be time enough hereafter to figure out how not to resurrect the Cold War Version 2, bring about the downfall of Western democracy and Eastern communism, in addition to preventing total global annihilation in the interim."

Olivia stood quietly in the presence of her colleagues but detached in a space of her own. She transferred her gaze to Stan in response to his subtle supportive nudge and inquisitive expression. "In some cultures, paying reverence at the grave site is a ritual to bring the deceased back to life. In this case, the choir of the avatar representing Leblanc as the choirmaster and all the deceased who will sing the truth. This legendary belief is evoked from sacred places in the realm of the mystic spirits."

"You seem to speak from experience," Stan quietly commented as if paying reverence to her wisdom. *How many cases could they have solved had they stayed together?* He asked himself.

Olivia whispered, "I mentioned a special place under the shade of the willow trees on our family farm in southeastern Alberta. It was a mystical place for me where apparitions would appear. Legend had it that the Blackfoot shamans came there to commune with the spirits of the buffalo. The spirits say that what we don't know supports what we do know. In one of my mystic dreams, I was reading poetry which was written in another language but I could understand it, like Émile Nelligan's poem. It appeared as an overlay of a verbal map. What just occurred with this solving of Leblanc's code was a déjà vu. It was there under the prairie willow trees. You were there also, in my dream because myths and dreams come from the same place."

Yvonne's voice signalled their return to the kitchen. "It is apparent that Leblanc knew all of this. So why didn't he do something about it?"

Olivia answered without hesitation. "Because, like us, he didn't know how to safely deactivate the pandemic bomb, the revelation of all the truthful details would unleash. He couldn't take the chance that any one of the treasonous traitors whom he had identified would assassinate him and use what we now know to their respective malevolent advantages. His best-case scenario was to hide it with a Hansel and Gretel trail of coded breadcrumbs until such time as he could develop a flawless exit strategy. I conclude he was never able to achieve that for whatever reason."

"Thirty years is a long time to remain silent," Stan said sceptically. "Did he believe that he was under surveillance every hour of every day? Was there no one he could trust? Was he so fearful of being found out? I find that very hard to believe."

"Is it possible for an inspector in the RCMP to just disappear off everyone's radar for that length of time?" Yvonne asked. "You were able to discover an address and send him an invitation to meet. So, I think there must have been another reason."

Stan shrugged. "Was our invitation to him his death warrant? Perhaps the question is rhetorical, given what we suspect has happened."

"We may never know for certain," Olivia lamented. "Our initial objective was to find out what happened to Davidson and Hamilton and why. We're getting close to answering those questions, ironically, as more bodies are added to the heap. I'm now more confident than ever that all the unknown dominos, whether dead or alive, will fall once any one is toppled, in addition to other innocent victims like the owner of the vacant garage where the black SUV was located."

CHAPTER 21

From the crackle of the radio on the morning of 5 November 1978: "Cancel Ident and GIS," the file never revealed the details of what would qualify as *untoward underfoot* shrouded within Leblanc's menacing arrogant reputation. Now the veil of secrecy had been breached and with it a torrent of information with potentially lethal national and international repercussions. The evidence was laid out on the table for all to contemplate. A shiver ran through those assembled in the ranch house knowing that the names on the list, some still alive, would be exposed for treason. Even the families of those deceased would suffer the consequences of the actions of their forefathers and mothers.

The search for the few secret squirrels who could have been involved in the investigation came up on the nominal roll of the Division headquarter. They were cross-referenced with the names that Leblanc had listed in his cryptic communiqué. Other conspirators were linked to the file to add to the growing list of potential huntsmen on their trail.

"We might not want to contact them but it would be valuable, if not simply enlightening, to find out as much as possible about the current whereabouts of these secret squirrels," Olivia suggested cautiously.

"Seeing a pattern here," Bernie muttered with guarded trepidation. "Not getting a warm and fuzzy feeling though." His expression prompted the others to focus on the monitors. "They are deceased, reported as having died on the same date. Both allegedly killed in the same motor vehicle accident. Both buried in the RCMP Cemetery in Regina. No further details available for either. Their status has changed from inexplicably absent to mysteriously missing, now permanently linked to correspondingly inaccessible graves of others listed on the nominal roll of deceased colleagues."

Stan sighed with frustration. "The probability of anyone exhuming their bodies is infinitely small. Even in death, they are silenced under lock and key, not to mention the *Official Secrets Act*. Their muted voices have been added to Leblanc's choir."

"On a positive note," Olivia added, "no longer are they suspected stalkers on our trail. We can safely assume they have already been successfully hunted. That leaves another unknown – two, actually. First, who is responsible for their supposed motor vehicle accident? Second, is that person or persons also connected to the untimely deaths of Davidson and Hamilton? Hackett?"

"And Leblanc," Yvonne added. "What is the connection?"

Bernie sat back and took a deep long breath. "This raises the stakes exponentially. It's safe to say that anyone associated with this case can be potentially added to the endangered species list, including us."

"There is more truth in stories than detail in facts," Yvonne stated. "I have a trusted friend who is with the Canadian Security Intelligence Service. We both served with military intelligence. When I say trusted, I mean absolute faith as far as absolute can go, ninety-nine point nine eight percent certain. We had worked together in Germany on a case that involved a senior member of the Russian State Duma who was on the verge of coming in from the cold, so to speak. We were double-crossed. Never did find out who the mole was. Our contact was assassinated literally steps from our safehouse. My friend was seriously wounded in the brief gun battle that ensued. I dragged her to safety. I tell you this because disclosure or even a hint of all the intelligence that we have unearthed thus far could immediately put all of us in the crosshairs, more so than we already are. So, we need consensus for any actions we take from this point forward, including my suggestion that I contact my friend."

"Thanks for sharing," Bernie acknowledged somewhat disquieted. He prided himself on knowing a great deal about his colleagues, yet he didn't know specifically about this aspect of Yvonne's military service. He was acutely aware that Canada had no legislative authority to engage in international covert espionage when Yvonne had served. That wasn't to say that Canada didn't gather intelligence. They did under the guise of military liaison officers attached to Canadian embassies. Any evidence of becoming involved in an exchange of gunfire would have been immediately and permanently suppressed to the same level as the circumstances of the mysterious death of the Doukhobor leader, Peter Lordly Verigin a half a century before. Likewise, any citations or medals of meritorious service earned for bravery would not be awarded or even informally mentioned.

Looking directly at Yvonne and Stan, Bernie assumed they had mined intelligence for other clients but never to this depth and never with such dangerous consequences. "Most importantly," Bernie said, "we conduct full background checks on all clients. If we aren't completely confident, we don't enter into any contracts. This file has exponentially more ramifications and the players are deadlier than anything James Bond ever faced with Q's innovative spy gadgets. The difference with this case is readily apparent. We are our own clients." He looked over at Olivia. "You are new to this game. At this juncture, suffice it to say that the genie can't be stuffed back in the bottle."

"More minds working on a strategy within the parameters of complete consensus is the only way forward. I want to enjoy retirement as much as anyone here." Olivia nodded, pausing only briefly to make direct eye contact with each person. Her gaze lingered longest on Stan. "I'm in full agreement with Yvonne's proposition."

The first order of business was to determine what Yvonne would say to her ex-military intelligence colleague and the means of communication that would ensure the maximum security and anonymity for all assembled. The protocol would be the same as she and Bernie had used on previous cases. The existence of the ranch would not be disclosed under any circumstances nor would the identity of current colleagues be revealed, or how many. The cover story would be a rendezvous with a friend to swap old stories on a social occasion. With the exception of Bernie, all would enter and leave the ranch henceforth via the tunnel that ran from the mechanical barn that bordered the treeline along the berm to the woodshed.

"Excuse me for a moment," Olivia stated quietly. "I need to enter into Bernie's private e-sanctuary." She returned moments later. "We need to take a day trip to the Wood Islands ferry terminal at Caribou just north of Pictou."

Her announcement was met with inquisitive stares. Nothing in any conversations or correspondence leading up to this point had mentioned Caribou or Pictou.

"Caribou? It is just a dot on the map, so small it doesn't even warrant a Tim Horton's," Bernie jested. "Its population increases twenty-fold when the Wood Islands ferry momentarily docks, and becomes deserted fifteen minutes later."

Olivia replied, putting her statement in context. "I found the address for Sergeant McNeill, the Bedford Detachment Commander. He is living in Caribou, Pictou County, Nova Scotia. Like the secret squirrels, I had forgotten about him as a potential resource to question. He had ordered us to turn all of our notes over to Security Services. He is listed in the e-phone directory so he may be still alive. He should remember the case if for no other reason than I doubt that there were too many files that landed on his desk with Top Secret designation stamped all over them. If I remember correctly, he had at least three rows of World War II ribbons stitched on his tunic, possibly four rows. Thus, he would have been acutely aware of security classifications. He would have lived by the adage: loose lips sink ships. That translates into commitment to forgetting every minute detail of whatever you think you might have seen or heard, for survival on the battlefield." She reminded herself, that she too could keep secrets about secrets.

"If you would like to check for snail mail at our post box in Amherst, Yvonne, I will provide a little home-grown security, along with one of our neighbours," Bernie suggested. "I would prefer to have Olivia and Stan remain here but only they know the Detachment Commander and, as a result, can speak with him regarding pertinent details. Our backup exit strategy will be the lobster boat which we will tie up at the marina within a stone's throw of the Caribou dock for the Wood Islands ferry."

Olivia's father had also served in the Second World War along with her grandfather who signed up in World War I. Although neither of them talked at length about their experiences, both were immensely proud to have served. It was all about duty to God, Country and King. Olivia believed she could coax now retired Sergeant McNeill into relating most details about the Hackett case by acknowledging his war decorations within the context of her own family's response to the bugle call. She would not ask Sergeant McNeill to violate the *Official Secrets Act*. Instead, she would express her questions around what he did not say. From those answers, she and Stan could derive additional missing pieces to the puzzle. She was feeling lucky.

"*When sorrows come, they come not as single spies, but in battalions,*" Yvonne pronounced with trepidation in a disquieting voice as if shrouded in an ominous prophecy.

Bernie, Stan and Olivia glanced at her in unison.

"Shakespeare's *Hamlet,*" she explained. "Claudius stated this, referring to calamitous events that seemed to plague Prince Hamlet as the plot unfolds. He meant that when bad events occur like accidents and deaths, they tend not to happen alone or in isolation, but instead in combination with other merciless incidents often simultaneously as if predestined and beyond anyone's control. I sincerely hope that Sergeant McNeill or others associated with him have not already become members of Leblanc's choir of silent voices."

CHAPTER 22

Olivia and Stan pulled into the driveway of a shorefront property overlooking the Northumberland Straits south of the Wood Islands ferry terminal. The name on the artfully refurbished mailbox positioned on the lawn adjacent to the house read Michael H. McNeill. Bernie and one of his colleagues parked on either side of the driveway providing surveillance and cover as circumstances might require.

A middle-aged man responded to Olivia's knock on the door.

"We are looking for a retired RCMP Sergeant Harold McNeill. Do you know of him?" Olivia asked.

"I am his son, Michael H. McNeill. My father passed away a few years ago. Why are you enquiring?"

On many occasions, Olivia recalled seeing a younger boy and an older girl entering and leaving the Detachment Commander's residence located behind the Bedford Detachment building. She could not recall ever meeting them though. Michael appeared to have his father's hazel eyes, fair complexion, warming smile and rugged physique.

"We served with your father at Bedford Detachment," Olivia replied with a noticeable hesitancy in her tone.

"And you are?" Michael pressed.

She paused, feeling a bit insecure about disclosing her identity, given the circumstances. "I am Olivia. My colleague is Stan."

Michael stared at Olivia, then Stan, then back at Olivia. His inquisitive expression morphed into a welcoming smile. "Would you like to come in?"

As they entered the hallway and followed him into the kitchen, Michael said, "Olivia Daniels and Stan Polanski. My father wrote about you in his diary. Let me explain but first can I get you a cup of tea?" He gestured to his guests to sit at the kitchen table. "I sense you are here because of what happened on a farm. Is that correct?"

Olivia drew her head back and glanced at Stan, not certain and seeking direction as to how to reply to Michael's congenial gestures and enticing question. "Yes," she quietly replied, "tea would be wonderful."

Michael poured three cups of tea. "Allow me to explain. I recall your names and the case from my father's secret diary because the two of you were people in his final and most detailed entries before he retired."

"Secret diary?" Stan repeated. *Why would a Detachment Commander have kept a secret diary? A diary, OK, not completely uncommon, but a secret diary?* he pondered.

"More a private diary which he diligently kept on a daily basis since joining the RCMP. My mother allowed me to read it to help me with my research when I was completing my Master's Degree and ultimately a PhD in clinical psychology. I was studying the effects of Post-Traumatic Stress Disorder on employment. His was a classic study of trauma relived from his war service when so many of his friends never made it off Juno Beach in Normandy. I say, relived because my father's initial PTSD resulted from the loss of so many of his war buddies. The deaths of the two constables and another corporal from the Bedford Detachment who just disappeared and was never located were too much. This case re-traumatized him. He attempted to drown his grief in alcohol after he retired. There were too many days when he would sit on this porch with tears running down his cheeks. Eventually, my mother could no longer console him."

They looked at Michael curious about his reference to his father's PTSD from his war experience and how it was exacerbated by the deaths of the two constables and the disappearance of a corporal. His demeanour seemed abrupt yet conciliatory, distant yet present.

Olivia assumed the constables were Davidson and Hamilton. Reference to the corporal, she surmised, must have been another unrelated incident which occurred before she arrived at Bedford Detachment if, as Michael described, he retired on the heels of the Hackett murder case. She wasn't sure why Michael was telling them about the details of his father's PTSD and his mother's supportive response. It was as if he was rambling, debriefing unresolved details from his own life somehow related to his father's war time and RCMP service. There was clearly much more to this case than just the shooting of Hackett in the barn.

"According to my mother, my father's faith in the hierarchy of the RCMP diminished over the years," Michael elaborated. "It hit rock bottom with this case when he was ordered by his superiors to say nothing, deny any knowledge of the case and the deaths of Hackett and the two constables and the disappearance of the corporal, in addition to directing his subordinates to do the same, to be dishonest. He was a stalwart, salt-of-the-earth person. Despite being the son of an RCMP sergeant, today, I have no confidence in the RCMP. I say that based primarily on how they treated my father with utter disrespect and contempt for his PTSD condition. They saw it as a weakness in his character. Perhaps they were envious of all the ribbons on his tunic which he had earned during the war, many for heroism and gallantry. As an aside, I also base my opinion of the RCMP on how the police have traumatized some of my clinical clients. That's not to say there aren't good cops. There are. My father wrote highly of the two of you. He hoped you would get together again. I gather you have."

"He specifically mentioned us and the other members of the RCMP who died?" Olivia asked. The tables appeared to have turned. The clinical psychologist was the client on the Freudian couch detailing his own reactions to family relations. She would provide a supporting shoulder if that helped Michael to fill in some of the pieces to the puzzle.

"Yes. He was re-traumatized over the deaths of the three members of the detachment – the two constables and the missing, presumably dead corporal. Davidson was the name of one constable. I can't recall the name of the other who committed suicide. My father wrote in his diary that he found it highly unlikely this other constable would take his own life. He specifically wrote that he was confident that this other constable had been murdered by someone within the RCMP Security Services. It was made to look like a suicide. About the constable who drowned, my father had serious doubts about the circumstances. My father said that he had the emotionally challenging job of gathering up all his uniforms and accoutrements and shipping them back to Headquarters. He had to do the same for some of his buddies during the war. What really caused my father to question the circumstances about his drowning was the fact that he could not locate any of this constable's notebooks, not one. Yet he knew that this constable was careful to keep copious accurate notes."

"What about the corporal?" Stan asked. He could not recall there being another member involved in the Hackett murder investigation or any other case before or after.

"The corporal was with the drug section. My father described him as self-centred and too focused on his career. He never wanted to share any information or work with anyone else for fear they would take all or even any of the credit. The corporal would introduce himself to his druggie contacts as a detective inspector."

"Did your father make note of his name, the corporal?" Stan pressed.

"He didn't. My father believed the three deaths were somehow connected to a murder on a farm at Hammonds Plains. He suspected Inspector Leblanc and the Security Service member who took over the investigation. He made a specific entry in his diary saying that he did not trust either of them."

"Did he record the name of the Security Service member?" Stan asked.

"He did but I do not recall. It was a German name. I just remember Leblanc's name."

"That's OK."

"There was a plainclothes corporal from the drug section who disappeared at the same time as the shooting at a farm. There was a big investigation and a Board of Enquiry. Constable Davidson gave evidence because he saw the corporal hanging around an abandoned dilapidated building just north of the farm. The corporal's car was found in a gravel pit near the farm. It had been burned out. There was some skullduggery going on. Constable Davidson had approached my father on a few occasions about the farmer who had been shot. This bothered my father considerably. He never recorded the essence of what Davidson had said only that it caused him considerable concern. My father deeply regretted not having warned Davidson to be more careful."

"Could we read his diary, just the reference to this case?" Olivia respectfully requested.

"I digress a bit. My mother died from loneliness within a year of my father's death," Michael explained with sadness in his lowering voice. "Just before that, she burned the diary, his old army uniform and his RCMP uniform in a fit of rage. I was able to rescue his medals before they were also condemned to Dante's inferno."

"I am so sorry to hear this. It must have been very difficult for you," Olivia empathized.

Michael held his head low while silence filled the space between them. He quietly explained, "I recall my father saying on some Remembrance Days his medals weighed what they did, a pound or so. On other days they were too difficult to wear. On most days in the latter years of his retirement, they were just too heavy to wear and bear. The war wounded him and eventually killed another brave soldier. It also took his life-long loving and devoted partner."

Olivia watched as Michael withdrew in grief. She sensed that the medals were a tangible link to his father. She leaned toward him. "Would you like to tell us about his military service?"

Michael stood, walked to the kitchen hutch where he retrieved a cork mounted rack of a dozen military medals which he humbly laid on the table. "He was too young to serve when the war broke out. He had an older brother who had died of what is now called sudden infant death syndrome, SIDS. In January 1944, my father took his older brother's birth certificate to the recruiting center. Due to his robust muscular physique and mature stature, he appeared older so was enrolled under his brother's name. He turned sixteen on 6 June 1944, D-Day. He was awarded the first of several medals for bravery on the Normandy Juno Beach. After the war, he kept his brother's identity when he joined the RCMP because he had to prove his military service. His Christian name was Michael. I was named after him. He knew more about leadership and caring for men than any RCMP officer."

Olivia and Stan gazed at the medals with awe. Michael had allowed them a glimpse into his father's life that few had ever known. They had an appreciation of why the deaths of Davidson, Hamilton and the unidentified corporal impacted him so deeply.

They needed to respect Michael's emotional state. Olivia felt it necessary to ensure he had some support so asked, "If I recall correctly, you had an older sister. Does she live close by?"

"Yes, Sarah lives in Halifax. She visits at least once a month, just about every weekend in the summer." Michael shuffled through a pile of papers in a basket on the table and retrieved a business card. It read simply *Sarah McNeill* and listed an email address and cell phone number. "You may want to speak with her about an incident regarding the murder at the barn and a student who was enrolled in the same German language class she attended at Dalhousie University. When she told me about it years later, it seemed odd. I remember it only because it seemed to relate to one of the comments my father made in his secret diary. My mother had burned the diary by then so I couldn't go back and check. I don't recall any more details."

Olivia responded with an inviting smile. "Thank you. We will follow up. You have been very kind and a gracious host. We do not wish to impose on your time any more than we have." She wrote her email address on a piece of paper and handed it to him. "Could you contact me if you remember anything else? I would be indebted to you."

Michael nodded. "The pleasure has been all mine. My father was a troubled soul which I seem to have inherited. I am so sorry that you could not read his diary as I did several times. There was something haunting in it. That is why I recall your names and all the details – well most details – of the murder case on the farm. In my heart of hearts, I always hoped we would meet. I pass along my father's unspoken words which he regretted not having said to Constable Davidson – *be careful, very careful*. If I remember anything more, I will raise the flag arm of the decorative letter box in the front yard and leave a note in the event I am out when you drop by."

"Well, wasn't that an interesting conversation," Bernie's voice sounded in their earphone as they pulled out of the driveway. "It validates what you already suspected. Did you know who the drug section corporal was?"

"I wasn't aware of his name," Stan said. "Within a week of the shooting of Hackett and on the heels of Olivia's immediate transfer to Ottawa, I had packed my bags and was Alberta bound for Assumption Detachment. The search for him was underway. Surprisingly, I was never interviewed. With all the hush hush and secret squirrels running around attempting to suppress all references to the murder of Hackett, they must have assumed that I was never there. Oversight on their part. I wasn't about to hang around to volunteer my time. It never crossed my mind again until Michael mentioned it just now. In retrospect, I do recall Davidson telling me that he thought he saw an unmarked police car parked by an old building on the adjacent property to the farm – same make and model as we typically used back then. That would have been just across the fence from where we dug up the metal box containing the Russian Makarov PB pistol and the documents in Cyrillic script."

"Would Davidson have been involved somehow? Or was he simply in the wrong place at the wrong time?" Olivia speculated. "When we dug up the metal box, I didn't look the length of the fence line specifically. I don't recall seeing a dilapidated building."

Stan raised his eyebrows and slowly shook his head from side to side. "I can't see the drug section corporal being involved in a drug deal with Hackett if he was all about himself, a detective inspector, as Michael's father described him in his secret diary. I can't see a trained disciplined Russian sleeper cell agent like Hackett risking his cover. Certainly, Ruslan would not have tolerated such behaviors. I can only agree with your second scenario, the drug section corporal was in the wrong place at the wrong time, unfortunately."

Olivia huffed in astonishment. "I find it intriguing that Sergeant McNeill kept such detailed notes about our case having been specifically ordered not to do so, in addition to reminding all the detachment members to omit all references. That level of disobedience must have come from his disgust for his superiors. I can only imagine what he thought about the arrogance of Inspector

Leblanc. His diary entries would have been his effort to debrief the re-traumatization from his war experience. Like using his older brother's birth certificate, the diary snubbed what he perceived to be incompetence of authority." Olivia smiled on reflection. "I would have loved to have spoken with him after he retired. What might he have said in person that he did not record in his diary?"

"Perhaps best that his wife burned the diary, given what transpired. Michael would have been sucked into that vortex for certain and become a secondary victim more than he already is," Stan added. "I'm deeply honoured that Sergeant McNeill thought so highly of us. He must have had some influence over our transfers, to safeguard our wellbeing. He was a true leader, caring for his subordinates like a shepherd watches over his flock to the end. I too would have liked to have met him after his retirement, to shake his hand in heart-felt gratitude. He deserved a better ending to his life. At least, he is finally with his colleagues who died on Juno Beach in Normandy."

"Our next conversation with Yvonne will be interesting," Stan commented with an encouraging inflection as he pondered the mystery of uncertainty which continued to shroud the case. It was now evident that Sergeant McNeill's involvement was a ninth tentacle in the case that needed to be re-examined carefully. He had grave doubts about Leblanc's integrity. That distrust bolstered his own feelings regarding Leblanc. Although he kept an open mind, Leblanc was taking on attributes of a corrupt cop, despite some evidence to the contrary as suggested in the decrypted documentation now laying on the kitchen table at the ranch. He could only hope that Sergeant McNeill's son would remember additional details regarding the conversation with his sister. Given the contempt that Michael held for the RCMP, specifically officers, he was confident that Michael would email Olivia if anything came to mind, however slight.

Bernie's cell phone vibrated repeatedly accompanied by a series of sharp beeps indicating an intruder was being recorded by the security CCTV cameras around the farmhouse. He monitored the image of a man on the back porch. He could hear Digger barking in the background. "Back to the ranch immediately and enter cautiously via the berm route to the tunnel from the machinery garage to the woodshed," his text to all read. He continued to monitor the CCTV cameras as they tracked the intruder as he attempted to look inside the ranch house in vain through the tinted one-way glass. He then walked around the livestock barn and the machinery garage again in a futile attempt to rattle the locked doors. He finally walked to the old single-room school house recently converted into a community center at the parameter of the property where he had parked his black SUV. The final CCTV recorded him driving in a southerly direction. However, due to the angle of the camera, the licence plate could not be identified.

Once they were back at the farmhouse, Bernie reactivated his system which he had automatically shut down when the intrusion alarm sounded. They gathered around the horseshoe of monitors and watched the replay of the path the intruder took as he wandered around the property, specifically the close up recording of him at the back door.

"Halt the camera," Olivia barked as she stared at the profile of the man.

"You recognize him?" Stan asked.

"Somewhere, we crossed paths," she replied as she slowly shook her head and squinted at the still image on the monitor. "Can you increase the size and resolution?"

Bernie complied with her request.

"Somewhere. I can't place him but I do recall cursing under my breath when we crossed paths. There wasn't much in the way of an exchange of pleasantries," she recalled. "It wasn't when I attended university at either Carleton or Calgary. At least, I don't think so. Can you display other still images before and after this shot?"

Bernie complied, holding each frame for several seconds until Olivia requested he advance to the next. She just stared in silence searching the Rolodex of pictorial files from her mind. Imprecise depictions remained blurred. A younger face, perhaps, an image from a photograph, a profile, a persona, a posture, an inexact mirage of an evocative pose or a lilt. Every Sherlock Holmes has a Doctor Watson. Was he someone else's assistant, in the background, his distinguishing features hidden in the shadows? Her head flicked up. Her eyes combed the elliptical orbit. Then, just as instantaneously, the ephemeral flash of the faint implicit echo of what might have been was lost like the fleeting projection of a revolving kaleidoscope ostensibly influenced by quantum forces beyond her control.

"It will come to me, just not now," she muttered in frustration as she stared blankly expecting clues would jog her memory. None did.

She had experienced similar intuitive sensations while resting under the shade of the diamond willow trees on the bluffs of the family farm in southeastern Alberta. Here, now, Digger stood silently, leaning faintly against her leg as if to say, "I share the aggravation of your frustration. I could help if you could understand me. Alas, we can both only hope for inspiration."

CHAPTER 23

Suzette was as elegant as ever, Yvonne conceded, as she hugged her. "The Château Laurier hasn't changed, which is reassuring in this era of replace everything regardless," Yvonne noted. She very much looked forward to catching up on what Suzette had been up to with the CSIS although she doubted that Suzette would reveal any secrets of the tradecraft, at least not verbally.

"Doucement, ma chère amie." Suzette pulled back from Yvonne's affectionate embrace. "On days like today when the weather changes and low-pressure systems descend on the Ottawa River Valley, I am acutely reminded of my mortality and that fateful day when bullets flew at the Château de Mercy in Metz." Some memories of yesteryear can seem like only yesterday. Other memories are repetitions, without the option to press the pause button or ideally to delete, as if there was never a past, only a present with the replaying of the graphic events.

"You saved my life." Yvonne bowed expressing her deepest gratitude. She too had experienced countless daunting dreams of the day the bullets flew. The flashbacks of the images haunt her, often at inappropriate times.

"My recollection of that landscape of the soul is different. It was you who dragged me out of the line of fire and saved my life," Suzette countered.

"A toast to us," Yvonne replied, raising a crystal goblet of Pinot Noir. Even the nuances have nuances.

"Yes, to us," Suzette replied with a smile as she gently massaged her shoulder.

Yvonne put her glass on the embossed coaster and reached for her cell phone. She discretely displayed an e-photo which drew an invisible yet conscious response from Suzette as the bells in the Peace Tower tolled eleven times.

"I had a premonition that your text to meet was more than just a social call," Suzette commented. "Perhaps we should go for a walk along the Rideau Canal," she whispered under her breath all the while shielding her lips.

Yvonne finished her wine. Her candid gaze conveyed her acknowledgement of the caution that would define their communiqué to follow.

Suzette gulped back her double Scotch neat. "I won't ask, at least for now." Her shoulder twitched with a jolt of sharp searing pain. Real pain or perceived ghost pain were now indistinguishable, having long merged into one and the same. "Once in the game, always in the game. That's a given."

"I won't tell, at least for now," Yvonne muttered under her breath.

Once away from the earshot of passers-by and careful to hide their lips from long-distance electronic video surveillance, the intended dialogue immediately became the focus of their rendezvous.

"Connected to our Duma, tovarishch?" Suzette asked, her voice trailing off to a faint whisper. The details of the encounter were as clear today as they had been in Metz. "News of who betrayed us and who pulled the trigger remains unknown. I continue to doubt they are one in the same." Her response was more of a question than a statement of fact.

Yvonne nodded discretely. "Getting closer I believe. I kept this photo of the assassin in full confidence that he would eventually show up like a bad penny. It's ironic that the penny is no longer in circulation in Canada, yet this former KGB assassin circulates in the shadow of these perhaps not-so-hallowed Houses of Parliament, the seat of supposed wisdom yet persistent deceit. As Agatha Christie prophesied, *'old sins have long shadows.'* All sinners, especially politicians and mandarins, would be wise to take heed."

"What can I do to help you?" Her offer was obliging, as required by their prior bilateral oaths of allegiance, yet hesitant. Suzette knew that as long as the case remained unsolved there was a chance that Charles Dickens' ghost of Christmas Past would again rear its ugly head. Today was as good a day as any, better perhaps with Yvonne by her side.

Yvonne was nonchalant in her reply. "I am retired, so I can't officially get involved. You are in an ideal position to initiate action as a CSIS analyst. I'll provide you with the intelligence. You take all the credit. You deserve it as the culmination of a deserving career."

"And I naïvely thought I would slide into an anonymous retirement to muse over past exploits with the aid of the finest scotch."

As Yvonne revealed only the details agreed upon by her farmhouse colleagues, the consequences became increasingly apparent as did the pain in Suzette's shoulder. Ottawa housed many of those whose names were listed in Leblanc's encrypted communiqués, including several employed within the bowels of the Canadian Security Intelligence Service, a relatively short taxi ride from the Rideau Canal, shorter as the covert crow flies.

"This goes exponentially beyond the KGB assassination of our Russian State Duma comrade. We are going to have to think this one through, including all conceivable scenarios."

"We have come up against the Deep Black State before but not to this degree," Yvonne conceded. She was more comfortable having some level of command and control. As a junior military intelligence officer, she had learned how to master the art of situational awareness in fluid environments. She could become highly stressed or highly relaxed. The latter had more rewarding results, physically, emotionally and mentally. Age had the benefit of experience to draw upon but held a shorter fuse. Collegial support was always welcome. The list of those she could trust was markedly shorter than what it had been when they served together with military intelligence in Europe.

"The thumb screws will be secured and twisted for me to reveal all my sources. I need to backtrack to demonstrate that this intelligence surfaced as a result of my own hands-on experience in Europe and subsequent detailed analysis of the facts that surfaced from the KGB Duma assassination and the unknown mole. I'm confident that I can do that. You may be tracked down and asked to corroborate my story. They will be the facts as we knew them to be. So, no need to memorize other fabricated stories."

"Can do," Yvonne confirmed. "As you say, no need to memorize details that didn't occur. Any variance we can chalk up to memory loss attributed to age."

"The existence of the Hackett sleeper cell can be concealed under the *Official Secrets Act*. The connection to the FLQ Crisis and murder of Pierre Laporte is another matter altogether as are the murders of constables Davidson and Hamilton, in addition to Inspector Leblanc and his subordinate secret squirrel. Once Pandora's box is opened up, it's anyone's guess. As you suggest, Cold War Version 2 is a viable yet far more fearful scenario." She rubbed her shoulder as the political low-pressure system descended onto the meteorological pressure already present.

"Sir Francis Drake had it easy with his Royal Proclamation to plunder all manner of Spanish and French shipping on the high seas and arrive back at the steps of Greenwich Palace with his ships brimming over with gold and a sundry of other treasures," Yvonne summarized with a light-hearted chuckle.

"It is somewhat different under the umbrella of the current privacy legislation and international laws of the sea," Suzette qualified with a more sombre tone.

"Ah, for the good old days of the Cold War Version 1 when we were unburdened and unfettered. Well, perhaps less burdened and less fettered with greater latitude would be more accurate."

"With just the two of us, we could openly discuss options. I don't have that leeway today," Suzette lamented. "On the contrary, I need to be very careful about what I say and even more selective who I share my thoughts with. There are too many with two or more income streams. Budding relationships with the sole purpose of developing great friendships are today minefields for even greater betrayal among those wanting to advance up the promotional ladder either internally to the CSIS or externally to a detestable cabal. So, I'll want to think this one through. Off the bat, we need to alter our communications."

"Agreed," Yvonne confirmed. "Do you remember our system of bidding when we played bridge? We used the established bidding rules when the game was to our advantage. We used our modified non-traditional rules when it was to our opponent's disadvantage."

Suzette nodded. "We'll continue to use text and emails for chats as we have always done so as not to draw any undue attention to any change in routine habits. Otherwise, the sequence of the senior suit remains the same: spades, hearts, diamonds and clubs. A no trump modifies the sequence to activate and deactivate."

"I look forward to working with you again," Yvonne confirmed. A warm smile filled her face. "I miss all those occasions when we would engage in conversations that mattered over some fine Moselle valley wines. After you retire, we should take a Rhine River Cruise to re-acquaint our taste buds."

"I'll hold you to that invitation." Suzette's smile was brief, shadowed with a tic of a nod and a twitch of a grimace.

"All OK?" Yvonne asked. She sensed a *je ne sais quoi* in Suzette's manner, an ever so subtle hesitancy only a close colleague and long-term devoted companion would notice.

"All good," Suzette replied conscious of her friend's concern. She needed to respond with a plausible explanation. "There are days when my shoulder reminds me of my mortality. This is one of them," she repeated. Her eyes suggested otherwise. Clearly, there was pain but also something else she could not hide completely.

Yvonne held her gaze as it seemed to drift, unsure of the full veracity of her response. *We all change. It had been a long time since we had shared personal issues. Now is not a time to judge, to assume before confirming all the facts, first hand,* Yvonne reflected. There was something there that she would need to explore beyond the façade of Suzette's good-humoured reference to her mortality.

⇥ ⇤

AS YVONNE SAT IN THE Air Canada Maple Leaf lounge at the Ottawa airport awaiting the flight to Halifax Stanfield International airport, she reflected on her introduction of Suzette to her farmhouse colleagues. She had decreed with absolute confidence that she trusted Suzette ninety-nine-point-nine-eight percent, as close as statistically possible to one-hundred percent, the superlative of always. It insinuated absolute was without variance. An expression of misgiving, of uncertainty now flickered on her face like a black and white silent movie. There was something about Suzette that had changed. If she had to deploy, Suzette might not be there to the same degree as she had been when the bullets flew in Metz and the Duma defector was killed by the KGB agent. She would mull over her concerns in an effort to clearly identify what was in her craw before expressing her misgiving to Bernie. Perhaps it was just her health. Self-medicating with a double scotch neat was out of the ordinary for Suzette. She was an accomplished connoisseur of the fruits of virtuous vines, an accredited Master Sommelier. She had never been a consumer of spirits. Time changes our tastes, Yvonne supposed.

CHAPTER 24

"Coffee pot on?" Yvonne asked Bernie, inferring that if it wasn't, he should attend to the immediate need of a colleague desperate for a caffeine fix. She then proceeded to the e-womb of intelligence, inserted her thumb drive and brought up a series of photos depicting different poses of the same person. The others circled around the horseshoe display of oversized monitors.

"We can conclude that the meeting with your CSIS colleague was successful?" Olivia enquired anticipating additional positive results.

Yvonne nodded. "This is Viktor Titov. Focus on his face, especially the scar on his left cheek. I previously told you about my CSIS friend, who shall remain anonymous for now. We both worked in Europe with the Canadian Armed Forces Military Intelligence at the same time and were involved in the defection of a Russian State Duma bureaucrat." She paused briefly to allow the others to focus on Titov's profile as she took a long sip from her steaming mug of coffee.

"Is this the mole?" Stan asked.

"The plot thickens. We are confident that Viktor Titov is the Russian mole who pulled the trigger. My friend and I followed Viktor from the Canadian Forces Base in Lahr, Germany to Metz, France. That's when I took these photographs in front of the Château de Mercy. It had been 1 Division Headquarters of the Royal Canadian Air Force until 1967 when President de Gaulle took France out of NATO and, in doing so, ordered the expulsion of Canadian and American military forces from French soil. My CSIS friend identified Viktor Titov as a KGB and later FSB agent. For reasons yet unclear, Titov came to Canada sometime thereafter. He initially lived in Ville Jacques Cartier, south of Montréal, in a suburb adjacent to Canadian Forces Base St. Hubert. There he spied electronically on Canadian military operations. Subsequently, he became a sleeper cell handler like Ruslan was with John and Sylvia Hackett."

"Does your friend know those in the upper chain of command? I ask because we may unknowingly have someone else on our trail," Stan pressed, thinking of the unidentified prints he had lifted from the Russian Makarov PB pistol, silencer and documents hidden in the metal box that Hackett had buried beneath the fence post on the farm at Hammonds Plains.

"Not sure," Yvonne replied. "I'll check when next we communicate. She didn't mention it but she might know. Viktor Titov began his career in Canada as a federal bureaucrat around the same time he became a sleeper cell handler. It was interesting that he quickly advanced to become a senior mandarin. He supposedly retired from government several years ago but not before recruiting and mentoring other Russian agents in what is today a comprehensive infestation of alien agents in government. There is a strong indication his mercurial rise was aided by one politician, a communist sympathizer or perhaps another Moscow agent who had risen to become a senior bureaucratic. That person has since died. The CSIS believes Viktor Titov still manages several sleeper cells."

"With this disclosure, might we conclude that your meeting with your CSIS contact was successful," Olivia uttered. "Did she have any thoughts on the letter we received supposedly from a CSIS agent?"

"She stated in no uncertain terms that it was bogus."

"The mercurial rise of Viktor Titov. Leblanc had an equally accelerated rise in rank while serving with the RCMP. Is that coincidental or might he have been helped by the same senior politician or mandarin?" Stan proposed. "Perhaps you could pass this by your contact also. We need to be ever more conscious of tripping landmines."

Yvonne nodded and glanced over at Olivia. "Do you think that Uri would be a good candidate to work with me?" Yvonne had an ulterior motive in asking. Uri could be a source of intelligence for her to feed to her own CSIS contact, Suzette. He had stated emphatically that he held a passionate hatred for the Russians for what they had done to his fellow Ukrainians during the pre- and post-World War II years. An opportunity to seek revenge after all this time might be sufficient motivation to form an alliance. If he agreed, he would find out soon enough who would be the senior senator in the relationship and it would not be him.

Olivia reflected for a moment. "There's a good chance if you approached him tangentially. Not possible if I sent the invitation. He would rightly suspect a disingenuous intention. He isn't a stupid male. Far from it. He still might suspect that something untoward was underfoot, but I will leave that to you to identify the best tactics to employ in order to achieve the objective."

Yvonne's slender smile and subtle nod confirmed receipt of the intended connotation. In addition, Olivia would want to maintain not just a discrete distance from Uri but an absolute separation in the event the Russian bear had him under physical and electronic surveillance. Even setting up the lobster boat rendezvous was pushing the security envelope with the two suspected students in his class, one of which he surmised was a Moscow agent, the other being either CIA or CSIS.

"One last point," Olivia added. "Uri removed himself from the din of rattling sabres and the clamour of ideologies in search of some peace. Service with the Russian special forces, the Spetsnaz, was too intense, a bridge too far for him. This quest remains unmet so it is one of his underlying aspirations. Just some food for thought."

"Interesting. I'll bear that in mind," Yvonne confirmed.

Olivia continued with her psychological assessment of her ex. "Uri is a complex mix of needs that are in constant flux. To be successful, you would be wise to gauge your proposition in a way that will balance both his desire to seek retribution for the suffering of his fellow Ukrainians and his equally deep desire for inner peace. Some mornings, he would rise early in order to practice savate, a form of French kickboxing. On many if not most occasions, I could sense the seething vindictiveness of his pent-up anger. In the evening, he would engage in yoga with deep spiritual self-hypnotic meditation. Depending on his mood, the fulcrum could move and the balance shift. Best to keep your distance while he is wrestling with his inner demons. I can assure you he rarely wins. The match ends in a stalemate at best. Under such circumstances, just give him space and time to achieve a state of inner calm. His underlying motivation is to seek better soundtracks in his life. He was never able to achieve that in his unremarkable life growing up in Ukraine and certainly not in the higher profile elite Spetsnaz, Russian special forces."

"I need to ask, is he a violent person?" Yvonne followed up.

"No, he was never violent with me or anyone else that I was aware of. As I said, he is a troubled soul. To his credit, he knew it and used his savate and yoga to sedate the inner demon."

Yvonne nodded in appreciation of the personal analysis of Uri's psychological and emotional state. This allowed a refinement in her own assessment of Uri, based on Olivia's intimate knowledge and her own pragmatic analysis. It reminded her of the need not to assume but instead to gather additional background information before drawing conclusions, all the while remaining open to the requirement for on-going re-evaluation.

Yvonne reflected on her recent meeting with Suzette. She had no second- or third-hand independent evaluation, instead just her own personal appraisal which she acknowledged was coloured by the bias of their long-term friendship and the shooting at the Château de Mercy in Metz. She would gather additional background information before their next meeting.

Olivia's cell phone boogied across the table from the vibration of an incoming message. It was marked as urgent. The sender was Michael McNeill. "Had a visit from a man and a woman who said they were CSIS agents, yet they failed to produce any identification. I was too flustered, upset, fearful to enquire. They asked about my father and anything he might have said about his time in Bedford. I told them I was only a child back then so didn't know anything. I did not mention my sister. They were very rude and arrogant. We need to talk about his military medals and their connection to the killing of the farmer in the barn at Hammonds Plains. In my father's unspoken words, *be very careful*."

Bernie motioned for Olivia and Stan to remain in the kitchen as he held his index finger to his lips. He returned momentarily with an electronic motioning device which he used to scan each of them separately. He then examined and scanned their cell phones. Thereafter, he whispered, "you are clear."

"I was thinking the same thing," Stan said. "There would have been only two viable explanations for Michael McNeill being interrogated by these supposed CSIS agents after all these years. Either we were being electronically monitored or it was coincidence. We have pretty well ruled out the former. Our cell phones are clean as are we. That means these people are thinking like us, Olivia, but are one step behind."

"Agreed," Bernie replied. "To remain on the safe side, the two of you maintain a lower profile. If you do have to leave, you do so via the tunnel to the machinery barn, and along the berm to the woodlot. Being one step ahead of the black hats is good but far too close for comfort. On a positive note, as far as the file is concerned, it confirms that we are on the right path and getting close to finding out who killed John Robert Hackett, other members of the choir including Davidson and Hamilton, in addition to the choirmaster, Inspector Leblanc."

"We need to speak with Michael's sister, Sarah McNeill, and soonest," Olivia announced.

CHAPTER 25

The late morning dense fog hugged the rocky outcrops of Peggy's Cove. It was doubtful that the early fall sunshine would be powerful enough to break through and show its face. Only a few tourists had started to brave the opaque veil and trickle into the parking lot behind the restaurant. The sound of the waves alone on the shoreline without the graphics of the lighthouse architecture was more alluring for some.

"Lobster and Chardonnay," Uri replied to Yvonne's proposition. "This is becoming a habit. May I surmise that you are seeking my assistance once again?"

"Not so much what you can do to assist me, but what I can offer you," Yvonne replied with a subtle yet inviting nod.

"I'm all ears." Uri replied.

He enjoyed the sound of the ocean surf and the vistas even when masked by nature's misted shroud. At this moment, they were secondary to the immediate ambiance that he found to be aesthetically pleasing more so because it allowed him to become invisible, like an obscure stowaway on a square-rigged clipper that once plied the Atlantic coastal waters. In the classroom, he was the protagonist, very much the extravert. When offstage, he sought out opportunities to disappear into the shadowy peaceful ambience of the anonymous introvert.

Yvonne showed him a cell phone photo of a smartly dressed man with the Capital Parliament Buildings slightly out of focus in the background yet clear enough to confirm the location where the photo had been taken.

He studied the image, perhaps a moment too long. "A narrow field of focus with the 'f' stop suggesting that the individual is the intended subject of the photographer, not the Ottawa landscape. The image is also a bit grainy suggesting a high ISO to accommodate for low light, and a high-quality telephoto lens."

Despite his effort to appear neutral, Yvonne noticed that Uri slumped as he focused on the facial features. He continued to scan the e-image and frowned as he met her steadfast stare.

He had enjoyed a relatively uneventful life as a child and adolescent growing up in Kiev before being drafted into the Russian army, and again in Ottawa before being accepted as tenured faculty at Carleton University. But the pleasant aspects of life have a habit of being altered by unsolicited interruptions, some more haunting than others. On two occasions and again at this moment, the image in the e-photo caused him to experience acid indigestion. At a different time and place, he might shrug off the sensation and self-medicate with a liquid lunch.

Yvonne held the upper hand. She was not showing him family photos as a preliminary step in improving their interpersonal relationship. "A ghost from Christmas Past?" she asked, more a prompt than a rhetorical question.

"To which Christmas ghost might you be referring?" he asked. "I have a few, several to be more accurate."

"How about we begin with the first?"

He scanned the immediate environment out of habit. There was no one in sight. Thus, he concluded that no one could clearly see them. The dense Nova Scotia fog would muffle their voices as would the din of the accompanying silence.

Yvonne waited patiently, holding his stare with an encouraging coy smile. He was within her sphere of influence. He just wasn't fully aware.

"Russia invaded Afghanistan in 1979. My unit was part of the vanguard. I had just returned from a mission to our rear echelon base when we came under a mortar attack from the Mujahideen.

They fought using guerrilla warfare tactics backed by the U.S. which was supplying them with expertise and high-technology weapons. A KGB agent had been injured, a shrapnel fragment had struck his face leaving a V-shaped scar running from his left cheek to his nose and eye."

Yvonne raised her eyebrows and pointed to the man in the photo.

Uri nodded discretely. "Viktor Titov was the KGB agent. He would not have been able to identify me because my face was concealed with camouflage paste. At least I don't believe he would recognize me. I applied a shell dressing to his face that further impaired his vision before dragging him to safety. I didn't see him again until years later when I was in Ottawa teaching a course in Slavic Studies at Carleton University. He was meeting with someone along the Rideau Canal walkway close to Lisgar Collegiate Institute and the Canadian military's Cartier Square Drill Hall. He and this other person covertly exchanged envelopes. Neither of them smiled, which is a cultural norm of the Soviet era. You are taught not to trust those who smile in public. I saw him a few more times in Ottawa after that as he was entering and leaving various federal government buildings."

Yvonne put her arms around his neck and kissed him. He did not need an invitation to reciprocate yet remained cautiously curious. "I don't usually kiss on the first date," he jested. *Should I say thank you or step back?* he wondered.

"I think we are being watched." Her whisper was more forthright than her thoughts that commanded her immediate attention. Her disquiet was more compelling than her tone that communicated an urgent need for concern. "A dark-haired young woman in a red Ford two-door just pulled into a parking stall. Look over your shoulder to your right. Follow my lead." She reached for his hand and started to walk toward the mystery woman. Uri scanned the vehicle and its sole occupant in a broad surveillance sweep as they passed by, strolling in the general direction of the iconic lighthouse, now only a misty outline broadcasting the moaning foghorn.

"Let's take a rain check on the lobster," she suggested. He voluntarily leaned over, tucking his face into the nape of her neck and her flowing hair, tied in a loose ponytail.

"Do you recognize her?"

"Not sure but she may be one of my students, quiet yet always conscious of her presence in her immediate environment."

"One of the two students from your class when I visited? The FSB and CIA or CSIS agent?" Yvonne pressed.

"No. Instead, a student from another class who may have a crush on me. Maybe not. Not certain," he probed seeking validation for his tentative assessment. Most students in any term were a blur, the exception being those very few who were exceptional or the increasing numbers who were lost causes needing to take a gap decade as opposed to simply a gap year to explore the world and discover themselves.

"Go back to your car and drive out," Yvonne directed. "I'll stay back and watch to see if she follows. Turn left on Peggy's Cove Road and left again on Highway 3. Pull into the French Village Station Café. If she follows you into the café parking lot, confront her inquisitively but politely. If she follows you but doesn't enter the parking lot, head back to Halifax via the St. Margaret's Bay Road. Regardless of what she does, I'll keep her under surveillance at a discrete distance which in this fog will be slow and close."

She kissed him again but this time held the embrace long enough to slip a cell phone wrapped in a note into his pocket.

"Like your cover. We should meet more often," he murmured. He had practiced what he preached, done his homework. Yvonne had a reputation for being a passionate lover or a vengeful viper as circumstances dictated, both perfected in the pursuit of essential intelligence. He had experienced glimpses of the duality at their initial meeting in his classroom. He would offer her a wide berth if she adopted the persona of the serpent under the guise of an amorous rendezvous or the cloak of a Red Sparrow.

She watched as he walked towards his car, swiftly disappearing into the wet fog that had become even more impenetrable in the moments since they first spoke. He then briefly reappeared as he drove out of the parking lot, gesturing with her cell phone gift that he discretely held in his hand as they made brief eye contact.

Moments later, the red Ford reappeared and just as quickly disappeared in pursuit. The dark-haired woman did not reciprocate like Queen Elizabeth with a corresponding royal wave to Yvonne. Perhaps she had failed to see Uri's companion in her light beige jacket blending in with the grey mist against the white siding of the restaurant. Or the mysterious woman had, in fact, noticed but purposely snubbed her perceived rival. Yvonne stared after the ghost that too had been enveloped by the fog, her own inquisitive reflection equally imprecise, not to be wholly dismissed.

Yvonne sprinted into the mist toward her own car. She pressed the unlock button on the key fob. An audible chirp and a brief series of fuzzy flashes from her running lights confirmed its location. She knew the road and its twisting turns like the back of her hand having worked part-time at the restaurant several summers while attending school. Regardless, she still crawled at a pace closer to that of the focused tortoise rather than the more agile albeit carefree hare.

Unequal partners, the tortoise using cognitive skills of ingenuity and chicanery to overcome the hare who perceived its physical strengths and agility to be supreme, Yvonne mused as she carefully wended her way along the narrow road guided only by a single centred white line barely visible through the fog. Neither Uri, the suitor, nor his tentative dark-haired suitress appeared to be aware of the Aesop adage, *festina lente*, the fortitude to hasten slowly.

She had learned the essence of the pragmatism of knowledge taught and the intuitive awareness of knowledge gained through experience, the latter less so from any academic or intelligence lectures. Instead, it was gleaned from *sophia*, the mythical feminine personification of wisdom and its sibling, *phronesis*.

As she followed the red Ford back to Halifax, Yvonne remained troubled by her recent assessment of Suzette as they had talked while strolling along the Rideau Canal walkway. She was bothered by her behaviour which seemed different somehow. Yvonne couldn't put her finger on it. It was that fuzzy intuitive implicitness which concerned her the most. She would continue to mull over her misgivings and level of concern before chatting with Bernie. For now, she would focus on Uri and his mysterious dark-haired pursuer who, apparently unbeknownst to him, appeared to have entered his orbit. Curious, Yvonne thought.

A second thought crossed her mind. Had this dark-haired female followed Uri to find out who he was meeting? Yvonne, the mysterious intruder into the classroom, or someone else perhaps? A second thought, had this driver of the red Ford been dispatched by Suzette? On her return from her Ottawa rendezvous, Bernie had clandestinely scanned her cell phone and those of Stan and Olivia, anticipating that they were potentially being electronically monitored. She would speak with Bernie sooner rather than later regarding her misgivings.

CHAPTER 26

Olivia and Stan approached Michael McNeill's shorefront home, as before accompanied by Bernie and his colleague for surveillance and security purposes. Parked in his driveway was a marked RCMP vehicle.

"Keep driving by," Bernie's voice sounded in their earphones. "I'll stop and ask what's going on."

Olivia and Stan could hear the subsequent conversation via their monitoring devices.

"Who are you?" the constable asked Bernie in a cordial yet terse manner.

"What's happening? Is Michael OK?" Bernie replied.

"Are you related to Michael McNeill?"

"I'm his best friend, have been since our days at university. What's happened to him? Is he OK?"

"Does he have any family?" the constable followed up.

"Both of his parents are dead. He has a sister in the Halifax region. I think he has some cousins in the valley around Wolfville. Why do you ask?"

"I regret to inform you his body was found under the wharf at the Wood Islands ferry terminal. He appears to have drowned. His sister was here. You just missed her."

Bernie drew his hands to his mouth for theatrical effects. "Oh, no. This is terrible. He had called me to come and pick up my late father's military medals which he had cork mounted. If he wasn't in when I arrived, he told me to collect them from the top drawer of the hutch in the kitchen. Can I pick them up?"

"I am sorry. I can't allow you to enter the house. Everything will be dealt with through the estate."

"Oh, I have to get them back for my family. My father had been awarded them for conspicuous bravery with the North Nova Scotia Highlanders Regiment in the Second World War. He landed on Juno Beach, Courseulles-sur-Mer, Normandy. They are to be presented to the Regimental Museum. Their home garrison is just up the road in Amherst. I'm sure you visited the RCMP Museum when you were training in Regina. You would know from that experience the importance of maintaining the heritage, the history of the Force," Bernie pleaded. Crocodile tears flowed from his squinting eyes. He rubbed his shaking hands together in a pretence of anguish.

"Perhaps I can retrieve them for you. You said they would be in the hutch in the kitchen. Can you describe them?"

Bernie cried, "Oh Mother Mary and dear Sister Olivia, help me." He crossed himself, moaned sorrowfully, and slowly drew his fingers over his eyes and mouth hoping for an accurate speedy response.

"There are twelve medals in total, several for bravery, including the Military Medal which his father won on D-Day," Stan replied.

Bernie reiterated Stan's reply to the constable. "Being in the Force, I'm sure you will know your decorations and medals for bravery and heroism," Bernie said, anticipating the young constable would not want to admit ignorance.

"Wait here," the constable said. He returned within a few moments, the medals in hand. He passed them to Bernie keeping them out of sight as best he could.

"Oh, thank you so much," Bernie exclaimed. "This is community-based policing at its best. I will write a letter to your commanding officer commending you, if you would like."

"That won't be necessary at all. Please do not," the constable immediately replied, his voice accented with a tinge of trepidation.

"It's just part of the job. Nothing outstanding, certainly not worth any mention or commendation."

Bernie shook his hand with a double clasp of deep appreciation. "Again, thank you so very much. The Regimental Museum will be so pleased. At your request, I will keep this between us."

As he pulled out of the driveway, Stan's voice crackled in his earphone. "Slick, partner, very slick. That takes me back to our Watcher Service days in Montréal when we talked ourselves out of many tight situations when we had to think fast on our feet in order to create cover stories."

"Certainly, an Academy Award for best actor," Olivia added.

※ ※

"Yvonne, can you contact your CSIS friend to find out who these two supposed CSIS agents were who spoke with the now deceased Michael McNeill?" Bernie asked. The tone of the request signalled urgency, concern and caution.

"On it," Yvonne replied as she texted Suzette with equal earnestness for a prompt response if at all possible. She would scrutinize the speed and accuracy of her reply carefully.

"Another body added to this file and Leblanc's choir of silent voices," Olivia muttered with deep disquiet. "Hackett, Davidson, Hamilton, Laporte, Leblanc and possibly his secret squirrel subordinate. What is so important about this case to muster so much attention? More pressing, what is it about his father's medals that Michael McNeill mentioned them in his text message to me? He didn't just say he would like to speak to me. He said he needed to speak with me about his father's military medals and their connection to the killing of the farmer in the barn at Hammonds Plains. He referenced the medals specifically."

They stared in awe at the mounted medals that lay in the center of the ranch house kitchen table. Individually and collectively they represented individual acts of heroism which Sergeant McNeill had been humble to acknowledge. More importantly, Michael McNeill believed they were germane to disclosing the truth regarding the shooting in the barn at Hammonds Plains. Michael was now silenced as were others connected to this case.

Stan turned the medals over. The dark blue felt material had been carefully cut away from the cork mount along the edge of the right-hand side. A raised indentation indicated something had been removed. On closer examination, it appeared to be an impression of a folded paper, perhaps.

Yvonne looked up from her cell phone. "Just received a reply from my friend. No CSIS agents have been making any enquiries regarding Sergeant McNeill and Bedford Detachment as far as her colleague could discern." The brief coded text ended, "Keep your radar up and tread carefully." Maybe Suzette was OK and I am over sensitive because of her health, Yvonne reconsidered. The sense of *je ne sais quoi* continued to haunt her.

Olivia reviewed the email from Michael McNeill. "He said that if he was out when we dropped by, he would leave the red flag up on the refurbished decorative mail box in his front yard. That would indicate he had left a note inside."

Bernie texted his colleague in Pictou who had accompanied him on the two trips to Michael's shorefront home. Within the hour, he returned Bernie's text, "Have the mail in hand. Will meet at our usual rendezvous."

※ ※

BERNIE'S NOVA SCOTIA RANCH HOUSE kitchen table once again doubled as the conference table. All watched while Olivia examined the note. In its folded state, its outline matched perfectly the impression of the dark blue felt material on the back of the cork-mounted military medals. She gently unfolded it confident that she was the first non-family member to do so since Sergeant McNeill had penned its communiqué.

"It must have pained him more than battlefield wounds he suffered on D-Day to write this," Stan said in a solemn tone. "I can feel his anguish, his sorrow. No wonder he turned to alcohol to help him to get by, day to day. A true hero reduced to such a state. No one should have to end their life like that. How sad, how very sad," he lamented.

"I can appreciate Michael's hatred of the Force and its officers, and why it killed his mother," Olivia added. Anger boiled up inside her. Sergeant McNeill had been her first and only Detachment Commander. She had looked up to him in admiration as a father figure, and as a leader and decorated war hero, as she had regarded her own father and her grandfather. She could not have imagined the horror of battle they had endured and the inherent loyalty for comrades in arms.

Every word of what Sergeant McNeill had written verified what Olivia, Stan, Bernie and Yvonne had deduced thus far. Hackett's death had been covered up for reasons that Sergeant McNeill found to be very suspicious. He wasn't new to the realm of secrecy. Secrets from World War II remained forever embossed in his memory, but they were secrets of honor. He was unsure of Leblanc's loyalty to the Force and its motto, *Maintiens le Droit*. That bothered him the most.

Stan hissed in ultimate disgust, "Leblanc had threatened to destroy Sergeant McNeill's distinguished career and reputation if he so much as whispered a word of this case to anyone. The murder and cover-up simply did not occur. I never held any officer I worked for in the Force in high regard, in any regard for that matter. The operative expression is *worked for*. You never worked *with* any officer. At this point, I wholly sympathize with Michael. I hold all officers in utter contempt."

"So where to from here?" Yvonne asked after a respectful pause as if a pause was necessary in order to process deep personal emotions.

"First, we take a break. Then we re-evaluate what we know for certain," Bernie replied. "The Montréal connection is our weakest link because we know virtually nothing about Leblanc's meanderings and associates while there. Stan, I will contact one of our Watcher Service colleagues and have him snoop around. He currently lives in the Mount Royal district so shouldn't be long in getting back to me. In the interim, scan your own memory banks for clues as to what we may have missed thus far. Olivia, review your notes regarding your brief encounter with John Robert Hackett, perhaps not so much what he gasped in those dying breaths or what he may have gestured, but what you may have seen in the barn. Anything. I appreciate that it has been a long time."

Olivia added, "We need to contact Michael's sister, Sarah, before whoever is responsible for Michael's death gets to her first. The rendezvous needs to be somewhere away from Halifax and Michael's house overlooking the Deer Islands ferry terminal at Caribou. No doubt, she will be upset with Michael's death."

"The Hammonds Plains farm choir has increased by one more silenced voice," Stan uttered with sombre concern.

"I agree with Stan," Bernie said. "I am reluctant to contact Sarah for fear of signing her death warrant."

"Who apart from us is a common denominator?" Olivia reflected out loud. "We find the common denominator and we identify the source of the leak."

"It has to be linked to Inspector Leblanc, now his ghost." Stan paused in mid thought as he followed a thin thread to a related concept forming in his mind. "Or someone very close to him. Doors immediately started shutting on us as soon as we began making enquiries on-line in your condo in Calgary. Then when I emailed my Ident contact who I trained, he warned me to be extra careful. Michael recited his father's words to us, to be very careful."

"My money is on Leblanc or someone very close to him, either one step above or below," Bernie concluded. "I'm thinking an associate of Leblanc. Someone who you may have crossed paths with or knows of your involvement. Whoever it is, they want to block all efforts to open this case up because they have too much to lose. The ramifications have to be beyond national. I'm talking global, geopolitical, certainly Cold War which seems to be heating up with links to Russian sleeper cells past and present."

CHAPTER 27

Olivia awoke as the sun was about to break the horizon, her mind spinning like a roulette wheel on steroids. She slipped into Bernie's office and ran a search sequence. A name appeared on the monitor, Elmer Andrew MacDonald, with a list of professional credentials and several academic articles he had published and others presented at conferences. A subsequent search revealed an address, 579 North Street, Halifax, Nova Scotia. The 1978 census showed Elmer Andrew MacDonald and Edith Marion MacDonald as the residents and joint-owners of the heritage property that appeared to have been in the MacDonald family at least since the Halifax explosion in 1917. A search for the current census listed Jennifer Lynn MacDonald as the occupant and registered owner. "The gods of research may be with us," she quietly muttered.

"The gods may be with us?" Stan repeated in a muffled voice as he looked with blurry eyes over her shoulder. "I won't ask what you're doing up at this hour."

"When I initially searched for a coroner's report related to Hackett's death, there was no record listed. Nothing. Nichts. Nichego. Rien. I was and remain baffled by no mention of John Robert Hackett. It slipped my mind to follow up. On 5 November 1978, the chief coroner for Halifax County was Dr. Elmer Andrew MacDonald." She pointed at the name and associated census data on a second monitor. "The current owner and occupant of 579 North Street is Jennifer Lynn MacDonald. Good chance that she is related, perhaps Elmer's daughter. She could have inherited the property. Like good Maritime families with roots back to the previous century and beyond, they rarely throw away heirlooms and keepsakes. Instead, they end up in the attic making room for the next generation of collectables. She might have his coroner's notes."

"They would have been kept in his office under lock and key consistent with the Charter and Privacy Legislation," Stan replied.

"The *Constitution Act* came into effect in 1982. Hackett was murdered in 1978, four years before. I kept my notebooks prior to 1982. Perhaps Elmer MacDonald did the same – kept his notes, at his residence."

Stan leaned forward, placed his hands on her shoulders and gave her a slight squeeze. His breath stirred her hair. He gently kissed her cheek. "*Mirabilis es*."

The gentle imprint of his fingers lingered. "*Mirabilis es*, Latin for…?" she repeated with a curious tone.

"Latin for you are miraculous, wonderful."

She smiled up at him with a faint blush as she reached over with her left hand and placed it over his. She reflected on how much his sincere compliments had meant to her, complemented now by his gentle gesture. They seemed to be skipping steps in the customary courtship ritual as if they were close confidants from another time, picking up where they had left off as if nothing had happened in the interlude. Nothing had happened in Bedford yet both had been impacted, each by the other. She reflected with a slight nod. Her smile said it all.

His words just seemed natural, like endearing expressions uttered by couples who had been together since puppy love days as high school sweethearts. Such intimate attributes had been absent with Uri whose emotions were more often akin to those of a caustic Cossack. But it takes two to tango. She accepted her role in the remnants of the matrimonial bond with eyes wide open, albeit with unseeing and naïve fairy tale expectations. Although she had an academic PhD, she had come to the realization long ago that she had less than stellar credentials when it came to mastering untutored youthful emotions. In her teens, she had not engaged in any close relationships. Neither had she entered into any close relationship since her divorce from Uri, for that very reason. At this moment, her thoughts ran the gambit of both concerted trepidation and fleeting anticipation.

"Double double, *s'il vous plait, monsieur.*" The predictable aroma of brewing coffee beans floating up from the kitchen brought a warming smile to her face which Stan responded to in kind.

"Ton plaisir est mon plaisir."

She would approach Jennifer MacDonald under the pretence of research into the history of coroner services in Nova Scotia. Getting away from the ranch house would have its added benefits. She would see the real world again without the lens of tinted windows and sheer lace curtains, but with heightened awareness of the need for continuing security.

"Sounds like a plan," Bernie agreed when she explained her motivation to follow up on her latest research findings.

⊰ ⊱

YVONNE TOOK A SLOW BREATH, having thought about Olivia's plan over breakfast. "May I suggest a Plan B? The CSIS may not be actively on your trail, at least not yet, although certainly curious as to your previous enquiries and current interests. My colleague in Ottawa confirmed that. Factor One, those who are pursuing you are looking for a man and a woman. They could very well have photos of the two of you. Factor Two, whoever they are, they have left a lethal trail of bread crumbs in their wake. Factor Three, we know the Russians are involved and they have only one rule in their playbook. That is, there are no rules. I have some experience operating in their free-for-all colosseum. Factor Four, the Russians use very sophisticated mobile CCTV cameras strategically positioned, among other covert tracking devices. Again, I have some familiarity with their modus operandi. So, I suggest I change my appearance and play the part of the researcher. I still have a closet full of disguises amassed over the years, each with their own rehearsed personalities."

"Although I am experiencing a bit of cabin fever and would like to get out, I have to admit that Yvonne's Plan B would be more prudent at this juncture," Olivia reluctantly agreed. "We have stayed one step ahead of the black-hatted bad guys. No need to give them the advantage of securing even a toehold anywhere near the foothills let alone the summit of the commanding heights that we currently maintain."

Olivia followed up, "Perhaps Yvonne could also contact Sarah McNeill and ask to meet at a location convenient to both. Yvonne could mention the German language class she and a foreign student had attended at Dalhousie which Michael had referenced. That is specific but still broad."

The others nodded in agreement with Yvonne's Plan B and Olivia's addendum to the schedule to contact Sarah. If Sarah failed to reply, nothing would be gained but, perhaps most importantly, nothing lost. Olivia was specifically thinking of Sarah not following in her younger brother's footsteps and joining the silenced voices of the Hammonds Plains farm choir.

"I should be back by midnight tomorrow," Yvonne announced. "That will give me ample time to interview Jennifer MacDonald, lay low for a brief period, contact Sarah McNeill and arrange to meet if at all possible, then change disguises and exchange vehicles." She would finally follow up on a related matter. She winked at Olivia who acknowledged her intent to cultivate her newest informant of East European ethnicity.

Olivia lamented the fact she would not be there to observe first-hand the puppet's response to the puppeteer's finesse.

Peering at Yvonne, Bernie admitted, "I'd be happier if one of our colleagues provided backup while you are visiting the MacDonald residence. If I were after Olivia and Stan, my first strategy would be to figure out how they think. Olivia would be the easiest to identify because she has a CV full of academic-related conference and published research papers. Stan is less in the public sphere but his resumé has a fusion of strategic and surveillance successes which puts him in an almost unique spotlight."

Yvonne thought for a moment before responding. "The list of viable options to get pertinent information is getting shorter as the list of known cadavers increases. God only knows how many others are missing in action."

"I can think of a few other cases we have worked on like this," Bernie acknowledged. "I suspect the pursuers have probably figured out we are amassing compelling evidence and a growing nominal roll of the fallen."

Yvonne smiled with confidence. "To our advantage and their disadvantage, we can conclude they do not know where we are, otherwise they would have launched a torrent of rocket-propelled grenades or surface-to-surface missiles at this quaint rural heritage hideaway. To their advantage and our disadvantage, they have fewer suspects to cover and we are all in one place. Find one and they locate all. Find one and we are still figuring out how to locate the next one."

"As with our historical cases, we err on the side of caution. Best we have backup on all future excursions, starting with this one," Bernie directed as he looked at Yvonne.

Yvonne nodded. "I agree, just in case."

CHAPTER 28

Jennifer MacDonald was on her way out to an appointment when Yvonne knocked. She assumed that Yvonne was the Dalhousie researcher. "Thank you for being so prompt. I had received a call from the Dean's office at Dalhousie University, Faculty of Medicine, about any notes my father had related to his work as the coroner. They said that someone would be right over. This is the only box of files I could locate. I sincerely hope that they contain the information you were seeking."

Yvonne replied somewhat perplexed, "Thank you. I need to respect your time so I will be on my way."

Jennifer locked her front door, walked to her car that was parked on the street ahead of Yvonne's. She drove down the North Street hill toward the Angus L. MacDonald bridge.

Yvonne was loading the box into her car when her earphone crackled. "You have company. Suggest you get out of there fast. I'll block your exit. Take your immediate right and then next left. I recommend that you not follow Jennifer across the bridge to Dartmouth but instead take Connaught Avenue, out the Bedford Highway, and connect onto the 102."

First, she would attempt to contact Michael McNeill's sister, Sarah. The subject line on the text read: Personal condolences on Michael's death. The text was terse only referencing a fellow Dalhousie University student in her German class that Michael had passed along in connection to her father, in addition to her text address.

Sarah's immediate reply was equally brief, "Yes."

Yvonne responded, "Can we meet here in Halifax?"

"I will be departing shortly to deal with some family estate matters. We can meet at my home in Waverly now or make another appointment," Sarah replied.

"Be there in half an hour," Yvonne confirmed.

"Your text piqued my interest," Sarah said when they were settled at her kitchen table, "especially reference to a fellow student in my German class at Dal and a connection to my father that Michael mentioned. I had only spoken to my brother about that. So, I can only conclude that you are somehow connected to a case my father was involved in when we lived in Bedford. My intuition tells me not to delve further into how you are involved if for no other reason than my father was very closed mouthed about it. The connection to another student in my German class was equally mysterious." Her tone was both inquisitive and cautious.

"Your brother strongly suggested that I speak with you. I would very much appreciate hearing anything you can offer," Yvonne replied.

"First, let me say that I am extremely bothered with the circumstances surrounding Michael's supposed drowning. I say supposed because all the way through his adolescence and especially his teenage years, he was an accomplished swimmer winning numerous awards. He never swam around the Wood Island ferry dock because he knew the currents could be treacherous and the waters were often filled with jellyfish which had paralyzing stings. There are warning signs along the shoreline of the Northumberland Straits cautioning swimmers to stay out of the water around some beaches. He only swan in the water opposite our cottage."

Sarah continued with the deep emotion of disbelief in her voice. "No one swims around the ferry terminal because the water there is polluted with diesel fuel from all the boats, especially the ferry. No autopsy has been ordered because the RCMP have classified the drowning as accidental. Why? An autopsy would not find diesel contaminated water in his lungs because he died elsewhere.

In addition, he never swam in the Northumberland Straits without wearing his wet suit. He did not have it on when his body was pulled out of the water. The tide flows south along that stretch of the coast. So, if he was found adjacent to the Wood Islands dock, he would have had to enter the water north of the terminal. North of the ferry dock was too far to walk and his car was still in the driveway of our cottage which is located south of the ferry terminal."

Sarah glared at Yvonne. "Ask yourself, how did he get there? Don't quote me on this but whoever dumped his body there where the current was static was clearly not from this area. I find it difficult to believe that the RCMP are that incompetent to suggest his drowning was accidental. Michael would have believed it though. After he read my father's diary, which I also read, he was convinced that there was little if any secrecy by provenance when the RCMP Security Service was involved. Instead, it was more about secrecy by seduction. He had said on numerous occasions that a culture of integrity never was their strong suit. Sorry for the rant. This entire matter thoroughly irks me. It took my father. It took my mother. It has taken my brother," Sarah apologized as she hung her head low.

"I can appreciate your frustration," Yvonne replied with compassion in her manner. Her immediate thought: *I sincerely hope it will not take Sarah.* "Can I ask you about one other related matter?"

Sarah took a few moments to take several deep breaths. She then peered at Yvonne and nodded.

"Michael said that the student in your German class caused you considerable grief, not so much during the class but a few years after the course had ended and you had graduated. Can you tell me about that time?"

"His name is Hans Schrödinger. He introduced himself to me as an exchange student from the Netherlands. That was the first of a few well researched lies. He was older than me, mature and charming. Our relationship soon became intimate… He said that it was appropriate that I introduce him to my parents. He had done his homework regarding my father's military exploits. He knew my father's military unit. They bonded well after he said it was my father's unit that liberated his hometown in the Netherlands in November 1944. After the class ended, he abruptly returned to the Netherlands, or so I thought – another lie. I was devastated to say the least. I wrote to him but never received a reply."

Yvonne sympathized with Sarah and her emotional plight.

"That was phase one of my relationship with Hans Schrödinger. Let me give you a bit of background regarding phase two and our reuniting. When I was in first year university, I enrolled in the Canadian Forces Communications Reserve as a signals officer with what is now 36 Signal Communication Regiment Headquarters, Halifax. By the time I graduated, I had qualified as a captain. That fall, I attended a NATO military exercise in Germany. Low and behold who shows up to provide a security briefing but Lieutenant Colonel Hans Schrödinger of the German Military Counter Intelligence Service. I confronted him and he admitted to the string of lies. Hans dated me to get to my father in order to secretly find out as much as possible about a Russian sleeper cell. He never told me any names but after I read my father's diary and put two and two together, I concluded it must have been John Robert Hackett who was murdered in a barn at Hammonds Plains. His wife, Sylvia, disappeared shortly thereafter. John Hackett had a German connection. Hans was on a mission to find out as much as he could about him. That was all he told me except that he had strong feelings for me and sincerely missed me after he left. He received my letters but could not reply for security reasons that I understood. I believed him because my father had written about the murder at the farm. His explanation didn't sooth my bruised emotions much.

In fact, I thought about him after the military exercise ended and I returned to Canada. He had given me a new mailing address but I never wrote him again. I continue to think about him though."

Yvonne sat silently commiserating with what Sarah referred to as her emotional plight before offering some wisdom. "One hundred and fifty years ago, John Greenleaf Whittier wrote these words in a poem about Maud Miller who experienced lost love. I recited them many times after I experienced the pains of lost love when my first romantic relationship ended tragically: *For of all sad words of tongue or pen, / The saddest are these: 'It might have been.'* Again, I extend to you my deepest condolences for the loss of your brother, Michael."

"Thank you," Sarah replied. "Talking about it really does help. Michael reminded me of that. I will miss him. If you are in Halifax again, please drop by."

"I will do that. Until we bring some closure to Michael's death and this case that your father wrote about in his diary, best not speak with anyone else. Please contact me via the text message address I used if anyone does contact you."

Sarah nodded slowly. She didn't need to know any more details.

CHAPTER 29

"You're back early," Bernie greeted Yvonne as she climbed up the staircase from the tunnel, holding a tattered cardboard box and appearing a bit harried.

"As always, you are a wise director of these operations," Yvonne replied. "The coroner's house became a hot location." Glancing at Olivia, she said, "Due to the urgency of the situation, I felt it best to trim back one of the agenda items before returning. I was, however, able to meet with Jennifer MacDonald who gave me this box of her father's files. Let me first brief you on the conversation I had with Sarah McNeill, Michael's older sister."

After relating the essence of the conversation with Sarah, Yvonne concluded, "Facts regarding many of the players we have identified to date reinforce our suspicions, including Hackett's international connections, specifically his German links. Let's discuss within the context of the box of notes I retrieved from Jennifer MacDonald."

They spent the late afternoon reviewing handwritten notes by the coroner in view of the absence of any official printed record of Hackett's death. Doctor MacDonald had made an extensive entry in his diary regarding the cause of death. Hackett had been murdered. His death was not suicide. The angle of the weapon, the trajectory of the bullet and dearth of gunpowder residue on his clothes were consistent with a weapon discharged from a distance and by someone else.

"You were correct on your call in the barn," Stan congratulated Olivia. "You called it a murder when I suspected it could be a suicide. The coroner's notes support your astute observation. You are good!"

Pinned to the page of the coroner's entry in his diary for 6 November 1978 regarding autopsy John Robert Hackett was a large sealed envelope addressed to the Chief Coroner Halifax County. Inside were two smaller envelopes. "Permission to Release the Body" had been handwritten on one. "To Whom It May Concern" had been penned on the second. The letter in the first envelope was dated 6 November 1978 and signed by Inspector J.P.R.C. Leblanc, RCMP Security Service. It directed the coroner to release the body without delay to the wife of the deceased, Sylvia Hackett. It further directed that for reasons of national security, the coroner was to record the death as a suicide. The wording had a connotation of an order, not a request.

"The 6th is the day after Hackett was shot and killed!" Olivia exclaimed, her voice both assenting and enquiring. "Long enough to conduct an autopsy if it became a top priority and to falsely record a cause of death, assuming it wasn't obvious from the wound. Or short enough to prepare the body for expedient and judicious release to the next of kin, Sylvia Hackett, or her representative."

Stan turned the letter over. The back was blank. He opened the second envelope. It contained a single handwritten note dated 13 November 1978 but without a signature: *'Buried together where they lived happily graced by God in holy matrimony under the fountain that brings forth the water of life. Christ en Croix.'*

Olivia compared the writing on all documents, including the signature. "The hand writing appears the same. I conclude that they are written by the same person, more than likely Inspector J.P.R.C. Leblanc."

"Wife shoots husband with aid of comrade. Doesn't sound like happy holy matrimony to me," Stan commented with a glib tone.

"*As* they lived would be a normal description, not *where* they lived," Yvonne remarked. "Is there an inherent message here for the interpretation of: To Whom It May Concern?"

"Christ en Croix. Christ en Croix. Christ en Croix." Olivia repeated. "It's Hansel and Gretel a.k.a. Inspector Leblanc leaving a trail of breadcrumbs, clues."

"I've lost the connection," Yvonne stated.

Olivia explained, "*Christ en Croix*, the title of the poem that Leblanc recited to me when all this began. The poem was a masquerade of open encryption pointing to the clue which helped us break the code. It can be one of the best methods to communicate sensitive intelligence."

"What goes around comes around?" Yvonne reflected.

Olivia grumbled, "We are back to the proverbial square one. Is Leblanc a good cop or a corrupt cop? He was certainly an obnoxious bully, regardless."

"I agree with your characterization. He was an asshole. We need to be careful not to allow that emotion to bias our perspective. He is involved, somehow. No doubt there," Stan confirmed. "But in what context and in what role, choirmaster and leader or a member of the choir under the direction of another choirmaster?"

Olivia sat motionless as she tried to reconcile what seemed to be a folly of contradictions. Was it better to be an honest villain or a dishonest champion? The quintessential question in many academic debates regarding the myth of the hero. Her frustration was obvious. "I don't know anymore. Maybe it was just naïve wishful thinking on my part that he was a good cop after all, perhaps just a figment of my fertile academic imagination."

"Leblanc recognized your potential. That was why he asked you to join him," Stan suggested. "You said you told your students that their intuition was never wrong. It was just their misinterpretation of their intuition that sent them off-course. So, follow your intuition."

Olivia nodded slowly. "Good point. I'll grudgingly take my own advice, at least for now."

Bernie let that caldron simmer before asking, "How deeply is he involved? Temporarily not revealing a murder, treason, cover-up as a strategy? Instead, clandestinely recoding the details to fester in files for someone else to find and ultimately reveal? Someone like Olivia. Is that what Security and Intelligence did back then?" Bernie asked, not certain of the answer, yet curious enough to press for clarification.

"*Remember, remember, / The fifth of November, / The Gunpowder treason and plot; / I know of no reason / Why the Gunpowder treason / Should ever be forgot!*" Olivia chanted.

Yvonne regarded her, bewildered.

"My father would recite that every year on the fifth of November. I recall mumbling it in the barn immediately after we found Hackett, shot. The words have been rumbling in my mind ever since."

"You turn over a rock searching for a lead and you find yourself inundated with an infestation worse than you could imagine finding in Pandora's box. I think that another conversation with my colleague in the nation's capital is in order," Yvonne proposed. "But first I need to follow up on a loose end."

"Would there have been a formal policy that dictated how a coroner should respond to directives from other government agencies like the RCMP Security Service regarding the *Official Secrets Act*?" Bernie asked.

Stan raised his eyebrows in skepticism. "To suppress evidence, withhold information, lie convincingly like Pinocchio gaping at the reality regarding cause of death, that's serious stuff. The handwritten directive for the coroner to falsify the records was from Leblanc. It was not an official typewritten document from the Prime Minister or another senior executive in the PMO. I was never aware of any remotely similar documentation as an identification technician," Stan replied. "A cabinet minister or senior mandarin would have been summarily dismissed for even suggesting such behaviour. To fabricate evidence in court would constitute perjury, an offence under the *Criminal Code*. That's not to say that it didn't happen with the wink of an eye or suggestion that one's career might benefit with clandestine compliance or be stinted as a result of nonconformity, all the contrived cousins of provenance."

Yvonne added, "I very much doubt that Leblanc would have engaged in a come-to-Jesus, heart-to-heart conversation with MacDonald in which they conspired to go beyond ethics to cover up the truth. Perhaps the notation that MacDonald made in his private diary was his way of dealing with his dilemma, his conscience, not to completely falsify his records. *Entre le loup et le précipice* – between the wolf and the precipice, colloquially translated in English to mean between a rock and a hard place."

"Leblanc was an emotional vampire," Olivia proposed. "Stress is another all too frequent common denominator associated with this file." She focused on Stan seeking validation for her assessment. "As soon as Leblanc's voice crackled over the radio to cancel Ident and GIS in the wake of Hackett's last breath, your stress went up as did mine. By his own admission, Sergeant McNeill became stressed as did his wife, in addition to his son and daughter by association. Now the coroner in his diary acknowledged the stress he was under."

Bernie held up his index finger in a gesture of a hiatus as he monitored an incoming email. There was no content. Only one word in the subject line: Hermes. *Gravitas* – gravity hung heavy.

"Need to contact Hermes," he announced with a guarded tone.

Only Olivia returned his gaze with curiosity. Stan and Yvonne nodded in validation of his communiqué.

"Hermes the Greek god of messages, communication, akin to the Roman god Mercury?" Olivia enquired.

As Bernie departed their company for his office, Stan reached over to Olivia, rested his hand on hers and whispered, "Hermes is a request from a confidential source to talk by the most secure means. It is only requested under dire circumstances."

CHAPTER 30

Bernie dialed into his encrypted voice scrambler. He adjusted his head phones while he waited for the acknowledgement code to uncouple. Both authenticating green lights appeared on his module. An audible click confirmed the secure connection.

"What have you got yourself into this time, Bernie? Whatever it is, you want to be constantly watching over your shoulder."

"There is considerable breadth and depth with Cold War and FLQ implications, *mon ami*," Bernie replied. "I sense that you have bumped up against something."

"I don't know whether the ramifications associated with the Russians or the Front de Libération du Québec has raised more hackles. Individually, each is at a heightened level not seen since I don't know when. Together, they are so high, no one has contingency plans mapped out to even think about the consequences. The CSIS, Sûréte du Québec and Montréal Police are tripping over one other. The Russian Embassy is screaming and the Prime Minister's Office is demanding minute-by-minute updates. The bodies have already started to pile up here in Montréal."

"I heard on the news that there had been a shooting and names are not being released pending notification of next of kin," Bernie replied.

"Because it is so murky, let me give you a chronology," His contact replied. "You asked me to snoop around and find out what I could regarding Inspector J.P.R.C. Leblanc. As it happens, he was living in a condo in the Mount Royal district, a stone's throws from my place. My cover was easy, I was simply walking in my hood. Last evening, a neighbour of Leblanc's called the police to report a break and enter in progress. A patrol car was dispatched and the police officers confronted a suspect in Leblanc's condo. Shots were fired. One officer was killed and the second critically wounded. The intruder was also killed. As it turns out, he was supposedly a military attaché with the Russian Embassy in Ottawa although he had an identification card that listed him as a delegate to some international cultural conference. He had in his possession some documents he had taken from Leblanc's place that related to the FLQ crisis. Intriguing, the pistol he used had a silencer attached. The CSIS agents seized everything and secured Leblanc's condo. They were seen carting out boxes of documents including some books, mostly poetry, according to the neighbour who attended poetry readings that Leblanc hosted."

"How did the CSIS happen to be there so quickly? As you describe the scene, they must have been on the heels of the patrol officers," Bernie asked with a quizzical tone.

"According to one of my contacts who was on duty in the communications center, the CSIS had Leblanc's place wired and under 24-hour surveillance. You might want to make enquiries if you have a CSIS friend."

"What about the Russian military attaché? A silencer on his pistol? That sounds like an FSB agent, not a businessman attending a conference unless you consider breaking and entering a business. What is the word on the street?" Bernie pressed.

"Very hush hush. The Russians have demanded that his body be turned over to the Embassy immediately. When they say the body, they mean the body and all his possessions. Apparently, he was wearing a two-way communications bug which indicates he was not acting alone. The Russians also demand no autopsy be conducted. They will not negotiate on that point."

"You said your contact works in the Montréal Police communications center. Sounds like a screw up in not passing information along to the patrol officers who unknowingly walked into a hot

CSIS surveillance operation," Bernie responded. "Was it intentional sabotage, someone on the inside? If so, it won't be the first time an individual was on the payroll of another nefarious organization. Or was it your normal inter-agency federal-provincial SNAFU? Or was it simply serendipitous?"

"Oh, yes. There is a serious inter-jurisdictional pissing contest underway. The head of the Sûréte du Québec and the Montréal police chief are in the hot seat. Miscommunication directly resulted in the death of the one patrol officer and seriously wounding of the second who were unaware of the CSIS operation. Germane to your case, neither the Feds nor the Province want the FLQ crisis resurrected. There are too many local, national and geopolitical skeletons in those closets. Word has it that Moscow was involved, instigating unrest at the height of the Cold War. Apparently, Igor Gouzenko, the post-war cyber clerk defector from the Russian Embassy, informed the RCMP that Russia had started to insert spies in Québec during the 1940s, and more in the mid 1960s to fan the flames of the separatist movement. The Mounties didn't believe Gouzenko initially on this and other matters because he was a low-level cypher clerk. It wasn't until after the October 1970 FLQ crisis erupted that they took him seriously. By then, much of his information was outdated. Too many politicians and RCMP officers at all levels had egg on their faces, but no one lost their jobs. If one incompetent domino fell, others would have followed in quick succession. No one wanted that."

Bernie dug a little further. "Any mention of Russian sleeper cells, specifically in Nova Scotia or other maritime locations?"

"In general, no more than usual. Mention the name Leblanc in the context of Russian sleeper cells and eyebrows immediately rise and people become closed-lipped in addition to becoming exceedingly nervous. They all run for cover. The CSIS grow atypically silent. Others tune their radar directly at you hoping to note the slightest of bleeps on their screens. Physiotherapists talk about an increase in client visitations complaining about upper body muscular pain from craning their necks in futile efforts to eavesdrop."

"Like your sense of humour. Speaking for myself, I still experience residual shoulder pain from one too many surveillance missions. Any mention of sleeper cells in Nova Scotia?" Bernie again pressed.

"Another yes. The Russians are uneasy. They want some property back that went missing approximately twenty years ago. Apparently, that was the motivation for the break and enter into Leblanc's condo. Someone thought he might have known or might have known someone who might have known. It was worth killing for, including police officers. So, it must have been exceedingly serious to raise so many hackles after all these years."

"Thanks," Bernie acknowledged. "Let me know if you hear anything new. We will be moving forward on our case soonest."

"Will do. In the interim, be *very* careful, mon ami."

"Just reading a news item, the wounded police officer has just died," Bernie advised with a lowering voice. "So very sad. Again, the name is being withheld pending notification of next of kin."

"Very strange. The deceased's family lives in Montréal, St. Bruno to be exact. I conclude that the police at all operational and political levels are stalling for time to try and figure out what the cover-up story will be, this time. Again, be *very* careful, mon ami."

※ ※

BERNIE RETURNED TO THE RANCH house kitchen conference table where he briefed Yvonne, Olivia and Stan on the essence of his conversation. "Nothing really new to add. Instead, just confirmation of what we already knew. The significance comes from validating what we suspected. We can confirm these people are not nice.

We need to have our radar screens up. The sad news, there are two more police officers added to the choir of silenced voices."

Yvonne interrupted the solemn stillness that had filled the kitchen. "It is not as if all the dying would stop if we immediately withdrew from this investigation. That is not an option. The choir started to attract muted voices decades ago, beyond World War II. They are all casualties of the Cold War which is officially over, yet not so and may never end."

Bernie added with a sincere fatherly tone, "We need to ensure that no one will witness our names on the nominal roll of Leblanc's choir of silenced voices."

All colleagues around the table nodded not just in acknowledgement and compliance with his directive but in commitment with his concern for their collective health and safety.

"One request, Yvonne. Can you ask your CSIS colleague if she knows anything about the surveillance of Leblanc's condo and the deaths of the two police officers in addition to the Russian military attaché?"

"I will be in communications with her shortly," Yvonne confirmed with hesitation and a tinge of trepidation. *Was less than ninety-nine-point-nine-eight percent trust sufficient?* she pondered. The trust she shared with Bernie and Stan was one-hundred percent. Statistics be damned. Even her faith in Olivia was fractionally higher than what she currently experienced for Suzette. If there was one thing she was sure of, it would be there is no room for second-guessing when the bullets fly. She never thought this day would ever come. Hence, she never considered the need to prepare contingency plans. *'Never' really is a very long time*, she supposed. Time to contact and evaluate Suzette's demeanour, if for no other reason than to reassess her own intuition.

CHAPTER 31

Uri's disposable cell phone buzzed. "I was wondering how long it would take before you called to renew our date for lobster and Chardonnay," he replied glibly with an acknowledgement that their dinner may never occur. Instead, the request would be a coded invitation to meet briefly. "You had omitted to include a charging cable with the cell phone you slid into my pocket. So, I borrowed one, assuming you might use similar models of disposable phones to schedule subsequent G2 Summits."

Yvonne did not reply with similar shallow banter but instead moved directly to the purpose of her contact. Her mood was strictly business, not social. "A couple of follow-up points. I tailed your admirer from Peggy's Cove. Just before she got to Hubbard's, she turned right off the shore road and right again on Highway 103. She then drove directly back to Halifax without stopping. She parked in the student parking lot at Dalhousie closest to the Student Health and Wellness Center and went into one of the dorms. Have you seen her since?"

"I haven't and have been reluctant to make any enquiries."

"What about the two women in your class, the ones you believe are FSB and either CIA or CSIS agents? Have they been acting differently?"

"Why do you ask? Do you believe the Peggy's Cove gal may be connected to one of them?"

"Not sure." Yvonne searched for a response from Uri regarding intelligence rather than a source of information. "Could be a backup to either. My intuition suggests that the intelligence world is heating up for some unknown reason. Best we be extra careful."

"The unknown being a connection to our mutual acquaintances

one of which I have had a closer relationship, or another entity altogether?"

Yvonne again lingered on his less than candid response before moving to a tangential topic. "We need to keep this and all future calls short. Do you have any questions regarding the instructions I included with this phone such as its immediate disposal and replacement?"

"Clear. No questions. Will turn off immediately after this call and then take the Halifax-Dartmouth ferry this evening and drop it overboard for cod bait. Will then pick up the next instalment as per the instructions. Anything you want me to do between now and our next e-communiqué?" A one-sided conversation, he thought. She was reluctant to answer the questions he posed. It was the modus operandi of a commander rather than an operational subordinate, he concluded.

"Watch the ladies and be vigilant about anyone else who may be paying extra special attention to you – your former employer, perhaps, someone with a visible facial scar. We will confirm lobster dinner at a later date. Above all, follow the protocol and the track discipline set out."

Track discipline. Haven't heard that military terminology since Spetsnaz days, he reflected. *Passionate lover or venomous viper? I think the latter and she has unfurled her battle standards and colours in preparation for an impending battlespace engagement.*

"As an aside," Uri commented before ending the call, "all hell has broken loose at Dalhousie University regarding research authority to access files off campus. We have been reminded – more like ordered – to follow strict university policies and procedures, especially when it comes to accessing government files regardless of whether they are held in bureaucratic archives or private libraries. Apparently, someone was supposed to retrieve some sensitive records, but they disappeared. It may be nothing."

"Interesting," Yvonne replied. "Be careful. I wouldn't want to have to postpone our lobster dinner date yet again." She sounded officious which was her inherent intent.

A nibble on a morsel of bait, Uri mused. *Perhaps a clue to pursue. A hint, comrade, podskazka tovarishch – friend's advice.*

※ ※

"YOU RECEIVED MY COMMUNIQUÉ," YVONNE replied to the contact request. A slight delay in transmission indicated that the call was being diverted through a coding device.

Suzette confirmed, "*Nous devons être prudents* – we need to be cautious. Our mutual acquaintance from the Château de Mercy in Metz has alerted two of his sleeping subordinates. They are en route to your neck of the woods. I don't believe they know you specifically but they have photos of two individuals, ex-members of the RCMP, whom you may have recently met. These two supposed retirees are in possession of property that has surfaced after twenty-plus years. We want this property, as do our cousins to the south, in addition to the Russians. It's more troublesome as new players in the sandbox from Beijing have also surfaced and expressed a keen interest. So, if you have any influence, have your acquaintances meet with us soonest."

"How did the sleeping subordinates get copies of the photos? From archived RCMP personnel files?"

"They have a source within the Force, a civilian employee, recruited several years ago, nurtured with monthly monetary instalments. We were aware of this mole, but this is the first time she has been activated that we are aware of. There has been an overall increase in e-traffic in addition to face-to-face encounters. Whatever is going on, it is being directed at high levels in both Moscow and Washington."

"And the recent shooting in Montréal of the police officers and the Russian military attaché?"

Suzette hesitated before replying. "Why do you ask?"

"It relates to what we talked about when we recently met. Is there a problem divulging any information?"

Again, Suzette paused. "I was there. I attached myself to that mission because I believed that our mutual friend from Metz who shot me is somehow involved. I did not see him at Leblanc's condo, nor was I expecting to see him. I just know that he is involved on the periphery, somehow."

"One more question, Suzette," Yvonne probed.

"Ask away."

"Would it be an acceptable practice to hide details away in related files if a CSIS agent believed that such action was the only viable option?"

Suzette was a bit cagey with her response. "It could be. Am I correct in surmising that someone has discovered intelligence that could implicate people at the highest level if it became known?"

It was Yvonne's turn to delay her response. The lack of a direct response filled the air yet the answer was implicit.

"Be very careful, my friend," Suzette cautioned. "We do not want a repeat performance of the senior member of the Russian State Duma being denied to us, in this case with you in the crosshairs. Perhaps you may wish to accompany your associates to a safehouse."

"Thanks for this update. I may call you in the near future," Yvonne confirmed.

"I need not repeat myself but I will. Be very careful, my dear friend." Suzette's voice dropped. "Reinforce your bastions, double the guard on the ramparts."

Yvonne noted, "I was watching the national weather channel.

Nice to see a strong high-pressure weather system stable over your region. How are you feeling?"

"Other unstable climate conditions are causing me considerable discomfort. Not sleeping well. I may attend a retirement seminar. Thanks for asking. Not many folks do or even take the time to notice," Suzette disclosed.

"Thanks for sharing," Yvonne replied. The communiqué was abundantly clear but the consequences less so. *I'm missing something. It's not personal, yet the impact will undoubtedly be personal,* she mused.

"Interesting the increase in e-traffic," Bernie commented. "Your thoughts on the response?"

"I'm not sure. I wish I was," Yvonne admitted reluctantly. "I wish I knew more. My numbers aren't the best right now. If someone read my tarot cards, I suspect they would reveal the same predictions. I'm in the first six months of the Typhon when I am subject to the physical effects of violence and accidents. I know that I'm off balance and need to be open to signs of danger. The looming negative consequences can be mitigated if I take care and remain vigilant."

Bernie shared her caginess. He was aware that Yvonne had inherited from her mother a mystic almost supernatural ability to read tea leaves and numbers with uncanny accuracy. It was wisdom older than consciousness itself. Her mother was Romanian by ethnicity with roots reaching back to the olden kingdom of Transylvania. In Greek mythology, Apollo gave his bride, Cassandra, the power of prophecy. Alas, she abused the gift and suffered dire consequences. Yvonne, in contrast, was always guarded with whom she shared the premonitions. Bernie constantly heeded her omens which she shared with equal respect. The pragmatism of technology was fine but not at the exclusion of other tools and resources. A singular strength taken to an extreme had the potential to become a weakness.

"Have an update to share," Yvonne added. "Where are the others?"

"Taking a walk in the wood lot, still within focus of our CCTV cameras and motion detectors. It was an opportune time to test our perimeter security. They should be back shortly."

Yvonne smiled with mild trepidation. She was aware of the increased attention that Bernie was giving to potential internal and external threat assessments. It wasn't uncommon for him to do so every so often. Lately, though, his uneasiness had become more palpable. She sensed he was confirming the security status more for specific reason than routine. On previous cases, he had commented that lethargy can be a harsh mistress as can paranoia. Experience had taught him that the correct balance was more often a matter of prudence.

CHAPTER 32

"There is a new colossus on the block that wasn't as prominent when John Robert Hackett a.k.a. Nikolai a.k.a. Oberstleutnant Brandt Felix Schmidt was murdered," Yvonne announced with a guarded tone. "Read the Beijing tea leaves."

"Hadn't seriously considered that scenario although I have been conscious of its presence," Stan admitted as he exchanged a wary glance with Olivia before transferring his attention to Bernie. "Admittedly, my focus has been waylaid by Soviet East European transgressions as opposed to the claws of the Beijing panda. In the malaise of a bilateral East-West standoff in which old foes were constantly grasping for excuses to joust, China has been rising in such a way as not to draw any undue attention. They are a wild card when it comes to considering additional bad guys on the periphery of our radar. They would certainly benefit were they to get their fingers on the file and selectively disclose the contents to their geopolitical advantage."

Yvonne continued, "Today, there are more traditional Lenin-leaning communists in Beijing than Moscow and are marching to the beat of a distinctly different drum. They engaged in the Cold War but mostly by proxy. If they get their grubby mittens on what you have, Cold War Versions 1 and 2 combined will appear to be child's play in comparison."

"Fear not," Bernie retorted with confidence. "We take on both the Russian grizzly and the Chinese panda. That which you deny, you entice with intrigue. We play the players to our advantage by exploiting tactical opportunities. Suffice it to say, both Moscow and Washington want to get hold of what we have in order to suppress it and eliminate us," he proclaimed with a rigid expression.

"They both have Cold War track records of being devious and ruthless. They both seek Canadian friendship and endorsement to bolster their own nefarious intentions. Each had their own seekers, hunters and gathers of intelligence. Beijing, on the other hand, is the primary emerging power on their respective radars. Hence, the Chinese Communist Party is strategically positioning itself for global dominance. All three view our part in this global Stratford theatrical performance as minor, in secondary supporting roles at best."

Bernie smiled, yet devoid of humour. "So, we maintain our façade of the protégé actor without the billing and play one against the other. We feed them all with misleading intelligence about what the others are doing and what quiet shy Canada may or may not possess. While they are chasing their perceived opponents and their own paranoid tails, we focus on shedding light on identifying all the players in addition to the suspected knowns and unknowns. In brief, we let the air out of their tires and, in doing so, take the power and ability to easily navigate away from them."

Olivia maintained Yvonne's distant stare. The others became conscious of the mutual relationship that had been developing between the two, one feeding off the other with Uri being the constant bait.

"Perhaps no surprise. There is a leak in the CSIS and the RCMP," Yvonne quietly announced. "A mole working in the RCMP archives accessed a photo of Olivia and Stan and released it to a Moscow agent. That's the bad news. The good news is the photos were taken when you joined the Force. So, you appear quite different today than you did back then."

Stan and Olivia exchanged worried expressions, each staring into their own distant pasts seeking moments when their private profiles may have crossed over the barriers into public domains. None surfaced for either as they sombrely scanned their memory banks for details of themselves in their respective wakes of professional initiatives like Hansel and Gretel leaving crumbs, certainly not within the context of intelligence research. Neither were seeing shadows where there were none.

"And...?" Bernie prompted, posing his inquisitive expression towards Yvonne.

"And I remain ninety-eight percent confident that my contact is a straight arrow. I've never doubted her loyalty in the past." They were both conscious of Eisenhower's adage that no plans survive first contact with the enemy. They would have to adapt and improvise in order to ultimately achieve their objectives, to find out who had killed constables Davidson and Hamilton.

"And...?" Bernie again prompted. *Her assessment dropped from ninety-nine-point-nine-eight percent to ninety-eight percent since last we spoke,* he reflected.

Yvonne slowly responded, "And I have no tangible reason to doubt her now."

Bernie pressed not to stir up a cauldron but for clarity. *Perhaps no tangible reason but what about any intuitive motivations to question.* He pondered. "So why were you questioning her integrity? If to re-evaluate the veracity of intelligence gathered to date, fair enough. You've never held back before. Now is not the time to start."

"Ghosts from Christmas Past." Yvonne repeated the conversation she had had with both Uri and Suzette. "Something isn't right, not adding up. Because the stakes are so high, I acknowledge that I may be over-thinking this."

"Something specific or just an uneasy feeling?" Olivia asked. She hadn't known Yvonne long enough to prompt for historical details. She only knew that unresolved events from her own past tended to surface at inopportune times. She knew that her intuition was never wrong. It was just her mis-interpretation of the intuitive message that sent her in the wrong direction. Although physically far away from the prairie bluffs and the willow trees on the family farm in the Cypress hills of southeastern Alberta where mythical dreams brought clarity to her misgivings, she had been able to transcend the essence of the separation. She remained cautiously calm.

Yvonne shook her head, troubled. "It has to do with my colleague and the shooting of the senior member of the Russian State Duma in Metz, France all those years ago when we both served with military intelligence. Also, something Uri said, or rather insinuated, about Viktor Titov. He's the KGB agent who was wounded in Afghanistan in the mortar attack by the Mujahideen and is now a sleeper-cell controller living in Ottawa. Perhaps it's somehow linked to the murder of John Robert Hackett."

Olivia held her apprehensive gaze. "A common denominator? Russia?"

After a brief interlude of silence, Yvonne asked, "Perhaps this is a stupid question, Olivia, but how well do you know Uri?"

"Both well and not well," she replied, a bit cagey but not wanting to appear evasive at the same time.

"From my very limited contact with him, he seems not just distant but mysterious as if not wanting to disclose the basics of a relationship. He appears to be constantly alert, on edge, purposefully probing as if scanning for predators sensed but not seen. More troubling, he interrogates himself, overshadowed by a silent deep groundswell of deception as if constantly morphing between the hunter and the hunted."

Olivia collected her thoughts before summing up. "That's Uri, and that's why he is my ex. Never is a very long time. Within that context, three years isn't a long time to be married but long enough to know the relationship would never mature."

Yvonne tilted her head a fraction and raised her eyebrows marginally more. She hadn't expected a non-committal interpretation to what she thought was a relatively neutral benign enquiry. She had sensed a level of acrimony between them when they met on Bernie's lobster boat. Perhaps they had merely agreed to disagree when they divorced. Her own marital relationship had ended under similar circumstances.

"At the time, I was so focused on completing my PhD, I didn't have the energy to invest in a relationship. It was only after I submitted my dissertation and had a moment to breathe that I realized our marriage was over before it started. The divorce decree came through on the same day I formally walked across the stage with my doctoral scroll in hand. He was and always would be a Spetsnaz fighting the same Soviets that had haunted him on the many nights he awoke in a cold sweat with terrifying nightmares. He believes they are still chasing him – they being the KGB."

"*They* as in KGB agent Viktor Titov?" Yvonne pressed for clarification.

Feeling empathy for his emotional condition, Olivia concluded, "Yes, I believe so. There are some places you don't go with Uri and that is one of them. I learned the hard way. In retrospect, I should have been more sensitive, more open to his emotional state." Her voice dropped off with that admission.

"Thanks for sharing," Yvonne replied. "It explains a lot." As she reflected, her disquiet lingered then faded, leaving only a faint trace like footprints under a light dusting of early winter snow.

Olivia proposed a related option. "Other denominators, but still Russian – other roles played by Viktor Titov."

"True," Yvonne admitted. "Viktor Titov shot the senior member of the Russian State Duma in Metz. Uri identified Viktor Titov as a KGB agent in Afghanistan. My CSIS colleague identified Viktor Titov as being a Russian spy and sleeper cell controller, currently living in Ottawa."

Olivia nodded, validating her deliberation without interrupting or rationalizing the potential consequences.

Yvonne again took a moment to reflect before continuing to list her concerns. "An unknown? Did Viktor Titov know Uri when they were both in Ottawa? If so, how well? We have no definitive evidence suggesting that Viktor Titov is directly associated with the Hackett shooting. I say *not directly* but what about *indirectly*? Could he have been connected to Ruslan as a potential protégé, trained by Ruslan to be a sleeper-cell controller? Ruslan retires and Viktor takes over his contacts. We know that Viktor recruited, trained and now runs an effective spy ring in Ottawa with tentacles that infiltrate the bureaucracy to the senior levels, not just limited to the Ottawa region. Finally, Viktor Titov remains one of the ghosts, absent without leave, on our list of tentative knowns."

It was Stan who pondered the probability of Yvonne's proposed scenarios. "Whatever the common denominator, Leblanc remains the tangible link. We can safely conclude that that's a given. From a metaphysical perspective, you embrace the image viewed by the photographer through the lens and the one in the mind of the photographer. What was Leblanc envisioning through his personal lens? What was his perspective, the image on the monitor in his own mind? What did he want to achieve by being elusive, playing these games? It immediately begs the question: *Would he have swept the moral dirt under the carpet?*"

"I'm starting to think that Leblanc had a penchant for selective truth depending on the circumstances in which he found himself." Olivia sighed without much enthusiasm. "Each person must confront morality from a personal perspective. They must have done some soul searching at one stage or another."

As *de facto* leader, Bernie summarized their possible scenarios. "We haven't arrived at the Rubicon just to go fishing. Let us agree for a moment that Leblanc was a good cop with a strong Christian belief. He was confronted by what he perceived to be an unthinkable crucible including Armageddon and the Four Horsemen of the Apocalypse as described in the *Book of Revelations* in the *New Testament*. He didn't see a viable option in the period following 5 November 1978 when Hackett was murdered in the barn. Accordingly, he hid the evidence, to be recovered at a later time when the global players were not as bent on destroying civilization as it existed within the context of the original Cold War. He crossed paths with Olivia and Stan. In the interim, and in them, especially Olivia, he saw a possible solution. He protected them as best he could by having them transferred away from the trajectory of the impending storm. He left a Hansel and Gretel trail and laid low, as did the other players it seems. It was a long shot but the best bet he perceived he had. Serendipitously, decades later, Olivia and Stan met at the Toronto Pearson International Airport."

With a confirming glance, Bernie reflected on his ephemeral summary before concluding. "And here we are today, up against the original Cold War combatants plus one new Asian player. As Uri suggested, all are adamant about resurrecting yet-unresolved ideological vendettas which reach back to the turn of the last century. To this end, China would be pleased if former East and West foes girded their loins, had knaves polish shields and put edges on swords, and did battle in the arenas of olden Teutonic knights. Our challenge, as I see it, is to defuse Armageddon, and have the Four Horsemen of the Apocalypse dismount, unbridle their horses and put them out to pasture, permanently."

"And we are still committed to finding out who is behind the deaths of Davidson and Hamilton," Olivia added.

All eyes met and heads nodded methodically in agreement.

"Life was simpler before 5 November 1978," Stan reflected. "Respective models for problem solving on that day had not been without fuzzy options. But the moral filters had fewer unprincipled implications that are now readily apparent. The choice between right and wrong seemed straightforward. However, arriving at the former was now fraught with the trappings of Armageddon with which Leblanc had wrestled two decades before."

"That pretty well sums it up," Yvonne commented.

Bernie concluded his assessment. "Thus far, we have been sequestered in this ranch house and for good reason. We need to move from siege mentality to a breakout strategy and go on the offensive."

"*De l'audace. Encore de l'audace. Toujour de l'audace.* Audacity. More audacity. Always audacity. Words shrewdly spoken by my stalwart partner," Stan proclaimed as he gazed at Olivia who smiled subtly. She did not blush this time in response to his compliment.

"As Leblanc correctly surmised, it is much easier said than done," Bernie followed up sombrely. "Now we begin the heavy lifting with the greatest risk. We need to plan for every eventuality."

"First, from what we know, who can we trust?" Yvonne asked. "Time to call in former colleagues. Second, we need to amass a list of those known former adversaries and antagonists. We must err on the side of caution if there are any questionable variables. An overriding modus operandi, *Laws of War* as defined in the 1949 Geneva Convention, were not designed for the multi-dimensional battle space of Artificial Intelligence and assassins gone rogue, which is our current reality."

Bernie nodded. "Basic rule, we can only validate individual allies who have demonstrated absolute integrity and loyalty. That does not include organizations like the Canadian Intelligence Security Service. We know for certain that Russian agents have successfully scaled its ramparts. We must also assume that the CIA has agent provocateurs strategically positioned within the CSIS parapets. An American culture of paranoia classifies them as allies with questionable commitment when push comes to shove. Again, I hearken back to the Avro Aircraft debacle among other classified examples. We have to assume that the U.S. would as easily install a not-so-Distant Early Warning – DEW Line – on the forty-ninth parallel fortified by their own military troops as they have done in the Arctic. Rest assured they have already developed detailed plans for that scenario. Enough said."

"A bleak picture but a necessary one," Yvonne confirmed. "Unlike the old KGB proverb, *doveryay i proveryay* – trust and verify, we verify first before we trust. There are no degrees to trust. In the immortal words of Obi-Wan, the *Star Wars* Jedi Master: *Do or do not. There is no try.*"

"Given the pace this case has taken, we don't have time to verify any new sources to trust. It's just us and our band of merry men and women," Bernie declared. "Howard Pyle had us in mind when he wrote *The Tales of Robin Hood.* The only difference is we are not the outlaws nor perhaps the Sheriff of Nottingham. An important yet subtle distinction. Certainly, some of the deputies are definitely not the good guys either. The tables have been turned and twisted."

Bernie thought back to their Watcher Service days. They had formed bonds that they knew would last a life time because the values they swore to in their oaths of allegiance were common to the core. Others in the Watcher Service they had rubbed shoulders with were less so, a few far less so. They each went their separate ways after graduation yet their vocations followed the same trajectory as if destined by the gods. Their commitment to one another remained steadfast. When Stan and Yvonne stepped back into semi-retirement, Bernie did the same. His was the perfect self-employment in his pastoral setting. He could choose the select few clients he wanted.

This case was different than any other. For the first time, the client was one of them – Stan, and Olivia by association. Virtually all other clients were in the intelligence business, removed from the front lines of their respective battlespaces. In less than a fortnight, more bodies had been accumulated than ever before. The three musketeers plus one where all in the crosshairs of multiple unknown assassins. Would this be their final hurrah? Bonds of a life time not broken but inevitably ended. Bernie would re-evaluate all physical security initiatives and electronic firewalls, and create additional redundancies where necessary.

CHAPTER 33

"We cross the Rubicon at this juncture," Bernie pronounced with Caesar's conviction. His delivery was deliberate and composed. A vision of Caesar's bloodied toga flashed before his eyes as if a haunting premonition. He had experienced reflections before on the eve of other missions as he contemplated the details of each stage of the critical planning process, but not with such lucidity which seemed to be shrouded with ill-omened caveats. And as before, he would keep his deliberations to himself. "Are we chasing spies or shadows?" His question was rhetorical. "No misgivings, now. We are in pursuit of spies and their moles. The only thing that matters now is achieving the end state and returning to the ranch to debrief as a team. It's time to set this strategy in motion."

His train of thought was disturbed by Digger who sniffed repeatedly at the back door sill each time drawing in a lungful of air, then pausing momentarily in an attempt to clarify the scent and ideally its source. He paced in an agitated manner in the kitchen between the back door, the entrance to the woodshed and the access to the tunnel. "What's got you upset, Digger?" Bernie asked reassuringly as he petted his head. On his cell phone, he scrutinized the images from the CCTV cameras. Nothing seemed out of the normal. He opened the back door to let Digger out. He remained on the porch surveying Digger's tracking route. It wasn't uncommon for Digger to become upset when routines in the ranch house were changed. Bernie would pay specific attention to changes in the sounds of his faint whimpers and pacing patterns. CCTV cameras could portray images but Digger could sense for the unseen. Once Digger returned, Bernie reached into his pocket and handed his loyal companion a biscuit as a reward. He then petted him again. "Good boy, Digger. Good boy," he whispered. He had learned long ago from the writings of an anonymous sage that there were times when the wolves were silent and the Moon howled. He had an inkling that Digger's restlessness was a premonition of one of those occasions.

Yvonne nodded. "I gave my CSIS colleague a call. She will join us in Halifax, although she won't know in advance where our safehouse will be. It's a precaution against potential alien ears and eyes in their respective bastions of intelligence, in addition to other unknowns."

Bernie cast a questioning gaze.

Yvonne met his stare. "She isn't one of King John's nefarious conspirators, I'm sure of that. She and I had spent time in the trenches as colleagues under fire. But she isn't one of Robin Hood's resources with a history of demonstrated loyalty, and proven steadfastness while under fire. The difference is subtle yet critical. Still at ninety-eight percent confidence, subject to change," she responded to Bernie's inquisitive expression. They shared the sensitivity of the moment.

"We few, we very few, we band of brothers," Bernie murmured.

"Shakespeare's *Henry V* on the eve of Saint Crispin's day and the battle of Agincourt. Let's make certain that we have planned for all contingencies," Yvonne added.

Olivia piped in, "What about the bait?"

Yvonne transferred her attention. "I've provided her with the three names from Leblanc's list including the one in the CSIS that we agreed on. I've also suggested she spread the word that she will be going to Halifax, to a farm on Hammonds Plains Road where, in 1978, a KGB sleeper cell agent by the name of Nikolai had been killed."

"And Uri?" Olivia followed up.

"I'll also meet with him," Yvonne confirmed. "There are a few loose ends to tie up." Her second declaration was more solemn suggesting a more ominous nuance. There was no subtle innuendo between her and Olivia as was evident on the eve of her previous trip to Halifax when she retrieved the box of Dr. MacDonald's coroner notes from his daughter, Jennifer. Of equal importance was information gleaned from her interview with Sergeant McNeill's daughter, Sarah. Yvonne's tone was exact and professional. There was no room for error, misinterpretation or unpredictable wild cards.

"Communications verification?" Bernie announced. "Check in by text message as you reach the designated checkpoints. I'll confirm. There is a time for redundancy and this is one of them. At each checkpoint, one of our colleagues will also confirm with me and follow behind you to ensure you are not being tailed. Questions?" Bernie made eye contact with each of them.

"I have confirmed all tracking and individual transmitting and receiving devices are functioning," Yvonne verified.

Bernie concluded. "The Makarov PB pistol and original documents with the metal box, in addition to Leblanc's coded notes, are secured in the garage. You all know where the safe and the combination are hidden."

Everyone nodded.

Digger remained alert to the increase in commotion and accompanying emotion. He continued to pace the kitchen floor and licking all hands on deck as they prepared to leave via the escape hatch in the woodshed to the subterranean tunnel.

Bernie affectionately scratched his ear. "*Armies on the Russian snow, / with cockade, sword and lance,*" he recited as he had done on the eve of other missions. Digger looked up in response to his master's reassuring voice. He snuggled against the pocket. His reward would be forthcoming.

"Those lines, by the poet E.J. Pratt," Olivia commented.

"Leblanc isn't the only one to cite poetry in times of importance," he replied.

Bernie made direct eye contact with his colleagues as a final parting gesture. "I will be monitoring your every movement and all conversations. As always, let's be safe in the sand box, ladies and gentlemen. There are still some unknown intervening variables." His parting stare reflected that of a commander on D-Day, his double handshakes were equally earnest. Both bore a tinge of wary reflection. He lingered with Yvonne. Their history was longest, their bonds strongest and more enduring.

Once all had departed, Digger curled up in his bed by the wood stove in the kitchen. Within a moment, he jumped to his feet and bolted to the back door, scratching impatiently.

"What's got you upset, buddy?" Bernie opened the door. Digger ran into the yard, then behind the mechanical barn. Bernie chased after him again checking the CCTV monitor on his cell phone. A yelp filled the space. A figure appeared at the back of the barn running in the opposite direction of the woodlot and the escape route along the berm. Bernie sprinted to the far corner of the barn. There he found Digger laying on the ground. A knife was protruding from his shoulder. Blood was seeping from the wound.

Bernie speed dialed the Cumberland County Rural Veterinarian. Doctor Simpson responded within minutes. As Bernie waited, he followed the directions of the vet for emergency First Aid following a stab wound. He applied pressure around the wound being careful not to dislodge the knife blade that impaled his shoulder. Digger whimpered as he stared up at his master and loyal companion as if apologizing for his inability to protect.

"You'll be alright, Digger," Bernie assured him. "Your friend Doctor Simpson will be here shortly."

Within an hour, all three were in the Rural Veterinarian Clinic. The general anaesthetic had taken effect.

"I'll keep him here overnight," Doc Simpson told Bernie. "He will wake up in about an hour. I will call you as soon as he opens his eyes. Go home. You can't do anything for now.' He repeated, "I *will* call you if there are any changes in his condition."

Bernie stared at Digger. He had never before left him alone. How could he leave him now? Yet he needed to get back to the ranch house and the communication system which was in direct contact with his team. He also had to review all the CCTV surveillance videos to ascertain if he could identify the person who had stabbed Digger. Facial recognition software could provide an identity profile if the perpetrator had been facing the scene of the stabbing behind the barn. All he had was what seemed to be a white patch on the back of the perpetrator's head. Bernie had colleagues who would attend to that task. Whoever it was needed to know that there wasn't a rock on this planet Earth where he could hide and where Bernie would not find him, drag him out, and ensure that justice was served. That wasn't a threat. It wasn't a promise. Instead, it was a fact, plain and simple.

CHAPTER 34

The team gained more confidence as they passed each checkpoint and picked up another associate who provided additional support like outriders and guards riding shotgun on a stagecoach transporting strongboxes of yesteryear in the Hollywood renditions of the Wild West. Yet they remained vigilant. The familiarity of Bedford brought additional tacit comfort and explicit memories. Yet their attention and scrutiny increased with even more shadows potentially masking unknown surveillance from eyes and close circuit cameras.

At the Upper Tantallon Detachment, a short fifteen-minute drive from Bedford, Yvonne made the introductions. "Stan, Olivia, this is Suzette, my good friend and colleague from the Canadian Security Intelligence Service."

"Last name?" Stan asked.

Her reply was terse. "Suzette is fine for now."

Stan and Olivia exchanged a quick glance accompanied with an almost imperceptible tic of a nod. Round One in the game went to Suzette. Her caginess did little to encourage collegial confidence and cooperation.

Olivia gave Suzette a partial list of names from the full accounting that Leblanc had identified in his coded communiqués. A few were repeats from the initial partial list that Yvonne had already passed along for bait.

"There are other senior mandarins and politicians at the federal and Québec provincial levels of government. In addition, you will note that there is one more name of a senior CSIS employee. This is not the only one." Olivia mused, *Check; checkmate with the next move.* She smiled inwardly as she awaited Suzette's response.

Stan interjected before Suzette could respond. "We can provide you with other names in the fullness of time. We are reluctant to include them at this time, just in case there is anything untoward underfoot. I'm sure you appreciate the need for caution." Stan stared down at the paper he had passed to Suzette. "Rest assured that if anything were to happen to us, and/or what is recorded here ends up in the hands of any unintended addressee, this information and the balance of the names will be released to the media and select members of Her Majesty's Loyal Opposition."

Both Stan and Olivia watched Suzette with neutral confident expressions. The surety of their communication was clear. Suzette was acutely aware there was no room for debate or negotiation on the terms of the release of future information including the global and national implications of such intelligence surfacing. The Canadian Security and Intelligence Service would be left to deal with embarrassing consequences. Neither Stan nor Olivia could care one way or the other. They had a lifetime of regrets. Round Two in the game went to Olivia and Stan.

"Any questions?" Olivia asked. Before Suzette could acknowledge, Olivia added, "One last point before you respond. Please note the partial photocopy of the original Cyrillic script and photos of the Russian Makarov PB pistol with silencer, its identifying marks, and the still unidentified fingerprints. I have provided a translation of the script in the event that you do not have command of the Russian language and the Soviet culture during the Cold War era circa 1978 when it was written. Please also take notice of the reference to the FLQ crisis and the direction to the recipient of this correspondence to use the Makarov PB pistol to kill Pierre Laporte. The recipient was a male partner in a Russian sleeper-cell duo code named Nicolai, a.k.a. John Robert Hackett a.k.a. Nazi SS Lieutenant Colonel Brandt Felix Schmidt. His sleeper cell partner's name was Sylvia a.k.a. Lada. Their Soviet handler was referred to as Ruslan."

Suzette let out a long breath before replying. "Your conditions are clear as is your wariness and amplified need for security. A few of the people identified are in very influential positions with equally influential friends in their respective fortified circles. Suffice it to say they could unleash a torrent of counteractions that would result in further casualties of the Cold War such as your colleagues constables Davidson and Hamilton."

"Thanks for this information," Olivia replied, maintaining direct eye contact and little else in acknowledged expression. "We have considered these and other potential variables in our threat analysis and mitigating strategies. By the way, constables Davidson and Hamilton were innocent victims as was Pierre Laporte. It was their families who were left to bear the burden of political incompetence and cover-up. If our disclosures help to reduce this burden, that will be a bonus."

Suzette paused before her final remarks. "I have no questions." Not wanting to initiate further antagonism and being aware of the commanding heights that Olivia and Stan held, she added with an amiable grin and a welcoming handshake, "My last name is Ouellette. Very much look forward to working with you on this file."

Yvonne entered the conversation. Addressing Suzette, she proposed, "We have established a tentative plan with contingencies based on several possible scenarios. We would very much appreciate your input and ability to bring resources to bear as you perceive as necessary."

Suzette scanned the summary. "Looks familiar and comprehensive. We had not included such a detailed exit strategy in our original plan for the defection and the senior member of the Russian State Duma in Metz. We learn from our mistakes, which is timely given the fact that I have been informed that Viktor Titov was spotted yesterday arriving at the Halifax Stanfield International Airport. He booked into a local hotel close to Bedford. That suggests he wants to be close to the potential action, the farm on Hammonds Plains Road."

Yvonne noted a slight falter in Suzette's voice and an absence of hesitation. She still trusted Suzette but perhaps the confidence level had dropped to ninety-nine point nine eight percent from one hundred and with a wider confidence interval. Bernie and Stan remained at one hundred percent, Olivia very close to that only because she had not previously worked with her. She thought back to her Watcher Service days, especially working with Bernie when loyalty was the defining attribute of their professional relationship. The bonds of loyalty had been challenged but never tarnished. Suzette's addition into her crucible of confidants was welcome. In retrospect, perhaps it was unfair to compare Suzette with Bernie and Stan. They were the original three musketeers, all for one and one for all. Suzette was a partner under different circumstances. Yes, they were a team. But, she wasn't a musketeer. *But* was the operative word.

Suzette added, "Unbeknown to Viktor, there were other luminaries from the foreign intelligence community on the same flight and at the airport to keep him under surveillance at a distance. At least, we don't believe that Viktor was aware. He certainly did not communicate with any of them or anyone else en route or between the airport here and his hotel."

Yvonne pondered, perhaps a mirror of Uri's classroom. Both predators and prey were auditioning for roles in this deadly theatrical production. The first act had followed the intended script. Like the convergence of high- and low-pressure systems, the elements of the perfect storm were building. She felt compassion for Suzette. Shakespeare was a visionary, she surmised, writing the play, *As You Like It*, with this Cold War Act II reality in mind. 'All the world's a stage, / And all the men and women merely players; / They have their exits and their entrances, / And one man in his time plays many parts.' *Today, more than one woman in her time plays many parts with her exits and entrances*, she mused with practiced confidence.

And what was Suzette doing in Montréal supposedly unofficially attached to the CSIS team as they monitored the comings and goings around Leblanc's Mount Royal condo within sight of the Russian consulate? At least one other defector from the former RCMP Security Service had lived in this neighbourhood. Coincidence? Convenience?

The three musketeers never withheld information from one another. Never. It was evident that Suzette was not divulging all details, perhaps crucial information. Yes, she was sworn not to divulge anything under the *Official Secrets Act. But. Yes, but.*

Yvonne had wanted to have a heart-to-heart conversation alone with Suzette to clear the air. The speed at which events had intervened and the pace of the investigation had unfortunately increased too quickly. Suzette's attention was focused on her employer, and rightly so given the exposure of additional names of infiltrators, one of which revealed compromising cracks in the CSIS façade. Other names exposed senior bureaucrats, some of whom had direct links to senior executives within the CSIS. They were influencing Suzette's decisions and less so her actions while she was away from her office in the nation's capital.

Suzette had been careful to assess events unfolding in her office, details that could potentially be used against her. She found herself *entre le précipice et le loup* – between the precipice and the wolf. Her superiors would have already known about her past relationship with Yvonne from documents she had completed on her application to join the CSIS, emails and other means of communications with Yvonne, including phone calls, all of which were purely social. Yes, *but*. There was always the *yes but* factor.

CHAPTER 35

Suzette's cell phone buzzed. She studied the screen apprehensively as she and Yvonne stepped away from the others. Without specifics, she chose not to notify or caution Yvonne. Instead, she requested verification of the text. Napoleon had likewise hesitated in order to confirm communications. That decision had cost him victory at the Battle of Waterloo and with it his dreams of a French empire. She tapped in a follow-up response, "Immediate verification needed," with an urgent icon attached. *Hopefully, this delay will not cost lives and result in my ultimate banishment to the Island of Saint Helena,* she mused.

Yvonne tilted her head but said nothing. Nothing needed to be said. The response to her silent question remained in the balance. Suzette responded with a single faint tic of a tentative raising of her eyebrows. Her communiqué was clear. They would need to talk in private, but not now.

Yvonne sensed her own mounting stress. She didn't like it. She and Suzette had perfected their signals as Intelligence Officers in the European arena to the level of a fluid team. They had earned the title from their colleagues and superiors alike as the Diamond Duo. Despite the perceived failure of that Metz mission, they remained committed to each other. Much water had passed under the bridge since then, though. Yvonne was all too familiar with her unease on such occasions.

"I need to update my superior in Ottawa," Suzette said in a slightly more confident yet still reserved tone. She had deviated from her director's concise directive to her because the name was one that Olivia had identified from Leblanc's list as being a confederate. With that revelation, Suzette's world had changed. There were other colleagues who were connected to that spurious link in the CSIS chain of command. There had been too many quiet discussions behind closed doors. One discussion had been with a retired colleague who had also served as a military intelligence officer in Europe at the time she and Yvonne were there. She had never trusted him before. Now her instincts were validated. Most of these colleagues had never proven their metal under fire as she and Yvonne had done in Metz. Most had never stepped outside the not-so-hallowed halls of the CSIS bureaucracy on Ogilvie Road in Gloucester.

Yvonne monitored her own cell as a text message from Suzette appeared despite standing within arm's length of her. "Need to talk soonest regarding Metz and Major Edwards." She stared at her previous partner with a perplexed expression.

"Major Mike Edwards," Yvonne replied in a shrouded whisper.

Suzette nodded without hesitation although she seemed distracted. Her breathing increased yet the depth of each breath was shorter and increasingly weaker. Her brow tightened and her pupils dilated as she scanned with greater acuity.

"The name Mike Edwards is on the list," Yvonne added.

"He left the military before compulsory retirement age and transferred into the CSIS. I worked with him indirectly," Suzette mumbled. They exchanged horrified stares.

"The leak. He's the leak, the treasonous traitor," Yvonne announced. "Had he pulled the trigger on their Duma defector? And me? Or was it Viktor Titov?" The answer was irrelevant to the Duma defector, at this juncture. It was very relevant to her Watcher Service colleagues plus Olivia at this moment. Mike Edwards had been the mole. Suzette ended up with the physical trauma from the bullets and emotional trauma from the circumstances of her wounding – betrayal, one of the seven cardinal sins that gave rise to other immoralities.

Suzanne delicately massaged her shoulder in response to the realization that her nemesis had been that close yet unseen for what he was. For all she knew, he may have been stalking her in the shadows of the Parliament Peace Tower. She corrected Yvonne's verb tense. "Was the leak. He died a few years ago. We suspected him of being in Viktor Titov's network but it was never proven."

"He was also suspect while working in Europe," Yvonne added. "This is all too coincidental." She had erred in her analysis. If you cannot identify the enemy with practiced precision in front of you on the forward edge of the battle space, then glance behind you. She had not done so and, as a result, was condemned to suffer the pain of her own omissions.

"He is the link to Viktor Titov who just happens to be here in Halifax today supposedly taking a Maritime vacation."

Suzette whispered, "Uri? By coincidence he happens to be here teaching at Dalhousie University. Just happens to have been a member of the Russian Special Forces, the Spetsnaz. He supposedly saved Viktor Titov from the alleged Mujahideen mortar attack in Afghanistan. Had his heroic actions been supposed or were they purposeful, to save a fellow *tovarishch* – comrade?"

"Is there something we need to know about?" Olivia interrupted. "I'm liking neither the vibes nor the implications."

Yvonne did not reply. Instead she continued to stare intensely at Suzette as her complexion became rugged. Her breathing became shallow. Her mouth became dry. Her heart began to pound, battling for space with her lungs that fought back in her ever-tightening chest cavity.

A reoccurring image flashed through Suzette's mind accompanied by searing pain in her left shoulder and breast where bullets had torn the flesh from her body on that fateful day. In her recollection, her eyes frantically searched for cover from the unrelenting hail of bullets. The source she could not identify. She was being dragged. The pain was increasing to an intensity she had never before known. Her breathing became sporadic and shallow. Yvonne's voice seemed faint and distant yet her arm was securely wrapped around Suzette's bleeding chest.

"Keep your eyes open. Talk to me, Suzette. Tell me what you are feeling. Tell me what you are thinking right now." A state of quasi-unconsciousness followed.

The immediate sound of her former partner's familiar voice at this moment, not a memory, brought her back to the reality of this time and place in Bedford, not Metz.

"Let's go for a walk," Yvonne said with reassuring tranquillity.

Despite feeling light-headed, Suzette agreed. *Du calme, du calme*, she repeated to herself as she took slow deliberate breaths in an attempt to regain possession of her intellect, her soul.

"How often do they occur?" Yvonne asked.

"Haven't had one this bad in longer than I care to remember. Facing the ghosts of both Viktor Titov and Major Mike Edwards triggered the anxiety. Time to retire from this game."

"We do not want a repeat performance of Metz," Yvonne said as she stared at her former partner. "It's not often you get a second opportunity to settle an old debt."

"Thanks for being here, once again."

Smiling, Yvonne replied. "My pleasure. That's what partners are for. All OK?" Her confidence in Suzette returned to ninety-nine percent. The disruptive impact of her trauma kept it from returning any higher.

Suzette's breathing had slowed. Her focus returned. "Just a bloody headache, some blurred vision, a bit of nausea and tinnitus screaming in my left ear. They always follow, sometimes for several hours, occasionally days. I've learned to adapt to this constantly merging normal. Otherwise, all OK."

Stan leaned over and whispered into Olivia's ear an almost verbatim account of the conversation between Suzette and Yvonne.

Olivia was wide-eyed. "Your hearing is incredible."

"Not so much hearing as reading lips. As I previously mentioned, my mother was born deaf. In addition to learning American Sign Language, I became an expert at reading lips. In school, I could pick up on all the gossip the girls were passing around. It broke up a few budding relationships when the lasses realized I could eavesdrop at a distance. Best be careful what you mumble," he warned. "I'm deadly seriously, Olivia. Others whose vocation is gathering intelligence can effortlessly do the same."

Olivia recalled the ominous warning that Stan had uttered on that momentous morning on 5 November 1978: "Strongly suggest that you only report what you observed at the scene and nothing of what the deceased may have said to you. Understand?" he'd emphasized. "I'm deadly serious, Olivia."

Today, Stan's stare was equally stern and ominous.

Olivia lingered, acknowledging his forewarning. She knew that he was as concerned for her safety as she was for his. She then asked, "Can you teach me to read lips?"

Stan nodded. "It would be my pleasure." *God, would I ever love to teach you about lips,* he ruminated.

Olivia approached Yvonne. "Is Suzette all right?"

"Yes. Flashbacks to Metz where she was wounded, betrayed. They can be overwhelming at times."

"Is our mission in jeopardy?" Stan pressed.

"Maximum flexibility with every mission," Yvonne replied with a tentative tone. "Suzette has been our liaison with the local constabulary and resources have already been confirmed. In the worst-case scenario, we can proceed without her direct involvement in the specifics of the mission."

"On the one hand, I share Stan's concern," Olivia commented.

"On the other hand, Suzette has already released to her CSIS colleagues the names and reference to the farm at Hammonds Plains where Hackett had been murdered. We might not get another opportunity."

"Hold that thought, Olivia. I need to call Bernie to bring him up to speed," Yvonne advised. "Also, I have to ask him to conduct a bit of research." She stepped aside to keep her conversation private, from whom, Olivia wasn't sure.

"You've known Bernie and Yvonne a long time," Olivia whispered to Stan. "She seems to portray one personality when around Bernie and another when away from his orbit and the ambience of the ranch. Is there some background, personal history between Yvonne and Bernie I should be aware of?"

"They both have strong personalities as do other associates. We are all aware of the dynamics, and have learned to respect what each other brings to the table in order to achieve the objectives for the clients. They have deep compassion for each other but I'm not aware that their feelings go beyond that. They could though. We were all very close back then but didn't always work together as a team on all missions. So, I could be wrong."

Olivia bowed. "Thanks. Good to know."

CHAPTER 36

Olivia watched as Stan rubbed his balding head. She had never felt so conscious of his presence, so hopeful and so whole since working closely together on this case. Yet she also felt unsure, something might derail the relationship, separate them once again.

He shot her a warm smile. "I had more hair before I got into this line of work starting with the Watcher Service," he quipped. "I think I need to retire completely before it's all gone and I am left only polishing the smooth dome like a billiard ball each morning."

She lamented, *perhaps living on a cul-de-sac in the soul of suburbia with the station wagon in the driveway of the three-bedroom, two-bathroom bungalow with two point three kids.* She dwelt on the thought. *Quit dreaming like a lovelorn schoolgirl. You weren't there so get over it. You've been living in a condo with a single secure parking space, on your own, with no one to impress, and now past the age of rug rats. Your books in your bookshelves have been your long-term companions, at times your cherished intimate partners. What are you doing gallivanting all over the country chasing after ghosts? Or after lost youth? Or after lost intimacy? 'Lying to oneself is more deeply ingrained than lying to others,'* she recalled Dostoyevsky having written.

Lately, she had been falling into the all too familiar rut of beating herself up in bleak periods of loneliness, of questioning her worthiness for love, to be loved. The retirement literature seemed to be accurate – at the fulcrum of the what-ifs. The what-if of what wasn't and the what-if of what could have been. *So, snap out of it, lady. Move on. Prove something, anything. Either commit heresy and take a yoga class, or pick up your foil and slay the dragon.*

Yvonne's voice jarred her out of her mental fencing lunge, parry and riposte with herself.

"Time to revise our battle plan," Yvonne announced. "Like Tom Sawyer, we get others to whitewash the fence for us. Specifically, we have a confidential source who has leaked to the media that a cold case with international implications dating back a couple of decades is being reopened. To further increase media suspicion, the local constabulary will be setting up roadblocks on the Hammonds Plains Road between Lucasville Road and Stillwater Lake. The entrance to the farm will be marked off with police crime-scene tape and opaque curtains erected around various dig sites including the windmill. Identification Units augmented with additional police officers will be seen excavating behind the curtains."

Olivia and Stan had been monitoring Suzette's recovery from her debilitating post-traumatic stress episode. With Yvonne's invitation and update, they were heartened that Suzette had rejoined the discussion, although slightly subdued by the gnawing headache between her temples that caused her vision to blur and her stomach to want to erupt.

Suzette had called her superior in Ottawa and brought him up to date, omitting certain details. Immediately after, there had been an increase in encrypted e-traffic from both the Russian and American Embassies in Ottawa confirming that the word had been leaked. An equivalent increase in e-traffic had been noted to and from the Chinese Embassy.

Stan approached Yvonne. "You mentioned you wanted Bernie to conduct additional research."

"A name on the list has been taunting me," she replied immediately. "Either that person in particular or another, a closer associate. We've worked together on enough cases to know that every stone has to be overturned to ensure that what is underneath is benign.

You know as well as I that to not do so can be fatal. Bernie should be getting back to me soonest. I'll let you know."

Stan studied her intently. His expression morphed from collegial curiosity to disquieting concern. Deep lines etched his face. He knew from experience that when Yvonne became unrelenting in her pursuit of something on the periphery, *a je ne sais quoi*, like a bulldog trying to validate a vague scent with nostrils flared, there was good reason. But which name had piqued her interest? More importantly, why? In what context?

He scanned the names again. Those he recognized were mostly bureaucrats, a few senior private sector executives, all prominent in their own influential circles. Some he did not recognize. Perhaps Yvonne had known or knew of them from her service with Canadian Military Intelligence. He was confident that had there been an imminent threat, she would have passed along her concern. Still, she seemed to be communicating in code, encrypted in such a way that he would have to be patient while the decryption was being undertaken.

"You're bothered," Olivia said quietly. "When you're bothered, I'm bothered and I don't like to be bothered. Care to share?"

"It's something Yvonne said or, more to the point, didn't say. She has asked Bernie to research a name on the list. Suzette is more than just an elephant in the room, allegedly because she can't talk about what she does as a supposed analyst at the CSIS. There is something pertinent to this case or someone lurking in the background that is influencing decisions. Suzette is Yvonne's friend, not one of our associates. We talked about trust with Bernie. For whatever reason, I just don't trust Suzette. She is holding back information from us, and possibly Yvonne."

"I share your concern. My scalp becomes prickly when she is around. When that happens, I get the feeling that something ill-omened is about to happen. Where is Yvonne now? We need to talk, to clear the air."

"She headed off somewhere. Not sure where," Stan replied. He sensed Olivia's apprehension and desire to keep apprised of the changing dynamics which were impinging on the tactics. They would have to coordinate should the circumstances dictate expedient actions. He too felt a growing need for wariness. On previous cases when working alone, his responses to changes on the fly were more flexible. He was now more conscious of the need to consider the impact of decisions on Olivia as a business partner within the context of a growing personal relationship. He knew that he would need to deal with the elephant in the room, to let go of the memory of his former wife, Betty, as a tenuous partner within a pragmatic civil relationship often devoid of expressed emotions. He concluded that he had been married but without a wife.

CHAPTER 37

"What's going on with your students?" Yvonne asked Uri in a forthright manner that demanded an immediate and concise accounting. Her voice was sharp and controlling, not coy or enticing as previously expressed. Naked silence lay exposed between them.

He met her unflinching stare. The venomous viper, not the passionate lover, was standing squarely in front of him with an explicit agenda. He had experienced such an authoritarian interaction as a junior officer in the Russian Army standing in front of his commanding officer with his heels together. He reined in his impulse to challenge, to engage in a reactive response. He studied her instead, her creased brow, her dour demeanour, her steely stare, all prompted by recent events tempered with her own ghost of a Christmas Past.

"The foreign national student, the one I suspect to be East European or more likely Russian, has been overly officious to say the least. Best described as pointedly abrupt, noticeably agitated, not just with me but with others in the class. She has absolutely no time for the student whom I suspect to be either CIA or CSIS."

Yvonne did not reply but instead maintained her steely stare as if to communicate that he had better be telling her the truth, the whole truth and nothing but the truth, so help him God. The Mujahideen mortar attack he had experienced when he rescued Viktor Titov in 1979 would pale in comparison to her impending viper strike should he deviate into the murky realm of less than forthright responses.

He broke the uncomfortable silence with an intentionally distracting question. "Can you give this pin to Olivia? It's for good luck. We may be divorced and the separation more acrimonious than amorous, but I am still concerned for her safety and wellbeing. I gave this pin to her when we were first married. She returned it to me sometime thereafter, and for good reason, the details of which are not important at this time," he admitted.

There was a tinge of remorse in his voice that Yvonne had not noticed before. She held his stare.

Yvonne examined the pin curiously. She recognized the design from intelligence briefings she had received. On this occasion, she was taken aback by its material existence now in the palm of her hand. It seemed heavier than what she had deduced from images in photographs.

"It was mine when I served with the Spetsnaz. It brought me luck on the missions that were particularly precarious."

An ill-omened shiver ran down her spine. The associations with the distant savagery of the Spetsnaz and KGB actions made her re-evaluate the truthfulness of the source and the extant circumstances in which she now found herself. The image of Suzette being wounded in Metz flashed before her. Her heart rate increased. Her palms moistened. Like Olivia, she too had married too young, too inexperienced, too naïve. Like Uri, she too held feelings for her ex notwithstanding the rancorous motivation behind their own spiteful separation and ultimate divorce. She reluctantly agreed to give the pin to Olivia. In her pocket, she detected the balance of its spirit, the power of myth like imbued Celtic amulets given amid Druid mantras.

"It is imperative that you contact me if any of these students fail to attend class, specifically the one you suspect as being Russian. Your next lobster and Chardonnay dinner will depend on it," she quipped devoid of overt humour. "Any questions?" Her presence reminded him of a Mujahideen guerrilla fighter psychologically committed to lethal combat akin to Japanese Second World War kamikaze pilots. Every culture recruited them, entranced them, and employed them like programmed robots to their political purposes.

He shook his head and smiled guardedly. It was neither the light-hearted court jester nor the passionate lover who continued to control the conversation. Instead, he found himself standing toe-to-toe with a potential predator that would leave him with battle scars on his face akin to Viktor Titov. Behind her chameleon façade was a non-debatable ultimatum as a final reminder of her rapt communiqué.

Uri debated whether he should just report the facts in response to her explicit questions or elaborate in greater detail regarding what he perceived to be relevant tangential information that would allow her to interpret the facts in context. The resulting analysis would, no doubt, alter the progression of her investigation. Whether she might change course, as a result, he would not speculate.

Alternately, he could take the initiative to research within realms she might not be aware of. How would she interpret the truth, the whole truth and nothing but the truth? But honesty by whose standards. That was cultural. And then there were some facts as he perceived them to be yet had not divulged even to Olivia during their brief marriage. They may be of interest to Yvonne but they were too private, too disturbing to share. Ghosts too frightening even for a battle-hardened member of the Spetsnaz to expose. He would take them to his grave as he would contemplations of what might have been the essence of a lobster and Chardonnay dinner.

He would not regret the outcome of such a gastronomic rendezvous nor fanciful nostalgic recollections thereafter. Instead, every day he repeatedly stared down at Viktor Titov's bloodied face in Afghanistan. On those occasions when nightmares would impair his ability to enter into deep REM sleep, he would take control of his kidnapped mind by replacing the violent illusions of vicious war with serene images of what might have been. He would forever love Olivia for the too few intimate moments that brought peacefulness to his troubled soul. But he could not reciprocate the love because of who he had become. He had thought about reconciliation several times since meeting in the hotel room only weeks before. Yet, he knew it could not occur any more than resealing the metal box with the Makarov PB pistol and Cyrillic scripted documents like Pandora's box with its infestations. Instead, he wished her all God's graces and happiness with Stan.

He again stared at Yvonne. He surmised that she too had experienced the violence of conflict perhaps not to the extreme of enemy hand-to-hand combat on a battlefield in Afghanistan. Regardless, she too was possessed with a traumatized soul forever doomed like the lost tribes of Israel to endless pursuit of harmony perhaps never to be found. Together, they might find a sense of common tranquillity if only fleeting. Even episodic periods of respite found in the tentative endearing embrace of another is sufficient to re-energize a sense of solace that sanctions subsequent steps forward.

CHAPTER 38

"Are you Ernst Gerard Wagner?"

"I could be."

"Are you the owner of a farm on Hammonds Plains Road, Halifax County, Nova Scotia?"

"Who wants to know?"

"I am Donald Munroe, Canadian Security Intelligence Service."

His cheek twitched. His face flushed. His eyes squinted as he examined the identification credentials presented by a tall muscular man whose physique resembled that of a linebacker for the Toronto Argonauts. Behind him stood two uniformed police officers of similar stature. Parked on the street in front of his house were two marked police vehicles and one blue unmarked car Ernst didn't recognize as being common in this otherwise quiet suburban bedroom neighbourhood. He scanned the front yard for a second pair of uniformed officers. There was none in sight. He assumed that they were in his backyard, one positioned at each corner of the house away from the line of sight or line of fire from any window. There were no pedestrians on the sidewalk or children playing in the yards. Vehicle traffic was conspicuously absent. These variances from the neighbourhood norm made him feel increasingly uneasy. His response to their question was as terse as his first answer.

"Why do you want to know?"

"We would like your permission to search your farmhouse in Nova Scotia and your current residence here in Toronto."

"Not without a search warrant."

The CSIS agent slid his identification into the inside left breast pocket of his jacket and retrieved a series of folded pages from his right pocket. "I have a warrant for your arrest, a search warrant for this premises, and a search warrant for the farmhouse in Halifax County, Nova Scotia, in addition to all other buildings and structures on that property. Ernst Gerard Wagner, you are under arrest. Turn around and place your hands behind your back."

He hesitated, weighing his choices, his clenched fists held out of sight behind his back. He heard a shuffling of feet behind him. He swivelled his head slightly to the left and right, and noticed from a peripheral view two uniformed police officers approaching up his hallway on either side of him. Escape via his backyard was now not an option. His neutral smile slipped to a frown as truncated thoughts raced through his mind merging into muted phrases of frustration. He left the interpretation hanging.

"You only want to consider one option. Don't be foolish," Munroe said bluntly.

Ernst slowly turned and felt the steely grip of the handcuffs being placed on his wrists by the two uniformed officers now directly behind him. One officer read him his rights. He suppressed a shiver that started to descend the length of his spine but was halted only by fortitude.

At the police station, he was put into an interrogation room. A uniformed officer stood outside the door. The CSIS agent who arrested him was joined by one other person dressed in plainclothes who entered the room with a thick file under her arm. She identified herself as a CSIS agent and again warned him of his rights.

"You purchased the farm on Hammonds Plains Road on 15 August 1986 at a tax sale. Is that correct?"

Ernst nodded reluctantly with a flicker of annoyance, then admitted ownership. "Yes, it was a good price because the previous proprietor had supposedly defaulted on their property taxes. I remember because I travelled to Vancouver that summer to attend Expo 86."

Donald Munroe stated emphatically, "CSIS agents and

uniformed RCMP officers are currently searching the farmhouse and outer buildings on your property in Nova Scotia. Other Toronto police officers are also searching the house here in Toronto where you were arrested. Is there anything you want to tell us?"

Wagner hesitated. He mulled over viable options. There was only one.

"I'm sensing that you want to talk to us," agent Munroe said in a calm convincing voice.

With tranquil civility in his demeanour and practiced conviction in his tone, Ernst replied as if engaging in a conversation of diplomatic etiquette, all in an effort to abate any paranoia of being a spy and delaying the guillotine: "I want to make a deal."

"I can't promise you anything," Munroe replied objectively.

"I understand that," Wagner responded all the while maintaining his neutral stance. "But I can save you time and help you find what you are looking for. With the CSIS involved, I conclude that I haven't been arrested for not paying outstanding parking tickets." He took a deep breath and lowered his head. After a lengthy gap in which no one said anything, he uttered in a resigned voice, "I'm tired of playing games."

"What kind of a games?"

His response was instantaneous. "I'm a paid informant for the Russian KGB, now FSB, and have been since just before I bought the farm. They loaned me the money. They also paid my flight and accommodation to Vancouver when I visited Expo 86. In return, I do things for them. You probably know that I am the Head of Procurement for Department of National Defence contracts. I am told by my KGB handler what to approve. The contracts are awarded once I give the green light. I then receive regular envelopes with cash. I can give you a list of who these people are."

"You seem to have advanced quickly in the Public Service," Munroe suggested.

"Yes. They told me what positions to apply for. I did and was quickly promoted up the ladder. I am now referred to as an SME, a subject-matter expert. I sit on hiring boards. Like the contracts, they tell me who to recommend to hire. There are others on the panel like me so the anointed applicants are guaranteed to be hired. These people also advance rapidly through the bureaucracy to executive levels of director, a few to assistant deputy minister. Occasionally, I sit on promotion boards for other government departments and agencies. There I recognize some familiar faces of other panel members. It's all a charade for the appearance of non-bias or non-prejudiced hiring and promotional decisions. You would be shocked at the number of government employees who are on the Moscow payroll like me. I can give you a list of who these people are."

"Who is your handler?"

"I call him Jean Paul. No last name. The one before was also called Jean Paul as was the one before that also. Again, no last name."

"Where do you meet?" Munroe pressed.

"Different locations, mostly in and around the greater Toronto area. Sometimes we meet in other communities like Peterborough or Barrie, always at a coffee shop. From there we walk and talk."

"When do these meetings take place?"

"No set times. Not like government meetings when you meet once a week whether you need to or not. I receive a letter, sometimes a text, with the date, time and place of the rendezvous. If it isn't Jean Paul, the person I am to meet with always carries a backpack with a Tour de France logo stitched on the right side. To confirm, I ask if they have raced. They will reply that they have not but always dreamed about racing."

Munroe kept the pace of questions. "You said that you can save us time."

"On the farm in Hammonds Plains, there is a derelict windmill behind the farmhouse. On the north side, you will find a shallow unmarked depression. It is a grave. I don't know who is buried there. I'm thinking more than one person because they, my contacts, once spoke in the plural, bodies. The windmill also serves as a communication tower with a camouflaged antenna secured to the top."

"What else?"

"There is a door behind the wood furnace in the basement of the farmhouse. Inside you will find a private armoury of select small arms in addition to cell phones and other high-tech communication devices. The only constant in my schedule is when I am told to take my holidays and travel to the farm. I have no problem getting away because the person I report to is also on the Moscow payroll. That way, it is always a job-related work assignment, not an actual holiday. I never have to use my annual vacation so there is no audit trail of time away from work. Different people come and go at the farm. They don't bother me and vice versa. Occasionally, I pick up people who come ashore in small inflatable watercraft. They disembark from a surface vessel just outside the mouth of Saint Margaret's Bay. A few times over the years, submarines have dropped off and picked up my passengers. I ferry them out and row back. The rendezvous is always late at night and I have to follow a set routine. Apparently, there is a GPS location where, for whatever reason, there is an almost dead spot for radar and sonar."

"And your house here in Toronto?"

"You will find a bookshelf beside the flat-screen TV in the basement suite. It swings out exposing a hidden shelf which contains numerous identification papers – passports and driver's licences and the like. I receive instructions telling me when and where to make the deliveries. New replacement documents are sent to me via Canada Post and by courier on occasion."

"I know you said that you didn't want to play the game anymore and you wanted to make a deal. Think about the option of working with us, being a double agent. You don't have to decide right now. Just think about it. We will talk again after lunch at which time I'd like to show you some photographs. I'd be interested to see if you can recognize your contact, Jean Paul or others."

※ ※

"SUZETTE," DONALD MUNROE INTRODUCED HIMSELF, surprised by the clarity of the encrypted cell phone reception. "You were correct. Ernst Gerard Wagner is a paid FSB informant who wants out. He may accept our offer to be a double agent. More importantly, he talked about his network and the extent to which informants are quickly promoted in government to influential positions."

Munroe told Suzette about the shallow grave in the shadow of the windmill, the storage room behind the furnace, and the intelligence regarding the pickup and delivery point for individuals coming ashore and departing from the mouth of St. Margaret's Bay. He also listed off preliminary names that Ernst Gerard Wagner had verbally provided of those whose careers in the federal government he had helped start.

Suzette lingered in the moment before asking, "Do you believe him, all of what he told you, the ghosts of the imagined Trotskyites and the communists nirvana of Homo Sovieticus?"

"No doubt he was lying and telling the truth, more than likely both at the same time in order to position himself to take tactical advantage from first contact with the enemy. Yet, every spurious detail he provided compounded the lie and negatively impacted the opportunities for détente. It was all an avid reminder of the chilliest days of the Cold War. As you are aware, the trickiest aspect of a lie is maintaining that lie. I am confident we will gain additional intelligence at subsequent interviews. At this juncture, I am unsure if he wants out of the spy game completely or wants to play both sides for purposes of confirming personal tactical advantage. If his underlying intent is to reduce his stress level, he is going about it the wrong way. Playing both sides invariably deals you aces and eights – the dead man's hand purported to have been held by Wild Bill Hickok before he was shot dead in a saloon in Deadwood, Dakota Territory. Based on what we already know, I would surmise that most of what he said contained an element of truth. In summary, he is a survivor from the swamp who has learned to take meticulous steps to cover his tracks and not step on the tail of another venomous serpent. He is also shrewd enough to make himself appear indispensable if push comes to shove."

"Thanks for this and thank you very much for briefing me first," Suzette replied with sincere gratitude. "I am reminded that black and white of truths in our tradecraft are dwarfed by countless shades of grey. *La nuit tous les chats sont gris* – at night all cats are grey."

With a sense of sadness and betrayal in his tone, Munroe said, "Not a problem. You hear about these things, and read about them in spy novels…" He lingered. "In retrospect, I suppose it was always inevitable. You were correct, Wagner confirmed the identity of two senior members of the CSIS who were KGB agents, now FSB. Suzette's immediate superior being one. He also identified one retired CSIS member who has since died. "Neither my partner nor I know who to trust. For now, only the three of us are aware in addition to Wagner and I'd like to leave it that way until we can figure out our next steps. I don't know how long we can keep this from prying eyes and ears, though. Ironically, the more good guys who know, the greater our chances are of staying alive and healthy. Next to you, Suzette, I just have one friend of a friend who will understand the *gravitas* – the seriousness of the geopolitical ramifications and the personal threat of just being aware of these details."

As they spoke, Suzette scanned the cross-referenced names with the short list of individuals Olivia and Stan had passed on to her. Others were a match, validating their veracity. "Good idea to keep it between us for now. I have a list of other names, many senior bureaucrats in Ottawa and Toronto, in addition to a few in Montréal. I should be back in Ottawa shortly. We can talk face-to-face in greater detail then. In the interim, I have mailed an encrypted copy to cottage country. There will be other names coming. I have no doubt they will match those which Wagner has provided. Take care."

"And the same to you," Munroe replied. "Play safe in the sand box."

Suzette thought twice about identifying Yvonne as her source in the cottage country correspondence. Ultimately, she decided against it in loyalty to Yvonne. Loyalty was everything. She had withheld too much from her already and was acutely aware that their relationship was under considerable stress as a result. That decision weighed heavily on her already anxious mind and aching body, causing her to experience more flashbacks and nightmares that even the best double malt scotch directly from the bottle could not suppress. It felt like yet another low-pressure system had descended.

CHAPTER 39

Police roadblocks were initially set up to check all vehicles on Hammonds Plains Road. Records were kept of licence plate numbers, names of drivers and any occupants. Residents became conscious of an increased police presence in the region between Bedford and French Village. Opaque curtains had been erected around the windmill and other locations on the property close to and at a distance from the Hammonds Plains Road, all within clear sight of those driving along the gravel road running adjacent to the farm. Most were a ruse merely to draw the attention of curious onlookers, some of whom were non-residents.

The Upper Tantallon Detachment had been set up not only as the command center for the operation but also as the temporary safe haven for Olivia and Stan. The shift commanders had been advised to brief the patrol officers to spread the word that former members of the RCMP appeared to be central to the amplified activities. These unidentified previous members of the Force had served in Bedford Detachment in 1978. The patrol officers were also advised to let it be known to anyone who enquired that there were agents from the Canadian Security Intelligence Service milling around.

The Force's public relations spokesperson replied to questions from the media with a scripted news release. They could neither confirm nor deny that the CSIS was involved directly or indirectly because the investigation was ongoing. This non-disclosure accomplished its purpose – to heighten speculation that new evidence had come to light regarding an old cold case.

"They found the shallow unmarked grave north of the windmill," the Detachment Commander advised his guests. "The skeletal remains of three bodies have been exhumed. The coroner on scene has indicated that two are male adults. The third is a female, also adult. The remains are being transported to the coroner's lab in Halifax for detailed examination. A .303 calibre Lee Enfield bolt-action magazine-fed repeating rifle has also been recovered from the gravesite."

The on-scene Identification Services technician arrived at the Upper Tantallon Detachment within half an hour.

"What's the serial number on the rifle?" Olivia asked.

The technician carefully rotated the rifle exposing all metal parts with markings including the stock.

Olivia compared e-copies of the photos of the rifle that she had taken in the barn on the morning of 5 November 1978.

"The rifle in your photos and this recovered weapon appear to be identical," the technician advised.

"I would agree," Stan confirmed.

"And who are you to say so?" the technician confronted Stan abruptly.

"I served with Ident Services and Crime Scene Analysis for about ten years," Stan replied. "Prior to that, this lady and I were the first officers on-scene at the farm when the shooting was reported. We know more about this case than anyone alive today." He gazed over at Olivia. "And we plan on maintaining our alive and healthy status."

"Sorry, sir. No offence intended," the technician back-tracked. "Can I help you with anything else? I took photos of the shallow grave, the remains of the three skeletal bodies, in addition to the Lee Enfield rifle. I can show them to you if you think they might help."

"Thanks for your kind offer. Perhaps later." Stan produced a thumb drive from his pocket. "There are some photos of latent prints on this drive. It would be interesting to compare them with any that might be on the rifle you recently seized in the shallow grave."

"We could dust now if you believe it might be of assistance. I'd be honoured to work with you. As you will understand, I'd have to do all the lifting of prints. You cannot touch any of the physical evidence."

Stan nodded. The last thing he wanted would be to be summoned back from anonymity to attend a hearing or a trial, although the latter would be highly unlikely given the lapse of time and the absence of any suspects.

After dusting the rifle and lifting the prints, the technician stared at Stan with a gratified smile. "I believe we have a match."

Stan examined the results. "I would agree."

"Who do they belong to?" the technician asked.

"That remains a mystery. When I last checked the database, there was no record." Stan didn't reveal when or how he had gained access to the Integrated Automated Fingerprint Identification System. "Over to you to determine the rightful owner."

"I can search now if you have time?"

"I would be obliged," Stan replied. "I'm aware of two possible matches, Sylvia Hackett a.k.a. Lada, and John Robert Hackett a.k.a. Nikolai a.k.a. Nazi SS Lieutenant Colonel Brandt Felix Schmidt. Both Lada and Nikolai are believed to be, believed to have been, partners of a Soviet sleeper cell in November 1978. They may also be two of the three bodies found in this grave at the base of the windmill."

The technician raised his eyebrows on hearing the two East European names and that of a Nazi SS officer. The mention of the names also drew the immediate attention of Suzette who had been standing in the background along with Yvonne.

Stan was not surprised when the technician advised that his attempt to access IAFIS had been denied. "Should the Ident technician need assistance gaining access to either the Canadian or the International fingerprint databases, maybe you could grease the wheels," Stan suggested, transferring his gaze to Suzette who immediately tapped in a text message.

Suzette suggested to the technician, "Come with me and bring your exhibit so you don't lose continuity. We don't want to screw this case up after all these years." She then transferred her gaze to Stan. "Have a coffee. It might take a while, especially if we have to go international."

The Detachment Commander interrupted. "I've been asked to escort you both to the farm. Your knowledge might assist the on-scene search commander in determining where the teams might focus their efforts."

Stan looked at Yvonne for advice.

She slowly nodded, agreeing with the request. Her response was guarded though.

"Constable Evans will be your chauffeur. He's our most experienced highway patrol officer. We will assign a second officer to ride shotgun. It's not far, only a fifteen- or twenty-minute drive." The Detachment Commander regretted his expression as soon as the words had left his lips. Ride shotgun had a sinister implication under the circumstances. He realized it was just the lingo of the vocation. Both his guests would understand. He knew better, though. Familiarity breeds permissiveness.

Olivia and Stan took a moment to re-orient themselves with the farm and the barn where they had discovered John Robert Hackett a.k.a. Nikolai lying on the ground gasping in pain as blood oozed from his gut. The scene seemed familiar yet alien, their recollections recent yet distant. Both slowly inhaled with equally deep breaths before again making eye contact.

Olivia scanned with a 360-degree perspective as her camera lens had done all those years ago, her memory a silent presence.

Any traces of blood would have disappeared over the years yet she could see in her mind the crimson red stain as if it were 11:57 a.m. on 5 November 1978. She heard his final gasps, the words garbled with the blood that had gurgled up into his throat.

She vividly recalled Stan's caveat that there was something untoward underfoot and that she needed to keep her distance from Leblanc for fear of ending up like Hackett. And his warning again as she took the photographs inside the barn, to hide her camera when Corporal Werner Hartmann, the Security Service agent, pulled into the farmyard. How true his premonition had been! She eyed Stan with the same sense of foreboding she had experienced on 5 November 1978. At this moment, his close proximity was reassuring. She found herself purposely leaning against him. She said nothing. Her eyes spoke volumes.

Sadness overcame Stan as he recalled Mike Davidson pulling up in his sparkling clean highway patrol cruiser. He had asked him in a jocular tone if it was a slow day at the office for highway patrol. Then the secret squirrel arrived. Farmyard dust swirled from the wheel wells. His throat became dry. He could smell the acrid air as vividly today as it had been on that fateful morning in 1978. The secret squirrel directed him and Olivia to report to their Detachment Commander. Little did they know that their destinies had been sealed through association. Today, Olivia and Stan were the last two standing. Were there others? Could they break the curse?

"Cancel Ident and GIS," Leblanc's voice had crackled over the radio. All the events came flooding back in full detail for both. They had obediently followed orders to attend the scene on 5 November 1978. It was their choice to be present today with all the rawness of reactions and sensations of Athenian actors in this modern-day drama. He sensed her closeness and returned the physical contact and its inherent communiqué.

"I don't want to seem presumptuous," Olivia said to the on-scene search commander. She stoically viewed the e-pics of the black and white photos she had clandestinely taken all those years before, their edges now frayed with age. She described in detail the scene as she had found it. She was surprised that the physical structure of the barn and them now being in the barn, were having such a profound impact on her. It was as if nothing had been altered since that fateful day. Perhaps it hadn't. Perhaps Lada and Ruslan had walked out and never returned. Perhaps Lada had been prevented from returning because Ruslan had murdered her sometime afterwards and buried her in the shallow grave with her husband, in the shadow of the windmill. It was as if John Robert Hackett was repeating his final words to her. "She did it. Inside the metal box; 321 degrees. Zhena Tovarishch."

Olivia's father's voice resonated with equal clarity: *Remember, remember, / The fifth of November, / The Gunpowder treason and plot; / I know of no reason / Why the Gunpowder treason / Should ever be forgot!* She had not forgotten, nor would she. She was good at remembering and keeping secrets about secrets.

"I didn't know there were any photos taken at the scene. Can you send copies to me?" the on-scene search commander said.

Olivia replied in a bland voice as if from a distant place. "Will do once we return to the detachment and I get internet access." Was she gaping into an abyss from the edge of a precipice?

Stan described the scene at the farmyard, pointing out the foundation outline of the now destroyed fox barn and recounting what he considered to be the peculiar circumstances of its existence and ultimate demise.

Stan and Olivia scanned the property holding their focus on the fence line where they had dug up the metal box and first gazed in awe at the contents – the Russian Makarov PB pistol and silencer wrapped in the burlap sack, and the documents written in Cyrillic text.

The on-scene commander noted their hesitation, their eyes pirouetting in elliptical patterns. "Something jogging your memory?" he enquired.

"Something," Olivia responded with a worried stare. "Perhaps not. It's only been a few years," she chuckled with a tentative smile. "Time plays tricks on your memory." She transferred her hesitant gaze to Stan seeking concurrence in continuity.

"To err on the side of caution, you may want to search the fence line. I seem to recall something but can't recollect specifics," Stan commented as he scratched his balding head. In the distance, stood the outline of a dilapidated building.

"Thank you," the on-scene commander replied. "I'll dispatch a team to search."

"One last point," Stan said. "The remains of one of the male bodies may be that of a drug section corporal who was reported missing on or about 5 November 1978. I seem to recall the burned remains of his unmarked patrol car being found in a gravel pit close by. Not certain where the gravel pit is but it should be on a local map circa 1978. Notation of it would be in the investigation file if it remains in the archives."

The search commander stood stunned by this revelation.

Olivia grabbed Stan's hand with the same gorilla grip that John Robert Hackett had grabbed her, as an image of the Security Service agent jolted her memory like a bolt of lightning. That day, 5 November 1978, his arrogant words: "Report to your Detachment Commander." Today, the words caused her to focus on his image as he had turned his head toward the barn. She recalled it in vivid detail and for the first time in all these years. Now she remembered it, recognized it, the distinctive white flick of hair over a birth mark just behind his left ear. It was the same distinguishing mark on the left side of the head of the man recorded on Bernie's CCTV camera at the back door of the ranch house. It was Werner Hartmann in both. She needed to contact Bernie immediately, inform him, warn him.

Being back in the farmyard triggered Olivia to also recall Stan's words of wisdom he had spoken when they were ordered to turn over the crime scene at the farm to Corporal Hartmann. Today, she leaned against him and whispered the words back to him: "'Rest assured, the day of reckoning will come, it just won't be today, nor will it be tomorrow.' On 5 November 1978, your voice brought with it a sense of tentative comfort and security for me as it does again now. I sense that day of reckoning is close," she whispered again.

Stan nodded slowly. "I agree, that day of reckoning is close. With that sense of comfort also comes a heightening need to remain vigilant, partner."

By the time they had arrived back at the Upper Tantallon Detachment, Yvonne had returned from her meeting with Uri. More pressing, Suzette had been granted authority to access the previously denied fingerprint details. "Like the Ident technician, I must remind the two of you of the top-secret status of the results," Suzette emphasized. She remained close by as the technician provided the details.

"There were three sets of prints on the Lee Enfield .303 rifle. The first belonged to Sylvia Hackett a.k.a. Lada, a Soviet sleeper-cell agent, reported missing and presumed but not confirmed deceased. The second set belonged to a Soviet spy identified only by the code name Ruslan, and presumed but not confirmed deceased. His full identity has been removed completely, not just censored. A third fingerprint could not be matched. They had been smudged as if the individual had been wearing gloves. The prints that you provided on the thumb drive are those of John Robert Hackett a.k.a. Nikolai a.k.a. Nazi SS Lieutenant Colonel Brandt Felix Schmidt."

Olivia and Stan relaxed after this revelation that confirmed their initial trepidation, that something untoward was underfoot. John Robert Hackett's prints were not on the rifle, proving he had not committed suicide, not that there was any doubt in Olivia's mind. If the Russian Makarov PB pistol had been the pistol used to murder Pierre Laporte at the height of the FLQ Crisis, and only Hackett's prints were found, there was no doubt in their minds that John Robert Hackett a.k.a. Nikolai had pulled the trigger on the fateful day in Montréal in October 1970.

"Thanks," Olivia replied. "It corroborates what we had suspected all along. Excuse me, I just need to send one email." She stepped away from Yvonne and Suzette.

Bernie immediately confirmed receipt of her message identifying Werner Hartmann as the mysterious intruder caught on CCTV on the porch of his ranch house overlooking the Northumberland Straits. His reply was terse, "Thank you very much. You have saved me a great deal of research time."

The on-scene commander acknowledged receipt of the e-copies of the original black and white photographs surreptitiously taken by Olivia on 5 November 1978.

Yvonne stared at them blankly. "I guess that news provides you with some sense of solace. But not so much for constables Davidson and Hamilton."

"I've been asked to bring you both back to our office in Halifax," Suzette noted matter-of-factly. "No non-domestic fish seem to have demonstrated interest in nibbling at our bait, at least not yet. We will resume tomorrow. In the interim, traffic on Hammonds Plains Road will continue to be checked."

"I'll ride with Suzette in one car while your chauffeur drives you in the highway patrol chariot of fire," Yvonne stated more in the form of a directive that was to be obeyed without any room for debate.

Olivia stealthily slid her hand over to touch Stan's that hung by his side. He turned his head slightly toward her and searched for a reason why she was wanting to communicate. Had their return to the murder scene in the barn and the farmyard heightened her level of concern? Her déjà vu? Was there another reason? He curled his baby finger around hers. She reciprocated with a firmer grip. Stan concluded that if they were going to work together as TOFIS sleuths on future cases, they would have to work out a better way of communicating their respective concerns. For now, he would discretely whisper to her when in the semi-privacy of the back seat of the highway patrol cruiser.

Olivia cast a glance at Yvonne who nodded back reassuringly. All the while, Suzette maintained her reserved peripheral presence. It wasn't so much that Olivia distrusted Suzette. It was more that she didn't fully trust her, there was no history of earned loyalty. Olivia felt a closer tie to Digger and was confident that Digger felt the same way. It didn't have to be to the extent of Greyfriars Bobby in Edinburgh, Scotland, almost one hundred years earlier to its master although she was certain that both Digger and Bernie would lament that loss of the other with equal saddened emotion. There was a subtle distinct difference. Yet something else was gnawing at her, something related to both Digger and Bernie.

The *je ne sais quoi* was a shroud that held more secrets than Olivia carried. And then the portentous echo of her father: *Remember, remember, / The fifth of November, / The Gunpowder treason and plot; / I know of no reason / Why the Gunpowder treason / Should ever be forgot!* The familiar ill-omened shiver ran the length of her spine.

"I've already brought Bernie up to speed," Yvonne added. Her pronouncement seemed almost out of place, given the current context.

As have I just now, Olivia recognized.

Stan and Olivia exchanged glances each with a barely notable tic of a nod. They needed to speak with Yvonne privately about their reservations regarding Suzette and the revelation of Werner Hartmann as the mysterious intruder caught on Bernie's CCTV cameras. Had Bernie responded to Yvonne's request for additional information concerning the one name on the list, whoever it was?

CHAPTER 40

"We are being followed," Constable Evans announced as he monitored the manoeuvres of a black SUV in his rear-view mirror. He flashed his headlights to get Suzette's attention. As she braked twice to confirm, the SUV pulled alongside and crashed into the left side of the unmarked highway patrol cruiser in an attempt to knock it off the road. The SUV then pulled in behind. Simultaneously, the driver of the SUV fired a series of bullets striking the left side of the rear window and the trunk.

Evans slammed the accelerator to the floor and shot past Suzette, forcing on-coming traffic to swerve off the road and into the ditch. The SUV followed suit close on his tail ramming into the rear of Suzette's vehicle temporarily forcing it off the road. A second SUV of similar description sped past her. Evans ran the traffic light turning hard right onto the Bedford Highway accelerating south parallel to the shore of the Bedford Basin. He radioed his position and direction, and called for backup. Intersecting traffic driving north crashed as the drivers steered to avoid the trio. A marked police cruiser pulled into fourth position in the race, and then another marked cruiser into fifth. Suzette had recovered and was following at a distant sixth but closing in at a rapid rate.

"Hold on tight," Evans barked at Olivia and Stan as he negotiated a sharp right hair-pin turn up Lodge Drive. A car exiting Lodge Drive was struck by the first SUV causing it to spin 150 degrees out of control. The SUV then accelerated up the hill in pursuit of the unmarked highway patrol car. Smoke rolled off all tires. Dust from loose dirt on the shoulder rose like a dense smog obscuring a clear line of sight. The second pursuing SUV overshot, barely negotiating the turn. A car approaching from the north cut across oncoming traffic, forcing a transport to jackknife and careen off the highway through the safety rail down the slope and onto the railroad tracks close to Prince's Lodge.

"You know where you are going?" Stan asked in a loud voice.

"We had worked out some counter manoeuvres in the event of such a situation. We seem to have lost your friends though, but not to worry, we have other sufficient resources."

Olivia rapidly read the text message from Bernie: "Your tracking device is jammed – suspect a second device interfering."

Stan turned quickly to look through the rear window. "Not to worry?" he questioned their chauffeur's confidence. His heart sank as he saw two black SUVs bearing down on them, blue and red lights flashing close behind this duo.

Evans swerved left off Lodge Drive and then quickly right onto Kent Avenue. In less than a minute, he slammed on the brakes as the road ended at the parking lot for the Prince's Lodge's Heart-Shaped Pond. Other marked and unmarked police cars converged out of adjacent driveways from all directions. Officers exited with weapons drawn. *A perfect pincer movement,* Evans smiled crookedly. *Well, almost perfect. Just lost the ladies. Another slow day on highway patrol*, he chuckled to himself.

"Follow me," Evans yelled at Olivia and Stan. They ran from the parking lot along the south path bordering the pond.

"OLI, *DOWN!*"

Olivia turned to see Uri motioning her with both hands signalling her to drop down to the ground. She immediately fell, Stan beside her.

Out of the corner of his eye, Uri noticed Viktor Titov duck to the ground in a similar manoeuvre. Uri rose awkwardly from his knees amid a hail of bullets and bolted toward Olivia but fell in front of Viktor.

Viktor stared up squinting at Uri curiously while wiping a widening trail of blood that had leached from a crease wound along his forehead into his left eye and down along the scar on his cheek. "Do I know you?" he asked Uri as if he was only an apparition.

"Afghanistan, 1979. I saved your sorry ass during the Mujahideen mortar attack. You got that scar on your face then."

Viktor recalled with terrifying clarity, assuming that Uri was a Russian military colleague from that ill-fated political mission. "Help me again and I will reward you," he pleaded, his voice trembling as if he were a condemned man already standing on the gallows with a noose tightening around his neck, yet demanding clemency for time to appeal his death sentence.

"We make decisions that we live to regret. I will not make such a decision once more," Uri replied. "Ask yourself, Viktor, what is the use of position and false status in such times as you now find yourself. *Pas de grâce.*"

Courage often rests in the artificial wisdom and corrupt acclaim of KGB legend rather than individual actions, Uri mused as he glared down at Viktor's agitated stare that mirrored his pathetic begging. He had survived by moral cowardice, not courage, an attribute that Uri found repugnant.

Viktor searched Uri's expression apprehensively, his eyes frantically seeking redemption, atonement for past transgressions, yet finding only the frown of an unforgiving inquisitor.

A second silent shot struck the left side of Viktor's head. The splatter of blood was muffled. His cold black eyes bulged outward from the concussion of a bullet as it passed through his temple severing the optic nerves and crushing other frontal lobe grey matter. The clarion call of imagined Trotskyites was no longer a taunting quest.

Two shots, double tap, passed through Uri's back, one penetrating his heart. The force of these bullets propelled him flat to the ground beside his nemesis. He would never again be plagued by nightmares of Afghanistan and the Mujahideen.

Police emergency response team members advanced with weapons at the aim to the approximate position of the shooter. The occupants of the two pursuing black SUVs lay face down on the ground in custody. The sound of ambulance sirens became increasingly louder.

Stan gently held Olivia in his arms, her motionless body faintly sensing the cadence of his breath and his own pulse. Nothing could be said, needed to be said. They had been singularly present with each other since the first moment they met in Bedford all those years ago, rekindled in the nearness of the moment when they met again in the Air Canada Maple Leaf Lounge in the Toronto Pearson international airport only weeks ago, and now reaffirmed in the eternity of the ongoing throes of lethal confrontation between East and West.

She gazed up at him through glazed eyes, lingering, then lessening. Her shadowy smile fleeting, her feeble gesture waning. The lucidity of her intention faint and fading.

Suzette braked. Their car slid to a stop alongside the congestion of police vehicles adjacent to the parking lot. She and Yvonne wove and ducked their way alongside the path, taking cover behind boulders and trees – Yvonne clutching a pistol tight to her thigh.

Moments later, Yvonne stared down at Stan holding Olivia's motionless body in his arms. The acrid stench of gunpowder and accompanying scent of death lingered. Her heart dropped, her chest sank, her breath immobilized at the sight of Olivia's blood-stained blouse and ashen complexion.

Suzette gazed in the direction of the advancing Emergency Response Team members. Their combat camouflage for once blended into the forested environment whereas in urban settings it stood out like advertisement billboards illuminated with neon lights on steroids. One of the officers was kneeling alongside the immobile bodies of Viktor and Uri. Suzette froze as numbing nightmares of Metz flooded her mind.

CHAPTER 41

"You set them up," Yvonne yelled at Suzette with spite. "The list of names was supposed to have been the bait, not them."

Suzette stood with a blank expression manifested by conscious omission.

"I've never known you to behave without integrity, unable to adhere to moral standards. I guess that there is always a first for you." Yvonne hesitated gasping for a calm breath where there was none. It didn't come easily. "And a first for me to so terribly misjudge intent from anyone, especially you." Her glare left no doubt in Suzette's mind regarding what had been but would never again be a resolute relationship.

"It wasn't supposed to have gone down that way," Suzette replied as exasperated as her former partner at the confusion and carnage that confronted them. "There must have been a leak that we didn't know about, hadn't plugged."

Yvonne glared, dumbfounded, paralyzed by the revelation that Suzette had not been completely honest with her, a labyrinth of lies, a maze of mistruths, obscured in the mist of time. She stared down at Olivia's motionless body cradled in Stan's arms as he gently rocked back and forth.

"As I mentioned, we knew that Viktor Titov had flown from Ottawa to Halifax. Here he met with one of his associates. That person passed through the police checkpoints on Hammonds Plains Road. So, we knew that Viktor had taken the bait, he was aware of the names on the list that you had provided to me. We also let it be known through one of our own informants that the safehouse where Olivia and Stan were housed was adjacent to the Heart-Shaped

Pond on Kent Road. Perhaps I should have told you – at risk of some unknown surveillance possibility. For that I apologize. Physically, it was a perfect location to complete the pincer manoeuvre to trap them, capture them. And it worked." *Almost*, she lamented.

"I can't believe that you didn't tell me, tell them. They trusted in me, and in you because I introduced them to you. My God, what were you thinking or not thinking? From my perspective, I'd say in any statement that you had a vendetta against Viktor for shooting you in Metz. It was revenge that has cost lives. Here, today, Viktor was shot. Uri was shot. Olivia was shot. To add to the complete screw up, the shooter seems to have miraculously escaped. Gone. Disappeared through your supposed foolproof police net. The only trace of evidence is a Makarov PB pistol with silencer that was found, sullied with blood. We can surmise that when the police returned fire, the shooter was wounded but still managed to escape. It was another Russian-manufactured Makarov pistol. The model PB is the weapon of choice of the former KGB and now FSB, also issued to Russian special forces, the Spetsnaz, Uri's former unit. A variant is the Makarov model PM used by the Chinese. No one seems certain which model this one is."

Suzette replied in as reassuring a voice as she could muster. "For your info, the female student in Uri's class whom he believed was Russian was in fact an FSB agent. Moscow had sent her to follow Uri. Uri was also correct in assessing that the other student was either CIA or CSIS. She was one of ours who was tailing the FSB student. Another was the dark-haired female whom you and Uri had seen at Peggy's Cove. She was wearing a disguise. The FSB student has been picked up and is currently being interrogated."

"Can we conclude that if Moscow had sent the female student in Uri's class to follow him, Uri wasn't working for them?"

"We might conclude that but I wouldn't bet on it," Suzette

replied. "The purpose of her surveillance could have been to ensure compliance on Uri's part and report."

"So how the hell did Uri end up at the Heart Shaped Pond before us?" Yvonne barked. "What was his connection? Was it to Viktor?"

Suzette shrugged her shoulders. "We don't know for certain, at least not yet. There is no intelligence to suggest that Uri was on Moscow's payroll. He had to have had another link, contact, perhaps CIA. I don't know."

Uri had given me his Spetsnaz pin to pass along to Olivia, Yvonne thought to herself. *Had Olivia been shot because she had been purposely or inadvertently tracked? Had I misjudged both Uri and Suzette? Had both co-opted me into their own ill-fated plots? Was it all my fault? How can I now live with myself? How can I face Bernie and Stan? I had been so careful, checking and double checking every detail, every risk assessment for every scenario.* "Where is the God damned leak in your organization?" she challenged Suzette. "It sure the hell isn't with me."

Suzette hung her head. "I just don't know for sure," she replied in a lowering voice. "I have my suspects and their names are on the list you gave me for bait. I don't have the entire list and can fully understand if you don't turn that over to me. And I wouldn't ask you for them under the current circumstances."

"You had mentioned that some of those on the list were in very influential positions and, as a result, could unleash an unholy reign of terror. I conclude that the backlash has begun. Well, lock and load, lady. I don't know about you but I have had a good run. If I'm going down, there will be a litany of treasonous villains in my wake," Yvonne declared in a voice accented with controlled rage.

"I should have retired a few years ago. No loss to me. I understand if you don't trust me, may never trust me again, may never speak to me again. So, I won't ask to become involved any more than I have. If this is to be our last hurrah, I want you to know that I did not betray your trust."

Yvonne continued to glare at her former partner, dumbfounded, devoid of expression beyond tightly clenched jaw muscles. *How could she think, say that she had not betrayed my trust? What had happened between Metz and now?* Slowly, Yvonne shook her head in disgust. Suzette averted her eyes. She failed to meet her stare. Yvonne turned and left her standing alone.

Yvonne's focus was now on Stan, how she could support him. And then Bernie. The three of them had worked together on so many cases since their Watcher Service days, providing steadfast mutual support. The three musketeers, one for all and all for one. Loyalty had no gradations. She forced a shallow breath as the image of Olivia's bloodied body consumed her mind. Tears filled her eyes. She needed time to recover, to prepare for her reunion with Bernie.

She sent him a text in that regard, advising that she had a few outstanding issues to deal with. She would return to the ranch house by noon tomorrow.

Those at all levels in organizations have their own agendas, more so at the highest levels like academic intelligentsia whose reputations have been built on cultural and political influence. Suzette was no different. Her organization was renowned more than most for such less than integral tactics by some within its ranks. Yvonne had played that game while serving with military intelligence. She now gained some semblance of solace from the fact that she no longer had to play in that disingenuous swamp again, though she could not escape its permeating stench.

CHAPTER 42

Yvonne glanced down at a succinct text message from Bernie. It read: 57. She raised her eyes to a half-mast squint in guarded contemplation, and then wide open in committed resolve.

She carefully wended her way through the forest and tree lot to the berm line that added extra seclusion against potential prying eyes. She stepped quietly, stopping every few strides to scan and listen for indicators of alien surveillance or other imminent threat.

Bernie monitored her approach on close-circuit cameras along the berm, into the garage, down the stairs, into the tunnel, up the stairs and into the woodshed adjacent to the kitchen. No one followed. He would not press for further details immediately. They would be revealed in the fullness of time.

A familiar aroma of freshly baked bread and cinnamon buns greeted Yvonne as she entered the kitchen. She smiled in appreciation of his artisan baking abilities but she felt great regret for a less-than-successful mission. Their embrace was warm and full, first collegial then morphing into personal. But where was Digger? She reached down. There was no warm tongue to welcome her, no head to pat as she had done on all those other occasions when she stealthily returned from missions. Her eyes searched the kitchen. His bed by the old wood kitchen stove was empty.

Bernie explained. Tears filled her eyes. "Not to worry. I've done enough crying for both of us. Doctor Simpson called this morning. Digger is recovering well and, as a result, he will be bringing him back home this afternoon. He explained that, like people, animals recover best at home by the hearth and in their own beds."

Yvonne returned his gaze, alert for imminent indicators for the reason behind a 57-alerting text. Her eyes, still tear-filled, continued to dart in a pattern of disciplined scrutiny. She noted nothing of concern.

"All secure on the home front," Bernie assured her. "Digger had scared the perpetrator off. Received another text. The imminent threat has been neutralized. Now, just usual traffic. A couple of our colleagues reported a questionable character had stopped at a café in Oxford. Others of no apparent concern had registered in local hotels. The latter departed early although in what direction the proprietor was unclear. Given what had transpired, it was prudent to raise the level of security to a code 57. All is safe *now*," he reaffirmed. "Let me reiterate, all is secure. Digger will be home shortly." A reassured but still wary smile filled his face.

Yvonne's breathing relaxed. "The name I asked you to research?" she asked.

"He is the most senior contracted bureaucrat with a direct often unfettered link to the Prime Minister's Office and those in the tightest inner circle. You need to gird your loins, don your armour and raise all shields if you plan on engaging with him," Bernie said soberly. "This person wields more power and influence, like a Druid priest in Celtic society, more than all his predecessors combined. Even worse, he has driven a holly stake into the careers of many a rising civil servant while ensuring the mercurial advancement of otherwise unknown protégés. He controls and manipulates them with the ferociousness of a barbed male gauntlet. It is purported that a few others ended up like Leblanc, lobster bait."

Yvonne locked onto his stare, her attentiveness focused. She was steadfast and poised for mortal combat. "It's time to contact an old friend of ours who owes us a favour, big time."

"Moshe?"

Yvonne nodded. "Unless you know someone else, he's the only one I am aware of who can achieve the objective and who is not a member of the Five Eyes. If this got out, Canada's reputation as an

Intelligence partner would disappear through the cellar so deep that hell would seem a mere baby step away. Our economy as we know it would tank and not recover in my grandchildren's lifetime, and I don't have any offspring yet."

She sipped her coffee as Bernie typed in his request. A faint smile extended from the corners of her lips, her brow creased, her stare committed. Her demeanour remained calm and confident.

Now seemed the appropriate time. "How are Stan and Olivia?" Bernie asked with a grave tone.

"As you might expect." She hesitated. Her voice cracking with sorrowful emotion. "Olivia was still in Emergency when I left. Her prognosis remains critical. She had lost a great deal of blood. The attending surgeon was not hopeful. When last I saw Stan, he was attempting to wash her blood from his shirt and hands. The stain will remain for a very long time, its traces and scent forever."

Yvonne dropped her head which muffled her voice as she continued, "He hasn't fully dealt with Betty's death. Now this." She waited a brief moment before summing up. "He remains committed. He is tough. But, he needs time and support."

Bernie reflected as he reviewed his outgoing message, then tapped the send key. He transferred his attention back to Yvonne. "Who was the shooter?"

"We don't know yet. I say yet because whoever it was hasn't been captured. There is a strong possibility he had a Moscow affiliation. More likely another connection. Could be a she. Not sure. There was blood on a Makarov pistol that the police believe was one of the weapons used, but that has yet to be confirmed. Our colleagues are feverously beating the bushes. Their initial findings are perplexing, not directly related to Viktor as a player."

"And Uri?"

"No one seems to know how Uri ended up at the scene ahead of just about everyone else. One source suggests that he had an informant, someone who knew of Viktor's agenda. There are growing indications that there is at least one other agent in the sandbox, an unanticipated intervening variable operating in the intelligence environment either intuitive or counter-intuitive to the Russia card. Your enemy's enemy is your friend. Uri may have tapped into that Asian agent, an ally to some, an enemy to others."

"And the CSIS?" Bernie pressed.

Yvonne inhaled a slow deep breath, again taking time to consolidate her thoughts.

Bernie maintained his stare with a probing yet patient pose.

"Suzette is remaining tight-lipped."

"I'm sensing a confidence issue," Bernie suggested, as much a statement as an enquiry.

"She admitted to not having been completely honest with me. That is the death knell in any trusting relationship let alone this arcane vocation."

"Would you have expected anything different, given her employer?" Bernie asked with a tinge of hesitancy.

"I replayed that record over and over again as I drove back here. Yes. Maybe. No. I don't know. Going into this case, I had complete confidence in her to cover my back, as we did with each other in Metz when she was shot. There I dragged her to safety. Now she failed to reciprocate. She left me in the dark. As a direct result, Olivia is fighting what could be a losing battle for her life."

"Do you think Suzette blames you? Doesn't trust you?"

Yvonne gazed up, weighing the conversations she had shared with Suzette over the years, and most recently. "Not once did she ever give me any indications of that. To the contrary, she repeatedly conveyed to me, not so much in words, that that thought had never crossed her mind, nor would it. Ours was a storied existence of absolute loyalty and proven dedication under fire."

"So, where are you right now?"

"My faith has been cracked. Fractured. Does any amount of confidence less than one hundred percent count? You and Stan and I have that solemn pact. It's a cliché to say the Three Musketeers, all for one and one for all. But that's what it is all about for the three of us."

She and Bernie maintained eye contact as she dwelled on that conclusion.

"What are you thinking?" he pressed.

"Just after the dust settled, I challenged Suzette. She looked away. Just now, you and I maintained eye contact, never looking away. When I spoke with Stan, he and I maintained eye contact even as he held Olivia's limp bloodied body in his arms. That's telling, that's the litmus test. That's all I need to know. Doubt will forever remain between Suzette and me."

"The shooting is being reported to the media as a biker gang drug war," Bernie added. "Two tourists, a male and female innocently caught in the cross fire were also reported as being shot. No mention of deaths."

"Not surprising. The government can't acknowledge that agents of different stripes are scurrying around unencumbered within and outside of government, with impunity gunning down honest law-abiding citizens. That level of honesty would be political suicide. Consider the implications beyond the deception that would connect the Sleepy Hollow of Hammonds Plains to the metropolises of Ottawa, Montréal, Toronto, Moscow, Washington DC, possibly Beijing, and God only knows where else. Add in the international geopolitical ramifications, let alone relationships with the Americans. The longest undefended border would become heavily defended overnight with American military troops augmenting U.S. Border Patrol and U.S. customs agents. Trade could potentially grind to a strangling halt overnight."

"Biker gangs and drug lords are a convenient godsend to

government spin-doctors. They tend not to have public relations professionals to appeal such projections through media outlets. We've known about this unsettled separation of convenience for a long while, and used it for mutual convenience."

A confirming email appeared on Bernie's monitor. 'On my way. Moshe.' He shared the text with Yvonne. An extended quietness filled the space.

Bernie broke the silence when he concluded the time was opportune. "What happened isn't your fault. I know that you think otherwise. We have proven checklists and redundancies in our procedures to account for contingencies. We debrief after all missions and we will do so again once Stan has recovered."

"I know," Yvonne acknowledged after a contemplative moment. "It's just that Suzette was my resource. I sensed there was something off balance with her. There were enough red flags but I didn't follow up immediately. I chalked it up to her day-to-day work stress. I didn't factor in the added impact of post-traumatic stress. I erred in my judgement."

Bernie reached out to her, his smile non-judgemental. He then held her for what seemed to be an extended period of support. As they stood, he quietly whispered a Celtic Druid mantra three times: *'heal, heal; balm, balm; body heal and soul be calm.'* He then recited once: *'So be it.'* Home was where the hearth was and she was home, with him, and soon to be joined by Digger. The family would be complete once again.

Doc Simpson pulled into the farmyard. Bernie met him and helped carry Digger into the kitchen, to his bed. The dog wagged his tail and whimpered softly as his master fondly repeated, "Good boy. Good boy."

"I've given him a sedative because I knew he would be so excited to be home with his family." He bowed acknowledging Yvonne. Digger lay in his bed looking up at Bernie who knelt down and gave him a biscuit from his pocket. Digger left it for later, comforted that he knew it was there. "Here are some pills to help him manage the pain, one every eight hours as needed. Make sure he has drinking water close by."

Later, after dinner, Bernie and Yvonne walked along the trails in the woodlot behind the mechanical barn which protected the old grey F100 farm tractor amongst other machinery. They talked some more and stopped in silence on occasion to embrace as they had done many times before and would do again many more times. Digger waited in the kitchen, not worried that they would not return. He was where he needed to be, doing what he needed to do – protecting his home and his master.

DIGGER WHIMPERED, LOUDLY. BERNIE REACHED over the side of the bed and received a limp lick from a tired tongue. Bernie lifted the covers, stepped onto the floor and reached down to pet him, carefully stopping over the wound. It was warmer than the remainder of his chest. The veterinarian had cautioned Bernie to be conscious of too much heat as a sign of potential infection. He left instructions to call him, day or night, if Bernie was concerned. He sat on the floor beside him monitoring his recovery. After several minutes and a reassuring more determined lick, Digger seemed to fall asleep, his breathing having become less anxious although still not fully normal. The whimpering abated. Bernie remained beside him on the floor monitoring his progress with his hand on his head before crawling back into his own bed.

Approximately fifteen years ago, Bernie had found Digger as an emaciated puppy soaked with seaweed and shivering on a deserted part of the beach. He had carried him back to the ranch house in his arms and nursed him back to health with the aid of the Doctor Simpson who had just established his rural veterinarian clinic. Digger had been his first patient. Bernie and Digger had become loyal companions, never apart since that day. Yvonne knew that one day in the not so distant future Digger would not be there to give warm welcomes and receive biscuits from his master as a reward for being a good boy.

"он в порядке?" – Is he alright?" Yvonne asked as she snuggled up beside her loyal partner.

"да – Yes," Bernie replied with tentative reassurance, his own eyes moist with tears. He kept his hand extended over the side of the bed faintly resting on Digger's head while monitoring his breathing and heartbeat. He would not sleep for the balance of the night.

CHAPTER 43

'Received your cryptic request. It's doable. Call me now at this number,' Suzette's text message from Donald Munroe read.

"Thank you for agreeing," Suzette said when they were connected.

"The fate of the secret squirrels from the RCMP Security Service, as you described them, strikes too close to home. I wasn't aware. Some, perhaps most, of the history of those who served before the Canadian Security Intelligence Service was formed in 1984 have been boxed up and all but forgotten. I'm appalled. The death of any member should never be forgotten under any circumstances. As for constables Davidson and Hamilton, their deaths also need to be remembered beyond mere gravestones in the RCMP cemetery in Regina. Leave it with me."

"The list of names I sent you surfaced from the Hammonds Plains case," Suzette reminded him. "You will notice an overlap with names that Ernst Gerald Wagner provided. We can talk later regarding Inspector J.P.R.C. Leblanc. For now, I need to find out who killed constables Davidson and Hamilton. Their deaths certainly weren't accidental drowning and suicide as was previously reported."

"I'll get back to you," Munroe confirmed with confidence. "Take care."

"One last request," Suzette asked. "If you can access the service record of Werner Hartmann, it would be interesting to ascertain if any names on the list also appear on his file."

"Your suspicions have been correct thus far with Ernst, I'll follow up."

"Ernst Wagner, we need to talk."

Donald Munroe's voice rattled him in the same manner it had done when he had introduced himself the first time they met at the front door to his home in Toronto.

"What about? I told you everything I know."

"Perhaps not exactly everything," Munroe replied with a mixed tenor of simmering annoyance and a demand for obedience. "I appreciate that you were a bit stressed when we first talked and some details may have slipped your memory or other facts may have been confused."

"What exactly?" He felt unsteady like the first time they had faced off, the seasoned football linebacker against the rookie who had recently been called up from the juniors. His cheeks twitched. His face flushed. His eyes squinted.

"The unmarked grave on the north side of the windmill on your farm in Nova Scotia," Munroe set the stage. "You mentioned you didn't know who was buried there. I got the sense that you knew that there was more than one body. If you expect us to continue to work with you, protect you, you need to be completely honest. You need to tell me the truth, the whole truth and nothing but the truth. If you leave out any details, it will come back and bite you, if you are lucky. If not lucky, there is a high probability you could end up in your own unmarked grave with no one to keep you company."

Ernst hesitated momentarily. Beads of sweat began to appear on his brow. "I didn't know their Russian names. I only knew their Canadian names, Robert and Sylvia Hackett. Those were the names on the real estate documents when I purchased the property in 1986. I never met them. Instead, a lawyer acted on their behalf."

"That's where I believe your memory was a bit confused." Munroe leaned forward and glared at him. "Don't play games with me, Ernst. Think. Think seriously of the potential consequences. The people who this lawyer represented are not nice, and you know that. Their friends, Jean Paul's colleagues, are still hunting for you."

"John Robert Hackett. His Russian name was Nikolai. Sylvia Hackett's Russian name was Lada," Ernst blurted out, half mumbling. "That's all I know."

"That's better. Now why didn't you tell me that at first? It would have saved me a lot of time. You said that you could save me time. But you haven't, not really. I'm disappointed, Ernst. And I thought that you didn't want to play games anymore, in order to reduce your stress. Here you are playing games with me, your stress increasing."

"I feared you would think that I had something to do with their deaths, that I shot them, John Hackett and his wife. The both of them. I didn't."

"How did you know they had been shot?"

"The Russian controller, he never introduced himself to me by name, he just told me. I never saw the bodies."

"I know that you didn't kill Nikolai and his wife, Lada. But I also know that you are aware who did. So, you had best tell me who shot Nikolai a.k.a. John Robert Hackett a.k.a Nazi SS Lieutenant Colonel Brandt Felix Schmidt and his wife Sylvia a.k.a. Lada. In addition, I am aware that you had been a Russian informant before 1986 when you purchased the farm."

Ernst huffed. "Lada and her Russian handler, who I only knew as Ruslan, murdered him, Lada's husband, Robert. As I said, I never met the Russian, Ruslan."

"What was Ruslan's last name?"

"I don't know. I swear I don't know."

"And the .303 calibre rifle that was buried in the grave with Nikolai and Lada," Munroe pressed. He then fished for facts. "Your fingerprints were on the rifle."

Ernst pulled back, unsure of the suggestion that he had touched the rifle. It had been so long yet his never-ending nightmares made it seem like yesterday. "Ruslan used the rifle to shoot Nikolai. He later used it to kill Lada. I helped Ruslan bury them both. I must have handled the rifle then. Put it in the grave." Oddly, Ernst felt lighter with that more truthful admission. "I hadn't thought about the rifle for a long time. As you said, I must have confused the facts with all the stress. I sincerely apologize." *The thought had crossed my mind. Ruslan purposely had me handle the rifle in order to implicate me in the murders of John Robert and Lada Hackett. He could then use that fact to control me further. That's what controllers do, blackmail for the purposes of controlling. What else had he done to incriminate me?* Ernst pondered.

"Talk to me about an RCMP Inspector who headed the investigation. His name was Leblanc, Inspector J.P.R.C. Leblanc. He was French-Canadian."

Ernst furrowed his brow and pursed his lips as he attempted to recollect the name. Given the reality that Ruslan had cunningly incriminated him in the murders, he felt less loyal to Moscow. His memory was less fuzzy. "I never knew him personally, just heard about him. Ruslan told me to stay clear because he was a nasty cop." Ernst slowly shook his head from side to side. His eyes searched for greater clarity. "If I remember correctly, Ruslan didn't believe that he, Leblanc, could be bought, corrupted, trusted. I could be wrong, though." Ernst paused, staring into the distant past. Fewer facts were obscured. "There was one RCMP security agent who worked with Leblanc on this case. He came to the farm just after John Hackett had been shot. Apparently, this other Security Service guy had a reputation for being arrogant too. Ruslan told me to stay away from him, also. I moved to Toronto around that time and only visited the farm when I was told to do so. I never saw any other cops or security and intelligence agents around the farm after that, back then."

"What do you mean when you say, *back then*? Were there other times after that when you came across Inspector Leblanc or his colleague, Corporal Hartmann?"

Ernst considered carefully his response. He needed to provide Munroe with additional truthful but still limited information in order to keep fresh his usefulness as a CSIS double agent, all under the pretext that other expired information, no longer useful to Moscow, had recently come to his attention. "I never met Leblanc or the other agent back when John Hackett had been murdered but was advised by my handler, Jean Paul, that Hartmann might show up at the farm at Hammonds Plains. Jean Paul didn't say so explicitly but I got the impression Hartmann was a Moscow double agent recruited by Viktor Titov to report back on what Leblanc was up to. Someone superior to Leblanc in the chain of command made sure that Hartmann was always working for or close by Leblanc. As for Hartmann's purpose at the farm, he would need to be rowed out to another vessel loitering at the mouth of St. Margaret's Bay. I got the impression it was to be a one-way passage, but I could be wrong."

Munroe was aware of this detail. Molehunters within the CSIS had already passed that information along. "You didn't mention that before when we first spoke," Munroe barked.

"I was only told this by my current Jean Paul a short time ago, when we met."

"Fair enough," Munroe acknowledged. "What do you know about the two other RCMP officers, constables Davidson and Hamilton?"

Ernst dwelled in thought for a considerable length of time before answering. He wanted to be as honest as possible but still deceptive in his reply in order to maintain his cover story. If you made up stories, you had to remember what you said initially. It was better sometimes to just tell a truth even if it was vague. In his training to be a Moscow mole, he had been schooled in communist philosophy, including that of Felix Dzerzhinsky, the legendary founder of modern Russian Intelligence Services who often cited the Lenin adage: 'The West are wishful thinkers so we will give them what they want to think.' They accomplished that quite convincingly.

"In my own mind," Ernst stated. "I believed that Moscow was and remains paranoid. There weren't 'Trotskyites behind every tree', a false belief that prompted Stalin's pre-World War II great purge."

"Any more than there wasn't a 'red under every bed' as U. S. Senator McCarthy had warned in the 1950s," Munroe replied. "Now tell me what you know about constables Davidson and Hamilton."

"One of them, I don't know which one, was at the farm on the morning that Nikolai, John Hackett, had been shot. A male and a female RCMP officer got there first but left after Leblanc's colleague, Hartmann, arrived. Ruslan told me that these two had been transferred away so wouldn't be a problem. I don't know how Ruslan knew that. I never knew their names."

Munroe maintained his command presence, towering over Ernst with his football physique that cast a dominating shadow across the table.

Ernst studied him for a moment before continuing. "I heard from Ruslan that one cop knew John Hackett, he had stopped him a few times on Hammonds Plains Road not too far from the farm. I don't know his name. Both Ruslan and Hackett's wife, Lada, were worried. That cop was killed, drowned, because Ruslan was suspicious, worried he might have known too much, that John Hackett had told him something. Ruslan didn't know if he had talked to any other cops. So, this cop had to be killed. Ruslan was paranoid, constantly apprehensive about who might have known what."

Munroe stared at Ernst more intensely as if suggesting that he might be wavering from the truth.

Ernst blurted out, "Honestly. That's the truth. Shooting John Hackett was supposed to have been a simple case. Neighbours would have become suspicious if he had just disappeared so the RCMP were called to investigate the shooting at the barn. Somehow, it became messy, complicated after that. There was another cop who was somehow involved. He was shot, made to look like a suicide. I don't know how Ruslan knew that either. I concluded that Ruslan had a police informant. Ruslan always reminded me to be aware of any cops who might be snooping around the farm. I was to let him know if there were, take photographs if I could. I had been trained by Moscow to take pictures without anyone knowing."

"Who killed them, the RCMP constables?" Munroe pressed even more forcefully for additional details.

Ernst paused again, pursing his lips marginally, squinting slightly, staring intently, thinking deeply, a ploy to make it look like he was trying hard to recall more details.

Munroe raised his voice, wanting to maintain the momentum. "Talk to me, Ernst. I know that you have more to tell me. I know that some memories may be vague, repressed because you may not want to remember them. But it is important. I need to know in order to protect you. You do not want your current handler, Jean Paul, to suspect that you are a double agent, now do you? You need to remember so you can keep your facts straight for Jean Paul, and in doing so, reduce your stress."

"Some memories are foggy. I don't know," Ernst emphasized. "I swear I'm telling the truth, as much as I can remember. There is someone higher up in the government. There are dirty cops, I gave you the names of a few, in uniform and the other Security Service agents like you. I'm just not sure regarding Nikolai and Lada. I can't recall. After those two uniformed cops were killed, Davidson and Hamilton you said their names were, another cop disappeared. It became very stressful. You don't kill cops and expect that their deaths will be glossed over. There is someone else who had a lot of influence, who was calling the shots. He was senior in rank. He wasn't the hitman, he didn't get his fingers dirty. Instead, he got someone else to do the killing. Whoever that other person was pulled the trigger. That's all I know, I swear, all I can remember with any degree of certainty."

Munroe leaned into him within inches of his sweating face. He glared with greater intensity.

"I swear, I don't know," Ernst protested. "From being a Russian informant, I do know that you keep a low profile and not ask questions. When I met with my first handler, Jean Paul, in fact all the Jean Paul handlers, they individually reminded me to always be invisible, only do what they told me to do and only when they told me to act, like traveling to Hammonds Plains."

Munroe stepped back. He didn't want Ernst to provide false information just to escape the pressure to talk. Fewer correct details were better than a lot of false intelligence.

"I really looked forward to going to the farm because there was a lot of stress at work. There was stress on the farm but not as much. I could get away, go fishing by myself. Some of the people I helped get government jobs and get promoted just vanished. I didn't want to disappear like them. This senior person in government was involved somehow. He pulled all the strings. He was like a viral plague, always present but never seen, at least not by me. You just knew that he was always out there. Evil. Dangerous. That's why I wanted out. I knew the stress would kill me or I'd join the ranks of those who had evaporated, like the Hacketts and the two Mounties."

"What happened to Ruslan? Where is he now?" Munroe asked less forcefully.

"I don't know. Once the first Jean Paul became my handler in Toronto, I never saw Ruslan again. He was much older than me. So, I wouldn't be surprised if he is dead now, from natural causes or otherwise and in a communal unmarked grave."

"If you can remember anything else, you have my contact number," Munroe said in a more conciliatory yet still forceful tone. "Thank you."

"There is one other thing," Ernst blurted out. "I can't remember if I mentioned it before or not. I was told by one of the passengers I dropped off to an awaiting ship that the captains of the surface and sub-surface vessels had a second job besides conveying passengers. It was to study the coastline in order to update their maps, making note of the increasing number of potential strategic targets within the growing number of oceanfront communities. This passenger had been in some of these communities pretending to be a tourist but taking photographs."

Munroe merely nodded, acknowledging this additional information that Ernst had not previously mentioned. Its disclosure confirmed that Ernst had more accurate information to pass along. Munroe would have to extract that intelligence before Ernst joined the ranks of the vanished as he described those who had disappeared.

Ernst maintained his fabricated worried façade. He was Munroe's equal in this charade, trained by Leninist experts whose roots reached back almost a century. He knew more but wasn't prepared to reveal those facts at this juncture in his maturing relationship with the Canadian Security Intelligence Service. In the fullness of time, all things will be rendered vague, he surmised. In the interim, he would use other information as bait when he wanted Munroe to respond to his beckoning call. Like his latest

Jean Paul handler, he knew when Munroe didn't know but was instead fishing. Or he thought he knew. Ernst believed that he was a skilled double agent playing both of these employers against each other, and them against his latest Beijing contact who was actively courting him.

Munroe smiled to himself as they parted company, confident that Ernst wasn't completely aware of the constantly changing surveillance teams and the rotating electronic devices tracking his every move and conversation. He knew when Ernst wasn't telling the truth, the whole truth and nothing but the truth. Or so he thought. He knew that Ernst had not met recently with Jean Paul. So, Ernst must have known about Hartmann as a double agent recruited by Viktor Titov prior to this interview. How long before, Munroe wasn't sure. That would be revealed at subsequent meetings. The CSIS had identified the newest Jean Paul and Liu, the code name for the current Chinese agent.

CHAPTER 44

Yvonne scanned her text messages. Top on the list was from Suzette. It read: "Two points. First, I will be retiring next month. No fanfare, I'll just slide into anonymity with my heating pad and double malt scotch. Second, do you have time for java? About to take off from Ottawa en route to Halifax."

"What's up?" Yvonne texted back.

"I have been searching for an east coast property, ideally oceanfront, to buy and build a retirement home. For your information, I came across a real estate listing for a farm for sale on Hammonds Plains Road, Halifax County, Nova Scotia. It is an estate sale. Apparently, the owner, Ernst Gerard Wagner formerly from Toronto, drowned while fishing off the mouth of St. Margaret's Bay along with his fishing friend, Werner Hartmann, former RCMP from Ottawa. Their fishing boat was ostensibly overturned by a rogue wave. Neither were wearing lifejackets. Not reported in the media, only known to the CSIS, was the identity of the latter. Apparently, he had Ernst Wagner under surveillance. Hartmann's black SUV was located at the farm on Hammonds Plains Road. Suffice it to say, I will not be submitting an offer on this property. I understand that it has no ocean frontage, not even an ocean view."

After a moment of somber reflection and a tinge of forbearance, Yvonne, texted back, reluctantly. "The hunter became the hunted. Will meet your flight."

Bernie gazed up from his monitor. "Our colleagues have been busy little beavers. The dark-haired woman you saw in Peggy's Cove was one of Uri's Ukrainian contacts. She was a registered student at Dalhousie auditing some classes including one of Uri's. I say was because after our colleagues interviewed her in the wake of the shootout at the Heart-Shaped Pond, she withdrew. She has since disappeared into the sunset."

Yvonne asked, "Did they say whether she mentioned anything about a pin or brooch which Uri had passed on to Olivia?"

"They didn't say. Why do you ask?"

"Stan thought that Olivia had been wearing a pin or brooch, something foreign. There is reason to believe it was a tracking device. The bullet had destroyed whatever it was, ricocheting into her chest. That is what apparently caused extensive trauma and blood loss." Yvonne bowed her head in silence reflecting of the image etched in her memory of Olivia's bloodied body in Stan's embrace.

Bernie explained. "This all came about as a chain reaction to Olivia's and Stan's first meeting with Uri at the hotel in Halifax after they had unearthed the metal box and its contents. Uri should have realized that once a Russian Spetsnaz, always a Spetsnaz. You never get to completely divorce yourself from that fiendish fraternity."

"Suzette is flying into Halifax Stanfield International airport. I'll keep that to myself when I meet with her," Yvonne said, her voice now sharp. "Trust is an issue once lost never again to be fully restored." She met Bernie's gaze. "Still too raw."

※ ※

AS SHE WAITED FOR SUZETTE'S flight, Yvonne scanned two breaking news highlights on the front page of the *Halifax Herald*. First, a senior aide in the prime minister's office had been found dead late last evening at the scene of a car accident close to Harrington Lake, the summer residence of the prime minister who was not available for comment. The police were unsure if his apparent heart attack had contributed to his vehicle careening off the road or the impact had contributed to the heart attack. Names had not been released pending notification of next of kin who were travelling outside Canada at the time the story went to press.

The sword of Gideon has found its mark, Yvonne mused. *The actions of Midianite have been decisive once again.*

The second news item referenced a federal government announcement concerning the retirement of several senior mandarins, most in the Ottawa, Montréal and Toronto regions. The government referred to it as a boomer phenomenon. The formal announcement confirmed that it would be advantageous for the up-coming cohort of middle managers as these positions would be filled mostly by such qualified bureaucrats. *The spin doctors in the public relations office have been up all night putting a positive twist on the events also,* Yvonne huffed in disgust.

"Some but not all dominos have been taken off the playing board," Suzette whispered as she pulled up a chair.

Yvonne did not stand to greet her. The purpose of the meeting was not social. This was not the Chateau Laurier. There was no warm affectionate embrace. There was no wine served in crystal goblets, just coffee in paper cups with wooden stir sticks and plastic lids. The topic of discussion required a walk but there was no pleasant ambience of a Rideau Canal. Instead, the outside balcony would mask all verbal exchanges with the din of airport traffic. In addition, they would face the runways to prevent potential eavesdropping or reading of lips.

"I was never here and you never heard this from me," Suzette started her disclosure. "I swear that I never knew these facts before we left Hammonds Plains for our CSIS office in Halifax."

Yvonne merely gazed blankly at her devoid of any expression.

"We knew everything there was to know about Moscow's involvement. That included Viktor Titov's activities. We suspected a new kid on the block, in this case Beijing. Viktor had his network including sleeper cells and a tightly knit string of informants who were employed as federal civil servants. The most senior person was a confidential close friend of someone in the prime minister's office. He died mysteriously in the car accident you were just reading about in the newspaper. On the heels of his death, many civil servants submitted their letters of resignation after extensive interviews with human management resource consultants who had been temporarily seconded from the CSIS to ease the workload on regular HR folks from the Public Service Commission. These CSIS agents had the respective retirement documents prepared, having received prior voluntary indication of their intentions."

"Is it wishful thinking by the CSIS that they know everything there is to know about Moscow's sleeper cells? Or is it their arrogance leading them to draw that conclusion?" Yvonne asked.

"I'm sensing some skepticism?" Suzette replied.

"If there is one thing I have learned, it is the more I think I know, the more I know that I don't know. And the more I learn, the more I learn that I need to learn more. I would be naïve to think that Viktor Titov is the last of the sleeper cell handlers," Yvonne sighed.

"We are Cold War old-school warriors, you and I. We never say never, even to the reality of new kids on the block," Suzette said.

"And Viktor Titov's death?" Yvonne asked coldly.

"As I mentioned, Viktor had his well-entrenched network. He figured out that someone had released a list of names of previous and current informants and defectors. He needed to get to the list first. The Beijing agent was also on the trail of those in possession of the list. But Beijing didn't want to get it to protect their network. On the contrary, Beijing wanted to disclose the names. If they had to kill to get possession of the list, they were prepared to do just that, and anyone else who got in the way. This was consistent with the Marxist-Leninist doctrine, adopted by the Chinese Communist Party to disrupt and leave chaos in its wake. Viktor needed to stop the Chinese agent in order to protect his network of active moles and passive sleeper-cell agents. That begs the question: who is still active but not on the list?"

"A few missing pieces of the puzzle," Yvonne muttered under her breath. "But it doesn't explain how Uri and the unidentified shooter got to the Heart-Shaped Pond first."

"The name of one of our agents who was on the list was playing CSIS, Moscow and Beijing at the same time. That is how they all became aware of our plans to trap whoever was chasing Olivia and Stan at the Heart-Shaped Pond. We still don't know who tipped off Uri. We may never know. Having said that, we do not believe that Uri was working for his former employer. We surmise that he went to the Heart-Shaped Pond to protect Olivia, his ex-wife. Loyalty based on love runs deep for some people."

"You said that you knew everything there was to know about the Russia card. What about the two uniformed members of the Force and the RCMP Security Service member who was working with Inspector Leblanc? Do we know who he is and, more importantly, where he is? He wouldn't be senior enough to have died of old age."

Suzette paused, lowering her eyes. "The Russians were involved in the deaths of constables Davidson and Hamilton. Ruslan, the sleeper cell handler who shot John Robert Hackett and later his wife, Lada, either killed constables Davidson and Hamilton or contracted out their killings. I doubt that we will ever find out who actually pulled the trigger so to speak. Likewise, for the Security Service member who had been working with Inspector Leblanc. Ruslan was involved but we may never know who was responsible for actually killing him. There are too many assassins out there, fast guns for hire, who sell their services. Many, perhaps most, are ex-military snipers trained by the best. Ruslan disappeared off the radar at some point. I think that it is safe to say he is in an unmarked KGB grave somewhere, another forgotten casualty of the Cold War."

Yvonne prophesized, "History is the knitting together of deception as defined by the victors. But not Viktor Titov this time. He was a loser in the game of *koti i mysh'* – Russian cat and mouse."

"You seem to have sensed that something wasn't right?" Suzette remarked with resigned suspicion.

Yvonne stared up and collected her thoughts for an appropriate answer within the new untrusting norm that had tainted the space between them. "I applied the smell test. It stank."

Suzette shrugged her shoulders. "The challenge to finding all the dots in the intelligence architecture in order to connect them is like following a pestering wolverine tracking and back tracking. Some you never locate but you remain mesmerized by their imprints and scent, and still others by their myths and purported reputations."

They gazed out at an arriving flight from China, both trained in disciplined scrutiny.

"You mentioned that you were seeking oceanfront property," Yvonne commented nonchalantly.

"I will be meeting a real estate agent here shortly. He wants to show me some secluded property around Mahone Bay, away from Hammonds Plains. I understand that I can get there by driving from the Halifax Stanfield International Airport south along Highway 102 and then west along Highway 103, thereby bypassing the farm at Hammonds Plains, which I mentioned is for sale because the previous owner had drowned while fishing at the mouth of St. Margaret's Bay."

"Let me know if you retire to Mahone Bay. My travels may take me to that neck of the woods," Yvonne replied. "The fluctuation in barometric pressure tends not to be as dramatic as you have experienced in the Ottawa River valley. Hence, you may not be reminded of your mortality as often." She handed her an envelope she had pulled from her pocket.

Suzette gave her a curious stare.

"The balance of the names that Stan and Olivia had discovered. They don't need to protect them anymore. Best you have them to deal with as you see fit. Perhaps as a retirement gift to your previous employer. I look forward to reading about a second wave of retirements."

"One last item of interest," Suzette offered. "And I tell you this in the strictest confidence. I had asked one of my colleagues, Donald Munroe, to check on a hunch I had. He searched Werner Hartmann's personnel file relative to any of the names Olivia and Stan had handed over. You won't be surprised at the results. Some of Hartmann's security clearance documents had been removed, others annotated. My colleague could not determine who had stripped the file. There was just a brief notation in the margin with the initials, ME. Mike Edwards. Now deceased, Major Mike Edwards, our military colleague from Europe who joined the Canadian Security Intelligence Service. My, our suspicions are now confirmed."

A silence occupied the moment. Nothing more was said. Suzette rubbed her shoulder.

"Take care," Suzette said as she turned and parted company.

Yvonne gazed back over her shoulder and spoke in a louder voice, "By the way, if you like fishing, you can charter a boat from Mahone Bay."

"I hate fish and fishing. I do like lobster, though."

A reed thin smile came to Yvonne's lips. She reflected with a tinge of lament, *Lobster and Chardonnay. I never did have to pick up that tab. The conversation might have been interesting, somewhere between actors in an Athenian comedy and a Shakespearian tragedy.* She was silent for a lingering moment.

CHAPTER 45

"Can thoughts exist in a vacuum?" Stan asked.

"Interesting concept. Thoughts are energy. We dream but often cannot remember the energy of the dream, the actual thoughts. That is one of the principles upon which Quantum Theory is based. Energy being finite. Einstein proposed the theory. Stephen Hawking wrote and spoke about it."

Olivia pointed to her cup on the edge of the table. "This has potential energy. Once it falls off the edge, it has kinetic energy. When it lands on the floor, it passes that kinetic energy into other forms of measurable energy such as heat or sound."

"I remember in training, the Ident instructor saying that at every crime scene something is left and something is picked up by the intruders. The instructor was talking about physical evidence like a thread from a perpetrator's clothing snagged on a splinter extending from a door frame, or a fingerprint or paint chip. I found that intriguing. Science has advanced so much, beyond not just blood types or DNA or latent fingerprints," Stan suggested.

"In the barn where Hackett died, he left his thoughts and energy at the moment he took his last breath. From your Ident logic of leaving something behind and taking something away, theoretically, how close is Crime Scene Analysis from capturing Hackett's energy? His final lingering thoughts?"

"Close, relatively speaking. We pick up what was left at the scene through our senses, smell, taste, hearing. Why not sense as in sensing energy? Presence? Essence? The challenge would be one of admissibility in a court of law. In the late 19th and early 20th century, a German physiologist, Wilhelm Kühne, proposed the theory of optography, of viewing and retrieving an optogram or image on the retina of the eye. The theory suggested that the last image seen before death would be permanently recorded. Some police photographed the eyes of the deceased in the event the theory would someday be proven."

"So, it's like the Great Victoria Night-hopping Marrow Looper that you talked about, the Loch Ness Monster and Ogopogo in Okanagan Lake. You just know that it's there because it leaves something behind and takes something away."

He patiently cajoled her. "You need to rest, now. Doctor's orders."

"I'm feeling much better but will comply with your command." Olivia gazed over at a miniature glass cup sitting on the bedside table which held the shattered remnants of Uri's Spetsnaz pin. His secreted cryptic communiqué had been destroyed by the impact of the bullet that struck her chest. The splintered fragments had caused lacerations to the flesh and cartilage around her sternum resulting in considerable blood loss. But the pin had prevented the bullet from penetrating her heart. It had saved her life, perhaps imbued with the shielding spell woven by the sender. It had brought him luck while on the Spetsnaz missions in Afghanistan, among others.

"And Two Old Farts Investigative Services, TOFIS. Every Sherlock needs a Watson," Olivia chuckled. "You could fill the role of the intrepid private detective's assistant. Any takers?" she asked in jest. "I guess I can train you."

"Or vice versa," Stan countered. "Of course, we would have to artfully refurbish a post box adjacent to our driveway like Michael McNeill had done. But ours would have the address 222B Baker Street painted on the side where the arm raises up."

Olivia closed her eyes at the thought. Other thoughts occupied her mind. She imagined her family farm in southeast Alberta, and the bluff overlooking the shading grove of prairie diamond willow trees. She was pleased not to be swatting pesky prairie mosquitoes.

They were rare in Victoria, only imported by prairie and foothill folks who came to winter in the milder climate on the west coast. She made a mental note to explain to Stan her previous reference to being able to keep secrets. He would find it amusing. As a child, she had spilled red wine on her mother's new white linen tablecloth. Her father had told her not to worry. He would launder it and no one would be the wiser. It had washed out completely although she would always see the stain. It would just be a secret between them, and it remained so. She could keep secrets about secrets.

For now, she would merely smile. Life would be more laid back in Victoria. They had a double garage and a driveway wide enough for two cars. Stan had sold Betty's car so there was ample room. He told Olivia he only put his car in the garage on those few occasions during the winter months when there was indication of a heavy frost.

There was an added bonus to living in Victoria. A close-knit group of west coast antique book collectors travelled to Seattle each October to attend the annual Antiquarian Book Fair frequented by avid international book aficionados.

Her eyes followed him as he quietly left her to rest. *Reading had become my intimacy, my escape, and now I have you.* She simply loved being in love.

Exhausted as she was, she did not want to sleep. She wanted to remember, never to forget, never to close her eyes for fear of never waking up. Her thoughts drifted off as she recited the poem, Maud Miller, by John Greenleaf Whittier: *For of all sad words of tongue or pen, / The saddest of these: it might have been.*

Stan paused in the doorway, and reflected on how he felt loved in the moment, unlike in his past with Betty, longing for something missing that was never to be but would now be.

CHAPTER 46

"Bonjour." – Hello.
"J'écoute." – I'm listening.
"Я буду на связи – YA byl v kontakte." – I have been in contact.
"Да. Принято – Da. Priznannyy." – Yes. Acknowledged.
"We need to fill the void opened up with the recent retirements before the market place is populated with new kids on the block. These pandas have been proficient in accurately identifying the soft socialist underbelly and infiltrating the ranks of a number of prominent academic institutions."

"Not to worry. A minor setback. We continue to have contingencies in place. We have our own people in senior positions on Boards of Governors and as Deans at distinguished universities in addition to a few presidents of other academic institutions, including select colleges. Viktor Titov had created depth and breadth in his network as had others. His most recently recruited candidates are amongst the up-and-coming who will be offered positions left vacant by the retirements of some of their colleagues. Although their rise may not be as mercurial in the short term, they are known to those who remain in positions to assist at the federal and provincial levels, and a select number of larger municipalities. A few have already been promoted in police departments to commissioned officer ranks and are destined to command influential enforcement organizations. One is multilingual – English, French and German. He is on the short list for appointment as the next Canadian representative to Interpol in Lyon, France. They don't know that he is also proficient in our mother tongue and has a working knowledge of Mandarin, an accomplished linguist and respected raconteur."

"Да. Спасибо" – Yes. Thank you.

Made in United States
Troutdale, OR
07/08/2023